# TRIALS OF THE HORSEMAN

## Book One of THE DARK SKY SERIES

## DEAN RADT

TRIALS of the HORSEMAN

This is a work of fiction. All character, organizations, and events portrayed in this book are fictional, and any resemblance to real people or incidents is purely coincidental.

Edited by Claire Bradshaw

Cover Art by Humbert Glaffo

Map by SketchRisk

First Edition, April 2021
Richmond, Virginia

ISBN  978-1-7364011-0-1  (hardcover)
ISBN  978-1-7364011-1-8  (paperback)
ISBN  978-1-7364011-2-5  (ebook)

Library of Congress Control Number: 2021905007

Published in the United States of America.

For Kim

# Acknowledgements

"A novel is a world of feelings."
                    -Randall Kenan

I started this adventure almost twenty years ago. The bones of it were the backstory for a character in a roleplaying game. The plot and characters have evolved since that point, and it took a lot of effort to make those changes work. Many people helped me along the way.

First, I must thank my wife, Kim, who put up with so much and took on extra work so I could finish the book. She's the wind and the star, ever steady and supporting.

To Michael, who kept asking, "When are you going to finish that story" and helped me close many plot holes. And Kat, who in many ways was my co-pilot on this flight. She provided amazing ideas for scenes and was an essential sounding board while I wrote. I cannot thank you two enough.

Jeff Gaines, who started the game for which the backstory was created and provided critiques and input as I continued to write. Thanks, bud.

Benny M. Burrell, author and mentor, who has inspired me in so many ways. Thank you for getting me to pen to paper.

Brian, who got me through the floundering in my early attempts at writing by prompting me to find a writing group. Without that advice I wouldn't have joined *James River Writers* and met my amazing writing partners, Val Brown, Renee Hill, and Fatima Mahdi. Gifted writers each. They have been tough on me when I needed it and encouraged me along the way. Thank you. You're awesome!

Many thanks to Nikolas Lloyd (Lindybeige) for the historical information on his website and YouTube channel, and his critique of the period weapon fighting in the book. ... Oh, and his waggish reminder to respect the English language.

Jerry Shepard, author and guide, who not only beta-read, but also helped me navigate the self-publishing process. This process would have been more stressful without his help. My sincere gratitude.

My beta-readers and proofreaders, who picked up on issues and helped me fix problems in the hopes that everyone else will enjoy a better story. Thank you, Pam Ayers, Louis Bausone, Marisa Bausone, Steve Baumler, Jenelle Cosby, Emily Gurley, Dana McLease, and Sussan Ayala Rodriguez.

David L. Robbins made time for me when he didn't have to. He helped me improve the book, my writing process, and gave me instrumental guidance in the our few meetings. Thank you very much.

I must thank everyone at Solstice. From Meg Kearney, the director of the *Solstice MFA Program*, who saw something in me and gave me the confidence to make myself a better person and a better writer. To my mentors, Steve Huff and Laura Williams McCaffrey, who sent me into dark caves to explore and emerge stronger. And my professors, Sandra Scofield, Sterling Watson, and David Yoo, who pushed me hard and challenged me. To my workshop partners who set high bars with their own works, taught me, prodded me, and motivated me, Cindy Abdalla, Megan Leduke, Susannah Cohen, Jason Christy, Hannah Woodcock, Rhonda McDonnell, Jim Naremore, and Ellen Parent. My thanks to you all. You rock!!

And to the readers who buy this book, thank you. I hope it entertains and keeps you intrigued.

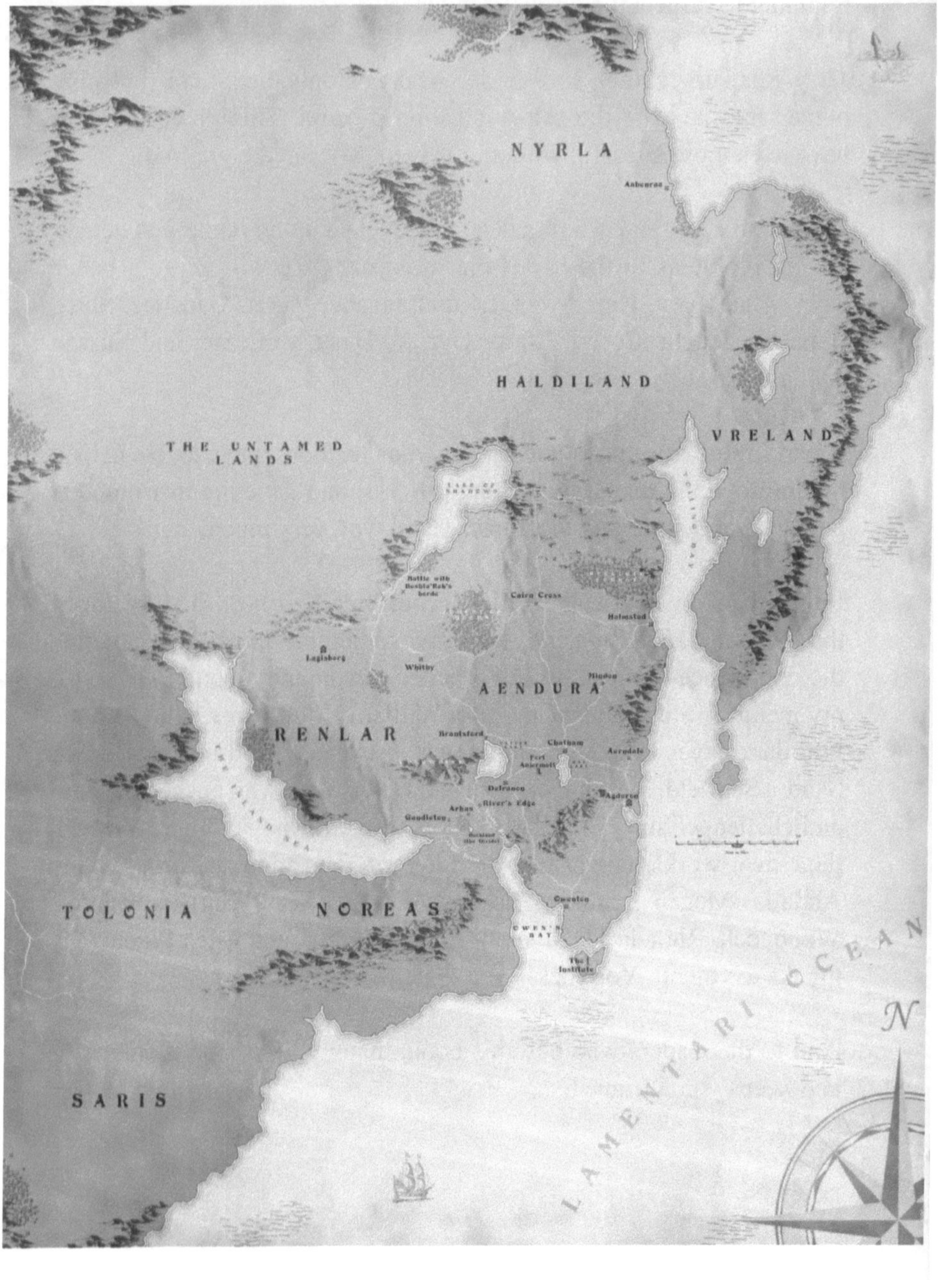
NYRLA
HALDILAND
VRELAND
THE UNTAMED LANDS
LAKE OF SHADOWS
Cairn Cross
Holmstad
Whitby
AENDURA
RENLAR
Chatham
River's Edge
THE INLAND SEA
TOLONIA
NOREAS
OWEN'S BAY
The Institute
SARIS
LAMENTARI OCEAN
N

Battle with
Beshta'Rek's
horde

FOREST OF
DEEDS

RESOLUTE
FOREST

Cairn Cross

Halmstad

Whitby

Minden

AENDURA

Brantsford

VASTER
LAKE

Chatham

Aerndale

EVERWHITE

Fort
Anjermott

GAV
LAKE

Delranon

Agderon

River's Edge

Arhus

Vaster River

Gandleton

Ebloes' Fane

THE
INLAND
SEA

Beckland
(the Divide)

Aryse River

0    30         75         150

Scale in Miles

OWEN'S
BAY

# CHAPTER ONE

It was not a pasture. And the narrow strip of dirt running through the middle of it was not a road. A farmer and a traveler might argue against that. The farmer might point out that the hundred or so acres of oval-shaped, knee-high grassland were perfect for grazing animals or a hay harvest. The traveler might point out that the strip of dirt, dry and firm and smooth, with a hundred yards of grassland on each side, was a road and a convenience.

Both would have been mistaken on this day.

Secreted in the field, and in the woods on both sides of it, were hundreds of cavalry troopers who saw the space for what it truly was. A place of death. It was no more a pasture and a dirt road than a snare was a bit of twine and a stick. Before nightfall, the snare would set and the picturesque scene would be changed.

In the western woods were three companies of cavalry. They lined up beyond the center point of the field, preparing themselves and their horses. Grimble, near the southern end of the line, stood next to his dapple gray mount. He closed his brown eyes and took a breath. The woods and the wildlife were getting used to their presence. The squirrel had stopped barking. Birds sang. The forest came to life as the men around him prepared to kill. All was well. He breathed out and opened his eyes.

All three companies were thirty yards deep into the woods. Shade from the newly leaved trees and the tall evergreens shrouded the regiment. The shadows that hid them also inched their way across the field. When the regiment eventually emerged, the sun would be at their backs. The location was excellent, the timing perfect.

"Set, Corporal," Eng said.

"Set," Kelban said.

"Rah." Grimble, of medium complexion with short, brown hair, kept his focus on the trees. He watched their movement in the breeze. A bead of sweat trickled down his back. Neither the light wind nor the shade was enough to keep him from sweating beneath the crimson-and-white gambeson armor each of the troopers wore.

A stillness formed in pockets among the line of troopers and horses of the 209th. In those spaces of silence stood the veteran troopers. Like Grimble, they had finished strapping barding to their horses and turned their attention to other matters. None prayed. They would do that when the battle was inevitable.

Grimble waited on one other member of his patrol to report.

"Shit," mumbled Goat. His cursing continued. Grimble shook his head.

Goat and the other "boots" spoiled the silence. They cursed and recited rote prayers between shallow breaths. They jingled their buckles and frustrated their mounts. To the veterans, the noise the boots made was like a fiddler rapidly stroking his bow across a discordant string. It even pushed Grimble's patience.

Goat mumbled on the other side of his horse, his head jerking as he repeatedly tugged at a leather strap. His mount tossed its head and shuffled its legs with each tug.

Grimble took a slow breath. This was not the time to yell at the recruit. Goat needed to be confident and focused when they faced the goblin horde. Everyone, boot and veteran, had some measure of apprehension over the coming battle. Understandably, the boots, with less than a month's training, handled that stress worse.

Grimble looked to Kelban, who stood by his own horse behind Goat. With every jerk of Goat's barding straps, the veteran's face reddened, his lip twitching and his scowl growing. "Fucking boots are gonna get us killed," Kelban mouthed.

Grimble caught Kelban's attention before the tall man snapped. He motioned with his hands for Kelban to calm himself, tilting his head toward Goat. Kelban's scowl retreated. He nodded in understanding.

The two veterans moved between their horses and the trees to finish securing Goat's horse's armor and check the rest of its tack. Goat stood off to the side while they worked. His face was unreadable. That blank stare was the very aspect that had earned him his nickname.

After strapping the barding to Goat's horse, Kelban walked over to the young man. At six feet and two inches, Kelban stood taller than every other man in the regiment – even Goat and Grimble, who were themselves among the taller troopers. Kelban was clean-shaven, but the hard lines of his weathered face and the intensity of his brown-eyed stare lent him a certain maturity.

He waited for Goat to look up and into his eyes and clapped him on the shoulder. "Keep listening to Grimble." Kelban smiled. "I'm tellin' ya, you do as he says and you'll stay in the saddle. He's helped a lot of us." He turned to Grimble. "Did we look this young seven years ago?"

Grimble chuckled. "I did, but you're like Dinger. You've always been hard. You never looked dough-faced like the rest of us."

Though they may have joined the regiment in a doughy condition, the troopers had been hard-baked by their training and the engagements they had survived. Because of that, every veteran seemed to have the same lean, trim physique. Grimble ran his fingers over his cheeks and the short hair of his brown beard.

*Would they recognize me back home?*

"Comparing me to Dinger Durinson? I don't know if I should be flattered or annoyed."

"Annoyed? How so? Dinger's better than any of us, save Roche, with spear and sword. You know that."

"Yeah, but I'm much better-looking," Kelban said as he stepped back to his horse. Grimble shook his head, but couldn't help smiling.

Goat took his horse's reins again. The animal fidgeted. Its eyes and nostrils were wide, its body tense. Grimble looked across the saddle into Goat's eyes. Like Kelban, Goat was clean-shaven, but unlike Kelban, it made him look boyish. The young man stared back. He was of lighter complexion than Grimble and Kelban, his face showing a gathering redness.

Grimble spoke evenly. "Slow your breathing."

"Yes, sir," said Goat.

"Don't speak, just breathe. Slower." Grimble rubbed the horse's neck and head, and watched as it relaxed. He took a drink from his canteen and passed it to Goat, who took a couple of sips between breaths.

"When we meet the enemy," Grimble said, "focus on your part. That's all you have to do. When fear and doubt enter your mind, and they will, turn away from them. Go to your training. Remember it. Maintain the line. Pick your target and trust that we will do our jobs."

"And if that doesn't work," said Kelban, "just stab the piss out of anything that doesn't look like us."

A faint smile tugged on Goat's cheeks.

*There's a killer in there,* Grimble thought. "All that shit with your brother back home," he went on, "use it. Let it motivate you. But when the fighting starts, keep your mind here."

"I can do this, Corporal," said Goat. "I won't let you down."

"I know. I trust you." *Gods, I hope we've had enough time to prepare.*

Before Grimble could return to his horse, Kelban asked, "You don't trust the scout reports, do you?"

"What?" Grimble asked. "What part do you have a problem with?"

"Almost all of it, brother. I'm tellin' ya, there's no way this Beshta'Rek's a goblin."

"Great gods, Kelban. The Ravens know how to do their job. Yes, I believe them."

"Too many things just don't make sense. First, he's a foot taller than any other goblin ever seen. And there's the size of this horde. Eighty? Biggest one I heard of before this was nineteen, and *that* was a large raiding party."

"I agree, it's strange, but given his size it's no wonder he's gotten a huge following."

"Okay, how about his using tactics, real military tactics, to hit the villages and towns along the frontier? And there's that advisor of his, T'Ugly…"

"Too'Ug," said Grimble.

"Right. He won't show his face – maybe he's human."

"Ha!" sniped Eng, turning his attention from the arrow in his hand to Kelban. He was the fourth trooper in the patrol, three horses away from Grimble. Eng did not tolerate Kelban's distrusting nature.

"How can you believe they're goblins?" Kelban asked him. "They move faster and have attacked deeper into Aendura than any other goblin raiders. They've avoided local militia and the king's infantry. Strangest of all, they take human prisoners."

"True," said Eng, stabbing the nock end of an arrow in Kelban's direction, "but their strange behavior doesn't disprove the reports. Your suspicious nature misleads you, brother. You're wrong here."

"A silver dula says I'm right."

"It's a bet."

"I hate taking your money, brother, but you make it so easy. I'm tellin' ya, no goblin could organize a horde that big… or be as big as they say Beshta'Rek is. Care to make it two dula?"

"Two it is. Careful, I'll own your soul before too long."

"Can't," said Kelban. "I traded that for a bottle of wine and a night of bliss the last time we were in Cairn Cross."

"Yeah," chuckled Eng. "Fun night."

Grimble smiled. *That was a fun night.*

"Care to get in on the bet, Grimble?" asked Eng. "You up for taking some of his money too?"

"Grimble doesn't gamble," said Kelban.

"Why?" asked Eng. "A Temple man?"

"Nah," said Kelban.

"I never win," said Grimble.

Kelban laughed. "He's a mule sack at it. I'm tellin' ya, he's the worst. Lost everything his first few weeks of training. Took him some time to get caught up with his debts."

"Thanks for being so honest, jackass."

"What are friends for?"

"Yeah, we had a guy like you in First Company," said Eng. "But he wasn't smart enough to quit, like you." He paused, his face turning solemn. "He was a good brother."

"Steep Ridge?" asked Kelban.

"Yeah."

A silence followed. The Battle at Steep Ridge, one of the last in the second war with the country of Renlar, had taken its toll on the men. It had also left the regiment below half strength for the better part of a year. Troopers had been moved internally to balance the companies, but the regiment remained undermanned. Three weeks ago, King Saevar's Lord High Constable, His Majesty's head of the military, had finally assigned replacement troops. But he had taken these men, all new recruits, from the ranks of an infantry company that had been disbanded.

The troopers of the 209th had heard the new recruits knew how to ride a horse, but it seemed their selection had actually hinged on the recruit swearing he had *seen* a horse at some point in his life. Grimble and the other troopers could not understand the lord's decision. They were the last light cavalry regiment in the King's Army. No other unit could fill their function.

The irregular beat of hooves at the trot brought the men's attention to a trail behind their line. The command unit of eight mounted troopers made its way along that trail, allowing Commander Dek the opportunity to check the status of the three companies.

Kelban did a double take as they rode by. He leaned around Goat to talk to Grimble. "What's Thom doing with the commander?"

"Dek found out these goblin pricks killed some of Thom's

family," Grimble said. "And even the commander knows how hot-headed he is, so Thom's been given the 'honor' of being part of Dek's personal guard for the mission."

Kelban nodded. "Yeah, I can see him leaving the formation if he got the chance to go after the chieftain."

Grimble looked down the line to his left, scrutinizing Goat, Kelban, and Eng. Seeing everything in order, he turned toward the other patrol making up the column. Master Sergeant Roche, the column's sergeant, stood at the far end. His dark complexion and close-cut gray hair and beard were almost as striking as his sharp jawline.

Two sun-bleached, crimson ribbons the width of a finger were sewn onto each shoulder of Grimble's gambeson. Running front to back, they noted his position as a corporal. Sergeants bore three such ribbons on each shoulder. The ribbons Roche wore were embroidered with gold thread, noting his status as a master sergeant. In Roche's more than twenty years in the army, none had bested him with weapons or in unarmed combat. He was a legend to his men.

When Roche looked his way, Grimble nodded. The sergeant tilted his head in reply and turned to the platoon's lieutenant on his right, letting him know the column's status. Roche looked back at Grimble. *Is he ready?* he mouthed.

Grimble nodded again, but thought to himself, *I hope so. Ihgel help us.*

He prayed he had done enough in the short time he'd had to ready Goat for this moment. As for the other boots in the regiment, their riding was not much better, and their acceptance of this hard life was questionable. None seemed proud or thankful for the opportunity to be among this elite unit. Not everyone could become a cavalry trooper, and fewer still could attain the proficiency required by the Wicked Spears of the 209<sup>th</sup> Light Cavalry Regiment, especially with a shortened training period. The indoctrination and bruising ministrations Grimble had received over half a year had been meted out to these boots in a few weeks. It was not enough time to make them confident riders, and certainly not enough to make them fully proficient in the tactics of the regiment.

Master Sergeant Roche had entrusted Grimble with fixing Goat's deficiencies. Grimble had helped quite a few in the regiment before. While not the greatest swordsman, he was a confident rider, and his superiors recognized his ability to build the bond between rider and horse. Grimble stroked the neck of his mount, Havoc, and shooed a fly from his ear before removing his helmet. He poured the rest of his first canteen's water into it, giving his horse a drink. The dappled gray, his partner of six years, nickered and turned his head to meet Grimble when he finished.

"Battalion!" came the call. "Moooouunt… up!"

The three companies, a total of twelve columns of troopers, mounted their horses as one. They readied themselves, checking their reins and equipment. Leather squeaked and the murmuring drone of one hundred thirty-four troopers' prayers saturated the woods. Boredom fled, apprehension worming its way into the void.

The enemy approached.

Grimble turned away from the anxiety. Beads of sweat ran down his back and soaked through his gambeson. His nose took in the odors around him, the day's languid heat and humidity intensifying the scents. When the wind picked up, providing some relief from the heat, Grimble could smell the men around him; and when it died down, he was left with his own acrid aroma. Neither was pleasant. He could not decide if he preferred the wind to blow or remain lifeless. He had been through many such days, but had never found an answer to that question.

Starting out of sight, from the far left, each trooper passed along the sign – a fist raised above the shoulder – to hold their position and to stay quiet. Eng held up his left fist; Kelban mimicked him, as did Goat. Grimble made the gesture and watched it pass along the rest of the column.

The horses, too, seemed to understand the command. Havoc shivered under his barding and dug anxiously at the damp ground with a hoof, shifting patches of thick black muck around. The vegetation around them had long ago been trampled into a mottled, loamy patch of wet earth. Grimble knew the courser could smell something; digging at the earth was one of his signals.

Moments later the other horses reacted. Alongside Grimble, the troopers fixed their gazes upon their own mounts. The horses themselves focused their attention ahead, toward the field thirty yards away. Over two hundred yards beyond, in the woods on the other side of the field, a dismounted company of troopers had secreted themselves in the dark. More waited out of sight in the field.

The horses' ears stood tall, their heads erect, but they stayed motionless, their gazes steady. A stronger sign came. Havoc and a handful of other horses reacted first. Their ears pinned back, and they lowered their heads briefly. The veteran troopers instinctively reached for the reins. The boots quickly followed suit.

Before Grimble had finished readying himself, he too picked up the scent. The stench, a mix of rotten vegetables and wet dog, crossed the field on the wind, creeping into the woods as an odorous wave, and striking the regiment in the face. This was good. If they could smell the goblins, the goblins could not smell them. The senior troopers did not react, but the boots grimaced and scrunched their noses.

*So that's what wet goblins smell like. Next time let's ambush them before they cross the river.*

Grimble looked left, checking on his patrol again. Goat stared straight ahead. Kelban and Eng looked at Grimble, Eng wearing a huge grin. Kelban, stern-faced, subtly lifted his fist, his thumb barely poking out between his ring and middle fingers. His eyes narrowed as he made the insulting gesture, a comment on the size of Grimble's virility.

Grimble shook his head, smiling, and silently mouthed back, *Stop showing off.* Kelban's stoic face cracked with the slightest of smirks.

Grimble turned toward the three boots in the rest of the column, the ones in Roche's patrol. Altogether that made four new troopers in the column – almost half their count, none of them tested.

*Too many boots.*

He prayed to Yahnn for leadership, and to Ihgel to guide their aim and give them strength in what was to come.

As one, the horses shifted their gazes to the left and trained their ears the same way. Whatever drew their attention did not hold it long. Soon they all faced the field again.

The odor grew stronger.

The road's entry point to the field was not in Grimble's line of sight, so by the time the goblin scout was visible, the creature was already near the middle of the grassland. Hunched, the scout skirted alongside the dirt road. The grass there was thick, higher than a man's knee, but the scout scuttled through it like a well-trained tracker. Occasionally he stopped to smell the air and listen, before hurrying his pace again a few seconds later. He kept his bow at the ready, shifting his attention from the road to the horizon while he moved.

Grimble, being a corporal, had been in on the attack briefing. He had learned that the Ravens, the specialists of the King's Army, had been tasked with addressing the enemy's scouts.

*Show the new guys something amazing, boys.*

The goblin used the hood of his tattered brown cloak to protect his eyes from the glaring sun, keeping his head low to focus on the road. Goblins did not tolerate sunlight well, and the fact that Beshta'Rek was able to push his raiders into starting their march while the sun was up was a testament to his leadership and tactical mindset.

Earlier in the day, the Ravens had dropped a bag of coins on the dirt road. It was intended to distract the scout, and it did its duty. The goblin paused near the bag. He darted his head this way and that, bending on one knee and scanning the woods. The sun was too bright and the forest too dark for his gaze to penetrate the shadows. The scout lifted his nose higher to sniff the air, and the hood fell back, exposing his gray, mottled head. His movements reminded Grimble of a dog searching for a scent.

The scout looked back to the hill behind him before turning his full attention to the pouch of coins. He reached out to snatch it. What happened next was over quickly – even Grimble, who was expecting something to happen, almost missed it.

As the goblin scout grabbed the pouch, the patch of earth behind him seemingly came to life. It was as if the ground had birthed a grass-covered man. The aberration wrapped its arms around the scout's head and fell back to the ground, dragging the goblin's body away from the road. There was no cry, no sound.

A few seconds later, both disappeared. The flanking scouts were no doubt being dispatched in a similar manner.

Grimble smiled. He turned to Master Sergeant Roche to see him smiling too. The boots exchanged looks, as if trying to make sense of what they'd seen. No one opened their mouths. Surprise was the order now, and even their mounts kept any protests to themselves.

A few minutes elapsed, and one by one, the troopers tensed. From left to right, the men raised their heads and took a breath of preparation. For many, this day marked the first time they had set eyes on goblin-kind, and the size of the horde added to the effect.

The raiders made their way into the pastureland. They were well equipped due to their fruitful pillaging. A vanguard of six goblins, three with bows, the others with spear and shield, led the horde. The main host followed about twenty yards behind, and trailing them was a rear guard of another six goblins. As end of day neared, Beshta'Rek's war party was a few miles into Aendura, confidently, but mistakenly, heading to their next target: the village of Grinnell.

Leading the main body was the war chief himself. Taller than any other goblin by almost a foot, he stood about six feet in height. For those who had believed he was not of goblin-kind, his pointy features and sickly gray skin were plain to see, casting their doubts aside. Beshta'Rek did not hide beneath a cloak; his eyes were exposed to the sun. The only things covering his body were his gambeson tunic, mail armor, and metal helmet. The latter sat upon his head like a child's cap, tipped to the rear. He might have been as tall as a human, but his head was too misshapen to properly wear a human's helmet.

Grimble saw Eng signal Kelban with two fingers. Kelban glanced sidelong at him, shook his head in concession, and muttered something profane under his breath.

Although a cloak did not cover the chief, the rest of his raiding party was outfitted with them. The goblin directly behind Beshta'Rek had covered itself to the extent that it was impossible to get a glimpse of his nose or chin. The Ravens had named this one "Too'Ug", claiming he hid his visage because it was too ugly for even the rest of the goblins. In all the time they had spied on the goblin encampment, not even the Ravens had been able to see his face. Too'Ug appeared to be the chief's counselor, not a warrior.

The vanguard marched upright, weapons at their shoulders, shields at their sides. They moved at close interval and practically in-step. The main host marched similarly armed, but they slouched, and their formation was loose. Their gaze and step were undisciplined and rough. A cloud of road dust kicked up around them.

As the vanguard arrived near the location of the scout's ambush, a crow called three times from the eastern tree line, opposite Grimble's position. Another crow called twice in response. Grimble noticed Too'Ug's steps falter; he looked left and right.

At that moment, ten troopers from First Company rose up from the tall grass about thirty yards to the front and left of the vanguard, and loosed their arrows at the lead goblins. Twelve more stepped to the edge of the woods on the eastern side of the road, eighty yards from the main host's left flank, and fired a volley of arrows into them. After firing, the troopers ran back into the woods to the east.

Cries and shrieks spilled from the raiders. In the vanguard, four of the six goblins fell immediately. One ran back toward the main body, an arrow protruding from his chest. He collapsed halfway back, attempted to crawl, and slumped, never to move again. The remaining goblin, an archer who was untouched, set an arrow and aimed at his fleeing attackers. Four small bolts impaled the goblin archer's body, and he fell backward, his arrow flying wildly into the air.

The remainder of First Company, mounted and twenty-six strong, rode onto the field from the south and loosed a volley of arrows at the main body of the raiders. Beshta'Rek shouted and the rear guard ran forward to join the group. Several goblins broke rank to charge after the troopers fleeing into the woods, but another shout from their chief brought them back into formation. The host raised a protective shield wall around itself, spears poking out all around. Beshta'Rek shouted all the while, gnashing his teeth at his raiders.

The twenty-six troopers of First Company's Second Platoon continued their advance onto the field, riding at a gallop between the goblins and the eastern tree line. They readied a second volley of arrows as they approached. On command, they stood in their stirrups, loosed their arrows, and kept riding to the north. More bestial shrieks sounded; two shields and their bearers fell, requiring the goblins to adjust and fill the gap. A few goblin archers replied with shots of their own, but their efforts were fruitless.

While the goblins were distracted, Commander Dek shouted, "Battalion!"

In unison, the captains of the remaining three companies in the western woods shouted: "Company!"

"Wicked Spears," the commander said, "assemble on the field by rank! Second Company is lead company! Yah!"

Second Company, followed by Third and Fourth, rode forward, dodging branches and emerging onto the field. Grimble checked on Goat as they advanced.

Under orders from their captain and lieutenants, Second Company formed a rank line of thirty-nine cavalry troopers, harnessing their spears and preparing their bows. Third and Fourth Companies took a position right behind Second, readying their bows as well.

By this time the horde had suffered through four volleys of arrows, alternating between the eastern woods and the mounted cavalry. Their losses were few, but the shield wall was no longer flush, showing small gaps here and there. The goblins' heads whipped side to side. Their confidence appeared to be diminishing.

The goblins facing Grimble's direction darted looks between their chieftain and the one hundred thirty-four troopers massing a hundred yards away. Too'Ug was making animated gestures, moving his hands as if trying to encourage those around him to steady the shield wall next to him; but his manner was foreign, and Grimble couldn't understand the signals. No arrow had yet found a path to either Too'Ug or Beshta'Rek. Both figures stood in the open and free of injury. The chieftain barked and shouted, keeping his warriors in line. The goblins managed limited replies with their archer volleys, but Grimble saw that his brothers, protected by their armor and speed, had lost neither horse nor man.

"Second Company, draw!" came the order, and a moment later a volley of arrows arced its way through the air. Before it could land, the captain ordered Second Company to a jog, and the group started its advance.

Grimble's company, and Third Company in front of them, drew back their bowstrings. Both companies loosed at the same time and a volley twice as large as the one before began its arc toward the horde. Third Company moved forward at a jog, while Grimble's company, Fourth, fired another volley.

"Fourth Company, ready... Spear!" ordered Dek. Grimble and the rest secured their bows, grabbed their shields, and unstrapped their spears, their horses beginning their jog toward the horde before them. The troopers moved closer together, each rider and mount pressing against those on either side until they moved as one unit.

"Goat! Get ready to stab the piss out of those fuckers!" Kelban bellowed.

Goat's ever-impassive face was a few shades redder than usual, his gaze locked on the goblins. Grimble breathed easier.

Another volley of arrows launched from the eastern woods, pelting the goblins, and a few more shields disappeared from the walls as their bearers fell. The screeching from the horde crescendoed. Thirty yards ahead of Grimble's company, Second Company stood in their stirrups, drew their bowstrings back, and loosed. Then the column turned right and, at a gallop, sped toward the south of the field. Third Company did the same, but wheeled around to take position behind Fourth Company.

"At the lope... Yah!" Commander Dek shouted. Fourth Company's troopers sped up and readied themselves for the charge. Grimble braced himself further, using his legs to apply tension between his stirrups and saddle. They were now forty yards from the horde.

Beshta'Rek shouted to the goblins facing the eastern tree line and pointed toward the cavalry charge coming from the west. Impressively, en masse, the bulk of them moved to bolster the wall facing the troopers bearing down on them. It was a commendable effort for their kind, but it would not be enough. Fourth Company was now thirty yards away.

"Spears!" ordered Dek.

"Rah!" the troopers shouted as one, lowering and couching their weapons.

It was too much for some of the goblins, and nearly a quarter of those remaining dropped their shields, fervently, fearfully fleeing the impending pain and death. It was at that moment that Too'Ug, directly in Grimble's line of sight, stepped closer to Beshta'Rek. The chieftain's lieutenant made a gesture in front of his face, like that of catching a hair blowing in the wind, and grabbed the chieftain's belt.

The two disappeared into nothingness. It appeared as if they'd been sucked into a hole in the air, like a scarf pulled through a ring.

"Wizard!" shouted Grimble and Goat, as the cavalry unit crashed into the shield wall.

# CHAPTER TWO

Bhen had grown up the son of gentry and accustomed to certain comforts. Even after he had been ordained in the service of the High Father he had found his life one of ease. But this past year had changed that. Specifically, serving this Devout Mother had changed that. His surprise assignment as a chaplain to Fort Anjermott, home of the 209th Light Cavalry, had shocked Bhen, but he had prayed it would be a pleasant and worthy station.

His hopes had been dashed upon his arrival. Khvoron, the town outside Anjermott, was small and offered few comforts, and the nearest respectable city was more than two days' travel away. There was no relief from life in the fort, and he was surrounded by wicked men. Nothing he had experienced had prepared him for the troopers' crude behavior and lewd conversation.

*Heathens.*

Still, the fort offered a proper Temple and chambers for him and his Devout Mother, Tara. That was, until she had announced a few weeks ago that they would accompany the regiment into the field, providing support for their latest mission. Bhen did not like that idea, but he withheld his doubts and hoped to endure.

Devout Mother Tara had been a revered and rising priest in the Temple of Truth as recently as a couple of years earlier, and Bhen had been proud when he was assigned to her ministry.

He looked around the tent, the acting Temple in the earthen fort. *Austere? Modest? Plain?* Bhen struggled to find a good word for it, so he settled for accuracy: *Disgusting.*

The bottom of the tent walls were splattered and stained with mud. Most of the grass within had been trampled into the dirt floor; a few tufts of green remained in unpredictable locations – for the sole purpose of making him stumble, Bhen was convinced. And the bugs – they crawled everywhere.

*Crawling. Flying.* He slapped at something on his face. *Biting.*

Bhen was thankful for the short brown hair that protected his scalp, and wished he was able to grow a beard or mustache to protect his face. He had wondered if they were attracted to his dark complexion, but he noticed them crawling on the light skin of the Devout Mother, too.

"Bhen? You're distracted," the Devout Mother said. "Focus."

"Yes, Mother," said Bhen. *Someone in her position should not have to endure such shabby conditions.* He looked up from his book and shifted his weight on his folding stool, attempting to find some relief from the hard wooden slats. He must remember to pack a cushion next time.

The Devout Mother's back was to Bhen, but somehow she knew he had lost his battle with discomfort. Her attention remained on the altar and candlesticks as she scraped the wax from them. She was taller than the average woman, five feet and eight inches, the same as Bhen. The blue edging of her white robe rippled in the lamplight. Bhen stared at the shimmering fabric, unable to focus on the scripture in his book. He found himself lost in the robe's woven fibers.

"Have the words miraculously transferred to the back of my robe?"

"No, Mother." Bhen gritted his teeth and shook his head. *Focus.*

"Then you must be telling me you've studied Raiyam's First Letter to Emperor Uldey long enough and you are prepared to recite it, without the Verity." Devout Mother Tara placed the tools on the altar and turned to face Bhen. He braced, expecting a harsh, judgmental glare. Instead he found her countenance soft and assuring.

"I have not, Mother. I..." Bhen paused. It was too early; the sun was not yet up. How could anyone focus on anything at this hour?

"You are distracted because so much is foreign to you now."

"This is true. But how can I avoid the influence of these conditions – the bugs, the lack of proper food, the ground? Sleeping on the ground, Mother, how can I not let that affect me?"

"We give our bodies to the High Father's service. When you finally accept that, things will not feel foreign." She stepped away from the altar toward a chest containing boxes of candles. She paused and turned to Bhen. "Wait – on the ground? Please, dear Bhen, don't tell me you've been sleeping on the ground. What of your cot? You are sleeping on your cot, aren't you?"

"My cot? Oh, yes, it's fine. I sleep on it every night." He hoped he had hidden his discomfort better this time. His statement was not a lie. His cot was fine, and he had been sleeping on it – the canvas portion of it, which was laid upon the ground. The cot's wooden beams and cross-posts lay in pieces near where he slept. Bhen had eventually given up trying to assemble the cursed contraption, and he refused to get help. He was too embarrassed to ask his Devout Mother how to assemble it and too proud to have one of the camp's attendants do it for him.

"There is more on your mind," Mother said.

"I will be alright, Mother."

"Very well, then. Since you are unable to recite the reading in its whole, can you tell me why Raiyam wrote the letter to Emperor Uldey?"

"It can be summed up in the closing lines, Mother. *'One would go mad trying to catch the seeds of the floccus tree in their hand. Seek not to place our church under your dominion. The word of Abbyon, the Word of Truth, spreads like floccus seeds. Seek harmony over control.'*"

"Did Emperor Uldey stop trying to take control of the children of Abbyon?"

"These are lessons I already learned in the seminary, Mother. No. He was too proud. He could not let something fall outside his control. He did eventually go mad, unable to bring the church under his dominion. Even if it was discomforting to him, he should have accepted things as they were."

Devout Mother Tara smiled. "I want you to think on that while we pray this morning."

Bhen nodded, wondering why she smiled. At her gesture, they moved from the Temple tent into the attached, smaller clergy tent. Bhen helped the Devout Mother prepare her area, a corner of the tent sectioned off with folding partitions and hanging scrims. After the incense was lit and her calming prayers intoned, the Devout Mother stepped onto her prayer rug and knelt, sitting back on her legs, hands on her lap. Her light skin and white robe contrasted with the dark-blue rug and dirt floor. She nodded, and Bhen returned to his area.

The unassembled cot lying on the dirt floor reminded him of their conversation. *Why does she want me to think about Emperor Uldey and his refusal to accept the way things were?*

Bhen prepared his candles and incense and knelt on his rug in preparation for his own prayer time. He cleared his mind and thought of nothing; a blackness. Errant images and waiting tasks insinuated themselves, or tried. Something crawled on his leg. He swatted at it. Bhen moved his mind to the tranquility, to the void, again and again, until he was distracted no longer. A calm crept over his body, starting in his arms and legs and working toward his torso, and finally, his head. His mind opened.

"Bhen… Bhen…" called the Mother. "Bhen." Her voice was weak.

The priest's mind closed and he was brought back to the *now*. The Devout Mother called to him again and he bolted to her. Throwing aside the scrim, he found her attempting to crawl toward her desk. Her pale skin glistened in the candlelight. Her long, black hair clung to her face. Her breathing was labored.

"Mother, what happened?" he asked.

"Please," she said, "help me to my desk. I wish to sit."

Bhen reached for her arm, trying to help her up, but his grip slipped on her sweaty skin. He caught her before she fell and helped her to the chair. She was weak – not the woman he had left minutes ago. Once seated, she let out a long breath and reached for her goblet. Bhen helped steady it in her hand while she drank. She finished and he poured her more water from the silver pitcher on the side table.

"What did this?" he asked. "Are you ill? Do you need something to eat?"

"No, no," she said, her breathing slowing. "I've had a vision. Abbyon showed me a vision."

Bhen stood there, clutching the pitcher to his chest as though trying to protect it from the Devout Mother's words. Visions were not unheard of, but remained rare. The messages one received through them might be confused for dreams or transient thoughts and images, and only the Shepherd was supposed to receive visions from the High Father. He said nothing, his voice far from his moving lips.

"The details must be remembered," she said. "I am still too weak. You must write this down, Bhen."

Bhen paused a moment before he set the pitcher down and knelt beside her desk, preparing the pen and paper. His hands trembled and he took several breaths to calm himself. When he was ready, he nodded.

The Devout Mother began. "I looked down on a large pond. The water there was shallow and the edges were ringed with patches of green grass and tall trees. As I watched, the shallows turned muddy. The grass died. The trees that remained were dead, without bark, and gray. It resembled a swamp. Those gray trees became giant spikes in the dark water, and there were few remaining green patches of grass. I could see small fish in the still water among the old tree roots and along the muddy banks."

Bhen scratched the words onto the parchment as fast as he dared. Dipping the pen's nib in the little inkwell made him the most nervous; he did so with an extra breath and prayed for a steady hand. He didn't want to miss anything, but feared that he would tip the inkwell in his haste and spill ink all over the parchment.

"The water was familiar," the Devout Mother continued. "No – it was welcoming. The patches of land felt like home. I peered over the edge of the land and into the water. My reflection resembled a bird. Then the bird wasn't me. I was looking at it. It was a white heron, standing motionless on a patch of dead grass at the edge of the water."

Bhen gasped. "The white heron. Abbyon himself?"

"I believe that is what the vision meant." The Devout Mother continued. "Out of the woods walked a white horse. It was beautiful and lean, and it moved gracefully to the edge of the water."

"Eblees?"

"The pond, or swamp, was now a stream. The horse raised its head high, pinning its ears back. It dug at the bank with its hoof. The heron raised its head and spread its wings. The two faced each other from opposite banks.

"The horse lowered its head to drink, and as it did so, five snakes and a songbird crawled from its mouth and lay on the ground by its hooves. The heron closed its wings and lowered itself to the ground. It stood again. Beneath it were five frogs and an egg."

"A frog egg?"

"No." Mother paused, thinking. "It was an egg like that of a small bird. White with brown speckling. One of the horse's snakes writhed on the ground and turned into eight snakes. Those snakes then slithered into the water and disappeared beneath the surface. I could not see into the water. The surface reflected the land around them.

"Two of the frogs jumped into the air above the stream. The two became six and they dove beneath the water's surface. The ripples created as the frogs and snakes entered the water grew large and violent, crashing into the banks and flowing up and downstream. Though they were separated by water, the horse lowered and snaked its head at the heron. The heron spread its wings and kicked at the horse. The ground shook." The Devout Mother took a breath. "That is all I remember."

Bhen finished writing the details of the vision, noting its receiver, the date and location, and his own name as the scribe. He blew onto the paper, drying the ink. His hands began to shake again as he realized he now held what may become an artifact in the Temple of Truth. Bhen worked to calm himself.

*Abbyon and Eblees. The two gods. The two churches. They've existed side by side – are they now to war?*

"Seal it," Mother said. "Then prepare the font. I must speak with the Council."

"Yes, Mother." Bhen rolled the parchment, produced a wax stick from the desk, and worked it in the candle's flame, preparing to seal the document. "How should I prepare the font? Are you contacting the Council of Mothers or Fathers?"

"*The* Council, Bhen. The Shepherd's Council. I must speak with the Shepherd."

"Of course," said Bhen. He sealed the rolled parchment with a blue ribbon and the Devout Mother's signet ring. "I'll gather the relics."

# CHAPTER THREE

Commander Loren Dek surveyed the landscape. He was struck by the stark difference a single night could make. Where yesterday's sun had set on chaos, it rose this morning to order – albeit a gruesome order. He gazed at the smoldering remnants of goblins on the burn pile. The stench from that mound and the blood-covered grass befouled the area. With every retch he heard and every repulsive breath he took, Dek thought about the alternative: a field fouled for months instead of days.

His thoughts turned to his men. They'd never been tasked with cleaning up the battlefield after an engagement. He knew that with the rise of the new day, every trooper would become aware of how long they had been awake. The light on their faces would renew them, however, and they would find a little more strength. Dek's brown eyes had borne witness to a great many things in his career. Yet he was ever impressed by the strength and endurance of youth. Horses he had ridden when he first served were older than some of the men he now led. Those steeds were long retired to pastures and farmlands, or no longer of this world. Occasionally he thought of them, and of the time he himself would no longer be able to dutifully perform his job; but he loved it so and he loved his men. Gray hair be damned – as long as he could step into the saddle, he would continue to fight and stave off the inevitable.

"Commander Dek," Lieutenant Trey Kani called.

"What's the word?" Dek asked his adjutant.

"Burial detail is complete, sir. Both men's lieutenants are preparing letters for the memorial service."

"What about the hunting party?"

"A mixed team of Ravens departed a few hours ago to hunt down the goblin chieftain and his mage, Too'Ug. Three Ravens remain with us for the ride back to camp. One of them completes his term of service in a few weeks, as I understand it."

"Excellent. Let's mount up and get these men back to camp."

Trey ran off to give the orders as Dek mounted up. His muscles and joints ached, but the saddle still felt natural. He patted his buckskin warhorse, Oak Warden, on the neck.

*Not too old yet.*

They had been on the road for half the morning when the first outlying homesteads of Talas appeared. The town of Talas had suffered an earlier goblin raid, and taking the quickest path back to camp meant traveling through it. The first home appeared uninhabited, overgrown grass and untended fields confirming the suspicion. The regiment soon passed several burnt-out houses and barns. As the main force rounded a bend, the forward scouts came into view. One kicked his horse into a gallop, passing the vanguard unit and riding straight to the command group.

"Commander Dek," the scout said, "our approach has been reported to the town. There's a crowd waiting. They appear unhappy, sir."

Captain Paul Gengler, Dek's executive officer, raised a finger to the scout. "Give us a minute." The scout moved his horse away from the command group and Paul turned to Dek. "I know you may not want to, but if we take the column around the town, sir, we'll likely avoid a political complication. The men are worn thin. All it will take is for one citizen to push our boys too far, maybe injure one, and we'll have a serious situation."

"I'm aware, Captain," Dek said. "Vasterland has always been on the edge of compliance with His Majesty. However, avoiding the town will make us appear weak and untrustworthy. Duke Haugo will seize that and further his efforts. We must win over the Duchy of Vasterland, not avoid it."

"Rah, sir," Paul said. "Scout!"

The scout rode up. "Yes, sir."

"Take position in the vanguard. We're moving through Talas."

"Rah, sir."

The regiment moved forward again and scooped up the other forward scout. As Talas came into sight, it was clear it had suffered greatly at the hands of Beshta'Rek and his goblin horde. Some buildings showed signs of fresh walls and newly thatched roofs, but several structures in the town remained burnt-out husks.

A man on horseback rode from the town and approached the column. The stout man wore gray pants above his riding boots, a black vest with a white shirt beneath, and around his neck dangled a brass medallion on a green ribbon embroidered with white thread. The medallion, a kite shield with wings encircling up from the sides, noted his status as the mayor. A scout escorted him the rest of the way to Dek, introducing the pallid mayor to their commander.

"We're just marching through, Your Honor," Dek said.

"Pardon, Mr. Commander Dek, sir," said the mayor. He mopped his forehead with a kerchief, his eyes wide and bloodshot. "But I think it may be better if you don't go through town. You see, a lot of the folks are – well, they're quite upset, on account of you moving on. Talk is you're doing so without – without finding those beasts, without finishing the job. Their words, sir. Many had loved ones killed or taken. No offense meant, sir."

"Mayor," Dek said, "you may inform your town that we met the enemy and left none alive on the field. The few who ran off are being hunted down as we speak."

Some color returned to the mayor's face. A shy smile grew across his mouth and ended at the corners of his eyes. "Thank you, sir. I will, sir." He rode back at once.

When the 209th entered the town, they were met by a distant mood. The townsfolk gave them looks like those on the faces of soldiers after combat. Each person appeared equally ready to tip toward violence or capitulation, like a dog with a blank stare. Everyone moved out of the regiment's way, save one woman.

Bent and weathered, she appeared to be close to sixty years old, but was likely much younger. Hours working in the sun and the hard fight she had given to make a home and a family so close to the wildlands had taken their toll. She stood in the middle of the road and stared at the ground in front of her, no emotion on her face. The column halted.

The mayor rode up to Dek. "That's Widow Saliese. Those filthy creatures killed her husband and took her two sons when they hit our town. She has no one left. Give me a moment and I'll get her to move."

Dek stayed the mayor with his hand, dismounted, and

approached the widow. His personal guard dismounted too, but Dek waved them off.

"Did you see my boys?" she asked. Her voice was delicate, tied between them with her last strand of hope and hanging in the air like gossamer, ready to snap. "Did you save my boys?" Her eyes fixed to the ground. Her face impassive.

"I'm afraid not, ma'am," Dek said.

Her eyes started to water, her face unchanging. She raised her head and looked at Dek. Her lips trembled. Her forehead wrinkled. Then she slapped him.

The guards and several other troopers started forward again. Dek turned to look at them, stopping their advance with his outstretched hand.

"Why'd you let them take my boys?" she cried. "Why'd you wait so long to do something? They took my boys. They took my Bren and Jarod." She broke into hysterical crying and fell to her knees.

Dek knelt and leaned in until their heads were inches apart. They talked about her sons, and he made her a promise.

After a while, Dek helped her to her feet and held her arm as they moved toward a few nearby townsfolk, who took her in and comforted her. They gave Dek unreadable stares. He walked back to his horse, remounted, and gave the order to move out. As they left Talas behind, he said a prayer.

It was his sixth prayer of the day. That many prior to a battle would be expected, but these had come after one. He wondered what had changed.

By midday each of the returning troopers had been up for over thirty hard hours. The warm sun and rhythmic walk of their horses lulled the newest among them into a saddle-borne, heavy-eyed trance. It was to be expected. To keep the troopers on their mark, Commander Dek gave the order to have all outriders paired up and relieved frequently. The 209th was inarguably the toughest unit in the King's Army, but the men were human.

The forward scouts came into view several hours later. Positioned on the road at the far end of a farmer's field, one kept his eye forward, the other watching for the battalion. Moments after seeing the main body, the rearward-facing trooper raised his spear above his head with both hands, as if trying to poke a low-flying cloud, and moved the tip of it in a full circle. The vanguard lieutenant raised his hand above his head, palm open, and the regiment came to a halt. Commander Dek and his staff moved off the road to take position in the field on the right. The captains shouted the orders to assemble and oversaw the formation of the battalion into its four companies.

"Wicked Spears." Dek's voice was strong and proud. "We have engaged a terrible enemy and emerged the victors. Whether here, with the priests, or sitting at the table in Ihgel's Hall, I am proud to call every trooper in this regiment my brother. You are the blood of the 209th, you are the saviors of this land, and you are the pride of King Saevar! Hold your heads high, for the denizens of the Abyss fear you and the ladies of Aendura wish they were yours." Dek paused for a moment. "Who owns the battle?" he shouted.

"Wicked Spears!" came the cry of over one hundred men.

"Swifter than wind…"

"Harder than steel!" the men yelled.

"Damn right! Parade column by company! First Company is lead company!"

The troopers aligned in formation, their saddle posture returning to its rigid state. Even the horses knew their part. The wind grabbed the regiment's battle flag as the color guard unfurled it, rippling its red-and-white quadrants.

"Battalion," shouted Commander Dek, and after hearing the proper echoes, ordered, "At the jog... Yah!"

The cavalry unit started its forward motion, outriders posting themselves close to the column. As the battalion rounded the edge of a copse of trees, their camp, a square-shaped fort, came into view. The redoubt was surrounded by eight-foot-high, hundred-yard-long walls of freshly dug earth with a loose palisade of sticks at the top. It was the standard that all Aenduran soldiers knew too well. Since there was plenty of forestland in this area, the bottom of each wall was further protected by an abatis.

Inside the walls the camp was broken into four quadrants. The tents and stables were arranged in such a precise order that any soldier or official, stationed or visiting, would know how to move about and find who or what was needed. Gaps between rows of tents, wagons, and other structures acted as streets and alleys, permitting natural movement for the troops within. The soldiers had named these byways, making it easier to give directions when specific tents needed to be located. The regimental colors flew over the camp, but beside it and matching its height was the green-and-gold pennant of the Earl of Lanrik, Kaye Anderson – a brazen display, indicating that Lanrik earldom was equal in station to the king and his army.

"The impudence," Lieutenant Kani said.

"I'm certain he sees it as appropriate," Dek replied. "I'd expect as much from any of Earl Anderson's knights, most of all his own brother."

"Shall I have the soup blanket prepared?" the lieutenant asked.

"That may be necessary," Dek nodded, and Trey smiled.

# CHAPTER FOUR

"Have you ever seen the commander rest?" Kelban asked, as they coached their horses to a jog. He was eyeing the man, awe plainly written on his face.

Grimble cocked his head. "No. Never."

"He never looks tired, either." Kelban's forehead wrinkled and his eyes got that faraway look.

"He's a beast."

"He's more than that. I'm telling ya, it's like he's an enchanted statue or something."

"What?" Grimble laughed. "Holy shit, Kelban. You sound smitten."

"I am. But it would never work out between us. He doesn't strike me as a cuddler, and you know how much I like to cuddle." Kelban couldn't keep the straight face. His lips pressed tightly, trying to contain a smirk.

Grimble chuckled. "Yeah, that's the first thing everyone thinks about when they see you, Kelban the Cuddler."

Kelban's look turned serious again. "I'm just saying, I'd follow that man to the Abyss. Those goblins gave us a serious fight and we only lost two, with about, what, a dozen wounded? I doubt there's a better leader in the army." He took a swig from his canteen and offered it to Grimble, who waved it away. Kelban finished the contents. "I may have been wrong about that chieftain being a human, but he has to be more than just a goblin. Those little shits fought like zealots."

"You may have something there. None of what happened yesterday was normal."

"I'm telling ya. Especially the wizard part. None of the lads I've spoken with have ever heard of goblins having a mage."

Grimble shook his head. "I almost missed my target because of that thing."

"You really saw it happen?"

"I don't know how you missed it."

"Maybe I was focused on my job and not daydreaming like someone else."

"Oh, it's like that?" Grimble smiled. "He was right in front of me – how could I not see it happen?"

Kelban's eyebrows shot up. "If he was in front of you, did you get a look at him? Could you see the ugly one's face?"

Grimble lost the smile, his face resolute. "Yeah. He was hideous."

"Really?"

"Yeah. Long face. Bug-eyed. Oozing pustules. Looked a lot like your last sweetheart."

"You son of a bitch."

Grimble smirked. "Couldn't see into his hood. Didn't see his face at all."

"That was good. You drew me in. Had me where you wanted me. You're getting better at this. I'll have to be more careful from now on." They rode for another minute before Kelban asked,

"Did you manage to ask anyone in Talas?"

"What?" said Grimble. "Oh. No. Didn't get the chance to ask about Ellie. None of the townsfolk were near me when we stopped. Not happy about that."

"Well, I did."

Grimble looked at Kelban. "And...?"

"She and her father hadn't been through Talas either. Sorry, brother."

"I didn't think they'd come this far west, but you never know. Thanks for checking. I owe you one."

Grimble got lost in thought again. The most promising replies he'd ever received to his questions and descriptions were "Don't think I've seen them in years," but most said they had never seen anyone resembling the merchant and his daughter at all.

*It's like they just disappeared. Damn it all!*

The fortified camp neared. "Look sharp, Goat," said Grimble. "Show those local boots what a real weapon of war really looks like."

Goat raised his head a little higher.

Kelban pressed his lips together, but nodded. He looked at Grimble and gave a thumbs-up. As glowing an endorsement as Grimble had seen Kelban give the boot to this point.

They approached the main gate of the camp in time to see men removing the obstacles in front of the opening in the dirt wall, an opening big enough for a wagon to squeeze through. Lord Albert Anderson's foot soldiers, assigned to guarding the camp while the regiment was out, moved the barricades for the returning cavalry troopers. Joining Anderson's soldiers were those who'd returned earlier with the wounded, as well as a handful of regimental support troopers and dozens of non-combatants who had stayed behind.

The troopers in camp rendered salutes for the returning cavalry as the regiment entered through a growing tunnel of personnel along Main Street. Grimble and the rest of the troopers simply wanted to make it to their tents, but nodded here and there to acknowledge the ones they knew in the gathering crowd. Ahead of the dust cloud, Commander Dek and his staff made their way to the headquarters tents at the center of camp. Fourth Company continued on until they reached their section.

Roche pulled up next to Grimble. "I need you to help Goat with his prayers and rituals."

"Worried about fights?" Grimble asked.

"Absolutely," Roche said. "You know these boys haven't trained enough. They saw their first action, they're fatigued, they're going to make mistakes. Thom and some of the other hotheads will no doubt jump their shit for it. I don't think these kids are going to take it today."

"Rah, sir," Grimble said. "I was thinking the same thing." Roche nodded and rode away to speak with Sergeant "Dinger" Durinson, Second Platoon's sergeant.

For the 209th Light Cavalry Regiment, the particular routine of tacking, untacking, and caring for the horse was akin to a religious ceremony, such was the reverence paid to each step and motion. So much so that in training a boot would suffer ridicule and harassment for days for missing a minor detail in the process; or worse, could be beaten immediately for dropping a critical step in caring for their horse.

Normally, by the time a boot had earned his spot to ride into battle with the regiment, he had mastered all the rituals and rites and could do them without thinking. But these were hard times for the King's Army and these boots had been sent into combat much sooner than ever before. Their current state would no doubt lead to mistakes, and that would lead to fights.

After the horses were cared for, the men were allowed to eat their rations while tending to their equipment. Armor, tack, and saddles were brushed clean and prepared for the next time, then hung on racks along with the saddle blankets in order to air out. Swords were deburred, sharpened, and oiled, and their scabbards cleaned. Spears were similarly cared for, and broken shafts were replaced with new ones. Weapons and equipment beyond repair were taken to the smiths at the workshops and reworked, reforged, or replaced.

Everything had to be ready in the event that the regiment was attacked or ordered to move out immediately. At that time, and not before, the men were permitted to wash up, get a few hours' sleep, visit comrades in the Temple's clinic, or mourn the loss of a friend. Grimble and Roche worked their way around, checking on the men, and were the last to get time for themselves. Grimble noticed Roche swaying ever so slightly as he stood up from one of the bedsides.

"Are you alright, sir?" he asked.

"Yeah. Yeah," Roche said, brushing off the moment. "Boot slipped. That's all."

Grimble watched him as they returned to their section of the camp, but everything appeared normal, and he soon dismissed his worries.

Commander Loren Dek was graced with the second-largest tent in camp. The Temple tent, several times bigger than Dek's, had the honor of being the most massive and the cleanest; though *clean* was relative, as nothing remained unstained in the field. The extra space in Dek's tent was not for luxury. It merely afforded him the ability to meet with his entire staff, protected from the elements if the front awning became insufficient.

Dek and the rest of his staff approached his mottled, mud-stained canvas dwelling. A magnificent chestnut stallion, tacked with an ornamented saddle and reins, stood posted beside the tent. Enjoying the shade under the awning were two of Lord Anderson's foot soldiers in their green gambesons. One leaned against his glaive, gripping it for support, his shoulders sagging. The other sat on the small meeting table, his glaive propped against one of the awning's support poles. Both soldiers' helmets sat upon the table with a similarly casual air.

The men appeared more like thugs than trained members of a military unit. Their unpolished demeanor was in direct contrast to the troopers of the 209th. Dek couldn't wait until the camp was free of their influence.

As he and his men made their approach, the two soldiers made a lubberly and disinterested effort to stand upright. One lolled his head toward the tent. "My lord," he said, "Commander Dek's arrived."

Dek studied the soldiers as he dismounted. He handed his horse's reins over to Trey and nodded. The adjutant smiled from his saddle. The two troopers assigned to his own guard seemed unable to ignore the failure to salute and show proper respect to the commander. Their gazes were locked on the foot soldiers, like hunting dogs on quarry. Trey and the rest of the staff turned their mounts and rode off to untack the horses. At the last possible moment, Dek's guards broke their stares and followed.

Commander Dek stepped forward, staring into the eyes of the closest soldier. In his mind were the five ways he'd already imagined he could kill the man, and he was working on his sixth – seventh – eighth. What bravado the soldier had had moments before hurriedly fled as he read the experienced warrior's eyes. The soldier averted his gaze and lifted the nearest tent flap so the commander could enter.

Dek donned a practiced smile as he moved inside, allowing the tent flap to close behind him. "Sir Albert, we have returned." He doffed his helmet. "I cannot thank you and your men enough for so courteously protecting our camp while we were away."

"Commander Dek," Lord Anderson said, "it was our distinct honor to fulfill this small part in the mission." His tone bore no inflection, no genuineness. "Congratulations on your victory."

The interior was much as it had been when the regiment departed. Dek's wooden cot was in a far corner. Upon it was Lord Anderson's pack and fur bedroll, already prepared for the journey home. At the foot of the cot was one of Dek's locked chests. In the other far corner was a small table like the one outside, with a vertical secretary of shelves and drawers secured to it by leather straps. There were barely two strides between the makeshift desk and cot. But it was enough room for Lord Albert Anderson to lounge in a chair, his right arm resting on the desk, and his booted feet upon Dek's other chest.

Albert focused intently on a sliver of dried apple held between his thumb and index finger. "My men and I are ever at the king's disposal." He chewed, seeming to contemplate the existence of dried fruit with little attention to the commander's presence.

"Would that the entire land were filled with men such as yourself."

"Yes, if only there were more men like me, then King Saevar could rest knowing these lands were well protected. His reign would be a mem – memorable one." Albert smiled and switched his focus to Dek for the first time. "Commander, I hope you don't mind – I happened across these tasty dried apples. They are delicious, and it seems I've finished off this entire sack. No doubt you have more stored somewhere and won't miss these, eh?"

Albert's dark eyes stayed focused on Dek's, as if trying to read him.

"What's mine is yours, Sir Albert," Dek said.

Loren Dek was a soldier, a warrior. He hated these moments of diplomacy and royal court play. The king ruled everyone, and the 209$^{th}$ acted under his authority. That meant Commander Dek was to be given every courtesy – but the king could not govern if unrest were created by his soldiers running rudely through counties and duchies, disrespecting the nobles charged with caring for them. The earls and dukes must not have their delicate egos damaged, lest they conspire against the ruling family. Orders given to the nobility must be veiled and colored as requests. It was a delicate balance. Courtesy was key. Dek's skill in brokering these meetings had excelled the last few years.

Albert, too, would know he had to be careful in this subtle game. Although this was a common man before him, Commander Dek's words had the power of the king, and the king's orders must be followed. Dek may not be nobility, but it was necessary to treat him as though he were. No doubt this frustrated Albert even more than looking after a feculent cavalry encampment. Dek, acting on King Saevar's behalf, had shown proper courtesy, and were Albert now to offend him, he would also offend his monarch and bring exaction. The other earls would not take his brother's side in this matter if that were the case. Dek figured it was Albert's goal to push him just enough to remind him who was of noble birth, but not provoke a royal response.

"You, sir, are a gentleman," Albert said. "It is a shame you had to ride so far from Fort Anjermott. Were Lanrik Earldom able to muster enough horses during this time of Planting, we could have saved you the effort. My men are well trained and absolutely lethal. Maybe we could remain in camp a few more days. We may be able to teach your soldiers a few of our well-known fighting techniques."

Dek let his smile fade. "His Majesty would not impose upon *his* nobles in such a way, forcing horses from the fields when they are most needed there. Our king is as just as he is wise, and ever aware of the obligations of the earls and their subjects. Besides, that is why you pay taxes, is it not? So we may ride in and protect his subjects in times of need, times such as these. And to your offer – indeed, your men do have their own way; I was witness to their military bearing just now. But I fear it would confuse my troopers, as our styles are different. There is no need to further impose upon your men – they already appear weary for the work they've done. No doubt all of you would prefer to spend this evening in your own beds."

A year ago, Dek would not have been able to stifle the derision trying to fight its way from his chest.

*Your men can only teach my men what* not *to do.*

As indicated by Albert's play, and his refusal yet to stand or even move from his relaxed position, he and his men would not go courteously from the camp. They would need encouragement. Albert had also played a card he thought would provoke Dek into making an impudent mistake, but it had failed, and he was now on the defensive. Dek displayed his best court smile.

A smile slowly lifted the corners of Albert's mouth, too, one side more than the other. It was a smile given by a competitor who knows the game has begun in earnest. "You must think me rude. I've kept your seat from you. Please, remove your armor and gear, have a seat, make yourself comfortable. It is, after all, your tent." He slid his feet from the chest, allowing his heels to scrape across the top of it, and stood.

Albert was a formidable man in his own right. Even seated, he was an arresting figure in his engraved steel and leather armor. Now standing, he took command of the tent without effort, but years of good living had rounded the harder edges of a body once accustomed to fighting. He did not move away from the chair.

"My thanks for your offer," said Dek, "but my work is not yet done." He was three inches shorter than Albert's six feet, but size mattered little to the seasoned warrior. Albert's intimidation efforts were better suited to his own men and the locals. Dek moved forward without hesitation.

"That's right, you cavalry types have quirky customs. Horse before man, or something like that."

"Something like that." Dek allowed the slightest hint of a growl to occupy the words as he locked his eyes on Albert. The lord held his stare; this was just his game. The two were within arm's reach of each other.

"Well, never let ick—" Albert stopped mid-sentence and appeared to choke on the very words he tried to utter. He tilted his head slightly to one side, raised an eyebrow, and breathed in, preparing to speak. He seemed unable to find the right words. His lips parted, twice, before he managed, "Never le—"

"Are you alright, Sir Albert?" Dek asked. He used his most caring manner, getting closer to the knight, practically face to face, as though examining the larger man.

The smell had reached Dek, and it was gloriously pungent, heavy on ammonia with debilitating notes of decay and waste, and a retching, gastric finish. Unpleasant as it was to Dek, he was able to tolerate the odor, as was every trooper in the 209th. The soup blanket was one of their earliest training tests – "soup" being a runny mixture of horse manure and urine, left to sit in a dark recess of the camp for days. Awash with the mixture, the blanket would be carried to its resting place – in this instance, next to the commander's tent on the upwind side.

"The aroma of one hundred fifty horses returning to camp," Dek said, "can be discomforting to some. I hope it is not offensive to you."

The foot soldiers pretending to guard the tent started coughing. "Gods!" one said.

Lord Albert Anderson's abdomen jerked, and a look of concern crept into his eyes. He hurriedly grabbed his kit from the cot and made his way toward the tent's exit. Once outside, he took a deep breath, but the look on his face improved only slightly. Albert turned to look at Dek one more time, confusion and concern written plainly across his face.

"I return the camp to your care, Commander Dek," he coughed, and mounted his waiting steed.

"You and your men have our gratitude," replied Dek slowly, torturously drawing out the formalities. "I have the watch now."

Albert turned to the soldiers guarding the tent. "Gather the men and assemble outside the main gate," he said. He rode off, adding, perhaps louder than he meant, "By all that is holy, what do they feed their horses?"

The two foot soldiers removed themselves from the area with equal fervor, calling for their comrades. Commander Dek suddenly found himself alone. Even outside, the soup blanket was painfully obvious, proudly announcing itself to everyone downwind. Dek worked to ignore it again. He stretched his body and arched his back. His joints loudly protested the motions, and his muscles silently resisted the effort, but he felt renewed. Securing the entrance flaps open, he reentered his tent.

Dek set about returning his personal chest back to its spot. As he was unlocking his military chest, removing the maps and journals within, and replacing them on the desk, a voice announced itself from the entrance.

"Trooper Wollter reporting." Wollter stood rigidly at attention, his armor brushed clean of road dust. He took a noticeable sniff of the air and smiled.

"Special orders remain per field operations. Carry on, trooper. Rah?" Dek said. He added a sniff and a smile, returning the inside joke.

"Rah, sir!"

Dek knew the trooper was tired, but he would fulfill his duty until relieved – if only to bring some dignity and military bearing back to the command tent, to show any of Lord Anderson's soldiers who may walk by what it meant to be a professional warrior.

Within minutes the buzz of activity at Dek's tent would start, and continue for several hours before the commander would be able to check on his men in the clinic. It began with Lieutenant Trey Kani, his adjutant. Trey entered with the commander's riding tack and waited. Dek, in the middle of retrieving his pens and ink, paused long enough to point to the rack in the corner of the tent. Trey secured the tack, as he'd done countless times before, then approached Dek and assisted him out of his armor.

"Commander," he said, "you'll be happy to know Lord Anderson and his soldiers are leaving camp and preparing to return home. Word's been sent to the brewer. The interim logistics sergeant advises the Hasty Report was sent by bird to

Anjermott immediately after the men arrived last night with the wounded. Third Battalion kept their anticipated shipment schedules, and the water teams have similarly met their requirements. Fodder and water supplies are at operational levels. The requisitions from the locals have not come through, and our stores of rations stand at four days."

Trey stopped briefly, watching Dek silently shake his head.

"I agree, sir," the adjutant said. "You'd think we'd receive more support from the locals affected by the raids. I have to wonder if something else may be afoot. Just the same, the paperwork should be to you within the hour. Lastly, Oak Warden is eating as we speak and ready for your visit. Shall I secure the apples for you, sir?"

"You can disregard that, Trey," said Dek. "Sir Albert found the store and deprived Warden of his treat. But don't worry – your efforts outside my tent made an uncomfortable departure for him. He paid for the apples he ate. And on that topic, now that he's gone, dispose of the blanket when you get the chance. You have my thanks for both tasks."

"Rah, sir." Trey dipped his head in quick acknowledgment. "Captain Gengler should be by shortly." The adjutant poured water into a basin on a tripod next to Dek's cot. "Your midday meal is on the planning table when you're ready. Please try to eat some, sir. Do you have any other orders at this time?"

"No, Trey. Thanks. See to your needs."

Dek's lunch rations would end up sitting on the wooden table under his tent's awning until after evening meal was served to the troops. This would not change their palatability one way or the other, but would be a tease and unheeded reminder as he moved in and out of the tent throughout the remainder of the day. In the late afternoon he would harass himself for not taking a nibble on the move, but challenge himself to wait for the evening's hot camp meal. In the end, that too would sit and grow cold. Immediately before he racked out, he would eat everything on the table and the next morning awaken in discomfort. His adjutant would not make a comment – he was too disciplined – but he would no doubt mentally chastise his commander.

Captain Paul Gengler, the commander's executive officer and second in command of the battalion, arrived a quarter hour after Trey left. Paul's visit interrupted Dek as he was writing his report to Regimental Headquarters.

"Commander, if you keep insisting on feeding the camp flies with your uneaten meals, may I suggest teaching them tricks, or at least naming them? I would quote policy on the prohibition of pets in camp, but as you're the —"

"Piss off, Paul," Dek said, his eyes remaining on the report. "You know it's too soon. My biscuit beetle died last week. I'm not ready for a new pet."

"Rah, sir," said Paul. His tone became serious. "I've checked on the wounded. Five needed no more than sutures or a burn, but eight remain in the Temple clinic. I've passed on tonight's orders to the company captains, as well as instructions for tomorrow morning's service for our fallen, and tomorrow evening's company time. The three cairns for tomorrow's ceremony – one other trooper did not make it back to the camp – will be in the yard, and the memorial cairns will be placed beside the Temple as usual."

Dek stopped writing, and he lifted his head from his report. "Three now. Shit! We should have overwhelmed those bastards. Wounded I can accept, but we shouldn't have lost a single trooper. Goblins don't fight like that, damn it all. We got sent in too early. The boots didn't have enough training."

"I agree with you, sir. On all counts."

"First we're left short for a year. Then they break up a couple infantry units and send us some untrained kids from one of them. Ihgel's arm! That's no way to run an army." Dek quieted. Paul was about to speak when the commander raised his voice. "And what in the Abyss is going on in the wildlands?" Dek let out a breath and rubbed his eyebrows, while Paul stood by and waited for the frustration to settle. "Who else did we lose?"

"Targer, Third Company boot. Bled out."

Dek closed his eyes and mumbled a few words.

Paul waited until the prayer was complete. "Speaking of the Temple, the Devout Mother requests your presence. She was insistent, and I don't think it was for the wounded men alone, sir. Her prayers and those of her priest have them well on the way to their recovery. Thank Abbyon."

"I'll make the Temple my first stop when I leave this tent."

"Oh, another thing." Paul fumbled with his belt and pulled forth a dark leather strap, about six inches long and two inches wide. "The boys found these around the necks of half the goblins, and a few others had them in pouches and pockets." He tossed the strap to Dek.

The commander examined the leather. It was darkened from moisture and smelled sour and rancid. He turned it over to find eight thin oval beads, rust-red in color, sewed onto the strap, one on top of the other. The leather bore no special inscriptions, stitching, or stamps. Dek looked up at Paul. "I've never seen anything like this on a goblin."

"None of us have. Could Beshta'Rek be more than a tribal chief? Could he be starting a new faction, using these as proof of loyalty or clan membership?"

"Perhaps," said Dek. "Another idea is that an outside group

is using these to pay or trade with 'Rek and his kind. Are they all alike?"

"The shape and color of the beads are, but not the number. Some straps are longer, some shorter. Most had a few beads. Eight was the most we could find on a strap. Only a handful of goblins had those."

"I'll include this in the report. Maybe someone back at Anjermott or even Agderon will know what these things mean." Dek set the strap on the desk. "What else do you have to report?"

Paul continued, pausing to answer questions or to give the commander a moment to recall something for his own paperwork. They discussed the team hunting down the goblin chieftain and made preparations for the regiment's return to Fort Anjermott once the wounded were ready for travel. When they were finished, the sun neared the horizon.

"Before you go," said Dek, "I've got one more thing I need you to do."

"Name it, sir."

"Get five volunteers from each company, preferably some with farming experience, and send them back to Talas the day after tomorrow. I promised Widow Saliese I would send some men to help get her fields planted and make needed repairs. They're to help her that day and the next, returning the morning after."

"Rah, sir. You know that isn't going to sit well with the men?"

"I'm aware. That's why we're going to offer them five nobs and a pass from guard duty for the rest of the month as incentive."

"Where are you getting the money, sir? How about this – we're almost through the Rising month of Planting. Let's make it no guard duty until the end of next month, the Heart of Planting, and no silver."

Dek shuffled through his papers and produced an envelope. "I advised you of our primary orders, but I didn't show you the entire dispatch."

"Pardon, sir? There was more?"

"I didn't share it with you because I wanted one of us to concentrate on destroying that goblin and his raiders. I didn't want anything else on your mind." Dek handed Paul the envelope, its broken seal still attached to the paper and ribbon.

Paul took a look at the envelope. His eyes widened momentarily when he noticed the king's own seal on the outside. Within it were two orders. The first he'd seen before, and he placed it aside. The second bore the king's seal, too, and gave orders for Commander Dek to conduct efforts, if possible, to counter the negative rumors spread by the duke and his earls. "*As we cannot alter the mind of the nobility —*"

"*— we must look to the people and win their hearts,*" Dek finished.

"King Saevar sent these orders himself?"

"Yes. He's long been dealing with his father's decision to change Vasterland from a march to a duchy. Apparently there's no winning that family, but why he'd go around the Lord High Constable and the war council, I can only guess."

"Glad I'm a trooper, and fight my enemies face to face. I'd never survive the politics of the court."

Dek chuckled. "They'd eat me up, too. I can barely play the game when it's one-on-one. But I guess if you have to, you learn to play or become a casualty."

"Alright, then, going back to the issue – where do we get the hundred dulas?"

"Since I was ordered to do what I can to improve the king's

image here, I'll request a bump in next month's pay to compensate the men."

"If they don't approve the request?"

"Then I'll pay it out of my account."

Paul's look of disbelief was unmistakable. "You're prepared to give the volunteers an extra week's pay from your own pocket for this stranger? You're not just doing this for His Majesty, are you?" he asked.

"No. This is more than the orders." Dek sat up straight and took a breath. "The army is all I have." Paul still appeared confused. Dek stretched his neck and took a deep breath. "I don't know if I ever told you, but my wife died in childbirth."

"I didn't know, sir."

"Few do. It was eighteen years and seven months ago. I have no children, no wife. The regiment is my family. These men are my family. That woman in Talas, Mrs. Saliese, lost her husband and her sons, all in one night. I'm sending some of my family to help a woman who lost hers."

"I support you, sir, but you can't blame yourself for the failure of the local nobles."

"I don't. It's the right thing to do and my special orders make it possible. Five dula and a pass from guard duty the rest of this month."

"Rah, sir."

"Send an officer with the men, two if we don't get any sergeants to volunteer. If the detachment has time, they are to help other locals as well."

"It'll be done."

A commotion started suddenly in camp. Not the urgent kind of disturbance that causes the hairs to stand up on the back of one's neck, but a series of noises and calls indicating something interesting moving through the streets. Within moments a horse approached at a fast jog and stopped in front of Dek's tent.

"Regimental courier, Commander," called the trooper on guard.

"Send him in," Dek said.

A road-weary trooper walked through the tent flaps, dressed in the uniform and armor of the 209th. His chest piece bore the emblem of Constable Dressel, the regiment's ranking officer. Every part of the trooper was dust-covered, and salt streaks trimmed his creases and joints. He came to attention and saluted. "Lancer Roux, with urgent orders from regiment."

Dek stood, returning the salute. "Come in, Roux." He held out his hand. Roux stepped into the tent and handed over the sealed dispatch. Dek put the trooper at ease before reading the orders. "Roux, see my adjutant, Lieutenant Kani, in the next tent. He'll set you up with a hot meal and a space to rack out. You can leave in the morning. I have several other dispatches to send with you. Rah?"

Roux came to attention. "Rah, sir."

"Dismissed." Dek returned Roux's salute and the trooper left the tent.

"Paul, how many Ravens returned with us?"

"Three, sir. Their lieutenant is with the others hunting down Beshta'Rek and his advisor. One of the three, a mage, is set to out-process at the end of the month."

"That's on hold now." Dek ran his hand over his head. "Master Sergeant Roche was a Raven during his first term, correct?"

"Yes, sir, but he didn't just serve and leave. He was forced out. Had an issue with his lieutenant, I hear."

"That's in the past. Roche has more than proven himself to me. Summon him. I need his help putting a mission together."

# *CHAPTER FIVE*

Page stepped out of the portalling shed, the spot designated for the company's mages to teleport into the camp. She was happy to trade the smell of pack animals and road dust, not to mention all the noises associated with the caravan, for these familiar grounds. A few nearby mercenaries reached for their weapons as she emerged, but re-sheathed them and greeted Page by name when they saw her. In moments everyone had returned to their business.

Page liked to believe she could blend in and appear as any other member of Iron Leaf. At five feet and six inches tall, she may have been a little shorter than the average member of the company; but with her short, sandy hair and the assigned traveling clothes she wore – a muslin shirt, black vest, and tan trousers – she thought she looked like everyone else. No matter how she was dressed, however, she was always recognized.

Page looked around at Camp Redemption. The Anvil.

*Home.*

With a nod to one of the men, she adjusted her backpack, lifted her carryall sack, and stepped toward Marston Hall. Even in her boots her steps were light, and she bounded, two at a time, up the wooden stairs leading to the timber-and-stone building. Page breezed through the main door to be greeted by Books' staff and guards. She dropped her luggage atop a bench outside the office, unstrapped her sword belt, and wove her sword through the loops of her packs. A short time later she was granted access to Books' office.

Books, Iron Leaf's commander, was already moving around his desk toward Page. The company's logistics and operations captains were in the room too, seated around a conference table. Books' assistant stood at attention beside the commander's chair. Other than a few maps on one wall, the room hadn't changed in the five months since Page had last visited. A fireplace and shelves of books covered the right wall, and trophies, paintings, and two large windows took over the one behind the desk. To her left was the map wall, and Page knew, without looking, that the banners of dozens of military units graced the wall behind her as she entered. The aromas of smoke and sweat loitered in the room.

*Does no one ever open a window?*

As usual, both the air and mood were stuffy. She was glad she had taken the time to doff her brigandine armor before arriving.

"Page!" Books said, extending his hand with a smile. He was as lean and hard-looking as ever, showing more salt and less nutmeg in his close-cut hair. The commander might be getting older, but he looked well.

Page smiled too, accepting the outstretched hand. "Commander. Good to see you, sir."

Books reacquainted Page with the two captains. Their gaze lingered longer than their handshakes, and one's smile betrayed his thoughts. Page ignored it all. That was the game.

*For now, boys, but you won't be able to get away with it forever.*

Books escorted the men to the office door, speaking to them along the way. "I'll get recruiting on it. Let me know if you come up with anything else." He turned back to Page and clapped his hands. "How long's it been, Page? Three months?"

"Five. Just over five."

"Shit. Like a river, it waits for no one." Books paused. "Or can *you* make it wait?"

"No, sir," Page said, smiling. "There's rumor of a spell, but they say it's beyond the skill of even the highest Grand Masters. Doubt even the Dark Sky Wizard himself could have cast it." Page took in the room from her spot in front of Books' desk, noting the new maps on the table and the desk as well as the wall.

"Something to eat or drink? Tea, brandy, whiskey?"

"Brandy. Haven't had a drink in weeks."

Books nodded to his aide, holding up three fingers. The man smiled and opened a small cabinet in the corner of the room, revealing several bottles. He poured brandy into three small blown-glass goblets, each set within thin, silver elm leaves upon a silver stem. Books continued as the aide handed them over. "All going well with your current assignment?"

"Yes, sir. We're between caravans as the patron resupplies the wagons. We head out again in a few days."

"Excellent." Books lifted his glass. "Iron Leaf completes the mission."

"Iron Leaf completes the mission," replied Page and the aide.

They all sipped from their glasses. Page savored the flavors as she rubbed a finger over the pommel of her dagger. *I love my job.*

"You're getting straight pay on this job," Books said. "Not your specialist pay."

"Correct."

"I've got a specialist assignment for you. Patron is paying rate and a half for the short notice, too."

"I like the sound of that, but what about my current post? I don't want to leave Ripper shorthanded, sir."

"I'll pull one from another team. We've got two teams in training cycle now, so I have the bodies."

"This new patron's asking for a mage?"

"A team with a mage," Books said. "You'll be temporary to Hammer's team."

"Hammer? I've heard of him. He's got a good reputation."

"Yeah, he's a good man."

"I'm in."

Books looked to his aide and made a scribbling motion in the air. The man nodded and left.

Once his aide was out of the room, Books relaxed. He gestured for Page to take a seat as he rested back on the front of his desk. He finished his glass and set it down. Page took her time, enjoying each sip.

Books turned toward her. "How you been, Emma?"

"Good. Doing good." Page smiled. She'd known their conversation would turn familiar once they were alone. She preferred it that way. Books – Niko – was more like a favorite uncle than a boss. No – he was more than that.

Page wiggled into the leather chair, pulling her feet up onto the seat. She looked over her shoulder and pointed at the wall. "Why the crude maps? Is that Noreas?" She took another sip.

"Yeah. Trying to decide if we answer their call. They say it's to push deeper into their frontier. But something's off. They've

56

called a lot of teams down there. More than I think necessary, and they really want us onboard. I don't know how they can afford us, but they say they'll pay. They want as much of the company as we can send. I don't know them well enough to know if we should trust them." He looked at the maps and back to Page. "Forget you saw those maps."

"Done."

"How's the job with Ripper?"

"It's the typical escort. Mundane, 'til it's not. Ripper's doing well. Negotiates with our patron on the important stuff, keeps us safe while giving him what he wants."

"Good to hear. It's his second post as team leader. I'll make it permanent."

"So, what's this new job, Niko? Who's the patron? Noreas?"

"No. Renlar."

Page raised an eyebrow. "Their war with Aendura starting up again?" She finished her glass.

"Not as far as I know. I'm pretty sure Renlar just wanted that land between the rivers and access to the coastline. Now that they have it all they don't need to start another fight." Books took her glass and refilled it. "This is something internal. The request came from the chancellor himself, says it has the king's support. He's paid for a week of your time, starting tomorrow, to secure the time to negotiate the job. He'll meet with Hammer and his team in Lagisborg four days from now. The team can decide at that point whether to accept the full mission or not. The chancellor understands we don't do suicide missions. If you agree to take it on, he'll continue to pay until the mission is complete. There is no end date yet." He handed the refilled glass back to Page.

"Long term." She took a sip. "Rate and a half. What's the

catch?"

"I don't know. So I want you to be extra cautious on this one."

"You know me, Niko."

"Yes, I do. That's why I'm telling you to be careful. I know you won't risk the lives of your teammates, but you might risk your own for the tuition money you need."

"Please."

Books held up his hand. "Emma, we've known each other nine years now. You were the youngest we'd ever recruited. I've put you through three years of training at the Institute so far. Shit, you're the only one who's dared to call me a jackass to my face."

Page suppressed a smile. He had really pissed her off that day. "What are you getting at?"

"You're like a... I just want to be certain you don't put money above all."

"I won't."

"The money's not worth it."

"I won't."

"There will always be another job."

"Shit, Niko. Don't be a jackass. I said I won't, alright?"

Books grinned and shook his head. "Okay, damnit." He moved to the other side of his desk. "Sometimes I wonder if you'd have been better off if I hadn't pulled your lazy ass off the streets, but most of the time I believe you're doing what the gods intended."

"What? Pissing you off?"

"That, and being the most lethal mercenary in this company." Books handed a piece of parchment across his desk. Page leaned in to take it from him. "This is the letter we received. Hammer and his team will arrive here tomorrow. Until then, reoutfit with what you need at the quartermaster."

Page looked over the letter and sipped her brandy. There was nothing special in what it said, but it was unique in the fact that it bore the official seals of Renlar and the chancellor. "Anything else?" She swallowed the last of the glass and set it down on the desk.

"No," Books said, turning his attention to a ledger. "Now get your lazy ass out of my office."

Page came to attention. "Kiss my lazy ass, sir." She turned on her heels and walked to the door.

Without looking up from his desk, Books cleared his throat and said, "Emma – it was good seeing you."

"You too," Page said. She paused. She wanted to say more. Instead she opened the door and stepped into the hallway.

# CHAPTER SIX

The routine and structure of the next day helped Grimble and the men get back into their rhythm. It started with feeding and watering the horses, receiving the day's camp rations, throwing the salt meat in a pot of water for later, and nibbling on some nuts and a broken piece of yesterday's stale bread. After that each trooper worked on readying his uniform and armor, polishing the buckles and buttons as best he could in the time he had before the formation and ceremony at mid-morning.

For the men closest to the three troopers who had given their lives, the ceremony was particularly hard. It would be the last time their names were called as part of the formation roll call. The sergeants in charge of each fallen trooper waited for the name to be read three times before answering that they had fallen in battle.

Goat and Elam Targer had been from neighboring farms. They had known each other from a very young age. Even though they'd been in different companies, the two had checked on each other frequently. A tear ran down Goat's stone face when Elam's name was called. Grimble understood.

The memorial cairns had been built as they always were. Each trooper's wooden shield lay on the ground, facing the sky, with his spear driven point-down into it. His riding boots were set atop the shield, filled with his bedding to keep them upright, and his helmet rested upon his boots, propped against the spear shaft. A single ribbon of white linen with the fallen trooper's name was secured to the top of the spear so those in Ihgel's Hall, the warriors' final resting place, could see it better. The horse slain in battle was similarly honored with its saddle, its rider's spear similarly placed and adorned as those of the troopers.

Following the ceremony, the troopers fell back into their camp routine. Groups were sent to forage for food, water, and wood. Some were assigned to guard mounts. Others were tasked with stable duty, getting the horses out, and giving them time to graze in a nearby field. Grimble watched as Havoc ran out to the field with the other horses. The dappled gray loved getting away from the confines of the camp, and pranced and shook his head happily as they ran to the gate. Watching the horses helped remind Grimble everything would be alright.

Evening meal call arrived before most expected and the troopers assembled in their companies. The bonfires were lit against the wall at the end of the company's line of tents. The men gathered their packs and stools, whatever they could sit or rest upon, forming a semicircle around the fires. Wooden or tin mugs dangled from their hands. The boots followed the example of their seniors. Grimble and Kelban sat among the group of veterans in their company.

Before long a murmur started. It grew louder as a cart creaked along Back Street toward Third and Fourth Companies. Third's captain drove the cart; seated beside him was Captain

Dean Radt

Sundersman of Fourth Company. In the back of the cart, sitting upon barrels, were the troopers and boots who had been evacuated back to camp the night of the battle. Those men, once gravely injured, now appeared no worse for their injuries.

The cart stopped, and as the captains moved to the back, the men seated on the barrels hopped down. One of them, a boot who had joined the regiment with Goat, ambled over to Fourth Company.

"Puddles!" the men cheered. He received pats on the back and a cascade of questions from his fellow boots. The slightest of smiles appeared on his face.

Captain Sundersman stepped into view, lugging a kilderkin barrel in his arms. Goat, near at hand, moved to help his captain. A strong hand grabbed his shoulder, staying the young man. "This is for him to do," said a veteran. "He'd be insulted if you tried to take it from him. It's one of the ways the officers honor us. The commander buys the beer and the captains and lieutenants serve the first round."

Sundersman carried the barrel to the middle of Fourth Company's camp, then went back to the cart and secured a second, setting it next to the first. The men cheered as he tapped the barrels and began to pour the beer. Moments later a matching cheer came from Third Company's campsite.

"Third Company's always lagging behind," Eng said, raising a good laugh from the men of Fourth Company. Sundersman smiled as he filled a mug.

Once everyone had a mug in hand, the captain stepped up onto the back of the barrel stand. Positioned above the gathered men, he shouted, "Fourth Company! The finest company!"

"Rah!" the men shouted.

Sundersman raised his mug. "Here's to the two-oh-ninth

cavalry!"

The men shouted in response. "The army's eyes, who thunder ride!"

"May our banner ever fly!"

The troopers continued, "Wicked Spears own the battle!"

"We're first afield! We never yield!" Sundersman shouted.

"Swifter than wind. Harder than steel!" the men concluded, and everyone drank deeply.

Sundersman pointed to Puddles. "Your wounded comrade is returned to you with the blessing of the Devout Mother and her priests. Thanks be to Abbyon, the Holy Father." His voice darkened. "Lads, we engaged an enemy unlike any seen before. Your valor and skill were proven again. To the Abyss with those goblin fucks!"

"T'Abyss!" the men yelled.

"This was no mere skirmish. Each company will receive a campaign ribbon. Brag about this battle, give account to your future children, know you fought well, but never forget those who fell beside you." The captain raised his mug again, and each trooper did the same. "We honor Jan Patel, Marco Fermaak, and Elam Targer. Good men. Good troopers. Courageous warriors. They've earned their place at the Great Table in Ihgel's glorious hall and will be placed in our Regimental Book. May they never be forgotten. To Jan, Marco, and Elam."

The entire company took a hearty drink and paused. The silence was long. Noises of the night crept into the ceremony, yet no one heard the calls of the wildlife or the cracks and pops of the fire. Like Grimble, they each thought on the men they had ridden beside. Brothers who would no longer be in their tents, no longer sit beside them at chow; no longer share guard duty, train, or simply complain about military life with them.

The captain's solemn voice slid into the silence. "Men, the regiment's been stricken these last two engagements. Much has been asked of you. Always you have answered the call. By the gods, I am proud of you and honored to fight beside you. This night is for you. Sergeants, have the men see to the horses and guard mount as necessary, but there will be no morning muster."

The men silently raised their mugs to the captain. With that, he and the platoon lieutenants left the company camp.

A few more logs were thrown on the fire as it burned next to the wall. The men of Fourth Company topped off their mugs and gathered in a semicircle around the flames. Goat took the opportunity to approach Puddles. For the first time in weeks, his face was possessed by a broad smile and shining eyes. Grimble watched as a handful of boots joined Goat to speak with the wounded boot.

"I can't believe it," Goat said. "An axe opened your... There was so much... We thought you were gone."

"I'd heard of the magic of the priests," said Yappy, another boot, "but never once had I seen its work. Gods!"

"I'd given up," Puddles said. "But the troopers who rushed me back kept telling me to hold on. Kept saying I'd be alright. I thought they were full of horseshit, I did."

"What was it like – you know, in the Temple?" Goat asked. They sat down, propping themselves against the packs and drinking deeply from their mugs.

"I don't really know how to say. I don't remember getting there, must have passed out, but I woke up when they were putting me on a cot." Puddles took another swig from his mug and stared into the fire. "There was a lot of white all around – white lights, but not like a lantern or the sun. I couldn't tell where the light was coming from, and it hurt when I moved, it did, so I didn't try to do much looking around. The priests stopped by, praying over me and putting some kind of liquid on my head and where that pig goblin hacked me."

He paused to take another drink, then looked into his mug and breathed in slowly through his nose, ostensibly taking in the aromas of the brew. Grimble remembered how colors had seemed more vivid and aromas more fragrant after he had been so close to death and healed by the Temple priests. Life had not been the same after that. As Puddles breathed out, he turned his eyes toward the stars above, appearing as though he were trying to count them.

"And...?" Yappy said. "Don't keep us waiting, man!"

Puddles returned his gaze to the men around him and, with a content face, continued. "The others, the other wounded, must have been all in the same area, because I heard the priests do the same thing around me several times. Then she came in – you know, the Devout Mother. I could barely see her from where I was, but I tell you, there was something different about her, there was." Puddles was lost in the moment. The eyes of the fifteen other company boots were glued to him.

"Just being near her I knew she was holy. Don't ask me how. I just know she's been touched by the gods. She was chanting in a language I'd never heard, and her face was turned to the heavens. I wanted to look at her better but was also afraid of her. I tell you I was."

Grimble understood. He'd been there before, as had most of his brothers in arms. He knew exactly what Puddles described and what was coming next.

Puddles took a long swallow, finishing the contents of the mug, and went on. "This feeling came over me, like I was relaxed. No... more than that. I can't describe it, other than it was the most calm I've ever felt. Felt like I was asleep, but my eyes were open, they were. Couldn't tell you how long it was, felt like maybe days; but it couldn't have been. One of the priests was pouring water into a basin when she started praying. When she stopped praying and walked away, and he was still pouring, I turned to watch her go, expecting the pain in my shoulder again, but it wasn't there. The pain. It was gone."

Grimble knew that calm, and the wonder of being whole again. Puddles tried to take another swallow and realized his mug was empty. A few of his fellow boots poured their mugs' contents into his, and he thanked them and took a swig.

"I reached up and felt my shoulder, I did, and it was all together, just some crusty blood on it." Puddles pulled his shirt open to show his left chest and shoulder. There was a thin, faint, almost silvery line where his wound had once been; no other sign of the severe laceration and compound fracture he had endured two days before.

"Abbyon!" Goat muttered.

"I bet she's an elf," Yappy said.

"Gods! Not that again," several boots grumbled.

"She could be. You don't know," Yappy said.

"We told you, there ain't no elves," said a boot from Second Platoon.

"Well," continued Puddles, "I don't know about any of that. But I tell you, the gods are real, and I thank the Father, will every day, for what was done, I will."

The boots fell into several different discussions. The rest of the company had finished settling in. A merchant stopped by with his cart selling distilled spirits and tobacco, and a selection of other vices. Many of the men took advantage of the chance and the merchant left with a smile and a heavier purse.

More beer was poured into waiting mugs. Stories of battle were started. A handful of the camp women joined the company around the fire, some for companionship, others happy to make extra coins during the evening's revels. One young woman arrived after the rest and made directly for the section of boots. With long black hair and copper skin, she was more attractive than most and seductive in the way she moved.

"Evening, boys," she purred.

"Good evening, ma'am," Puddles replied. Goat grabbed his arm and looked him in the eyes, giving the subtlest of head shakes. Puddles appeared confused, but heeded the warning and said no more. The rest of the boots stared straight ahead at the fire, giving her no heed. They looked like guilty men not wanting to see the evidence displayed before them.

"Please, boys, I won't hurt you, unless you like that sort of thing." She stepped between the men, raising her dress to tread carefully, but higher than necessary, showing off her legs. They were perfect, especially in the firelight; she could have been the muse of any sculptor. Some of the boots were able to maintain their focus on the fire, but a few glanced at her legs and seemed overcome with fear. Their eyebrows twisted in pained looks of concern.

"How about you?" the woman asked Puddles as she squeezed herself between him and Goat, her breasts rubbing against Puddles' chest and arm as she did so. "The fire is nice, but I have something much nicer for you."

"Uh, no thanks, ma'am?" Puddles said, and looked to Goat for confirmation.

The woman raised an eyebrow. She rolled toward Goat and nuzzled his neck. She twisted her body against him and ran her hand down his leg, raking her fingers along the inside of his thigh on the way back. "Gods, you're a good-looking one," she purred in his ear. "Wouldn't you like some company tonight?"

Goat held true to his name and stared straight at the fire, eyes open, mouth closed.

"It's no use, Svana," a veteran called out. "These boys proved themselves. We told 'em."

"Oh?" she asked in a kittenish voice, running a finger along the inside of Goat's thigh again. "What did they tell you?"

Goat swallowed. "Your brother's a Raven in Second Batt."

"Shit!" Svana exclaimed. The troopers laughed. Her entire posture and demeanor changed from playful to practical. She got to her feet. "Well, can't blame a girl for trying to make some extra money. Don't let this scare you away from my cart in the workshop area, boys. Sell or mend, leather or cloth, I'll see to your needs." She brushed off her dress, and while doing so, locked eyes with Kelban. It was subtle and brief, but Grimble was watching.

Svana gave a quick smile and turned to the women present. "Good night, ladies. Off to the tent." Thom and some of the other veterans exchanged looks and knowing smiles about "the tent."

"Good luck, Svana," several of the woman said as she left. The company returned to their drinks and conversations.

Grimble was not worried about "the tent," but wanted to know about the look Svana had given his friend. He whispered to Kelban, "What was that about?"

"What was what about?"

"That look. It's the second time I've seen you and her do that."

"It's nothing. Don't worry about it."

"Bullshit, man. Do I need to keep an eye out for her brother when he returns to camp?"

Kelban rolled his eyes and looked left and right. "I'm tellin' ya, forget about it. It's not what you think."

"All right. All right," Grimble said, showing his palms. "Didn't mean to pry. Just letting you know I've got your left side if her brother finds out."

"It's not what you think," Kelban said again. "Look, I helped her with a matter a few months back and I've kept it quiet. Okay?"

"Shit. Svana never asks for help. I've seen her change the wheel on her cart, her *loaded* cart. Thirty or forty men must've asked if she wanted help. Turned us all down."

"I've already said too much."

"Don't worry." Grimble patted Kelban on the shoulder and took a heavy drink from his mug. "I've already forgotten what we're talking about."

Later in the evening, two troopers pulled out a mandolin and a pipe and began playing. They meandered through several popular tavern songs. The company sang along with them. After the third verse of "Lock and Key, My Sweetie," Master Sergeant Roche moved between the men and the fire. "Troopers, I think now is a good time. Let them wait no longer."

Three other sergeants, one from each column in the company, joined Roche. The four gave the history of the regiment and its major campaigns – from one of the first engagements, when it received its moniker, "Wicked Spears," to the Battle of the Dark Sky, the Two Rivers War, and Steep Ridge. They ended with the routing and destruction of the Horde of Beshta'Rek.

The boots were brought up one by one to reinstate the use of their given names. No longer would they have to refer to themselves in the third person or endure being called "boot" – they were true cavalry troopers from that point forward. After each was called to stand before the sergeants, he stated his real name and told the company about his life and where he had grown up. This personalized every man and provided entertainment to the company of warriors, many of whom had not been home in years, some over a decade.

The first to be called, Snotball, tried to minimize his story, but between personal questions and harassment from the troopers, he learned to divulge as much as he could remember. Goat – Nolan Miller – was the second. He came from the outskirts of the capital city, Agderon. His family ran a mill and were doing well. Goat was the fourth son in a large family and not in line to run the mill. The girl he loved had married one of his older brothers, and Goat had decided it was better he leave and pursue something completely different. Having a lot of anger, and not many options, the King's Army fit his needs. By the end of his story, several troopers had promised they would give his pilfering brother a visit if they were ever near Agderon.

When he was done, Roche piped up, "The regiment welcomes you, Nolan Miller. Take your seat."

"Sir, may I keep the name 'Goat'?"

A buzz started among the men. Roche raised an eyebrow and looked at Dinger before turning back to Goat. "That's not unheard of, but why would you want to keep your boot name?"

"Sir, I left that life behind. Nothing good for me there." Goat looked into the fire. "Nothing."

"The company will have to vote on it," Roche said. "Their say is final."

"Understood."

"Men, what say you?"

The men turned to one another, mumbling and nodding. They looked at Grimble and received a nod. Finally, they turned to Roche and raised their fists in the air, as if holding spears point-up.

"The regiment welcomes you, Goat," said Roche. "Now sit your ass down. Yappy, you're next."

Yappy was from a village a day's ride from the current encampment. Although his family was near the areas raided by the goblins, their village had not suffered an attack; but Yappy feared they would, and was proud to have played a part in ending the goblin chieftain's raids. His family had contacts and distant relatives beyond the western border of Aendura, in the untamed lands from where the raids originated. Yappy told them the humans inside the untamed lands called it "the frontier," saying it simply needed to be settled like Renlar had been. They and others on the border called goblins by other names: wild-men, savage-men, and sometimes, ghouls. There were outposts in the frontier that traded with a few small tribes of goblins, and the groups tolerated each other.

Yappy had joined the King's Army to get away from his village and see more of the land. His hope was to one day see an elf in person. The new troopers rolled their eyes at this. Yappy intended to return home after his initial ten-year enlistment with enough coin to start a small homestead and woo a nearby farmer's daughter who had caught his eye.

Puddles was from Delranon. He and his family survived the Battle of the Dark Sky. This prompted numerous questions from the company, but no definitive answers. He had not seen the battle and could not tell anyone what the Dark Sky Wizard looked like; being a toddler at the time, he only remembered hiding with his family inside a food cellar. However, he had seen the wreckage of the stone tower, part of the outer fortification protecting the Spire – the seat of the Arcane Council. The wreckage had been brought down on the Dark Sky Wizard, ending the battle.

As beer and liquors flowed, tongues loosened, and the moon rode high into the night sky. After the last new trooper told his story, some of the senior troopers, who were either excellent storytellers or had interesting tales, were called to tell theirs.

Grimble hoped he would not be called upon. It had been well over a year since he had last told his story. Each time he had done so, his brother troopers seemed to be struck by Ellie and had wanted to know more about her. He didn't like sharing details about her – but whenever he spoke of her, his memories grew vivid again, and it was almost like being with her.

"Grimble," Sergeant Dinger called out, "why don't you tell us your story again? It's a good one, and we haven't heard it in a while."

Grimble winced.

"Yeah, Grimble," Eng agreed. "I haven't heard it yet."

"You don't really want to hear my story," Grimble protested. "I grew up on a farm, enlisted, the end."

"Don't make us call you out, Horsepiss," Thom said. He threw a rock at Grimble to accentuate his point, but missed. Grimble flashed a look at him and prepared to stand.

"Easy," said Kelban, putting a hand on Grimble's shoulder, staring at Thom.

"Ha! You supply train reject," Eng laughed. "I don't know why they issue you a bow, you can't hit shit!"

"I can hit your dumb ass," Thom said. He picked up another rock and threw it, hard. Eng managed to get his arm up in time to deflect it from hitting his head. His eyes locked on Thom with a determined look.

"Easy," came the calls from several troopers. Thom rubbed many of them the wrong way, especially when he was drinking. It was his nature. The newest troopers sat still, mugs close to their bodies, not knowing what to do.

Eng got to his feet. "You limp-dick, asshole-licking piss-bucket!"

Thom stood as well. The men nearby wrapped themselves around both troopers, preventing them from getting at each other.

"Alright!" Grimble yelled. "Alright, already. No need for this. I'll tell the story."

Eng and Thom stopped struggling, but continued to glare at each other.

"That's all I was asking for," said Thom. The tension left his body, and he put on a half-hearted smile. The men holding him eased up a little. Eng softened too, and the men around him loosened their grips. Slowly everyone sat back down. Eng and Thom wore faint smiles, but did not take their eyes off each other. Goat and the new troopers looked nervously between them and took a drink.

"Don't hold back on anything about Ellie," Thom ordered. "Less on the fuckin' house fire and your idealistic bullshit, more about Ellie."

"Gods," Grimble exclaimed. "It's like you plan to track her down."

Another trooper chimed in. "Well, you said yourself, she's not your girl. Don't hold back one bit."

Grimble got to his feet and stood in front of the company. "I first met Ellie…"

"Start at the beginning, asshole," Thom said. "Build up to it. Better that way."

"Fine," Grimble said, "you limp-dick piss-bucket." Both Thom and Eng smiled.

Grimble took a swig from his mug, looked inside it, and took a breath. He gazed out at the men and began.

# CHAPTER SEVEN

"I'm Corporal Grimble Broadleaf."

"Grimble!" his platoon shouted.

"For those of you who don't know, I grew up on a tobacco farm near the town of Minden in the Duchy of Ostergot. We've farmed that land since the time of my grandfather's great-grandfather, Quincy Geldirn. It was granted to him by King Brinar IV for his military service. It's not large, as farms go – roughly forty acres, some of it wooded; but it's provided our family with a means and a name for generations.

"We've got a particularly good spot for growing tobacco. Folks said our family tree must be a tobacco plant. Because of that they started calling us the Broadleaf family and our old family name, Geldirn, was dropped."

"What's the name of your tobacco? Have we heard of it?" a trooper asked.

"It's not sold on its own. Merchants buy our tobacco and mix it in with some from other farms. They make special blends that way. I know ours is used in King's Leaf and Tavern Time, but there are others too."

"Those are good smokes. Expensive," the trooper said.

"Quincy knew what he was doing. If we had more land I might have been a man of means, rolling in coin, not riding around with the likes of you bastards." Grimble smiled and a few troopers chuckled. "Ihgel has blessed us. Between the money made at the tobacco market and our own foodstuffs grown in the garden, we do okay most years.

"When I was six, my brother joined the King's Army. Both of my grandfathers were serving at that time as well. All three died in the Battle of the Dark Sky two years later. Their ribbons are at home. They're one of the reasons I joined up."

"Idealist," Thom said.

"Nah. Far from an idealist," Grimble said. "If anything I'm closer to a romantic."

Thom snorted. "Same thing."

"Says the man whose breath is stronger than his mind." Grimble shook his head. "After we lost them, my mom and grandma argued with my father a lot. A couple of years later, when I was ten, I woke up to find I wasn't going to work in the fields but was being sent to a new school near town. My sisters, Jenn and Rose, thirteen and fourteen at that time, went too. My dad didn't agree with my grandmother. He needed the help on the farm, and until that time education was not a priority for my family."

"You don't say," Thom said.

"Hey, shit-for-brains, you want the story or not?" Grimble snapped. The other troopers were equally dismissive of Thom's input.

"Alright, alright," said Thom.

Grimble continued. "I was one of the youngest there, and it was like being a boot just about every day. Things changed a little when I got the chance to play some of the after-school games the boys would start up. I was still that 'little kid,' but from then on, the other lads would ask me to join their teams after school."

Grimble took a drink from his mug. "Anyway, in Planting Season when I was fourteen, we had our first visit from Dahl – Dahlbren Vonderlehr. He's one of those traveling merchants, the kind who sell anything from a wagon or caravan.

"No one knew who he was at first. I was in town that day because Dad needed an extra hand with a delivery, and saw Dahl's caravan parked near the blacksmith's stables. Two large mules were tied up outside one of the stalls. The caravan itself must have been of a Haldish or Vrelish design. I'd never seen anything like it before, or since. It was large and made all of wood, no canvas – like a small house on wheels, painted green and brown. Its paint was faded and weather-worn, but you could see foreign lettering and symbols on the sideboards.

"While I was admiring the markings, I heard some shuffling inside the caravan. I walked to the back, where the stairs were set, and got ready to introduce myself. Figured I'd welcome the owner to town. I heard that unmistakable *scuff* of a misplaced footstep and knew someone was about fall, so when an arm appeared I moved to help them.

"Lads, I remember it like it happened yesterday. I expected a masculine grip, or some old man's hand. But instead, I caught hold of as elegant a hand as I have ever known. It was the kind of touch the bards sing of. Don't laugh, fellas. It's the truth. As I held her hand, she floated down the steps. She was dressed in green. That's all I can remember of her dress, because my eyes, boys, my eyes were locked on her face. All of a sudden I became aware of my dirty shirt and trousers and was torn between never wanting to leave that moment and wishing I were somewhere else.

"She appeared to be about fourteen, like me, and had long hair the color of honey. It practically glowed like gold in the sun. You don't need to say it, Thom – I'm pretty sure I looked like a fool. Brothers, her beauty was… pure, not something exotic; and not something you could tire of. Her eyes were amber, deep amber… They were hypnotic."

Grimble's voice faded. He caught himself a moment later.

"Where was I? Oh, yeah. When she spoke that first time it was like a warm drink on a cold night. Her accent was faint, one I'd never heard before – strange, like her caravan. I felt out of place but didn't want to leave. Though if that had been the only time I was going to be near her, I would have thought myself blessed by the gods. But it got better.

"She introduced herself as Ellie, and I managed to get my name out after a few 'um's and 'uh's. Eldaloren is her real name. She's Dahl's only child. The two of them are very close.

"Anyway, the blacksmith had stepped away, but his dog was there. His dog was always there. It's a scrawny thing, with thick black hair, knotted in places, but it had a face like a baby bear and everyone thought it was cute the first time they saw it. But when you approached it, or entered the shop while Krun was out, that dog turned into a monster faster than a shoe hitting the floor. Docile to demented in an instant."

Grimble opened his eyes wide and spread his fingers over his head. "Its eyes glowed, its hair stood on end, its lips curled back to show stained fangs, and it drooled as if its mouth were a spring." He stopped his charade. "Lads, I'm telling you this little dog went from fuzzy to frenzy as fast as Thom finishes with the ladies."

"Piss off," Thom said.

"I don't know if the blacksmith trained it that way," Grimble went on, "or if he received the creature from a denizen of the Abyss. Perhaps some demon tired of caring for such a terror and sent it here. Who knows? Wherever the blacksmith got it, that creature turned out to be the perfect watchdog for his shop. It took me years to find a way, but I finally made friends with it – not mastery over it; just friends with the beast.

"Anyway, Ellie and I made some small talk, and then she saw the dog and its cute face. She cooed and started toward it. Before I could say anything it did what it always does. That damn dog went full wrath and bluff-charged Ellie. She looked scared, but she didn't scream. She backed away.

"I explained to her about the dog's nature. She told me how much she liked dogs. That she'd had one at one point, but couldn't keep one in the caravan. It was tough enough for her and her father in the tight space. We talked some more about the weather and birds and her caravan, but she kept turning her head to look at the dog. So, I took a chance. I told her I'd found a way to befriend the dog and asked if she wanted me to teach her so she could pet the demon spawn." Grimble smiled.

"She stared into my eyes like she was reading something. She asked if I was joking. I told her I was serious, and to prove it, slowly walked up to the dog and pet its head and chin. When I turned to her, she was wide-eyed and smiling. 'Show me how,' she said.

"I walked her through the steps, and when it was all done, about fifteen minutes later, she was petting the beast. She beamed at me as she scratched the dog's neck. I can still see her face, lads.

"I told her I was impressed the dog hadn't scared her away when he charged. She said she'd seen some strange things before and told me a story of a place she and her father passed regularly called Barrow Gap.

"It's somewhere in the north of Haldiland. She said it's the strangest place they'd ever seen. It's a narrow passage between two rows of hills, about two hundred yards wide and a mile from one side to the other. Apparently, the land sinks there a little and the gap is covered at all times by a fog or smoke."

"See," Thom said, "I keep telling you all she's not that smart. She doesn't even know the difference between fog and smoke."

Kelban leaned over and punched Thom's arm. It sounded like someone slapping a horse's hindquarter and caused the beer in Thom's mug to foam and spill over the top.

"Ouch, you fucker," Thom snapped. He noticed Kelban's glare. "Alright, I'll shut my mouth."

"She said," Grimble pressed on, as if explaining something to a child for the tenth time, "that it acted like both, Thom. At night and when the sun goes behind the clouds, Barrow Gap is filled with a wet mist, a fog. But when the sun shines down on it, the place has the smell of a fire burning nearby and looks covered in smoke. The locals call it the White Terror. They said it was cursed by Eblees and told Ellie and her father to stay away."

"Eblees? Who's that?" Yappy asked.

"That's one of the gods Noreas and those countries to the south worship," Eng said. "Go on, Grimble."

Grimble nodded. "Ellie said the warnings weren't necessary. She said you can tell right away there's something wrong with the land there. Even their mules refused to go near the White Terror and stopped pulling when it came into sight. She and her father had to calm them and hand-lead them along the road. She said she kept looking over her shoulder at the mist. Finally, curiosity overtook them and she and her father walked toward the smoke. 'Just to take a look,' she told me.

"I never knew Ellie to lie about anything, lads, so I don't

doubt her story. She said that they felt it would be alright to get closer. The sun was out and everything felt normal. But that changed when they were about a dozen steps away.

"At first things were okay. They smelled the smoke; she said it was faint, but was there all the same. It cloaked the gap as high as the treetops. As they got closer she and Dahl saw shadows in the smoke. When she told me that, the hair on my neck stood up.

"Ellie thought birds had flown overhead and their shadow had slipped across the smoke, but there weren't any birds in the air. She said she looked again and saw the form of a person, nothing more than a silhouette or shadow, and it faded away.

"Other forms appeared and disappeared. They moved about, but their shape was never clear, never complete, and they never stayed visible for long. She said it was like watching moving human shadows, complete and incomplete. She said a chill ran through her. Ellie found out later the locals claim the shadows are the souls of those who ignored the warnings and went inside. They call them the Tombless.

"Well, Ellie and her father didn't know that at the time, so they called out to them. When they got no answer they moved a few steps closer. They called again. Still no one answered. That's when wisps of smoke appeared, like floating vines, and drifted toward the two of them."

"T'Abyss! I wouldn't stay around!" Eng said.

"Yeah, their thoughts too," Grimble said. "They backed away until they reached their caravan and left. She said they had to pass the place at least once a year. They passed it one time at dusk – not what they really wanted to do, but they did. The mules acted differently in the fading light. They actually moved *toward* the mist, ignoring Dahl's control on the reins. She and her father had to brake the caravan and lead the mules out of the area on foot. She said that while they walked they heard voices calling to them. The voices were faint, but felt friendly.

"Ellie and her father knew to ignore them. She said it might have been different if that had been the first time they'd encountered the White Terror, but it wasn't going to catch them off their guard. She says the smoke or mist seemed to be growing every year. Last time they had visited, the White Terror had moved almost a hundred yards out of Barrow Gap and was halfway to the road that passes by it.

"About that time, when Ellie was finishing her story, a group of kids started gathering. Before long, a few older and wealthier boys showed up. They approached and introduced themselves. They were all doing tricks and little things to try to impress Ellie. She seemed happy for the attention. My dad was done with his work and called to me from across the street. I moved away from the crowd."

A trooper spouted out, "You lost your chance, brother."

"Looked like it," Grimble said. "Dad said he'd seen me with Dahl's daughter and asked a few questions about her. He also said Dahl was looking for a nearby home or farm to park his caravan overnight while he did business in the area. Anyway, Dad apparently offered our farm for the two of them to use, but doubted they would take the offer. I agreed. There were wealthier families around Minden, and for my part Ellie appeared to be enjoying the company of the older boys. I doubted they would stop by our farm.

"So, was I ever surprised to see the two mules and that caravan on the road to our house a few hours before supper that afternoon. There was Dahl driving the mule team, his long, black hair pulled behind in a tail, but I couldn't see Ellie. Dahl stopped the wagon near our barn, didn't even lock the brake, and the stout bastard jumped down from the buckboard like he was a kid.

"Where Ellie is subdued and quiet, Dahl is animated and rowdy. On that first visit he and my father set to bargaining over what we had left of the past year's tobacco harvest. I wondered if that was the sole reason for the visit, because there was no sign of Ellie. After he and Dad had been negotiating for some time, Dahl called out, 'Bring that bolt of wool we picked up in the mountains.' And Ellie stepped out of the caravan with the fabric. She smiled when she saw me."

"Well played," a trooper piped up. "Well played."

Grimble grinned and continued. "We learned Dahl and Ellie had plied their wares for years near our northern border with Haldiland and made trips all the way into Nyrla and Vreland. But the counts and barons in Haldiland were at it again, fighting among each other, and safe travel became unpredictable. Since driving north was too dangerous, Dahl had decided to bring his wagon further into our country."

Grimble took another drink from his mug. "Dahl built a reputation in our area for providing what was needed without cutting into your purse. I heard plenty of stories of him 'looking into his store,' as he called his caravan. Sometimes folks would ask him for some hard-to-find stuff. Dahl would step away and return moments later with the very thing in hand. He didn't always have what you wanted, but seemed to have what you needed.

"Dahl and Ellie stopped by our farm four or more times each year. Each visit to our town would last for days, sometimes a week. The meals they shared under our roof were always memorable. Ellie and her father knew a lot. They read a lot. They'd been to cities and countries all over the land. Sometimes they'd bring us a rare dish or treat from their travels.

"Even though they'd been to a lot of places, they were full of questions about our little farm and the land around Minden. Dahl always asked my father about the changes to the land and the amount of rain since they had last stopped at our home. He listened to my father's answers as though they were the most interesting things he'd heard. Ellie and I took advantage of their distracted talks to walk off and be alone."

"Yeah, you would," shouted a young trooper. "Now it's getting good." The group laughed.

Grimble smiled. "You might be surprised. A lot of the lads, some better-looking than me, and many who were smarter, had similar thoughts on their minds. Heck, everyone who saw her couldn't help but comment on her looks. They tried to lure her away, but she spent most of her time walking with me. I don't know, boys, sometimes I wonder if it was because I was content to simply walk or sit beside her in silence.

"They stayed with our family every time they were in town or riding through. Even during years of poor harvest, Ellie and her father stopped by the farm. My dad and Dahl became more friends than business partners. They'd wander to the barn and discuss business, news, the weather. Ellie and I would spend the days walking in the forest and skirting the streams.

"Sometimes our talks went into the very smallest details of our lives. Other times we talked about stupid kid things. Since she traveled all over the land, she was full of stories about distant places. I enjoyed those stories the most. Those of you from small towns and villages know how it is. Sometimes that's the only way to get news and learn about the rest of the world. But Ellie seemed to admire *my* life, as I got to see the slow growing and passing of nature and time around me. It was strange that such boring things interested her.

"I'd point to a nest, tell of its builder and how they had lived their lives since she had last visited. She would point to a tree and ask questions, or listen to what I knew of the fish in a certain creek. Silly stuff, if you think about it, but she was enthralled. What I knew was basic, but Ellie made me feel like a genius."

Grimble ran a finger along his beard and neck and found himself hundreds of miles away and years in the past. Behind him the fire popped, and he was abruptly returned to the camp. "I'm sure you want to hear some lurid story, or at least wonder how far I got with her. You new guys – I have to disappoint you there. She never gave me a sign she wanted more than what we had, and I was afraid of scaring her away. You know when you're on a hunt and caught with your bow in your lap, and a buck pops out of the trees, not ten steps away? You know that if you reach for your bow and draw an arrow you'll spook the creature. So you sit there and take in the moment, and admire the beauty of the thing.

"We took breaks during our walks, sometimes by the water, sometimes under a tree. After a year, Ellie would hold my arm while we walked, or let me rest with my head in her lap, playing with my hair and singing. Those were good times." Grimble smiled again. His eyes stared far off into the darkness above the camp.

"She sang in languages I didn't understand. Songs she'd learned from her travels, I guess. The sound of her voice and the feel of her hands in my hair practically lulled me to sleep. For those of you who've been to the Temple's clinic to heal your wounds, the touch of her hand and the sound of her voice was almost like that to me. Trust me, if you ever met her, you'd understand why I was happy just to walk with her and didn't want to scare her away.

"During a visit in Tending of my eighteenth year, I – we fell into a creek. She was soaked head to toe. We had a good laugh, but things were different. Uh… We took one more walk after that. Just one." Grimble's voice quieted. "That was the last time she and Dahl visited. No word has been heard, no message sent, since then. For months I traveled as far as I could with a plow horse, and sometimes on foot. Never very far, because I had no money. But no city or town along their routes had any news.

"My folks knew nothing. My dad was as worried as me, but he and Mom wouldn't talk about it in front of me. Grandma wouldn't speak of it at all. I'm sure Ellie and Dahl are fine – they know too much to get caught somewhere they shouldn't be. I took the whole thing as a sign from Abbyon that she and I were not meant for each other."

Grimble took a breath and spoke louder. "Anyway, the farm wasn't the same after they stopped visiting, and after hearing about the world from the two of them, home became a very small place. So, a little more than a year later, in the Gathering before I turned nineteen, I made the decision to follow in my brother's footsteps and enlist.

"I joined up, and at indoctrination they found out I could ride a horse; so, they sent me here to ride with you. That was more than seven years ago." With a smile, he added, "And I've regretted that decision ever since."

There was some light-hearted laughter, a few feigned protests. Grimble moved back to his spot next to Kelban.

"Ellie – that's a girl I could love," Eng said, a distant look in his eyes.

"Hey," Oliver said, "what about that woman in Cairn Cross you always go on about? What's her name?"

"Tessa," Thom said.

"Yeah, Tessa," Oliver continued. "You keep swearin' you're going to marry her."

"Still going to, but that's not love. That's a financial decision."

"Financial?" Oliver asked.

"Yeah. Either I marry her or go broke," Eng said, getting curious looks in response. "She's a whore, boys, and a goddess under the blanket! I'm addicted, not in love."

The sergeants called on Thom for his story, saying he must be dying to tell it since he couldn't keep his mouth shut during Grimble's. Thom moved to the center to begin his tale.

Kelban leaned close to Grimble. "You need to be careful, brother. A few here are going to get the wrong impression and think you don't really love her."

"Whether I love her or not is beside the point," Grimble whispered back. "She's better off with someone of means, not some farmer's son, not some trooper."

"Then why do you ask for news of her or her father at every city, town, and market we pass?"

Grimble looked Kelban in the eyes briefly, opened his mouth, and silently brought his lips back together. His vision fogged. He looked away, turning his attention to his trouser legs and wiping unseen dust off the hems.

"I'm tellin' ya, if you don't stop acting like you're not interested and we *do* run across her, you'll have trouble with half a dozen guys in this company alone."

"Ellie can handle herself," said Grimble softly, his attention still focused on the condition of his trousers.

"But can you?"

Grimble didn't reply. He took a deep breath through his nose and tried to focus his blurring eyes on Thom. He knew Thom's story. He hoped it would distract his mind from the tangled thoughts it wanted to explore. But his mind preferred Ellie, her voice, her touch. He took another deep breath.

Kelban punched him in the shoulder. The man's fist was like stone. It hurt, but Grimble smiled. "Thanks."

"I've got your left, brother," Kelban said. They returned their attention to Thom.

The fire, burning strong and bright, suddenly began to dance. It diminished, returned to its full flame, and danced again. There was no noticeable wind inside the camp, but the fire acted as though gusts were pushing the flames in all directions. Sparks, here and there, continued to race skyward unaffected, but the flames moved like they were alive. The confused Fourth Company stared at it. Shouts of surprise and curiosity rose from Third Company's campsite.

"Crap!" Roche shouted, but his face showed frustration, not alarm.

Near the center of the camp came a bright flash, like someone had thrown gallons of oil onto a bonfire. At the same time a thunderclap resonated through the camp. Several ladies screamed in surprise. Cries of alarm arose, and the men of Fourth Company kicked up dust and scrambled to their tents to arm themselves.

"Stand down! Stand down!" Roche shouted. "Stand down! As you were!" He repeated the order over and over, shouting to the men of Third Company as well. The troopers looked at Roche, many with spear or sword already in hand, fighting their urge to run to the noise or the tops of the camp's walls. The sergeants of the columns gathered around Roche in the middle of Back Street. Grimble stood nearby, waiting for orders.

"The officers will be here soon," Roche said. "They'll

confirm it's nothing."

"How can you be sure?" a Third Company sergeant asked.

"It's Flicker, I'm sure of it," said Roche.

"Flicker? Candles and lamps, yeah, but this? Never heard of him doing this."

"This is Flicker. He's enraged beyond any point we've seen, but it's him. Have your men stand down. One more drink then they rack out is my suggestion."

"Alright, Roche." The other sergeants returned to their company, ordering their men to stand down. Roche and Sergeant Dinger did the same for Fourth Company.

The troopers reunited and refilled their hastily discarded mugs. Questions and rumors flew about as they drank. Before long the talking ended and happy singing resumed. The bonfire burned with no sign of what had happened before, and Grimble watched Roche slip away toward the center of camp.

# CHAPTER EIGHT

The flames were gone, but the embers burned and the few remaining logs in the bonfire continued to crack and pop. The scents of the charred logs, smoke, and spilled beer mixed together and were a pungent reminder of the night before. Black was turning to blue above as the sun prepared to peek over the camp's wall to shine upon the interior, and one of Third Company's platoons had been assigned watch and morning duties, so Fourth Company was hard asleep, enjoying the rare opportunity.

First to stir were the women who had kept company with troopers the previous evening. Their services rendered, they quietly gathered their effects and crawled out of the tents, returning to their cots or workshops. Some troopers stirred from their places of rest. A few slid to their own tents, but most paid a visit to the urinal buckets before stumbling back to their companions or the comfort of the bedrolls and more sleep. Three troopers sprawled on the bare ground near the ashes of the fire, their mouths agape, drool pooling beneath their cheeks. They gave every appearance of dead men, save for their snoring and the random twitch of an arm or leg.

Moving at an official pace, one trooper made his way from the center of camp, passing the horses in the stable area along Back Street and arriving at the first tent in Fourth Company's site. He knelt down and shook the nearest of the two men. They exchanged words, and the sleepy trooper lazily raised an arm, pointing a finger further down the line of tents. The kneeling trooper stood up, moved to the middle, and picked a tent. He knelt again, stirred the occupants, and whispered to them. They grumbled, and one muttered, "That tent," motioning with his head.

The trooper gritted his teeth and rolled his eyes. He stood again and took the few steps to Grimble and Kelban's tent. This time he remained standing. He kicked the shoulders of the two sleeping men.

"What?" complained Kelban. "We're sleeping, asshole! Third has duty."

"Corporal Grimble Broadleaf?" the standing trooper asked.

"That's me," Grimble answered in a hoarse voice.

"Take a piss and splash some water on your face. You're to come with me to the command tent. Commander Dek's orders."

Grimble peered out and blinked his eyes clear. The trooper standing above him bore Dek's insignia on his armor. Dek's runner.

"Alright," Grimble said. He crawled out of the tent, to the protests of his body and head, and prepared himself to meet the battalion commander.

This was far from a normal event. In fact, the commander rarely spoke directly to the troopers unless it was a passing "Excellent" or motivational "Rah, trooper!" So rare was a summons to the command tent that Kelban and several others who had heard the order stirred awake and watched as Grimble got ready.

"What does he need to bring?" Kelban asked.

"Just him," the trooper said. "Armor and weapons are not necessary. Haste is the word." Grimble pulled on his boots and stood to follow the commander's runner.

"Ihgel's with you, brother," Kelban said. Grimble nodded and fell in behind the runner as he walked off.

When they were clear of the ears of other troopers, the runner whispered to Grimble, "I don't know what it's about, but you probably already guessed you're not being called to the mat." Grimble knew he wasn't being brought up on charges. He would have known he was in trouble long before being called by the commander, but he appreciated the courtesy. The runner continued, "He called others before I came to get you. Ravens are involved. Planning something."

"Thanks, brother," Grimble said, tucking in his shirt.

There was a noticeable change of aroma as they approached the center of the camp. The campfire smoke was accompanied by another charred smell. Grimble's stomach growled. The sounds of an argument, with one raised voice, came from ahead. The voices did not come from inside the commander's tent, but beside it.

"No, no, no, and I say again, no! That will not do!"

"It's not a denial of your claim, it simply means…"

Grimble rounded the outside of the tent with his escort and saw Dek's adjutant speaking with a non-combatant. Grimble recognized him as one of the traveling merchants, a cobbler; but he currently had the appearance of a blacksmith. His clothes and face were marred with streaks of black soot, matching his black hair.

"I've already spent the night working to salvage what I

could, and you want me to do more work when it is clearly not my fault," railed the merchant, wagging his finger. "Most of my stock is destroyed, my cart is barely useful, and you —"

"Sir, we've told you, it was probably a rare case of —"

"No, no, no, no, NO!" the merchant interrupted, slapping the back of his right hand into the palm of his left to accentuate the words. "It was not swamp gas or lightning, nor did I leave a lantern burning on the cart! My friends tell me one of your – your – your *strange* warriors yelled like a madman and my cart blew up like an alchemical tinder bundle." He threw his hands apart and shouted, "Boom!"

"My good man, you cannot think that the king, in all his benevolence, would deny compensating you for your troubles," the adjutant said. At the mention of His Majesty, some of the fire left the merchant. "We are simply asking for patience while we forward the claim through our command and up to the palace."

"Right. Well, I'm a loyal man. I certainly would not impugn His Majesty's grace," the merchant asserted, a look of reticence on his face. "I'll return to the tally and get it to you when it's done." He stepped away, scowling briefly at Grimble and the runner.

"Thank you, sir," the adjutant replied. He turned to Grimble and his escort. "Broadleaf, yes?"

"Yes, sir," Grimble replied at attention.

"As you were. Stand by under the awning." The adjutant turned to the runner. "Thanks, Vasqez. Get some chow."

Grimble stepped under the command tent's awning and waited. One of the commander's guards stood three steps in front of him, manning his post beside the tent's entrance. The adjutant lifted a flap and stepped into the tent. Grimble could not see everyone inside, only some legs and shadows, but the interior looked crowded. He had walked past the tent numerous times before, but never had he been this close. Lying on the ground near the entrance was a metal plate with a towel on top. Grimble had seen this many times before and knew it was the commander's meal.

"Does the man ever eat?" he asked Blackfoot, the guard on duty. The response was a smile.

As his ears became accustomed to the morning noises, Grimble started picking up the conversation inside. It was not held at a whisper, but voices were kept low.

"I don't like it," a deep voice said. "We have to accept Roche to command this. Not my choice – no offense – but alright, I'll go with it."

"None taken," Roche said. Grimble recognized his sergeant's patient tone.

"Then he brings in Dinger. Okay, Dinger's got a good rep as a fighter, everyone knows him, and I understand we need an overwatch. Since the rest of our team is gone, we gotta take what we can, no offense."

"None taken," Dinger said. His tone was not patient. There was a pause.

"Now we gotta take another along, this Broadleaf trooper. If we really need six, why not Kelban Kupreson or Sergeant Ferns from Second Company? I hear Kelban got his sword stuck in a goblin during the fight and beat two more to death with his fists. Broadleaf can ride, sure, but we need to know whoever joins us can hold his own and think fast. Agreed?"

"Agreed," a different voice said, hushed but audible.

"The lads agree with me," the deep voice said.

"We didn't hear from him," came Captain Paul Gengler's voice.

"If he disagreed, he'd let us know," the deep voice replied.

"We need two for overwatch," Roche said. "A sixth man on the team barely increases the footprint and it gives us more options and better support. Baz, you know me well enough. I was on the team when you joined. Trust that I do not add personnel without reason. If we had enough Ravens you wouldn't question taking six on this mission, but they're not here. They're off hunting down the horde, trying to find their launch point. We need six, and you know we do."

Roche slowed down. "He may not be the swordsman Dinger is, but he's a warrior through and through. Enough that I put him above some in your unit. He grew up in the woods, can ride better than any man in the regiment, and he's resourceful. He fits this mission and our needs. Commander, you chose me to lead this and asked what I needed to get the mission done. Grimble may not be the best man, but he's the right man, sir. We need him and Dinger to accompany us."

There was a pause.

"The candle is already burning on this one. Regiment sent orders for this mission two days ago, gentlemen," Dek said. "They anticipated we had access to every member of Scout Company. I'd hoped the Ravens would've returned by now, but that is not going to happen. We cannot wait any longer and I will not pull those men off the search for Beshta'Rek and his mage. If you have any compelling reasons to exclude Corporal Broadleaf, speak now." Dek paused. "We have our team, then. Bring him in."

The adjutant opened the tent flap and motioned for Grimble to step in. Grimble ducked through the entrance and was about to come to attention when Dek interrupted. "As you were, Broadleaf. We have too much to cover. We'll dispense with protocol here."

"Yes, sir," Grimble said. He looked about the interior of the tent. Dek was on the opposite side of the table; to Dek's right was Captain Paul Gengler; beside Gengler was Roche. Sergeant Dinger Durinson stood at Grimble's left.

To Grimble's right and moving around the table toward Dek were three men he did not know. They were not dressed like troopers, which left him with no doubt that they were Ravens. The man to Grimble's right was slight of build, medium-complected, with long, wavy brown hair. He kept his focus on the table, one hand scratching his chest and the other close to his sword's handle. He did not turn to face Grimble.

The man beside that one was lean like a warrior, but with large muscles like a blacksmith and taller by a few inches than everyone else in the tent, almost as tall as Kelban. He was dark-skinned and his black hair was cut close, as was his beard. His hands rested at his hips, one on his knife and the other on his sword's pommel. His face was stern, with a scarred eyebrow and another scar at the back of his jaw that led to a missing earlobe. He gave a small nod to Grimble.

The last Raven was the thinnest of the three with a pale, gaunt face. His long black hair was brushed behind his shoulders and he sported a trimmed black beard. His right sleeve was rolled up, revealing a well-defined forearm as he absentmindedly stroked his mustache and stared, unfocused, through Grimble. He held his left arm behind his back.

"Corporal Broadleaf, thank you for coming so quickly," Dek said. "Before we go any further, and before you say anything else, I need to make you aware of some items. Master Sergeant Roche recommended you for an assignment, but we need you to understand what to expect. You would be accompanied by

Sergeants Roche and Dinger, as well as Sergeants Kurt Melovet, Baz Acheson, and Flicker Ringwood from Scout Company. It will be extremely dangerous. The team will be on its own in enemy territory, and if you're caught you will likely be killed, or imprisoned and tortured for information. No ransom will be paid for your return. This is an important, but perilous mission. What say you?"

"I'm in, sir." Grimble had spent enough time in the military to know that turning down an assignment after recommendation led to your military death.

"Excellent. Let's get to it." Dek dismissed Paul Gengler and turned over the papers on the table. Lowering his voice, he continued. "As I lay this out, feel free to speak up. I want to give you everything you need to be successful. Clear?"

"Yes, sir," the men said.

"Gentlemen, a high-ranking member of Renlar's army wants to turn spy. He claims to have information vital to the safety of our beloved Aendura. Our agents learned of this only recently, but they place his reliability at high. You will meet with him, determine his trustworthiness, learn what intelligence he can provide, and set up codes and drops for future contact. We will address this person as the Baker. Clear?"

"Yes, sir."

"The meeting will take place inside the river divide we lost a year ago, in a farmhouse outside Gandleton. There is expected to be a lot of movement in the Divide, which Renlar now calls Beckland. Renlar's King Heselov has offered free land to those who will work it, and we have word Noreas has put a call out for mercenaries to help them explore and expand into their wild lands. With new farmers moving in and mercenary groups moving through toward Noreas, you can expect the roads to be busy."

"Who determined the meeting location?" asked Baz, the larger Raven.

"The Baker did," Dek said.

"I don't like it," Dinger said. "We'll be picked up quickly with that many eyes on the roads."

"No, it makes sense," said Kurt, the Raven next to Grimble. "It's far from Lagisborg, in the middle of nowhere, and the Baker's given us a cover story for being in the area. I think this Baker may be genuine. Is he waiting on us, or do we have a time window?"

"The Baker will be at the farmhouse between the twenty-eighth and the thirty-first of this month," Dek said. "That's thirteen days to travel and four days to validate him, negotiate the terms, and conduct the intelligence work."

"Do we know which farmhouse outside Gandleton?" Baz asked.

"Not yet," Dek said. A few of the assembled men cocked their heads; the others furrowed their brows. "This is the way it is. You men will need to remain flexible."

"I don't trust the Renlarans," Baz said. "They warred against us over a hundred and fifty years ago, breaking away and turning Lagis March into Renlar. They start another war with us three years ago for the Divide, and now one of their officers wants to help us out? Sounds like a set-up before they move against us again. I don't like it."

"You need to be suspicious," Dek said, "but we can't pass this up without looking into it. If the Baker's genuine, he's putting his life on the line as well. He's informed our agents he worries he's close to being discovered by his people. That could be why he's shielding his dice right now. He's claimed he'll take precautions to prevent discovery on his end and will provide the exact location of the meeting in the next few days."

"I like this guy," Kurt said. Baz and Roche glared at him. "Relax. I don't trust him, but I like the way he thinks. He's planned this out."

"There's more," Dek said. "If Renlar knows he's trying to meet with us, they may use their assets here in Aendura to determine where the meeting's taking place. There are few spots we would launch a mission like this. The Ravens are one. You'll have to be careful from the start. I'll let Roche take it from here."

"Lads," Roche began, "two couriers brought messages about the mission to this camp on consecutive days. We may be watched at this very moment, and I don't want to risk the interception of a third courier en route here. When we leave this afternoon we will bear no military insignia, look as conspicuously civilian as possible, and carry no weapon bigger than a knife. We head by horse to Whitby and then to Brantsford, where we will receive the final details of the mission, including the location of the farmhouse. Any questions yet?"

"Are we by horse the whole way?" Dinger asked.

"No. We ride as far as Brantsford. Right now the plan is to throw off anyone watching us by portalling from Brantsford to a town close to Gandleton. The closest our mages can get us is River's Edge, which is on our side of the Vaster River. It may be in Aendura, but we'll be only a river crossing and two days' travel on foot to Gandleton. The other team we link with in Brantsford will further throw off any followers by pretending to be us as they travel to Agderon.

"Once we're inside Renlar, we will stay there until the mission is completed or aborted. I know what you're thinking – 'Once we determine the Baker is genuine, why can't we portal in

and out of the farmhouse or some other nearby spot every day?'
Ripples, gentlemen."

Two of the Ravens turned their heads to the gaunt one
stroking his beard – Flicker. Dinger and Grimble followed their
lead, waiting for him to speak.

"Mage-sign," Flicker said, his eyes staring unfocused
through Grimble. "He's talking about mage-sign. To mages it's
like ripples in a pond or sound in the air. The more powerful or
frequent the magic use, the bigger the disturbance."

"There's always some of it about," said Roche, "but if it's
big enough and frequent enough it attracts attention. Portals are
powerful spells. We'd make too much mage-sign, too many
ripples. I'm sure we'd be detected."

The other Ravens looked at Flicker again, but he said
nothing more.

For the next couple of hours, they went over the details
several more times. Their heights and weights were recorded, as
was their overall appearance. Roche and the Ravens were to
conduct the meetings and negotiations. Dinger and Grimble were
to provide cover as an overwatch team and would not be party to
the meetings.

Shortly before the noon meal, Dinger and Grimble were sent
back to their campsite to gather what they needed. Roche and the
Ravens stayed behind to work out more details.

Grimble and Dinger walked in silence as they headed back
to Fourth Company's campsite. Grimble focused on what he
might need and worried how the rest of his kit would make it
back to Fort Anjermott. Lost in thought, he bumped into a trooper
who had been charged with stable duty. Grimble realized he was
next to the paddock fence, and he let Dinger continue on to the
tents alone. Havoc would be taken out to run and graze shortly

and Grimble wanted to see his partner before leaving.

He moved up to the rope barrier and whistled. A few horses turned or lifted their heads, but Havoc walked briskly to his rider. He sniffed Grimble's hand and arms, nickering softly. The two friends put the sides of their heads together, gently pushing on each other. Havoc raised his head and used his lips and teeth to feel Grimble's hands.

"I don't have anything right now, bud. Wish I did." Grimble rubbed Havoc's neck. "I have to leave for a little while. Your brand – heck, your temper – would give you away as a war horse. Take care of yourself and help keep an eye on Goat while I'm away." He gave Havoc one last pat and looked him in the eye. Then he let out a breath and walked to his tent.

Kelban sat on a stool outside it, chewing heartily on some stale bread. As Grimble approached, Kelban stood and broke off a thick piece of the loaf. He tossed the chunk at Grimble, but it went wide of the mark, forcing Grimble to reach out and catch his breakfast before it hit the ground.

"Not awake yet, are you?" Grimble asked.

"Apparently not," Kelban said, picking up a wedge of hard cheese.

"Just hand that to me." Kelban smiled and did so. "I need to pack a few items and get ready to leave. They're sending a few of us to some training near Agderon."

"Mm-hmm," Kelban mumbled, still chewing on some bread. His eyes disagreed with his voice.

"Could use you securing my kit and keeping an eye on Havoc and Goat. Hope you don't mind."

"Mm-hmm," Kelban murmured in support, taking a bite of cheese.

Goat approached from his tent, picking his front teeth with

101

his pinky finger. "Training? What kind of training?" he asked.

"Training," Grimble and Kelban stated together.

Goat stopped in his tracks and looked at them, then changed the topic. "I can help keep an eye on Havoc, if you'd like."

Grimble knelt at the entrance to his tent. "Appreciate it. And stick with Kelban. He'll keep you straight. I'll be back before long." He started going through his equipment, packing what he thought would be necessary or helpful. Nearby, Thom noticed Goat and Kelban standing over Grimble.

"What's Grimble up to?" Thom asked.

"Training," Kelban and Goat said together.

Thom's eyebrows furrowed and he huffed away, throwing up his arms. "T'Abyss! Fine, don't tell me."

Kelban's face turned serious. "Word is the Ravens that made it back to camp are preparing to train too. Whatever you have going, Grimble, be careful. Don't trust people in secret groups. They'll choose their own over outsiders every time."

Grimble nodded. He understood his friend's distrust. Kelban's father had been a respected cooper in his province. He'd thought he would make a better life for his family and had moved everyone to the capital city of Agderon. However, the trade guilds there saw otherwise and had prevented Kelban's father from plying his craft. The family struggled now, and Kelban clutched to his distrust of guilds and other select organizations.

Grimble quickly changed into the new clothes he'd been given. They were nondescript, resembling the clothing of field hands and laborers. He rolled several of his chosen items in his bedroll and stuffed more in a sack, and got to his feet. "Thanks for breakfast," he said. Kelban nodded, still chewing. "Tell the lads I'll be back, not to get used to my absence."

Kelban held out his hand. "Wish I was training beside you."

"Me too." Grimble would feel much better about the whole thing if Kelban had been selected too. He clasped his friend's hand and looked him in the eye, trying to thank him wordlessly for always being by his side. Kelban's hands were strong and his grip always surprised Grimble. They embraced, loudly slapping each other's backs. Grimble released his grasp, took a bite of cheese, and stuffed the rest of the wedge into his sack. He threw the sack over his shoulder and reached out to take his bedroll from Goat. The three men looked at each other once more, and without another word, parted ways.

By the time Grimble returned to the center of camp, Dinger was securing his gear to his saddle. Roche and the Ravens stood together, their kits already secured to their mounts. One of the four horses raised its head and danced, pulling its tethered reins tight. Dek watched, through half-closed eyes, from the front of his tent. One horse remained with empty saddlebags and no bedroll. Grimble walked up to it, letting it smell and get familiar with him. He checked the horse's tack and hooves before securing his bedroll to his new saddle and packing the saddlebags.

Grimble handed his sword and scabbard to Roche, leaving only his knife on his belt. Roche lay the sword alongside five others on a canvas tarp, rolled it tightly, and bound it with leather lashings. Dek took the bundle and placed it inside the command tent.

Dinger and Grimble were thrown new traveling cloaks decorated with embroidery and other embellishments, making them ostentatious enough for the job. The other four members of the team wore similar cloaks. As Dinger and Grimble donned theirs, Dinger remarked, "Can't say I approve. Too flashy for me."

"We know," Roche said. "That's the point."

Baz rapped Kurt on the shoulder, and without speaking, the three Ravens left their horses and headed toward the Temple. Roche motioned for Dinger and Grimble to follow, but Dinger hesitated. He took a breath, casting his head back, then plodded behind the team.

They were met outside the Temple tent by Captain Paul Gengler. Paul led the men inside and walked them to the altar at the far end. Grimble attended services, but was not among the handful of troopers in regular attendance. Although he was faithful to the High Father, Grimble and his family fell in line with Ihgel, the god of farmers and soldiers. They prayed to Ihgel more frequently than any of the other gods. That said, Grimble had faith in Abbyon, the Father on High, and worshiped him dutifully. This was not unusual in Aendura, Renlar, or Haldiland. It was typical for people to honor and pray to the Father of the Gods, even if they aligned themselves more closely with one of the others.

Grimble knew the new priest, Brother Bhen, would arrive shortly and bless the men for their journey, saying it was right in the eyes of the High Father. The priests did this before every mission and battle; however, it was most often conducted in the yard outside the tent.

The men stood in silence, waiting for several minutes. Then a woman entered. Grimble and the others blinked and averted their eyes reflexively, as if stepping out of a dark room into the sunlight. It was several seconds before they could raise their heads to look at her. Dinger made three attempts to keep his eyes open and head up before being able to do so.

The Devout Mother was rarely seen in camp and never blessed the troops before battle. For her to stand among healthy men, men not on death's door, was a thing unheard of to Grimble.

This was the closest he had ever been to her. She was alluring, charismatic. The lines on her face indicated she was past her thirties, but everything else lent her a younger image. The blue accents on her white hooded robe matched her eyes. Her face was both at peace and firmly confident as she held her head high. Grimble felt a sense of calm in her presence. Her walk to the center of the altar space was slow and measured, each step a gliding, purposeful act followed seamlessly by the next.

"These are the men preparing to leave on the journey?" she asked in a melodic voice that held its own charm.

"They are, Your Excellency," Paul said.

She smiled and scrutinized the six men, lingering a moment on each, looking them directly in the eyes. Her eyebrows and the corners of her lips twitched, as if she were conversing silently. "No more than five were thought necessary. Who decided on six?"

"I did, Your Excellency," Roche said.

"So it is," she replied. She walked back to the altar and with a small, metal spoon heaped six measures of powdered incense into a brass bowl. A thick, gray smoke drifted upward as each spoonful hit the hot coals. It had proliferated into a cloud by the time the Devout Mother finished the sixth.

She faced the altar, her back to the troopers. The smoking bowl of incense, now hidden from Grimble's view, continued to send smoke heavenward. The Devout Mother looked to the roof above, chanting low, almost inaudibly, her arms raised above her head, palms up. Her arms slowly lowered until they were stretched out wide, parallel to the ground. The smoke slowed, no longer making its way to the peaked tent ceiling; instead it gathered into a nebulous shape in front of her.

The Devout Mother placed her left hand on her chest, and faster than any of them thought she could move, she spun to her left to face the men. Her right arm arced up and down as she moved. The flow of her robe caught the incense smoke, and it moved toward the men like an aromatic gray tide. As the first waves hit them, she chanted louder. The language was foreign to Grimble; but he had never expected to understand it. The last wave hit them with a strange force, waking them in body and spirit. Grimble's eyes opened wide. His body's reaction caught him off guard. The Devout Mother finished the prayer and silently bowed her head for a moment before focusing on the men again.

"It is imperative you are strong," she said. "You must be resolute. I cannot say what awaits you; only the gods know that. However, I know failure will lead to suffering." With that, she touched her forehead, her lips, and her chest with fingers of her left hand. Grimble, Roche, Paul, and the large Raven did the same. The Devout Mother bowed her head and slowly left the room.

Once she was gone, Paul led the men quietly from the Temple and back to their waiting mounts. "I will pray to all the gods for you and your success," he told them, said his goodbyes, and left.

"Before we leave," Roche said, "Dinger, Grimble – there is no rank on this mission, and no one is to be addressed by rank. Names only. Lads, this is Baz, Kurt, and Flicker."

Grimble shook Kurt's hand first. He was the Raven who had stood next to him in the briefing. After Kurt, he clasped hands with Baz, the large one. More muscular than the other troopers in the 209th, Baz had a grip to match his frame, firm and strong. He looked Grimble in the eye, his face a scowl, and held on to

Grimble's hand a little longer than necessary. Grimble did not back away from the challenge, matching the strength of the shake with his own grasp and holding firm, preventing Baz from rotating his hand into an inferior position. All the while he met Baz's stare until they both released grips.

Grimble turned to the last man, Flicker, the one with light skin and a gaunt face. He too looked Grimble in the eye as they shook hands. The grasp was light at first, but Flicker's fingers twitched unexpectedly. His eyebrows scrunched and he cocked his head to one side. Flicker grabbed Grimble's hand more firmly and looked at their clasped hands. Grimble was surprised by this unusual display, but he maintained his firm grip on the man's hand. Flicker leaned in to peer into his eyes one at a time, then released his grip.

"You were right to add this one, Roche," Flicker said.

# CHAPTER NINE

*I should have seen that coming.*

The right cross connected with Grimble's left cheek. It rocked his head and shook his sinuses, filling his nose with that snotty smell he hated. He stumbled sideways. For a moment the world faded away. Then it rushed back. Grass prickled his face.

*Grass? I'm on the ground?*

He tried to focus on something, on anything. There was something he needed to do. His mind fogged. He needed to think.

*Danger. Dangerous man. Watch for the dangerous man.*

Enough of his mind remembered there was a threat. He needed to be on his feet, needed to be ready.

Grimble canted as he pushed the ground away from his face. He swayed as it moved under his feet.

He stood, wobbling, against his head's objections.

The fog drifted away. Pain plunged in. The world righted itself.

Grimble put his hands up to protect his head and turned to face…

*That rat bastard, Baz!*

Surprisingly, the Raven had not closed the distance, had not come in for the kill. Baz held off several steps away, a smirk on his ordinarily passive face. Rage welled up in Grimble. This was stupid. They were supposed to be working together, not tearing into each other. Yet Baz apparently felt it necessary to test Grimble. And he was not holding back.

Throughout yesterday afternoon and again this morning, Baz had complained about everything Grimble had done. He had collected too little firewood. He had collected too much firewood. Grimble's horse made too much noise. Grimble's cloak was ugly. Grimble ate breakfast too loudly.

Grimble knew he was being pulled into a fight. The question was, when would Baz tire of the banter and make it physical? Until that time, Grimble gave back what he received. The constant effort frustrated him. He wanted to focus on the job at hand and complete the mission. Roche said nothing as the process wore on, showing tacit approval of the affair. Dinger chuckled and watched the whole thing unfold. This morning, Baz had finally snapped after returning from his morning necessaries to find Grimble heating water for the group's tea.

"Demons and damnation!" Baz yelled. "You're incompetent. You're a fucking idiot! Look, asshole! You got ash in the damn water."

"You're a miserable cuss, Baz," Grimble said. "Nothing satisfies you. You're worse than a jealous wife. You know what? If you're going to act like my wife, why don't you come over here and suck my dick."

Baz's face twisted in fury. He charged at Grimble. Grimble had expected the attack to come; he had been expecting one every time he had returned Baz's vituperation. Baz came in low, meaning to grapple with Grimble and take him to the ground. He was older than Grimble, possibly by five years, but he was bigger and he was quick. However, Grimble had a secret Baz didn't know about. Over the last couple of years he had been training with Kelban, who was considered the regiment's premier pugilist.

Grimble had learned much in that time.

Baz attempted to wrap his arms around Grimble's legs, but Grimble shot his legs back and put his weight on the back of his attacker. The two tussled for a while, each trying to get the upper hand, but were soon pulled apart and forced to step away from each other. Baz was strong. Stronger than Kelban. Grimble knew he had to keep him from making it a wrestling match.

Baz shot in again, but this time he threw a few jabs and punches in combination, testing Grimble's defenses. In that exchange, Grimble managed a blow to Baz's ribs, but he held back, trying not to take the man out of the mission.

He wouldn't make that mistake again. Baz's second attack combination was designed to pull Grimble's left hand away from protecting his head. Grimble recognized the feint in the middle of the blows but failed to weave in time. The blow that followed had been the one that knocked him down and put his face in the grass.

It seemed like forever, but seconds later Grimble was back on his feet. Baz looked fresh and his smirk remained. As Grimble squared off against him, Baz gave a slight tilt of his head and raised an eyebrow. "Your funeral," he said. He moved forward, left foot first.

Grimble waited, and as Baz moved his right foot, he stepped in, beginning a series of blows meant to test and feint. Baz countered and danced, keeping Grimble at a distance, but his smirk disappeared.

*He's not as good as Kelban.*

Baz's next attempt to close with Grimble was more cautious, and the two exchanged blows and blocks, with no real connections. Baz also tried again to grapple with Grimble. He failed. The two backed away from each other. Kurt and Dinger cheered, egging them on.

This time Grimble closed with Baz, using the same attack combination that had landed a blow on his ribs. Baz recognized it. He lowered his left arm to block the expected punch, but it did not come. Grimble stepped to the right and threw a left-handed uppercut. It connected with Baz's chin. His head flew back. His arms opened. Grimble twisted his body, planted his right foot, and using his weight threw a right punch at Baz's face. It connected with the man's nose.

Baz stumbled backward. His arms flew wide of his body and he fell to the ground. Blood gushed over his mouth and down the sides of his face. Grimble did not hesitate. He closed in on the downed man, intending to pound him into submission. But before he could, the arms of several men wrapped him up, intending to stop the fight. "Easy. Easy," they called.

*What? No!* Grimble struggled against them. "Let me go!" he roared. "I'm gonna finish the bastard!"

"EASY!" the men yelled. Their hold was firm.

"We're supposed to be working together!" Grimble shouted at Baz. "Not fighting each other! You better stay down, asshole!"

"Whoa. Easy."

Roche put his head next to Grimble's. "Stand down, Grimble," he said. "It's okay."

Grimble relaxed his body, but threw a look of disgust at Baz. Flicker helped Baz to his feet and handed him a clean rag. Kurt held a cloth out to Grimble as well.

"What?" Grimble snapped.

"Your cheek," Kurt said. He motioned to Grimble's left cheek. Grimble touched the area and, seeing fresh blood on his fingers, snatched the rag from Kurt's hand. He placed the cloth over the wound and applied pressure, working to calm himself.

"Holy piss, you've got a punch," Baz said, catching his breath. He stood and bent over, pinching the rag to his nose and looking sideways at Grimble.

"Should have taken our word," Flicker said.

"I think I will next time." He held his head up and removed the rag from his nose. It had a spectacular bend in it now. "How's it look?"

"Oh, it's broken," Kurt said. "Relax, eh? It improves your appearance." He let out a small laugh.

Baz's nose started bleeding again. He reached up, his thumbs on each side of his nose, applied pressure and pulled down. A cringe-worthy crackling emanated from Baz's face, followed by a snap. Baz removed his hands, revealing reduced blood flow and a swollen but straight nose.

"T'Abyss! You've ruined it now," Kurt complained. Baz smiled like a schoolboy.

Grimble's breathing slowed. He removed his rag and asked Roche, "Sew or singe?"

"Neither," Roche said. "You'll be alright."

Grimble looked at him in confusion. He could feel the gap in the cut skin and knew it required some kind of attention.

Roche pointed at the pugilists. "You two. Get down to the stream and wash up. Try to get some of the blood out of your clothes, too. It's over now. Any more blows and you answer to me."

Flicker handed Baz another rag and something shiny. Baz took them and headed to the stream. Grimble followed. His adrenalin dump had faded, the wound's sting becoming apparent.

Baz knelt by the stream and looked at his reflection in the slow-running water. "Good show, that. Wouldn't you say? You tagged me good. Doubt if my family would recognize me now."

Grimble knelt on the muddy bank a few steps away and looked at the older man. The swelling had grown around his nose and under his eyes. That, coupled with the blood around his face and on his shirt, made Baz an awful sight to behold. The Raven sat back and breathed out.

"What the fuck's your problem?" Grimble asked him. "This chest-thumping game of yours has slowed us down. Our injuries hurt the mission."

"Don't question my devotion to the mission. This wasn't a fight for top cock."

"I know how your kind operate, Baz. You always have to show your rank to the new guys. Remind them where they stand. We have plenty of guys like you in First Batt. I expected more from a Raven."

Baz clenched his teeth, took a slow breath and relaxed. "You're a thinker, Grimble. Nothing wrong with that. Most of the time. Flicker and Kurt are thinkers too. But I've known too many thinkers who hesitated when they needed to act. I needed to know you had the fight in you and wouldn't hesitate – that you wouldn't quit even when your body was telling you to quit, even when you were on your own."

Baz drew the shiny object from his rag. It was a metal flask the size of a deck of cards. He unstrapped a cup not much larger than a thimble from the top and uncorked the flask before he spoke again.

"I know you've been through several battles, always holding the line. It's easier to stand brave when there's a man beside you. I needed to know how you are on your own. Roche vouched for you – that helped. And somehow Flicker got a good feeling about you. Don't understand that, but I really don't understand his ways."

"Sounds like you have trust issues. Maybe you need some help."

"Now who's nagging? Maybe you should come over here and…" Baz spread his legs and motioned to his crotch, his eyes wide open, asking the question.

The two stared at each other for a while. Then Grimble laughed. Baz smirked.

"I needed proof, not words," he said. He poured a little brown liquor into the small cup and drank it down quickly. He scrunched his nose and exhaled through his mouth.

"Trust goes both ways," Grimble said. "I don't know you either. Don't know if *you'll* be there if I need you, or if Roche or Dinger need you."

Baz poured another portion into the small cup and handed it toward Grimble. Grimble stared him in the eye, not taking the cup. "Take it," Baz implored.

Eventually, Grimble did. "Sharing a drink after an orchestrated fight doesn't bring about trust," he said. "Especially when that fight causes us to be liabilities to the mission. I heard you Ravens were a different lot, but I had no idea." Grimble slung the contents of the cup into his mouth and swallowed. The odd flavor struck him right away. It had all the burn of alcohol but was accompanied by a horrible, organic nastiness. It was the worst tea he'd ever tasted, with a metallic finish, and burned like the purest alcohol he had ever drunk. Grimble looked into the cup and back to Baz. The Raven sat back, his smile growing.

His opponent's face changed before his eyes. The swelling diminished. Grimble felt the flush he had expected from the drink, but it did not warm his throat and stomach. The warmth was in his face, specifically his left cheek. It itched and burned for a few moments. Then the sensation subsided, gone as quickly as it had started.

"Now we can wash up," Baz said. They knelt at the stream and washed the blood from their faces. Grimble took a look at his reflection and saw the ruptured skin of his left cheek whole again. Baz's nose appeared similarly healed. The two went about rinsing the blood out of their clothes as best they could. "The other thing I like about that stuff is that it gets rid of riding and training aches, too."

"What's in that flask? I'm sure you have to know where to get something like that. You don't just pick that up at the market square."

"It's something one of Flicker's friends makes – an alchemist mage. That little drink you had cost more than a year's pay," Baz answered, scrubbing a particularly big stain on his shirt.

"Is that the reason we don't use it after battles? The cost? It could save lives. We wouldn't have to train new soldiers as often. That's money saved, too."

"I see your point, but the king's war council might disagree with us on that. But no, that is not the reason. It is good for small injuries alone. It won't heal major wounds." Baz stopped what he was doing and looked hard at Grimble. "Grimble, I'd give you the last drop of this to see us back to Fort Anjermott when this is all over. Each of us – Flicker, Kurt, me – any one of us would lay down our lives for you to see this mission through. If you need another opinion on that, ask Roche. I know you trust him. We're not going to leave you behind. That said, if it means the mission or one of our lives, you need to be ready to cut us loose or be cut loose. The mission is bigger than us all."

Grimble nodded.

"Just needed to say it," Baz said, wringing out his shirt.

"Hey, you two!" Kurt yelled from the campsite. "Are you done holding hands and hugging down there? We're about packed up and ready to head out."

"I started in the King's Army, like you," Baz said. "Joined for king and country. Keeping my family safe. Kurt there came by another path. Flicker still another. They'll behave differently than the troopers you're used to riding with, but they're good men. They won't let you down." Baz slipped on his shirt and offered his hand to Grimble. The two shook hands.

They walked up the embankment and emerged through the undergrowth to step into the camp, finding Roche pouring leftover tea on the coals in the fire circle. The hot coals and earth hissed in protest, sending steam back at the pot attacking them. Roche smiled as Baz and Grimble emerged with wet clothes and clean faces.

Dinger paused while rolling up his bedroll, his face a bright display of shock as the two men returned without scab, scar, or swelling. Grimble walked past him without a word and hustled to secure his gear. As he prepared his horse for the long ride ahead, Roche walked up and held out his hand. Grimble reached out, not knowing what to expect. Roche dropped two silver nobs into his palm.

"There was some wagering," Roche said. "This is your winnings."

"Baz knocked me pretty good," Grimble said, taking the

coins, "but I can't imagine it was hard enough to make me forget I'd made a wager."

"No. I put the coins on you. I knew he wasn't going to be satisfied until he put you through the gauntlet. Baz is that way. There are few he trusts. But he's a good man and an incredible soldier. One in a hundred. Anyway, I figured you should profit from his disagreeable nature."

"You could have stopped this."

"I'm building a team. We're stronger now. Had to happen." Roche paused and looked into Grimble's eyes. The look was sincere, almost pleading. "You need to pay attention. I need you to pay attention. Learn."

Grimble cocked his head. "What do you mean?"

"Nothing further. Just pay attention."

"Alright," Grimble said, unsure of the gist. "What about Baz?"

Roche wore a wry smile. "I think he's warming up to you."

"Fine," Grimble said as he mounted his horse, "but the next time he wants to dance, I pick the music."


The six rode southeast, cross-country for most of the second day before picking up the road they needed. There they continued east at a brisk clip, alternating between walks and jogs, trying to reach the next way station before dark.

Being able to ride two abreast at this point, Kurt pulled his horse next to Grimble.

"Eh, buddy," he said. "That was an impressive show this morning. I haven't seen Baz knocked down in... Well, I can't recall ever seeing that happen." Grimble nodded once in acknowledgment. Kurt continued. "I can tell you're more than a simple farm boy who made it into the army. You must have studied somewhere. Makes me think you're holding stuff back, not giving us all there is to know about you."

"What's your point?" Grimble asked.

"Relax, I mean no offense. But it's not right keeping information from the team. Makes it impossible to predict things. You know, like who's better with their sword, who's better with their fists, things like that." Grimble remained silent, waiting for Kurt to come out and say it. "I mean, if I'd known you knew how to bare-knuckle fight, that you weren't like the other troopers – well, you know."

"I'm afraid you have me at a disadvantage, Kurt," Grimble said. He suspected he knew what was coming, but mustered as much sincerity as he could. "What do you mean?"

"A craftsman must work with the material he has. Bad leather makes bad shoes, poor-quality iron makes bad tools, and bad information leads to bad bets."

"Ah." Grimble smiled, then dropped the expression as quickly as he could, forcing his face to go blank again. "No, I still don't think I understand."

"Okay, let me get down to it. If I'd known you knew how to fight I wouldn't have bet against you."

"Makes sense."

"The way I see it, you owe me two crowns."

"Whoa – that's a big bet on someone you don't know. Two gold crowns? Who does that?"

"I know Baz and his skill."

"Maybe you should take it up with him."

Kurt looked at Baz, then turned back to Grimble. "Yeah, that's not going to happen. You owe me two crowns." His face was grave.

Grimble looked at Kurt for a moment and smiled. Kurt

cocked his head in confusion. Grimble turned to face forward again, pursing his lips and sucking in, causing a high-pitched, almost inaudible squeaking noise. Kurt's mare jumped suddenly and bolted forward. It was evident by his reaction in the saddle that Kurt was not a skilled rider, but he managed to get his mount under control.

"You okay, Kurt?" shouted Baz.

"Yeah, don't know where that came from." He rode back to the spot beside Grimble. "Something must have spooked her."

"Sure looked like it," Grimble said.

"Well, back to business. It pains me to say it, but you owe —"

Grimble looked at him, pursed his lips, and sucked in.

"Holy —!" Kurt exclaimed, his face in shock, as his mare reacted to the noise again.

"Great gods above, Kurt!" Baz exclaimed. "What are you doing to your horse?"

Kurt recovered a little more quickly this time. He laughed like a man who has suddenly realized how the magician fooled him. "Playing a game on an uneven field and underestimating my opponent. You ought to understand that danger, eh?"

"Ouch," Baz said. "Below the belt, you complete git."

Kurt rode back to Grimble's side once more. They looked at each other for a moment. Kurt gave Grimble a knowing smile, and Grimble nodded.

"Had to try," Kurt said. "It was two crowns."

"No offense taken," Grimble replied. Kurt kicked his horse and moved to the back of the line.

It was past suppertime, but before dark, when the tavern came into view. This particular way station was one of the countryside's least impressive. A nominal wayside tavern, no more. The enterprising farmer of the land on which it was built had merely erected a barn beside the road for the extra income it could generate. Such endeavors were supported by the local earls, as they brought in extra taxes.

The building was nothing more than a large, three-sided pole barn with a loft, but it was a welcome sight for travelers wishing to get out of the weather and safely stable their horses for the night. The fees for the accommodations and fodder were low, but over time the farmer had earned enough coin to add a second, smaller structure next to the first. The new building was proudly called a tavern, but in truth, it was merely a large shed in which the farmer had placed a few tables and benches, so he and his family could charge for meals and drinks as well. The roads were dotted with these small way stations, and weary travelers thanked the god Gavel for them.

As the six men approached, a middle-aged man exited the small farmhouse at the far end of a plowed field and mounted a donkey. He made his way to them, sitting sideways. The team dismounted to shake the saddle out of their bones and stretch their bodies. Roche handed his reins to Dinger and walked toward the approaching farmer. To Grimble, it seemed to take Roche longer than usual to get the saddle out of his walk.

Roche talked with the farmer for a minute. He pulled his pouch from his belt and counted some coin into the man's hand. The farmer returned to his home on the donkey as Roche gave the men the thumbs-up sign. They gathered around him.

"Hay and grain are behind the barn, get what you need for the horses. There are two other guests, but only one using a stall, so there are enough stalls for our mounts. Sleep in the loft above or with your horses, your call. There's no hot food left, we got here too late, but he's bringing some bread, cheese, and a few items from the cellar to the shed – the tavern over there." Roche pointed to the small structure next to the barn.

Grimble and the rest went about untacking and caring for their horses. The three Ravens did not tend to theirs with the deliberation the cavalry troopers did, but Grimble was pleasantly surprised to find they showed a measure of deference to the animals they rode. The three Ravens finished stabling their mounts before the troopers and left as a group for the tavern.

Dinger's horse was in the stall next to Grimble's. After the Ravens left, Dinger motioned with his chin to the rafter overhead. "Do they really think that makes a difference?"

Grimble looked up at the large symbol for Gavel pegged to the rafter. It was roughly carved from wood. The flat horizon appeared to be a whittled tree branch the length of a forearm, and the half-risen sun set upon it was no more than half a disk sawed from the trunk of a six-inch-thick tree. He smiled. "I don't know. It makes me feel good. My folks told me it was the intent, not the appearance."

Dinger set his brush down and began cleaning his horse's hooves. "You really think that will protect you?"

"I believe Gavel watches over us. The symbol just makes me think of him. That's enough for me."

"And you're worried a hole from the Abyss will open up if you don't worship the gods?"

"What? No. All those stories of monsters and fey creatures crawling from the Abyss through dark holes and cracks in the ground are for kids. Gavel's blessings are real."

"You worship Gavel? I thought you worshiped Ihgel?"

Grimble pinched his horse's leg and secured a hoof for cleaning. "We worship them all. Urel, Gavel, Rafel, Yahnn,

Ihgel, and especially Abbyon, the High Father. We're closer to Ihgel. We're farmers, after all."

"I just don't get all that spiritual shit. I put my faith in steel and training."

Grimble shook his head.

Roche removed his horse's halter and walked out of its stall. He lowered the wooden beams that closed it off and stepped over to Grimble. "You two done with your heart-to-heart?"

Grimble smiled. "We're done."

"You did well today. With Baz and Kurt."

"The wait was the part that frustrated me." Grimble emerged from his stall. "I kept wondering when Baz would stop talking and finally get to it. Wondered how Kurt would try me too."

Dinger smiled. "How you handled Kurt was a good laugh. I needed that."

"You're welcome, brother." Grimble gave a short bow.

"How'd you figure that one out?" Dinger asked.

"It was a coincidence. Before we left the camp yesterday the water cart passed by us twice, once when I walked up and the other time after we came out of the Temple. Its axel needs grease. Kurt's horse bucked a little and tried to move away from the squeaking both times. Last night while we were eating, I tested her by making the noise I used for getting the attention of our dogs on the farm. She reacted to it. Figured it would come in handy if or when Kurt took his turn poking me."

"I remember her getting riled up last night," Dinger said.

"She could have been assigned to any of us – it was my good luck Kurt rode her. Now I suppose it's Flicker's turn."

"You don't have to worry about any more drama at this point," Roche said. "Flicker's not like that, and it's best to leave him alone."

"What's with his staring?" Dinger asked. "Sometimes he's normal, and then sometimes he looks like his mind isn't with us, and he stares through you like you're not there, even when you talk to him."

"That's a mage thing," Roche answered quietly. "Something about their studies and how they learn their spells. Some have it worse than Flicker, some so bad they never recover and lose their minds." He tapped his forehead for emphasis. "Don't worry – he's always there, even if it looks like he's distracted."

Dinger's eyes widened. "Damn it all. Flicker's a mage?" He looked at Grimble, but Grimble was trying to take it in too. "Gotta be honest with you, Roche, I don't know how I feel about that."

"Quit the superstitious shit, Dinger," Roche said. "There are a few in Scout Company. They've supported the regiment for years. You should be thankful we have him along. I know I am."

"But why would they want to join the King's Army?" Dinger asked. "I thought they were all about learning and swore off their fealty. All about devotion to the Institute and the Spire, or something like that."

"The Spire Council are the only ones that swear off any allegiances they had. The rest of those from the Arcane Institute can return to their countries to use their talents as they see fit. They can join mage guilds or freelance. It's up to them. A few, like Flicker, are attracted to the king's offer to pay off their debts for two or more years' service as a battle mage. Flicker's time is up at the end of this month. He's short. That's why Lieutenant Panyyl let him go back to the camp instead of backtracking the goblins. It's also why the cobbler's cart was burned up. Flicker got pissed when Dek ordered him on the mission, and the cart was the first non-living thing Flicker ran across after receiving the order."

Dinger whistled. "Alright, don't piss off Flicker."

Roche jerked his thumb toward the tavern. "Enough talk. Let's get some food."

They stored their saddles in the loft before heading to the tiny tavern, crossing paths with the two other guests, a man and a woman, who gave the men a wide berth. The Ravens were inside and seated at a table made of rough-cut lumber. An empty stool and an old bench sat next to the table, waiting for the last of the team. Two other tables, one with some dirty dishware, several seating benches, and a counter completed the interior decorations of the dirt-floor establishment.

Untouched on their table beside a jug and a pitcher were two loaves of dark bread, blocks of cheese, and a collection of dull turnips and carrots. The latecomers joined those waiting, and together the men dined.

# CHAPTER TEN

*Pardon the intrusion, Commander. The Devout Mother and I must take your leave – ugh.*

With the sun nearing the horizon, Bhen almost failed to see the horse dung lurking in the camp's long shadows. Thankfully he managed to sidestep it at the last moment, avoiding the strung-out clumps by inches. He was getting more nimble after several days in the camp. Now if he could just get used to the smell.

He started again.

*Pardon the intrusion, Commander. The Devout Mother and I must take – Agh! Where are those servants with the muck cart?* His foot, already on its downward motion, almost landed in another pile, but Bhen managed to leap. He landed on the dusty road and not the stinking mess, and he thanked the High Father. Where were the camp's indentured servants tasked with collecting the manure? Bhen's family had a large livery, and his family's staff were never this inefficient. He reminded himself to say a prayer for them this evening.

Before he could practice again Bhen found himself at Commander Dek's tent. Its sudden appearance caught him off guard and he stared at Trooper Wollter, searching for the words.

"Are you here to see the commander?" Wollter asked.

"Uh, yes. Please."

Wollter poked his head through the tent flaps. "Sir. Brother Bhenkeragor here to see you." There was a reply, but the noises of the camp drowned it out. Wollter stepped to the side and opened the flap. "Step right in, sir. But be careful of the —"

With his first step Bhen kicked the metal plate and bowl on the ground in front of the tent. They flew with a clang across the grass and dirt under the awning. A small loaf of bread and wedge of cheese tumbled into the road. Beans, wet and cold, sprayed across the ground, the tent, and both Wollter's and Bhen's clothes. The towel that had been covering the dishes lay impotent and clean across Wollter's boots.

Bhen flushed and leaned over to clean up the mess, but Wollter stopped him. "I've got this. The commander's waiting, sir."

Embarrassed, Bhen stepped inside.

Commander Dek rose from his seat. "Brother Bhenkeragor, it is good to see you."

"Please call me Bhen, sir."

"Will do." Dek's eyes focused on the hem of the priest's robes and the black beans clinging to the thick brown cotton. "Ah, I see you brought me my supper." Bhen stammered for a few seconds and fidgeted with the prayer beads hanging from his robe's belt. Dek shook his head and smiled. "I forget you're not used to me yet. Don't worry about the chow." He motioned for Bhen to have a seat at the planning table. "No harm done. It's my own fault. I should eat my meals when they arrive – and not cast aside today's meal for the promise of a larger one tomorrow."

Bhen waved off the chair, but smiled at Dek's words. He had

seen Dek at services on Temple Day, but not on a regular basis. He had never expected the military commander to be a faithful follower and reader of the texts. That he was familiar enough to paraphrase the Prophet's sermon on the dangers of greed showed Bhen that Dek paid attention to the scriptures. Bhen felt a measure of comfort return. "Thank you, Commander."

A distant shout rose above the camp's evening din. It was repeated several times, getting closer with each call. Dek held a hand up to Bhen. "Give me a moment, please. Our conversation may be delayed."

"Understood."

Wollter popped his head into the tent. "Arriving Raven, sir. Headed this way."

"When he gets here, send him in without delay. I've been expecting him." Dek turned to the priest. "This is important, Brother Bhen, and may take a few minutes. You're welcome to stay, but as per our agreement between the Temple and the King's Army, what you hear is for your ears and those of the Devout Mother alone. Understood?"

"Understood, Commander," said Bhen. He fully appreciated his duties as a chaplain to the troopers and would not betray that oath. He elected to stay, as Mother Tara had sent him on this errand and he was going to see it through before leaving the tent.

The commander cleared his desk of some maps and other loose items. A white handkerchief with a blue embroidered "S" was revealed underneath one of the maps. Dek's hand shot out and snatched it, eagerly stuffing it under his jerkin. He tilted his head, as if trying to see if Bhen had noticed. Bhen, playing the dutiful part of an oblivious guest, looked to the tent's ceiling as though he had noticed it for the first time.

Dek breathed out and his shoulders slumped for a second

before he sat upright again. He removed some paper from a shelf at his desk and pulled out the ink bottle and pen. Two candles in brass holders sat ready on the desk and Dek lit them with the lamp hanging from the tent's center pole. He placed a second chair next to his desk and waited.

There was a murmur outside the tent, then the flap snapped open so abruptly that Bhen jumped back. The stink of sweat and the grime of mud and ash stomped into the tent before the man himself slid through the entrance. Bhen had a hard time seeing him as a soldier. He looked wild; his bedraggled appearance hid any discipline. He was in his early thirties, bearded, slightly shorter than Bhen and most of the fort's troopers. But he was formidable. His bearing was menacing. That the man domineered the ground and the air and the very light that he permitted to touch him was beyond dispute. Bhen took one – two steps away from him. The man lowered his hood, moved around the table, and stopped a couple steps from Dek. He saluted.

"Command Sergeant Gad Skarren reporting as ordered, Commander Dek."

Dek returned the salute. "Relax and take a seat, Command Sergeant Skarren. I've been expecting you." Dek sat while Skarren removed his dark-gray cloak and sat it across the back of the chair. Beneath it he wore mottled green-and-gray trousers and tunic, and a dark-brown boiled leather cuirass. His belt held his sword, two knives, and a pouch. His boots were laced, and Bhen could not tell what color they were supposed to be for all the dirt and stains they now carried. Skarren cast a glance at Bhen before he slipped his gloves off his hands and sat down.

"You're in good company and free to speak," Dek said. "I trust the regiment's priests."

Even from the side Bhen could see Skarren raise his

eyebrows in distrust, but the man did not protest. "Did Vakos contact you personally, sir?"

"Yes," Dek said. "It's a strange sensation getting a voice in your head. Have you experienced it?

"Yes, sir. I agree. Unnerving."

"How far behind are Lieutenant Panyyl and the others?"

Skarren scratched the skin under his thick, dark beard. Bhen could have sworn a beetle fell free from its bushy confines. "When Vakos portalled me they were not ready to leave the village, and it was a long track. Hmm." He ran his hands through his tangled, dark hair. "Two days from now, possibly before noon. That's when I'd expect them."

Dek dipped the pen in the inkwell and started writing. "Alright, sergeant. Give me your report, starting with the status of Beshta'Rek and his advisor."

"Unfortunately, the chieftain, 'Rek, and his advisor were not located and their whereabouts are unknown."

Dek looked frustrated. "So we can expect more raids?"

"Sir, I don't know. This whole thing looks like a wink and smells like a fart."

"Alright then. Go on."

"It wasn't hard backtracking the horde. We moved northwest for a few hours and crossed the Karak River into the untamed lands not far from Falun." Dek nodded and Skarren continued. "The crossing there was not deep, and several ropes had been strung across the section. It looks like they were tied to aid the crossing. They had not been there long – days, not weeks. Another hour west into the untamed lands we found a camp. It was abandoned, but it had three long-term structures and two large cooking areas. Lots of sign, all of it days old. Trails converged on the location from several different directions. Only one trail going out. It appeared 'Rek used it to gather his horde before making his march. Some scattered items remained, but nothing of value."

He paused. Bhen and Skarren watched Dek dip his pen repeatedly and write feverishly, catching the highlights for the report he would write later. Bhen had always thought goblins were animals and warred with anything that was not of their own village or tribe. He was trying to comprehend the creatures coming together for a common purpose when Dek spoke. "Go on."

"We were assessing which trail to track when Vakos said he felt mage-sign. The ripples were continuous. He said they originated north of us, far away, but they came from strong magic. Two trails arrived at the camp from that direction and one of them showed more signs of passage than the others. We estimated somewhere between thirty and forty goblins had come along that one trail to the camp. If 'Rek used goblins from different villages for his raids, he probably made sure he took the most from his own village. He could trust them more. So we started backtracking that one.

"We tracked 'Rek's trail the rest of that day and all the next. There's some weird shit out there, sir. The going was slow. Vakos collected some plants and made some drawings of other things we saw. He says the guild mages will be very interested in what he's bringing back. It should keep them wanting to work with the army.

"Near the end of that second day we smelled smoke and death. Lots of death. Early the third day, yesterday, the trail led us straight to a village. We knew it was bad before we even laid eyes on the place. It was a good-size village, crude, but organized. Most of the huts were burned down. The others were heavily fire-damaged or knocked to pieces like a windstorm had come through. We could see the bodies everywhere, sir. But we watched it for a while, not wanting to fall into a trap. After a couple hours and no movement, the lieutenant sent a couple of us in to be sure it was clear. It didn't take long to confirm the only living things there were the critters eating the bodies." Skarren paused again and shook his head. He reached into his belt pouch and pulled out two items: a folded piece of paper and something the size of a deck of cards bundled in a rag.

"We didn't bother counting the huts," Skarren said as he unfolded the paper. "But the dead numbered – one hundred eleven. Best we could tell: twelve adult males, thirty-two adult females, and the rest were children. There were some weapons lying about. But whatever defense they put up couldn't have been much. Most were burned. Alive. Judging by the bodies." Skarren lowered the paper and took a breath. He gazed at the far corner of the tent. Dek stopped writing to look up.

"The kids, sir," Skarren said softly. "Burned. If I didn't know they were goblins, I never would have been able to tell. They looked no different than —" Skarren turned his face so Bhen could see no more than the back of his head.

"Finish it, Gad. I told you we're in good company." Dek looked hard at Bhen, who straightened and nodded his assurance. His oath to Abbyon forbid him from betraying the confidence of the flock.

*Is there more to these men than I believed? Is this what Mother Tara sees? With all their bluster and bravado and callous talk, does the killing and death actually take a toll on their humanity, their souls?*

Skarren spoke again. "Sir, they looked no different than our own children. Just like the families the Norean units burned in the Divide at the end of the war. That's all." His posture returned to its rigid state. "Anyway, some were hacked up. We found those goblins in pockets outside the village. Must have tried to hide and were hunted down. The ground was trampled, footprints everywhere, but we were able to make out two sets that seemed to have made their way throughout the village, side by side the whole time. Both sets were larger than any other goblin spoor."

"'Rek and his advisor?" Dek asked.

"That's what we're thinking. Vakos said it would have taken a Master or Grand Master to have caused all that destruction. So, not only is the advisor a mage, he's more powerful than we thought." His tone changed and he looked from the paper to Dek. "None of us had ever heard of a goblin mage, sir. Have you?"

"No. No, I haven't."

"There was something else, too."

Dek looked up from his notes. "What?"

"We found what looked like an altar in the largest hut. The hut was mostly burned down and not much remained of the altar, but on the wall behind the shelf was a patch of daub that was not charred. Like something had hung there and shielded the wall from the heat, and had been removed after the fire."

"Go on." Dek dipped the pen and started writing again.

"Whatever hung there was not smooth. It looked like it had edges or blades on it. We checked the other huts again for anything that might leave that kind of shadow or mark. We found this." He started unwrapping the bundle. "If there were more, they burned up." He pulled out a charred piece of carved wood and handed it to Dek, then rubbed his hands free of the soot.

The item was flat, the size of a man's palm, and pointed like a compass rose with eight points, four longer than the others. It was charred; the points were dulled and much of the design appeared to be missing. "Some kind of navigational tool?" Dek mused. "But why on an altar? What did Vakos or Panyyl make of it?" He placed the item on his desk, wiping the soot from his hands.

"The lieutenant suggested that too. Vakos wondered if the goblins have a religion we don't know about."

"Do you mind if I take a look?" Bhen said. Dek motioned him over.

"Was it 'Rek's village? Was it his hut?" Dek asked Skarren.

"We think it was. The bedding in it was longer than any others. We also found a pair of partially burned sandals in the hut. Comparing them to the feet of a few dead males showed us the owner was a bit larger than them. The sandal length also roughly matched the length of one of the two tracks we followed around the village."

Bhen picked up the piece of wood and stepped next to the lamp, turning the item over in his hands. He wondered how goblins handled their dead. Did they have a religion? A fleeting thought of trying to convert them flew through his mind. He looked again at the piece of wood and held his thoughts for later.

Dek put his pen in the inkwell and left it there. "Why would they do that? Kill and burn everyone and everything?"

"We wondered," Skarren said, "if 'Rek believed someone in the tribe betrayed him. Maybe he blamed some of his tribe for our attack." Skarren chuckled. "Maybe he was just that pissed off at losing and needed to take some heads. I've never heard of such a thing before, but it could be their way."

"I've never heard of that either."

The fire smell of the charred wood reminded Bhen of an incident at his home when he was a youth. "Perhaps he —" Bhen started. He stopped when he heard his own voice, afraid to enter the conversation.

"What?" both soldiers asked.

Bhen was taken aback at first, but knew he had to finish. "Perhaps he was trying to get rid of any ties to him, any evidence."

"How did you come to that?" Dek asked.

"Back at my family's estate, before I joined the seminary, we had a theft of some of our silver and gold table settings and dishes. My father and the master of the household interviewed and questioned and searched for the items among the staff. They found no leads. The day after the questioning started, a cottage housing one of the groundskeepers, a bachelor, caught fire and burned to the stone foundation. A search of the ruins found some of our dishes and two bodies. A man and a woman.

"I was there when the other groundskeeper's assistant, Artem, ran up to the burned cottage. He was pale, but said nothing until it was revealed the deceased woman was missing her left index finger. At that news Artem wailed and fell to his knees. His wife was not at home or at her post and she had lost that finger in an accident when she was a youth."

"How does this figure into the goblins, priest?" Skarren said.

"Artem," Bhen said. "He confessed to stealing our settings and dishes, conspiring with the other assistant, the dead one, to that end. Their plan had been to leave when the search was called off, but his friend was getting nervous. Artem decided he would kill his co-conspirator, plant some of the items in the cottage, and burn it all to the ground; thereby implicating his friend and ending the search. What he didn't know was that his wife was having an affair with his friend and he had interrupted one of their illicit trysts. She must have been hiding inside the cottage when Artem killed her lover and could not escape after he had set the fire. Artem hanged himself in his cell that night."

The two soldiers looked at Bhen, unblinking.

Dek was the first to speak. "I see."

"He was weak," Skarren said. "Should have kept his mouth shut. Could have gotten rid of a cheating wife and backstabbing friend in one blow."

*And back to being the indifferent brute. I don't know why I expected better.*

"Alright," Dek said, "the goblin chieftain was either exacting revenge for a perceived betrayal, simply enraged and murderous, or getting rid of possible clues about him or his methods." Dek picked up the pen again. He wrote a few lines and, keeping his eyes on the paper, told Skarren to finish.

"The rest of yesterday was spent trying to locate any survivors and clues. We found nothing and extracted a safe distance before bivouacking. This morning Vakos used the sandal to try to locate 'Rek, but couldn't find him. We circled the entire village, sweeping wide, hoping we would find something. Anything."

"Nothing?" Dek asked.

"Nothing. That's when Lieutenant Panyyl ordered me to report back to you with our findings. The team will bring what little we found and maybe the lieutenant will have some more answers for you."

Dek stood. "Get yourself some warm food."

Skarren snapped to his feet. "Will do, sir. Is there anything else you require?"

"Not at this time. Thank you, Master Sergeant Skarren. You're dismissed." They saluted and Skarren grabbed his cloak, his eyes cold and face hard. Bhen could see no signs of the concern or empathy he had heard moments before. For a heartbeat Bhen feared for his safety, but the soldier left the tent without a pause or glance toward him.

Dek turned to Bhen. "Now to your business, brother."

"Before we get onto that, commander, I may have something to add about this symbol." Bhen returned the piece of wood to the desk.

"Go on. Your insight has already been helpful once."

"That could be a holy symbol for Eblees, the Lightbringer."

"The father god Noreas and the countries to the south worship?"

Bhen nodded. "I believe so. But they don't worship him like a father. He is seen more like a commander or chieftain to his gods. Their religion is about who can rise to the top and lead the others. The Church of Light focuses on the greatness of the individual. Who has the most power, the most strength, the most —"

"Understood, brother. What makes you think this is his symbol?"

Bhen nodded, reminding himself Dek did not need a seminary lecture. "Eblees' symbol is an eight-pointed star. Sometimes it may be four, but that's typically in quick drawings."

"Do you know if goblin-kind worship Eblees too?"

"I've never heard of such a thing, but maybe the church is trying to convert them. I've heard Noreas looks to expand into their untamed lands, or 'wildlands,' as they put it. Perhaps this is a part of that effort."

Dek's face showed genuine interest and appreciation. "Thank you. I'll be sure to include those possibilities with my report."

"You're most welcome." Bhen cleared his throat. "Now, if I

may —"

Dek interrupted. "You're here to let me know you and the Devout Mother must leave camp."

"Uh. Yes, Commander."

"You need some horses?"

"Yes. Yes, we do." Bhen rubbed his head.

"Two or three?"

"Two, please."

"And you're leaving another priest in charge of the Temple?"

"Sister Yanise, sir. Brother Heiko and the surgeons will assist her."

"Will we see you before we return to Fort Anjermott?"

"That is unknown, Commander. The Devout Mother has petitioned to meet the Shepherd, sir. It may take some time."

Dek whistled. "Headed to Aerndale. I hope to make that trip one day. I would like to speak with you about it upon your return, if you don't mind."

"Not at all," said Bhen. The commander continued to surprise him. "We plan to travel to Whitby and from there portal to Agderon or Aerndale. The Temple and the guilds have had a good relationship. We're sure we'll be able to find someone who can get us close to our destination. If not, we will join a caravan headed to another large city and try again. If I may ask, how did you know my purpose here?"

Dek smiled. "This is a military camp." He said no more. Bhen cocked his head, trying to understand the meaning, but gave up. Dek offered his hand. "May Gavel light your way."

"Thank you. And to you and your regiment as well." Bhen clasped and shook hands with Dek. The commander's grip was strong. It hurt, but Bhen managed a smile.

# CHAPTER ELEVEN

In the center of Lagisborg, Renlar's capital city, was Frontier Plaza, with its namesake fountain nestled at the northern end. On top of the fountain's pedestal was a stone statue of two figures facing west. One was a woman carrying an infant. The other was a man holding a felling axe over his shoulder. With one arm around each other, they stared with joy into the wind at some elusive wonder, a marvel unseen by the fountain's visitors.

During the day the plaza was alive with activity and buzzed with business. It used to be so at night as well. Dozens of magical lanterns sat upon posts throughout the plaza, providing a soft illumination that was considered by couples to be very romantic and was treasured on special nights. A year ago couples had walked hand in hand. Artists had performed. Plays and concerts had entertained.

But now it was a lonely place. No lovers stared into each other's eyes in the muted glow. The streets were silent and practically devoid of life through a self-imposed citizen curfew.

This was due to the soldiers who had returned home without a trade or craft following the Two Rivers War, and had turned to robbery and ransom as a source of income. The city watch continued to patrol the streets, but they could not be everywhere. And too often their approach was betrayed by their noisy armor and weapons, making the effort to avoid them a simple one for people who were trained to watch for an enemy. The mayor consulted and planned and acted, trying to change the situation. But nothing had worked.

This late night was warm and humid, and a mist created halo globes around the plaza's lanterns. It was Page's first night in the city, but she was not admiring the sights. She watched for the unseen. She stood with Hammer beside the fountain and its stone couple. She felt the eyes upon her, the eyes of the watchers hidden in the shadows. Hammer's posture said he felt them too. Both were dressed fashionably, like Renlaran gentry. Even if Page was not fond of the clothing style, she had to admit they made a striking couple. They oozed wealth. They also radiated their status as apex predators, and the eyes recognized that. The watchers kept their distance. The watchers wanted prey.

Page and Hammer remained close but did not touch. They looked toward, but not at, each other. No words were spoken, no smiles displayed, no subtle signals sent. They simply stood, waiting.

Long before it could be seen, the coach could be heard. The four roads leading to the square were stone-lined, and the strike of the horses' shoes and the scrape of the wheels' metal rims heralded the coach's approach along the eastern road. Page and Hammer did not move or turn to look in the direction of the noise.

Pulled by two impressive draft horses, the black coach rounded the corner and turned northbound toward the fountain, its own lanterns lighting the way. As it neared, Page and Hammer turned to the street and slowly walked to intercept the coach. The driver slowed and stopped the horses. A male voice, measured and eloquent, spoke from behind closed curtains. "A beautiful fountain, is it not?" he asked.

"I hear there's one in Vreland twice as big," said Hammer.

The door to the coach opened. Page gathered her dress and, accepting the hand offered from within, entered the cab, followed immediately by Hammer. Two knocks on the floor signaled the driver to proceed, and he did without delay.

Page sat upon the cushioned leather bench. She could tolerate her stylish dress; she knew it was part of the game and enjoyed dressing nicely on occasion. But the silk hood she wore to hide her short, sandy hair bothered her. It hampered her hearing and limited her peripheral vision.

Hammer sat on the edge of the bench next to her in his tailored doublet and knee-length breeches. She knew he did not like dressing up, but he too had a part to play. A pair of poorly dressed commoners could not be seen getting into Chancellor Sala Nesar's coach. Page looked in the chancellor's direction. His face was obscured in shadow; the small lantern inside the coach cloaked all but his legs. She noted the stick he had used to signal the driver. It was lacquered and inlaid with gold, and too short for a walking stick.

*A sign of his station, or used for some other purpose?*

"I hope your wait was not long," Chancellor Nesar said. His left hand played with a string of worry beads, moving each brown-and-yellow stone bead between his fingers one by one, its golden tassel dancing with each movement.

"It was not, Your Grace," said Hammer. "We are honored you've selected Iron Leaf. This is Page, and I am Hammer."

"Your people told me there would be two, but a beautiful woman was not expected," the chancellor said.

"Please forgive, my lord," Hammer said. "No deception was intended. We thought a couple in the plaza would blend in better."

"There is nothing to forgive. I believe you misunderstand me," Chancellor Nesar said. Turning toward Page, he added, "Your presence is unexpected but very refreshing. I am pleased you've joined us, Miss Page."

"Page, my lord," Hammer interjected quickly. "Simply Page. She is not employed as cover, nor distraction. Page is an Iron Leaf veteran."

"Hmm, even more charming." Nesar paused a moment. "How many in your team?"

"Seven, including the two of us," Hammer said. "I was informed you were looking for a team of five to ten, to include at least one mage, preferably one with combat experience. There were some other requirements. We meet all of them, sir."

"Splendid," Nesar said. His voice rose: "Oh, yes, 'Page.' How appropriate. I see no ring, so you must keep your…"

Page smiled and demurely tapped the center of her chest, where her mage's medallion hung from its necklace.

"Thank you, my dear," said Nesar. He went back to manipulating the beads. "If things go well on this first job, you will see more work immediately."

"We are at your disposal, my lord," Hammer replied.

"Your group is highly revered and comes with a reputation for discretion and maintaining client confidentiality. Need I remind you of the importance of holding to those ideals while in our employ?"

"Of course not, my lord. To betray our clients would be Iron Leaf's death and our own. We understand this too well."

"Splendid." Chancellor Nesar moved forward in his seat, the

lamplight finally revealing his face to Hammer and Page. He was light-skinned, almost pasty, and his build showed that he enjoyed indulging in the foods his wealth provided. "A high-ranking general openly disagrees with King Heselov and his council on certain prominent matters. This general and his staff are under our watch and appear to be acting in concert against the good of Renlar." Nesar paused.

"Understood," Hammer stated. "No questions so far. Please continue."

"We lost track of the general three days ago. Our attempts to locate him, both mundane and Arcane, have been unsuccessful; however, we were not overly vigorous in our efforts, as we did not want to give warning that we searched for him. We fear the influence of outside agents. Order must be restored, and the safety of Renlar maintained. With your help, we intend to resolve this matter."

"Why do you need our help?" asked Hammer. "You have your own soldiers and Institute mages. Aren't they capable of conducting your investigation and search?"

Page looked hard at the chancellor. "You fear those loyal to this general will not work against him," she said. "He must be well placed, beloved, or both."

"Both, I fear," Nesar said. He gave Page a subtle smile. "Using our own soldiers is too risky. The king's most trusted men, his personal guard, must remain focused on their duty. We cannot spare them, especially if enemy agents are operating in the country. The members of the city watch are similarly not an option for us. They are comprised of either former military whose loyalty to their superiors following this recent war may compromise their fealty, or of brutes who are better suited knocking about ruffians and robbers. No, we require discreet, outside assistance."

"I understand your situation now," said Hammer. "When will work start, and who will we deal with? Who is to be our contact for you?"

"You will work with me, and no other. Much of what is to be learned and administered must be through my hands. Work begins tomorrow. We cannot let this wait. I'll give you the details as they become necessary. We will meet tomorrow before moving forward to finalize the plans. Your entire team must be on hand."

The coach negotiated the intertwined streets of Lagisborg for a few more minutes, gently rocking the three occupants. All the while the chancellor questioned them about Iron Leaf's history as a mercenary company. The coach eventually stopped a block from Hammer and Page's inn and deposited them before making a quick departure.

In the short period since Page had joined Hammer's team, she'd learned some of his methods and his approach to matters. She also knew he was respected in the organization and well known for his ability to accomplish his assignments with well-constructed plans. He was direct and concerned himself with the money, the contract, and the team's job. However, he refused to look into the heart of the issue or the true purpose and intent of their patrons.

Page liked knowing more.

Something about Chancellor Nesar did not sit well with her. It could be as simple as her dislike for the wealthy and the nobility, one of the strong opinions that remained from her time in Delranon, homeless and begging for money. It could be Nesar's refusal to shake hands with Hammer at the end of the conversation, as though Hammer were beneath him. Whatever the reason, she would have to work it out later, as her time now was better used for learning a few new spells. She watched as the cart and its light slipped noisily away.

"Page," Hammer called to her. She turned to find him already a dozen steps away, looking over his shoulder as he walked toward the inn. Page took a last look at the coach before hustling to catch up with Hammer.

"Is there anything you need to tell me?" Hammer asked.

"No," Page said. "At least, not yet. Something about him puts me off, but I can't place it. Might be I can't stand wealthy pricks." She said the last with a smile as she turned to Hammer.

"Me either, but his money's good enough. We've done a few jobs for the titled of various countries. They always have some political motive they don't share, but that is none of our concern as long as their money flows into our coffers."

"True," Page said, her myriad thoughts distracting her again.

"Page, I'm honored you're with us," Hammer said. "Your name and reputation are good in the organization. It can't be easy putting your trust in a team you don't know, but I hope you will take my word: we won't let you down, and we'll see you back to your team as soon as this job's done."

"I've bounced between a few teams because of my training. I'm used to this. You and me? We're good. Don't misread me."

Hammer nodded, and the two made their way through the door of the inn.

The pallid, sweaty innkeeper was busy trimming candle wax and cleaning the virtually empty common room. He gave Hammer and Page an indifferent nod as they entered. Pike, seated at the inn's long counter and nursing a disagreeably diluted drink, stood and fell in behind Hammer and Page as they made their way toward the stairs. Shortly after the trio reached the lodging floor, Sword, stationed in an alley outside, came in through the same doors the couple had and followed them upstairs. The innkeeper, expecting a new customer, looked up with a practiced smile, but seeing only a patron heading to his room, returned to his work, the smile removed.

The next afternoon, after midday mealtime, Page found herself back in her favorite leather tunic and leggings. She sat on a horse hitch outside the walled military barracks. Her sword waited for her elsewhere, but her pouch of arrowhead darts was joyfully on her belt, and the symbols of several spells were etched in her mind. Smiling, she traced her finger over the filigreed pommel of her dagger, enjoying the day.

Further away, Axe, dressed as a soldier of Renlar, waited too. Page was not pleased to be working with Axe for this portion of the plan. Sword was more level-headed and able to think on his feet, but Axe was the only one of the group who could mimic a true Renlaran accent. Page suggested Sword could have practiced the few lines and been believable; but Hammer disagreed. Page respected him, but he sometimes made poor decisions.

She and Axe waited for their target to leave the barracks as they had been told he would. According to the chancellor, Commander Rish Landar, General Batal's executive officer, kept a mistress near the barracks, and visited with her early in the afternoons. Page hoped she would be asked to hurt the commander. She could not stand philanderers.

The two Iron Leaf mercenaries did not have to wait long. Commander Landar walked through the gates and moved with alacrity toward the pleasure he thought awaited him. Focused on his destination like a sailor on the open ocean, he did not even look in Page's direction. Nor did he notice Axe approaching until the mercenary was mere steps in front of him.

"Commander," Axe said, coming to attention and giving the open-hand salute of Renlar's military. "We may have a problem, sir."

"What is it, soldier?" Landar asked, returning the salute. He was so focused on his lover waiting for him that he did not notice his bane closing in from behind.

Page moved to grab Landar's shoulder.

"I found a drunk officer over here," Axe said. He moved his hand as though to place it on Landar's shoulder, but instead grabbed Page's wrist as she grabbed the commander's shoulder plate. Landar tensed instinctively, and his hand started for his sword.

The world around them swirled and shifted.

In place of the streets outside the barracks was a long, whitewashed corridor with a stone floor. Candle chandeliers high above their heads lit the passage, showing that the way forward was empty, a single door at the end sixty feet away. Landar grabbed his sword, but several more words from Page caused him to pause and wobble for a few heartbeats. When Landar finally recovered and turned around, his sword was partially drawn, but he secured it in the face of the five crossbows and two swords now pointed at him.

"Remove your belt," Hammer ordered, maintaining his crossbow's aim at Landar. The commander unbuckled his belt.

"Whoever ya are, you're making a grave mistake," Landar stated. "I am not nobility. Ya will not receive a ransom for me; nor will this end well for ya if I am not returned to the barracks immediately." He removed the belt but held onto it.

Chancellor Nesar entered the corridor through the door

behind the mercenaries. "Drop the belt, Rish," he ordered softly.

Rish Landar let the belt drop to the floor, a puzzled look upon his face. "Chancellor? What's this about, my lord?"

Nesar moved between the mercenaries and walked toward Landar, his worry beads in his left hand. His approach to the kidnapped soldier was calm and disarming. Page had expected the commander to attack the chancellor or attempt to take him hostage, but he allowed Nesar to approach and to put his arm around him. The Iron Leafs lowered their crossbows as the two walked down the corridor to the other end. There the two men of Renlar spoke quietly, Nesar standing in the middle of the hall, Landar a few feet from him. Their conversation was carried to the mercenaries by the stone floors and walls, but was quiet enough that the team heard only fragments, most of the discussion coming across like a series of hisses.

Page sheathed her sword as she watched the defiant commander's gestures grow less animated, as his shoulders slouched, as his head sank. Nesar was calm, occasionally accenting his point with a gesture or two, but otherwise very reserved. Something about Commander Landar reminded Page of her father. She could not put a finger on it, but the man's look and demeanor reminded her of home, and she did not like that. She didn't hate her father, but she didn't love him either. He had never given her the time for that bond to build.

"Are you catching any of this?" Pike asked Sword.

"They're too far for me to get all the details," said Sword. "Need to be close to really read their lips, but I'm seeing enough. Seems the commander may have known about the conspiracy, but looks like he doesn't know where the general is now."

"So much for your vaunted training," Axe said. After the mercenaries had watched the two men for several more minutes, he growled. "Hope this shit doesn't take much longer."

"Hold your tongue," Hammer ordered. Axe let out a frustrated breath.

Eventually, Nesar reached out and patted the commander on the shoulder, and slowly walked back to the group. Landar stepped back against the wall; he placed his hands on his hips and leaned his head back, looking toward the ceiling above. Nesar didn't stop when he reached Page and the others. He quietly walked through them to the door behind where they stood. As he opened it, he paused.

"Kill him. Leave the body."

Nesar walked through the door and closed it.

Iron Leaf was not a group of assassins; however, they were occasionally required to dispatch unarmed enemies. Ordinarily that was during or immediately following a battle, not after taking a prisoner. The unexpected and emotionless order caught the team off guard, and five sets of eyes turned to Hammer for guidance. Page remained focused on the commander, who seemed to read their body language, moving away from the wall.

"Allow me," Page said. She drew three metal darts from her pouch, each one five inches long with a bodkin arrowhead. She fanned them out in her fingers.

At the end of the corridor, Commander Landar turned to the locked door near him and tried, unsuccessfully, to open it. Page mouthed a few words and, with a flick of her wrist, threw the darts in Landar's direction. They left her hand and flashed through the air at Landar, who turned to face the mercenaries in time for the three darts to pierce his chest in succession. His look of anger turned to surprise. He stumbled backward and collapsed to the floor.

Page was reminded again of her father, and she thought of him dying. It saddened her, but only a little.

She could live with that.

# CHAPTER TWELVE

Grimble awoke to the sound of movement in the loft. It was not the light, skittering movement of mice, nor was it the soft, gentle pace of someone returning from the privy. It was the hush of someone avoiding notice, using the wind and other natural sounds to outwit the loft's intrusively vocal floorboards. By the time Grimble realized what he had heard and focused on it, the movement ceased. Grimble sat upright and snapped his head in the direction of the noise.

Nothing.

Kurt rolled over in his sleep – possibly. It was hard to tell in the dim predawn light. Otherwise, everything and everyone was as the night before. Grimble's rapid movement, however, stirred Roche and Baz, who opened their eyes to stare at him. Roche rubbed his forehead and began to stretch. Baz raised an eyebrow at Grimble. Grimble lay back, his hands behind his head, and stared at the rafters above him, wondering if he had dreamed the noise.

Before long Roche was up and securing his bedroll, joined in short time by Dinger and Baz. The flat boards of the loft felt good under Grimble's bedding, much better than the uneven ground he'd slept on the last several weeks, but he knew they needed to be on the move. He removed himself from his small part of paradise and packed his equipment for the next leg of the trip. They should arrive in Whitby by the end of the day, forty miles from the border with the country of Renlar. After that they would head toward Agderon, away from Renlar. In a few days they would reach Brantsford, their launching point into Renlar – roughly a hundred miles farther away from it than where they had started.

*That only makes sense in the army.*

"Shit!" Flicker said, searching through his pack.

"Leave something behind?" Baz asked.

"No. Found them. Riding gloves were wedged at the bottom. I thought I pulled them out last night." Flicker pulled his gloves free, secured them in his belt, and buckled his pack shut. Within a few minutes, everyone had completed their packing and morning necessaries. They grabbed their saddles and walked down the stairs to the stables below.

"I'll see what the farmer set out for us this morning," Kurt said. "We can eat on the road, eh, Roche?" He grabbed an empty sack and collected the group's canteens, and headed to the shed next to the stable.

The horses were saddled and packed by the time Kurt returned with their full canteens and a sack of food. He made his way among the group, handing out their water and shares of the bread, boiled eggs, and dried fruits.

"You splurged on breakfast, Roche," Dinger said.

"Didn't want to hear any of you whining between here and Whitby."

Weeks of hard biscuits and suet pemmican awaited them in

Renlar. Any chance for a normal meal before they entered their enemy's country would be relished.

The men rode single file into a headwind as they hastened toward Whitby. Roche ordered a quick pace, wanting to arrive at the city before supper and hoping to eventually make it to Brantsford a day early. Early was protocol in the military. Grimble, who volunteered to take point, did not question the pace. But the morning wind and flying dust took their toll on both him and his horse. After a few miles Roche started switching the lead rider out more frequently, allowing the former lead to be shielded at the back of the line.

The wind slowed by mid-morning, allowing the men to ride two abreast when the road was wide enough. Grimble noticed Flicker spent most of the time in his saddle with a distant look upon his face – the very thing Dinger had asked about the night before. The battle mage spoke briefly with those riding beside him, but most often stared down the road, far in front of them.

Grimble knew there were mages in the King's Army. He had even seen a few summon fire and lightning on the enemy during the Battle at Steep Ridge. However, they were so rare that most soldiers knew nothing about them. As Roche made his way among the men, checking on their condition and giving updates, the curiosity became too much for Grimble. "What's wrong with Flicker?" he asked.

Roche looked ahead at the mage, who was riding lead. "What do you mean?"

"I know you said the staring was a mage thing, but he does it a lot."

"I'm telling you he's alright. If his mind were taken, he wouldn't be here." Grimble's confused look prompted Roche to continue. "The Taken lose their minds either when they start the Institute's training or during their time as an Initiate, an apprentice mage. He never would have made it to the level of a Master Mage if there was a problem. There are —" Roche paused as if trying to find the right words. "There are burdens some mages bear, a price they pay for their talents and abilities. Some show no signs at all. Flicker's not Taken, he just stares like some do. It's one of his burdens."

"The Taken?" Grimble asked.

"Have you seen a mage's spell book?"

"No."

Roche stretched his back in the saddle. "You can teach anyone to ride a horse; some will become better horsemen than others, but everyone who wants to learn can be taught to ride. Correct? Not so with magic. Not everyone can become a mage. The body and the mind have to be the right kind. The person has to be born with the ability to accept the energy and release it on command.

"Mage books are full of ornate colored symbols, each symbol being a different spell. I'm told that when a mage studies their spells to memorize them, the symbols in their spellbook become imprinted on their mind. The mage can see every detail of the magic symbol until they cast it and the energy it stores is gone. Since the symbols are always present in their minds, they cause some to appear distracted – to have that detached look, the stare."

"Like when someone in a conversation has their mind on something else," said Grimble.

"Yeah, like that. They say the Taken have their mind clouded by these symbols. Their minds are 'taken' from them by the Arcane magic they study. They can't let go of the spell or the energy it collects. As they continue to study, they build up more spells and more energy inside them. Beginner mages are able to remember a handful of spells, but those who become Taken continually build up these spells until their mind is gone."

"Wait," said Grimble. "Mages like Flicker have limits to how many spells they can cast?"

"Yeah," Roche replied. "They're not like gods. By the time an Initiate leaves the Institute they should be able to cast four or five simple spells. Their minds cannot hold more symbols and their bodies cannot hold onto more of the energy those spells need. Flicker can probably memorize more than a dozen simple spells. The more powerful ones, like portalling and his exploding fire, are harder to remember and require his body to store more energy. He can only remember a few of those at a time."

"And the Taken keep memorizing spells?"

"Yeah. I'm told they don't even realize they've memorized a spell. They can't recall the symbol and so they keep studying, taking in more energy and cluttering their mind. Once they become Taken by the magic, they live their lives constantly detached from everything around them. They walk around like zombies. If you put food in their hand, they'll eat. That's about all the reaction you'll get from one. You'll see them mostly in Delranon and Agderon, and a few of the other large cities, but rarely in the open elsewhere."

"How do they survive?" Grimble asked. "I've heard the cities are full of thieves and robbers. I'm surprised the Taken aren't set upon."

"The cities are not that overrun with rogues, country boy," Roche said. "But that's not the reason. Some believe killing or harming one of the Taken will bring bad luck. Most fear they'll release the energy stored in their minds all at once if they are killed or hurt, and anyone nearby will suffer the effects. Because of that, folks stay as far from them as possible. But there are a few who take pity on them. Provide them with food and water. The priests of Yahnn and her worshippers are some. They care for the Taken."

Grimble chuckled. "You don't believe the warnings, do you?"

"I'm not superstitious, and I don't know if it's true, but I don't want to test it. Arcane magic is not to be taken lightly, nor should its power be lightly dismissed. You'd do well to respect it, Grimble."

"Alright, alright." After thinking a moment, Grimble asked, "Arcane magic? There are other kinds?"

"Of course. You've experienced it. The magic of the Temple priests is a kind of magic."

"I figured that was the power of Abbyon and the other gods."

"It is, but it's still a kind of magic. And there's another even older than those two that no one's seen in hundreds of years. They say it was the beginning of all the others. Ancient magic worked by an ancient people who no longer walk the land, a people long dead."

The two rode side by side in silence for a time. Roche pulled some dried plum from his haversack. He stared at it, turning it about in his fingers before popping it in his mouth and savoring it as he chewed. "We think we'll never get old," he said to the air, or maybe himself.

Grimble did not know how to respond. He looked around them, trying to find something to talk about. He set his eyes upon Flicker again. "You said the staring was a sign, and that there were other signs too. Flicker has another sign, doesn't he? The one that gave him his name. That's why you knew the fire in camp was not an attack. The campfire flickered and danced before the explosion."

Roche smiled. "You got it. The staring thing is fairly common, but the other effects are rare. I knew one mage who caused the temperature to drop when she was about to cast a spell. I've heard of another who makes the air smell like smoke. Flicker makes flames jump and dance without wind when he's upset. But it's usually small flames, candles and lanterns. I knew he must have been angry enough to kill when the bonfires started dancing. We're lucky it was only a cart he blew up."

"He's that powerful a wizard?"

"There are others more powerful than him, but he's probably the most powerful in the King's Army. He never planned to be a combat mage. He worked his way up the ranks in the Spire, the one mage guild that governs all the guilds and the individual mages. He was in line to be an Arbiter. They're the mages tasked with investigating suspected violations and meting out punishment. They're a tough lot. But something changed – don't ask me what. The Spire stopped supporting him, and his old guild won't take him back. He's here now, earning a scholarship and a sponsorship from the king so he can attend his last year of training at the Institute."

"I had no idea."

"Few do," Roche said. "Good for you to know these things. A good leader understands the people they work with. Besides, I doubt he'd tell you himself. Flicker doesn't like being around people and doesn't say much, as I'm sure you've noticed. If you get more than a dozen words out of him at one time, play cards or dice that night; for surely you are the luckiest man in the land."

Grimble smiled. "Got it. Thanks."

The team continued their southward journey for several

more hours, alternating between riding at a jog, walking, and leading their horses to keep them fresh. They rode through and beside numerous farms, garnering the attention of farmers and farmhands as they did. The sun had neared its zenith when the call came out from Roche for them to take their midday break. A small creek lay ahead, with a few trees providing shade nearby, and Roche could not pass up the opportunity for the group to care for their mounts.

Everyone dismounted and led their horses to the creek. The animals nickered at their fortune, drinking their fill. After that, the men hobbled them with ropes on the nearby grass, permitting them the chance to graze. Once the horses were tended, the team met under the copse of trees for their midday meal.

There wasn't much talk. Each man kept to his own thoughts. They all downed their food with the rapid efficiency of the soldiers they were, making time for other tasks. Grimble and Dinger removed their boots to air their feet and extract any foreign objects. Then Dinger stretched and lay back against the trunk of a beech, his eyes closed. Grimble did as he had done since his days on the farm: took in the life about him with all his senses, soothing his mind with the wind in the trees and the smell of the nearby fields. The gentle, intermittent rustle of the copper beech leaves reminded him of home, taking him away from the dangers of the awaiting mission.

The horses enjoyed their grazing. Kurt, back among them, clumsily searched one of his saddlebags for who knew what. Roche and Baz ate and conversed, looking at the sun's position and conferring with the hasty map Roche had drawn from the regimental maps of the area.

A chickadee flew to a nearby branch, hunting for insects too small for Grimble to see. It pecked at something a few times, gave its throaty call, looked about, and flew away. Chickadees were Ellie's favorite bird. He had never understood that. There were more colorful birds, birds with prettier songs, yet she loved the little chickadee. Grimble loved the birds of prey; the hawks and eagles – but owls were his favorite. They were sentinels and silent hunters. He shook his head, thinking of Ellie and her little chickadee, and wondering what she was doing at that moment. He prayed to Ihgel and Abbyon, asking them to watch over her.

When Grimble came out of his prayer, he looked about again. Dinger was out, eyes closed and face slack, enjoying the break. Flicker, not far away, held half his loaf of bread in his hands. He chewed slowly and smelled the loaf, a look of puzzlement and worry on his face. He broke off another chunk of bread and tentatively took a bite. After a few chews, the worry disappeared, and he threw the remainder of the piece into his mouth.

"You alright, Flicker?" Grimble asked.

"Yeah," Flicker said, without lifting his eyes off the bread.

Before long the team was up, refilling canteens, readying their gear, and remounting their horses. They crossed the small stream and continued south along the road toward Whitby. Grimble was in the rear this time and could tell something was wrong with Flicker or his mount. The mage shifted in his saddle, trying to find an eluding comfort. He pushed his stirrups out to the side with his feet and looked at them, then eyed the saddle he sat upon. He rode for some time before taking his right foot out of the stirrup and stretching it. Grimble couldn't be sure, but from his vantage point, it appeared the right stirrup was shorter than the left. Flicker must have compensated for it in the saddle during the morning ride, but it seemed to be troubling him now. His frustration increased throughout the afternoon, and his horse too showed signs of agitation. The mage never complained, suffering the inconvenience stoically.

They kept to their morning routine of jogging, walking, and leading their horses. Kurt displayed a wry smile every time Flicker shifted his position or stretched his right leg in the saddle. Throughout the day they passed or met with other travelers: merchants, farmers, and others using the road. Each time the team was given the right of way and eyed curiously as they passed. They were no longer dressed as troopers or soldiers, but their appearance and demeanor must have belied the civilian nature of their clothes and mounts. Grimble was thankful there was another plan for travel inside Renlar, as the team was getting more attention now than if they had been in their uniforms.

For five or six hours they kept their pace. The routine was taxing on the horses, and the extra work and road dust made for dry mouths all around, especially as the day wore on. He was taking another sip from his as he heard Flicker mutter, "Shit!"

Grimble looked toward the mage to see him tipping his canteen back. Little more than a trickle poured from the spout. Grimble clucked, urging his horse to a jog, and pulled alongside Flicker. The mage was again looking forward, the empty canteen clutched in his hand.

"Here," Grimble said, offering his canteen to Flicker.

"Thanks." Flicker accepted it and took a swallow. He handed it back to Grimble with an awkward smile. "Stopper popped off mine. Shook dry." Grimble was about to move back to his spot at the tail of the column when Flicker spoke again. "You're from Minden, I hear. Where is that?"

"East, a day's ride from the mountains in the Duchy of Ostergot. I'm told it's halfway between Chatham and Halmstad."

"Ah, and you come from a family of farmers and soldiers?"

"Yes," Grimble answered cautiously, not knowing where the line of questioning was coming from or where it was headed. He'd ask anyone else what they were getting at, but was too nervous to ask this man directly.

"No mages in the family?"

"No."

"Hmm." Flicker removed his foot from his right stirrup again and stretched the leg out.

"Your right stirrup might be a notch short," Grimble said. "You may want to let it out the next time we stop. Just a suggestion."

Flicker stopped his horse right there and dismounted. Grimble slowed and waited for him as Flicker moved around to the right side, lifted the stirrup, and examined it. The mage gave another utterance and started to adjust the length. Grimble looked at the group ahead of them. They slowed, but Grimble waved them on.

"They'll catch up, eh," Kurt said. "I'll take point here if that's okay with everyone." He hurried to the lead and kept riding.

Flicker finished making the adjustment and mounted his horse again. He bore a look of satisfaction as he started moving forward. The look slowly left his face, however, and the stare returned – but this time it wasn't a passive stare. It was a determined look, and he was staring at Kurt.

For the next hour, Kurt did everything he could to stay away from Flicker. The game of cat and mouse wasn't a long one. Their ride neared its end. The town of Whitby, the capital of the Duchy of Vasterland, came into sight shortly after the brief stop. Kurt's performance avoiding Flicker made for an entertaining end of the day for everyone else. Grimble had expected Roche to put a stop to it, but Roche too appeared to enjoy the bounty of excuses Kurt used to ride at the front, or off the back, or to check on something he saw in the woods, each time maintaining his distance from Flicker whenever the mage shifted positions in the riding order.

Originally, Whitby had been a frontier town situated at a riverhead among tall, rolling hills. It had prospered early and grown in wealth as Aendura had. With no quarry nearby, the outer walls and fortifications were made of wood. Roche led the men across a short wooden bridge to the city's main gate, where they were checked by the guard and granted entrance. The streets were dirt, but the city had prepared long planks for foot traffic when the roads muddied during heavy rains. Pairs of porters with padded boards strapped between them waited to carry the most well-to-do across the dirty streets for a tip.

Mineral deposits and the fur trade had made many wealthy here. Shops with large glass windows mere feet from the dirt streets displayed delicate, brightly painted pottery, lace screens, fine jewelry, and the latest fashions, the latter of which were vibrant and hemmed to show the wearer's footwear. There was no better way to show off one's wealth than to display one's unstained, elegant footwear, and to stand out from the surrounding grays and browns as much as possible.

Dinger blinked as though trying to clear his eyes. "Shit. How can these folks live like this? Their clothes hurt my eyes."

"Peacocks," Kurt said. "Pompous and ignorant."

Roche turned to face Grimble and the team. "They do everything to the extremes. They will treat you like a family member or shun you like a stranger. They see the mystic as something amazing or profane. Rarely will you find one with an opinion in the middle this far west."

It was apparent the city had grown as the area flourished, and that no attention had been given to planning throughout its growth. The streets ran into each other and separated in random directions, narrowing and widening haphazardly. It took the better part of an hour for the team to find the inn they sought.

Grimble and the others dismounted and followed Roche, leading their horses through what appeared to be the main entrance to the tavern. However, instead of walking into a building they emerged into a large, square courtyard enclosed by two-story buildings on each side. They were met by a stable boy, a young man no more than thirteen, whom Roche spoke with briefly before returning his attention to the team.

"We can use the stables over there." Roche nodded toward the building on the right. "That young man will care for our mounts once they're untacked. Meet me in the tavern there when you're done." He pointed straight across the courtyard. Then he lowered his voice. "Eat and drink well, lads. This may be the last hot meal for a long time."

Roche left his horse in Dinger's care and set off to secure their lodging. The team led the horses to the stable and began untacking them. The inn and its stable were well maintained, and Grimble felt he could happily sleep in the stable if it came down to it.

"Ow!" yelped Kurt.

"That's for my gloves," Flicker said.

"What the...?" Kurt said. "By all that's holy, man... Ouch! Knock it off!"

"That's for messing with my bread."

Grimble looked over his stall at the two bickering Ravens. Kurt's back was to Grimble as he faced Flicker. Baz and his horse were in the stall between them.

"I didn't hurt you," Kurt said.

"I got a cramp in my leg, asshole. Oh, that's for my cramp." Grimble thought he saw the back of Kurt's hair briefly catch fire before the man slapped it out. Grimble turned to Dinger and shook his head. Dinger's eyes were wide, his mouth agape. He slowly crouched out of sight behind his horse's stall.

"Ouch, gods be damned!" Kurt said. "This is dangerous, eh. You could catch the straw on fire."

"I'm not mad at the straw," Flicker said. Kurt started dodging back and forth, dipping behind his horse in an attempt to avoid his attacker. "Not going to help. That's for my stirrup."

"You git!" Kurt slapped the back of his head. "Fuck! I already paid for that."

"No, you paid for the cramp. The stirrup was a separate matter."

"Baz, make him stop."

"Leave me out of this," Baz said. "I keep telling you to stop messing with him."

Kurt dodged toward the stall's door. As he grabbed the latch, a metal dart, the thickness of an arrow shaft and about six inches long, sank into the jamb not far from his hand, blocking the door so it could not be opened. Kurt's eyes flew wide. He turned to Flicker. "What the — That was close, man."

Flicker held another dart just like it in his hand. "That's not close. I could shave the top layer of skin from your hand. That would be close." He flicked the dart straight up. Kurt dove to the straw-covered floor. His horse danced away from him. Flicker mouthed a word and the dart changed its course, zipping toward the first and sinking into the jamb next to it.

Kurt hunkered down, trying to stay out of sight behind his horse; but it wasn't easy as the creature, agitated by the goings-on, shifted in its stall, keeping Kurt on the move. Kurt braced for the inevitable attack for emptying Flicker's canteen. Gray wisps of smoke swirled behind his head, and the smell of burnt hair lingered in the air.

"You can pay for the canteen later, Kurt," Flicker said. "Enjoy your dinner."

Kurt mumbled a curse. The team finished untacking their horses and left them in the care of a bemused stable hand. Flicker collected his darts and the team walked across the courtyard, stopping at the well to wash up before making their way to the tavern. Kurt trailed behind. Music and laughter met them as they approached the building, as did the savory aroma of roast meats and pies. Their pace quickened.

Inside they were well met by Roche, who escorted them to a table full of steaming bowls of stew, roast chickens, bread, butter, and mugs of ale. Grimble caught Kurt looking at the candles and lanterns throughout the large room. They danced and swayed slightly, even those within glass or paper lanterns. The corners of Kurt's lips frisked upward before he turned his attention to the food.

Flicker looked about the room, his expression on the angry side of detached. He ripped a loaf in half and cut the legs from one of the roast chickens. Dumping the legs and the bread in one of the bowls of stew, he turned to Roche. "I'm in no mood for company tonight." Flicker grabbed the bowl and a mug of ale and made his way to an empty table in the back of the room.

All eyes turned to Kurt. "It was harmless fun," he said, rubbing the back of his head.

Within minutes the whole thing was forgotten as the team ate and drank and enjoyed their warm meal. The minstrels were talented, playing a wide selection of music. The people of

Vasterland were a boisterous lot who loved their songs and stories. Many of those stories were of superstitions and bad omens, fairies and elves. Their songs were also of strange creatures and friendly fey folk.

*This explains a lot about Yappy and his obsession with elves.*

The food was long gone, but the beer continued to arrive. The men made small talk and told stories of their times at home or in the service. Grimble and Roche looked over at Flicker from time to time. He sat peacefully, leaning back against the wall and nibbling his food.

Another round was bought for the minstrels, and they asked what the crowd wanted to hear. So many names flew at the two men that Grimble couldn't tell what was being said. Finally one of the minstrels raised her palm up. "Okay, we got it," she said. "Wouldn't be a proper night in Whitby without 'Brave the Frontier.'"

The crowd clapped and cheered at the mention of Vasterland's anthem. The minstrels started the song slowly, and by the time they sang the first lyrics the crowd was clapping and thumping on the tables in time with the tune. Everyone inside knew the song and loudly sang along. Grimble and the team had fun pretending they were singing, though none of them knew all the words. Even Roche let loose.

The minstrels finished the three verses, and the crowd cheered and clapped enthusiastically. The few who were up dancing sat back down. The candle flames continued dancing, oblivious that the song had ended. They swayed and leaped vigorously as though pushed by a wind.

Grimble and the others turned to see who was coming through the tavern's door, making the outside breeze blow upon the candles; but the door was closed, and there was no wind. Yet the flames still flickered. The crowd watched in silence, brows furrowed in confusion. Grimble and the team turned their heads toward Flicker.

Standing at Flicker's table was a large man, sloshing a mug of ale about as he confronted the mage.

"Sir, I'm not in the mood, that's all," Flicker said. "Best to leave me alone."

"Everyone else was singing but you," the large man said. "You're an outsider, aren't you? You have a problem with our song? You have a problem with Vasterland and frontier folk?"

All eyes were on the two men and the dancing flames.

"Back off," Flicker said, a darkness filling his eyes.

"Back off?" the man said and slammed his mug onto Flicker's table. The flames leaped and danced wildly. The crowd gasped. "You're gonna sing our song, fucker, and you're gonna sing it right!

The man was interrupted as Roche and Baz grabbed his arms and the back of his scalp, forcefully moving him toward the door.

"What the…!" the man sputtered. He struggled against their efforts. "Lay off!"

"We're saving your life, asshole," Baz said as they dragged him out of the tavern.

Seven men at different tables got to their feet.

Grimble, Dinger, and Kurt snapped to a standing position, sending their benches crashing to the floor. That was enough to catch the attention of the men. The groups stared at each other.

"This is turning out to be a great night," Dinger said with a smile.

"Relax, friends," Kurt said to the crowd. "Your buddy is safe. No harm will come to him." Grimble and Dinger followed Kurt as he inched toward Flicker's table. Out of the corner of his eye, Grimble caught the motion of a man's arm. The man used his fingers to secure the knife on the table, ease it to the edge, and pull it below and out of view. His beard was scraggly, his face dark and gristly. The woman at his table simply watched Kurt.

"I don't think we trust your word, *friend*," said a large man three tables away.

"Do you trust my coin?"

A few more men and women in the crowd stood. The big man smirked and let out a chuckle. "I trust my fist'll knock out your teeth."

The team made it to Flicker's table, placing their backs to the mage. Flicker remained seated. He took a casual sip from his mug. Grimble glanced about but kept his peripheral vision on the man two tables away. The man turned in his seat. It would be easier for him to move from that position.

"You should trust my taglets," Kurt said, holding the two copper coins high in the air. "I owe you two beers for spilling yours." Kurt brought his hand down to his hip. From behind him, Grimble saw him slip the coins behind his belt.

"What?" said the large man. "You haven't…"

Kurt drew his hand back and acted as if he were throwing the coins with all his might. At that moment two copper coins flew across the span, and with a sound like a hammer on wood, knocked two mugs flying from the table beside the large man. Beer spilled, foaming across the table and floor. The men stepped away from the table.

The man near Grimble turned back to his table and returned the knife to the top of it.

"Like I said. I owe you two beers," Kurt said. "In fact, let me buy drinks for the whole tavern." Kurt looked at the faces around him, nodding enthusiastically. His face bore a bright smile. "You hear that? Drinks are on me. Drinks for everyone." He started clapping.

The people looked at him.

"Minstrels. A gold crown to start playing right now." Kurt motioned to the serving girl to bring beer to everyone.

Grimble watched as Kurt's enthusiasm affected the tavern. He was too vivacious to ignore. A few smiles spread. The minstrels started. The crowd warmed. The patrons, once angry and now confused, tentatively accepted their drinks.

Kurt sat down at Flicker's table, motioning for Grimble and the others to do so as well. He glanced sidelong at Flicker. "Nice shot."

"You almost blocked my view," Flicker said, nibbling on a chicken leg. "Might have been one mug and a groin." The men winced. "You're lucky I had two coppers."

Trying to take it in, Grimble asked, "How'd you —?"

But Flicker was too busy finishing his food.

"Same spell as the one for the darts," said Kurt. "Arrows or flowers, the spell can send them flying."

Flicker stopped chewing and glared at Kurt.

Kurt grimaced. "Sorry. Arrows or – or biscuits. The spell can launch anything that's not too heavy." He smiled and looked back at Flicker. The mage shook his head and drank from his mug.

Grimble watched the two Ravens. Dinger looked at all three before turning to face the other patrons.

Roche slipped in while the crowd was distracted and motioned for the team to join him and Baz outside. They gathered their gear and walked to their room, where they laid their packs on the floor. It was a large room of timber and plaster and had enough beds for ten. Roche had paid for them to have it to themselves. Each man grabbed a straw bed and made ready for the night. Grimble hadn't slept in a real bed since he'd left the farm. It was actually uncomfortable at first, but he managed to close his eyes as Roche snuffed the room's single candle.

A faint sizzle sounded in the darkness.

"Ow!" Kurt called out. "You son of a bitch."

"Canteen," Flicker said.

# CHAPTER THIRTEEN

Not long after daybreak Grimble and the team made their way down the interior stairway, packs in hand. They were surprised to find the inn's common room empty. No other guests broke their fast or moved about. All that remained were the odors of last night's hearth fire and the stale miasma of spilled drinks. Accompanying the smells was something heavier. Tension. It clung to the air, but hid from the sunlight streaming through the few windows. It was an uncomfortable contrast to the night before.

The team instinctively looked around, their hands moving toward their belts and the knives secured there. Kurt slid around the long tables, made his way over to a window, and peered into the courtyard. He looked back at the team and shrugged. Grimble checked behind the tavern's counter, but no secrets or dangers hid there either.

The sound of movement from a back room caught their attention and the team looked toward a curtained doorway as the owner of the Golden Trout Inn entered the room, his lips pursed, a look of chagrin in his eyes.

"Good morning, Samu," Roche said.

"Good morning, my friend," Samu replied. His look did not change. "May we speak?"

"Of course," Roche said, moving toward him. The team took positions inside the room and waited.

"I've always taken good care of you. Haven't I, my friend?" Samu asked.

"Yes. Always."

"Even when you were working, and I had that other place. I looked out for you, yes?"

"Yes, Samu. What's going on?"

"Last night. Last night scared a lot of folks. Your men scared a lot of folks. Both here and in the stable. The stable boy came in after you went to your rooms. He claims your men are wizards and almost burned the stables down trying to light each other on fire." Samu wrung his hands as he stole a glance at Flicker and Baz. "You must know I didn't believe his ignorant stories, but the locals did."

Roche smiled wearily. "We're leaving now. You don't have to worry about that anymore."

"I'm afraid that's not enough."

"What do you mean?"

"They know you and I are close."

"Spit it out, Samu."

"Regretfully I must ask you to never return."

"Never?"

"It must sound that way, but you will be forgotten by the Wanting season. Please, my friend, I hope you understand."

Roche grinned. "Samu, you needn't worry. You remain my friend, but we will make it sound as though you stood up to the Dark Sky Wizard himself."

Samu pulled a sack of food from behind the counter and handed it to Roche. "Good luck to you and your men," he whispered.

Grimble and the team stepped into the courtyard and headed to the horses, their packs slung over their shoulders. Grimble noticed that the half-dozen people in the courtyard had congregated in the two far corners, as far away from the tavern as they could be. It was quiet; the traffic on the street outside could be plainly heard. The men crossed the courtyard under the stare of a dozen eyes, and the looks they received along their way made the morning air feel even colder.

When they arrived at the stable they found the stable boy had become the center of attention and was basking in the adulations of a small group of adolescent boys and girls. They froze and stood silently, watching the men tack, saddle, and walk their horses out. Roche, at the front, was almost out of the stable when Kurt turned toward the youths and sneered. The stable boy paled and fled toward the alley behind the inn, his group of admirers tripping over each other behind him.

Before they left Roche paused in the archway leading to the road. "I've never been so offended! Never has anyone dared to stand in my way before! You will never see us again, you ungrateful son of a bitch!"

Grimble had never encountered such a group of superstitious people and wondered if their time along the border with the untamed lands had made them so. The team led their horses back through the opening as they left the inn, mounting them once they were outside on the street. Kurt gave Roche a nod of approval. "Nice performance," he whispered.

Their ride to the gate was unique. Word of the strangers visiting the Golden Trout and the omen of the dancing flames had

171

spread through the city like a chilling breeze. Each person they passed spat at the ground, shouted a warning down the street, or cautiously eyed them until they were out of sight. Small children were grabbed and pulled behind adults.

Roche rode through the glaring gauntlet stoically. Baz and Flicker's lips curled into silent snarls, but they ultimately endured the rebukes. Grimble, in disbelief, watched each act of defiance and disdain with mild curiosity. Kurt, apparently, could not abide the superstitious nature of Whitby's inhabitants. He made rude gestures toward some and aggressive, bluff movements toward others. The latter elicited screams or frenzied flights.

The dirt street narrowed before opening in the stretch leading to the city's gate. Heralded by the shouts and screams of Whitby's inhabitants, the team was met at the gate by the city watch. Nine armored men stood between them and the open gate. In front was the unit's leader, the watch sergeant, a good ten yards ahead of his men. In confident defiance of the approaching travelers, he stood in the middle of the street, one hand on his hip and the other held out with an open palm. Behind him, in two rows, were the eight men of his patrol, their poleaxes in a high ready position.

"Halt," said the leader. "Go no further. The mayor has words for you."

Roche said nothing and continued to ride toward the sergeant. Flicker reached into a pouch on his hip and Dinger placed his hand closer to the knife on his belt. Grimble made ready to ride hard or jump from his mount and fight. They continued forward.

"N-n-no further," the watch sergeant said. His eyes waxing. His confidence waning.

Roche and the men continued their ride toward the man. The

clop of their horses' hooves resounded against the buildings along the street and the wood posts of the city's walls. The sergeant melted away, watching them pass. The men blocking the gate lost their courage and skittered out of the way. The team left the city of Whitby and rode south-east, along the road toward Brantsford.

"It was the gate doors, right?" Grimble asked.

"Pardon?" Roche said.

"Neither the gate doors nor the portcullis were closed," Grimble said. "Was that how you knew the watch wouldn't fight?"

"Good eye," Roche said. "They didn't really want to lock us inside. The watch must be as superstitious as everyone else. The last thing they wanted was to trap us, the dangerous visitors, inside with them, making them the first targets of our wrath. It's easy for men in silk robes to order such things, much harder to carry out."

"The innkeeper was right, then. Not going back there anytime soon, are we?"

"No. Even more so because the watch will likely make up some grand story of how we used magic or summoned dark, fey energy to keep the gates from closing. I only hope Samu's inn wasn't ruined by our stay."

As they moved deeper into Aendura, away from the frontier and the border with Renlar, the team received fewer stares. It would be another four days before they arrived in Brantsford. The dirt road they traveled was more frequently used than the one they'd taken into Whitby. Albeit cared for, its heavy traffic had dug a trench three feet deep into the surrounding landscape in many areas.

The team encountered roadside inns and way stations every few hours, but Roche permitted their use for feeding and watering the horses only. They also met and passed merchants and trains of supply wagons headed to and from the small city. A good number of the wagon trains heading toward Whitby bore crates and barrels marked with a small insignia of a white, two-masted ship. The mark was the size of a boot heel, stamped in the crate's corners or near one end of the barrels. After Grimble noticed the first one, he kept looking for them among the passing caravans. He had never before seen that mark.

Progress along the road was quick and their pace was good. During the few stops and overnights when they rested their horses out of sight of the road, the men trained and sparred with whatever they had at hand. During these times, Grimble came to understand why Baz and Flicker put up with Kurt's jokes and insults. The man was fast.

Kurt preferred lighter blades and used smaller, thinner sticks while sparring against the rest of the team. Grimble was familiar with such narrowly tapered blades. While not as effective against heavily armored opponents, they were quick and lethal against lightly armored adversaries. And Kurt knew how to effectively use his speed. If the others, and occasionally Grimble, could keep Kurt at a distance with their longer-reaching "weapons," they won more than half the matches. But when Kurt got inside their reach, he won virtually every time. His hands whipped back and forth in a blur, and his opponent was left with red welts on vital areas of their body. After repeatedly striking at his opponent, Kurt would quickly disengage and move outside their reach before they could react or engage him in a grapple.

Back on his farm, Grimble had once seen a mother cat defend her kittens from two dogs. The cat lunged, scratched, and bit at the face of one dog, and before the dog could recover and bite back, she leaped directly from the first to the second, repeating her actions with equal ferocity. Once out of reach, the cat growled and hissed, her back arched. Both dogs were blinking and shaking their heads when she bluff-charged and sent them running. Kurt's method of fighting reminded Grimble of that mother cat. As if he were trained to engage more than one opponent at a time, as opposed to standing in a shield line.

Grimble's sword skill lagged behind that of his companions. He was used to fighting in a line with other shields at his side, and the spear was his favored weapon, not the sword. The sword training he now endured was humbling and frustrating. What frustrated him all the more was that he was trying to gain the team's trust, but felt as though his efforts made him look more the fool. The matches reminded him of his place among the team. Still, he worked to improve and to keep his temper in check, taking advantage of the lessons.

The only one he bested more times than not was Flicker. The mage's weapon skills were good, but he had clearly spent more time perfecting his use of magic. But Roche would not let Grimble spar against the mage often. In the end Roche ordered him to face Kurt in most of his matches. Grimble soon realized Roche was giving him the opportunity to improve his skill level. It was a good plan. A painful plan. And Grimble cursed under his breath at every single sting from Kurt's sticks. He struggled to keep the Raven at a distance. His failures were many.

At first Grimble thought Kurt took particular delight in meting out red marks and bruises. But before long he noticed Kurt using the same combinations over and over, disguising them with different approaches and feints. He would tell Grimble, "Watch my breathing," or "Watch my feet," or "Did you see how my elbow gave away that strike?" And Grimble watched, but the first day that was all it was: watching Kurt beat him with a stick.

The second day he started picking up some of the indicators and found he could counter some of the strikes. When that happened, Kurt had them repeat the drill with their left hands. After that he moved on to new attacks until Grimble picked up on those clues. Grimble had never trained so hard with his off hand. His skill grew and he began to appreciate the lessons, but only grudgingly, as Kurt continued to laugh and delight in the pain he dispensed. It infuriated Grimble, but he learned early on that showing any sign of frustration or anger motivated Kurt all the more. He soon got better at hiding his aggravation.

While they traveled, Kurt found another way of occupying the team's time: betting games. It started with Dinger and some card games, but once Dinger recognized Kurt's card game was better than his swordsmanship, he refused to play cards with the man. After that Kurt worked hard to talk the team members into making some of the most ridiculous bets. He took odds as to whether they would see a lame dog while passing a farm, or which horse would pee first after a water stop, or whether the next watchtower they passed would have someone on display in the pillory.

Kurt often lost, but the money changing hands was small change. Grimble got the feeling the gambling was Kurt's way of dealing with the monotony of the journey. He succeeded at enticing almost everyone into a bet or game during the first three days of the ride. He managed to goad Grimble into gambling once, and as was his luck, Grimble found himself the loser. He did not play any more games with the boisterous man. Only Roche avoided the betting. He gave Kurt a raised eyebrow whenever he was challenged. That was all the gambler received from the team's leader.

Immediately following breakfast on the fourth day, Kurt tried a different tack to pull Grimble back into the betting. Grimble watched it unfold, but did not see the end coming until it was too late.

Kurt started with questions: who was the best cook in the company, or the best swordsman. This got Dinger into talking about Grimble's horsemanship, claiming he was the best rider in the regiment. Kurt was adamant that title belonged to a Raven. The talking turned to goading as Kurt challenged Grimble to a race. Grimble did not bite. Kurt redoubled his efforts, offering odds and putting up silver coins. He went beyond dulas and straight to silver nobs.

"I'll match that bet. You're on," said Dinger. He turned to Grimble. "Shut this braggard's mouth."

Grimble rolled his bedding. He did not look up. "No, Dinger. I lost four nips when we passed that one-eyed, three-legged dog. It was only four nips, but he's not getting any more of my money."

"I knew you weren't that good," said Kurt. "Your reputation is fanfare."

"It's not your money, brother," Dinger said. "I'll cover the bet. Put him in his place."

Grimble knew Kurt was pushing him, trying to upset him. But he was not going to take the bait. "No. I'm not biting. He's setting us up. I know it."

Kurt looked hurt. "Fuck you. If you can't ride, admit it. Don't go insulting me just because you're not as good as they say."

"Can't ride?" said Dinger, striding over to peer down his

nose at the shorter man. "I could outride you myself, but I want to see you humiliated." He turned to Grimble, who was packing his kit. "Please, brother. Shut this fucker up."

"We don't even know the rules. He could make some crazy rule that guarantees him winning."

Kurt placed the blanket on his horse and turned to grab his saddle. "Relax, gentlemen. Simple rules." He looked down the road and pointed. "To that tree, around it, and back. First to pass the campfire wins. I'll even let Dinger give the word. It starts when he says 'Go.'" He placed his saddle on his horse and rested his arm on it, staring at Dinger. "That's a big responsibility. Think you can handle it?"

"You're starting to piss me off."

"It starts when you say 'Go.' That's a lot to remember."

Dinger was fuming as he walked back to Grimble. "Grimble, please. For me."

"I don't know," Grimble said. He looked down the road to the tree roughly three hundred yards away. "Around that first tree, the oak, on the left side of the road and back to the campfire."

"Yeah, horses start from where they stand now."

Kurt's horse was about twenty feet closer to the tree. Even though it was a little skittish, it was cold-blooded. The head start wouldn't be an advantage to him; Kurt's skill in the saddle was not much better than that of a new recruit.

*There's no way he can win. He has to be up to something.*

Grimble looked up at Dinger. The sun rose behind the warrior and Grimble was immediately struck by the last time he had seen Dinger's silhouette, more than a year ago. Dinger had been standing over him, outnumbered by their opponents, while Grimble had been on his back, sprawled and bleeding. He owed his life to Dinger. He had to do it, but there was something unseen floating in the challenge and he wanted to find it before committing.

He looked past Kurt to Roche and Baz, trying to gauge their reactions. Baz finished buckling his saddle and Roche, packed and ready, enjoyed his pipe. The smoke blew away in the breeze. Both men gave Grimble the *don't look at us* stare. Flicker stroked his beard and watched but said nothing.

Grimble stood and placed the blanket on his horse. He paused. He could not see any deception. If anything Kurt was at a disadvantage. He picked up his saddle. "Alright, you're on. Around that tree and back, first to pass the fire wins."

"We go when nipple-head here says the word 'Go,'" Kurt said.

Grimble nodded. "We go when Dinger says, 'Go.'"

"About time." Kurt pointed his thumb at Dinger. "If only jackass here can remember his part."

"Please, you surface-shitter," said Dinger. "How hard is it to say 'Go'?"

With that, Kurt shot from where he stood and ran toward Baz and Roche. Everyone watched for a second, trying to understand what they were seeing.

*Dinger said "Go,"* Grimble thought. "Shit." He dropped his saddle.

Kurt vaulted onto Roche's horse. Roche's spirited, warm-blooded horse.

"Hey!" Roche yelled.

The rogue kicked his heels into the flanks and cried out. Roche's horse lowered its croup and kicked off, stretching out into a gallop. Grimble looked at the other horses. Baz's was saddled, but it was cold-blooded like Kurt's. Grimble dragged the blanket off his horse, pulled on the quick release of the hobble and gave the rope a shake.

"You utter git!" Dinger yelled.

Grimble jumped onto his horse bareback, kicking it into a jog while he grabbed the reins. Kurt was ahead and pulling away, looking unexpectedly comfortable in the saddle.

The loosened remnants of the rope fell from his horse's foot. Grimble leaned forward and kicked it into a gallop. He spoke to it. He coaxed it. He stared straight ahead at his opponent. Kurt looked back. His eyes widened before he faced forward again to lean low over his horse's neck. Grimble gauged the distance.

*Shit, he may be too far ahead.* He locked his stare onto the oak tree on the left side of the road.

Kurt may have misled them about his riding skill, but he was not as experienced as a true cavalry trooper, and his horse carried more weight. But the glorious beast seemed to be giving Kurt everything he asked of it. Its tail flowed behind it, unfurling at the head of a blooming dust cloud.

Grimble urged his horse on. He challenged it. Wind whipped its mane like grass in a storm, roaring in Grimble's ears. Its hooves sounded like distant thunder. The gap began to shrink. The oak grew nearer.

Kurt's head start was enough for him to arrive at the tree about fifty yards ahead of Grimble. Kurt's horse took the turn wide. As they passed each other, Kurt on the return and Grimble arriving at the tree, Grimble thought he heard laughing.

Grimble urged his mount to take the turn tightly, almost scraping his shoulder against the trunk. The stress on Grimble's calves and the inside of his thighs was intense. They burned, but he gripped the horse with everything he had and prayed it would be enough. He felt the muscles of the beast flex and release; the bones and joints articulate. The horse righted itself and got its hind feet beneath it. It launched back toward the camp. Grimble sat astride the shoulders, telling it how strong it was. How fast it was. "Faster! Faster!"

Kurt's horse galloped toward the campfire. Grimble's closed the distance. About halfway back they were side by side, both animals stretching out in long strides, their heads thrusting with the tempo. Kurt shouted and cursed. Both horses, invigorated by seeing each other, renewed their efforts. The campfire neared.

The riders bent low along the shoulders and necks. Grimble gave another call. Kurt growled. He steered his mount to the left, pushing Grimble and his horse off the road. Their legs bumped. The horses crashed and rubbed against each other, trapping the men's legs.

*Oh, that's how it is?*

Grimble leaned into Kurt. He bumped Kurt's left arm, causing him to jerk away. His horse reacted to the motion and moved to the right. Kurt's mount fell back a full length as Grimble and his horse rode past the campfire first.

Dinger shouted in victory. Baz and Roche watched with smiles. Flicker stared through them.

Both riders took their horses around the camp and the nearby field to cool them down. Dinger shouted again. The animals' mouths frothed, their nostrils pumping with each heavy breath. Grimble smiled and looked about for Kurt. Even with the Raven manipulating the rules, Grimble had come out the victor. If felt great, especially after having to suffer Kurt's beatings when they sparred.

*Damn, that was a good race! Hope it shuts him up now.*

Grimble saw his challenger cooling his horse on the other side of the road. He rode to intercept Kurt, but the Raven moved away from Grimble and kept his distance. Grimble stared in confusion and cantered back to the campsite.

*What the f—*

Baz walked up to Grimble. "Give him a minute. He'll be alright."

"What's the issue?"

"He's not used to losing. I'm sure he's just calming down."

"He's lost bets on this trip before. Why's he mad I won this race?"

"He's not mad at you for winning," said Baz, "he's beating himself up for losing. Knowing him, he'd planned this whole thing out since he heard you were joining the mission. Those other bets didn't mean anything. I told you he was a thinker."

Grimble turned back toward Kurt to see him approaching. The man looked ready to murder. He stared Grimble in the eye, his teeth clenched, took a breath through his nose, and said, "Good race. Congratulations." Then he turned his horse and walked away before Grimble could reply.

"He better not have a limp after this," Roche said.

"Relax," said Kurt, dismounting with a blank face. "I just warmed him up for you." He handed the reins back to Roche.

It was not until after lunch that Kurt returned to his spirited self.

The sun was past its zenith and midway toward the horizon when Brantsford came into sight. The road crested a hill several miles away from the large city, affording the team the view even though they were more than an hour away from their destination. The city was larger than Whitby and protected by a stone wall. From this distance the wall looked smooth and perfect, a light gray against the greens and browns of the farmlands around it.

Brantsford was situated on the northern end of Vaster Lake, Aendura's second largest. The fruits of farming, fishing, and abundant trade made it a hub of commerce. Even miles away from the lake, Grimble could see several ships. Their white sails stood out against the lake's dark surface. He had seen them in artworks and heard tales of them from Dahl and Ellie, and hoped the team's travel through the city would bring them close to the harbor. Grimble could only imagine the country's capital, Agderon, would be as beautiful as this one was.

*If Brantsford is this amazing, Agderon must indeed be a jewel.*

An hour later the team reached the section of the road from which the city received its name: the ford across Brants River. It was at a broad segment of the waterway with firm ground beneath shin-deep, slow-moving water. Those preferring to reach the other side without removing their footwear could pay a copper taglet to the ferryman a quarter mile up the river. Most travelers kept their purses shut and got their feet wet.

Grimble and the team rode their horses across the ford and up the path on the other side. They approached Brantsford from the north. Light-blue-and-white vertically divided banners hung from the walls and from poles on every tower of the city, flapping in the lake breeze.

They were minutes from the main gate when Roche raised his cloak's hood, fully covering his head. He motioned to the others to do the same. The cut and color of their cloaks would linger longer in the minds of those who looked upon the team, which would aid the decoys who would ride out of town the next day wearing those same cloaks.

Once at the gate Roche showed the city guards the group was

not indigent, paying the toll for entry. Grimble expected the soldiers to give them curious looks, like so many others had along the road, but happily the men disappointed him. They seemed genuinely disinterested as the team rode past them into the city.

Grimble had forgotten which day it was – one day melds into the next when serving in the army, especially for those deployed and working outside the routine of barracks life – but it appeared to be early in the workweek. The city teemed with pedestrians and carts. Travel through the congested, stone-lined streets was slow. Grimble knew by the well-stocked vendor carts and the inhabitants nearly bumping into each other that Templeday had been one or two days before their arrival. From his memories of helping his father sell their tobacco, and of how the tide of goods ebbed and flowed, he speculated further that a ship or supply barge may have recently docked.

The inhabitants were not as flamboyantly dressed as those in Whitby. Although the finer cuts and bright-colored fashions that blared in the wood-and-dirt capitol of Vasterland would have blended in with the stone and painted plaster buildings of this commerce hub, most clothing was practical by design. There happened to be a lot of it, though. It seemed in Brantsford that the higher a person's status was, the cleaner and more numerous the garments they wore. Grimble saw one man, a flock of people around him, wearing trousers, a shirt, a surcoat, two vests, a frock, and a shoulder-draped stole.

"This is much better," said Dinger. "I expected another city full of peacocks. I don't know if my eyes could take another attack like the one they suffered in Whitby."

"Their feathers may be subdued," said Kurt, "but you can pick out the ones who puff and preen."

"They're far less superstitious, too," Roche said.

Kurt smiled and winked at an overly dressed young lady. She blushed and looked away. By the time she looked back at Kurt, he was already making eyes at another young woman.

Grimble shook his head and smiled. Before he could say anything, he caught the scent of a familiar tobacco and tried to locate the source. He had often wondered how far his family's tobacco traveled and tried to recognize the specific leaf or blend he smelled. He looked around, standing in the saddle and trying for a better vantage point. The source was nowhere to be seen.

"What is it?" Dinger asked.

"Nothing," Grimble said. "Got a little smell of home back there. But it's gone."

Dinger nodded but was soon distracted by a good-looking couple. He watched them with a smile as they passed by.

The layout of the streets was better managed in Brantsford, but it took the team the better part of an hour to reach their inn, such was the traffic they faced. The noise and smells changed almost immediately once they turned off the main street and onto a side one leading to their destination, The Wagon Wheel. It was a mere stonecast from the tumult of the bustling street, yet the aromas were more agrarian and less a mix between pleasant and unsavory. Grimble took it in. These were the smells he loved.

The Wagon Wheel occupied most of a city block. The land was taken up by the inn itself as well as the outbuildings, stables, and a paddock. It was set up for, and utilized almost exclusively by, traveling merchants. The stables were large, the barn spacious and well stocked, the paddock groomed, and several covered stalls offered a safe and secure location to store a cart or wagon. A spacious courtyard, large enough for several teams of horses to be hitched to wagons at the same time, sat in the middle of it all.

Roche led the team onto the inn's lot. A stone well stood across the courtyard and next to the paddock. A long trough near the well ran between the paddock and courtyard, sharing its water with animals in both areas. A light-complected man in his early twenties wearing a threadbare shirt and pants stood beside the well, a pack at his feet. He donned a blanket as though it were a cloak and turned toward the courtyard's entrance. He bowed his shaved head upon seeing the group.

Roche looked around the courtyard, his brow hinting at a furrow. He led his horse toward the well and the team followed. Grimble looked in the windows and doors and dark recesses of the inn. He wondered what had Roche confused or worried.

Roche looked at the bald man. "We've had a hard ride this day."

"Such is the way, yes?" the man said. "One day hard. Another day easy. Yet it is how we use each day that is important." He turned and motioned to the well and trough. "The water is delightful. Plenty for you and your horses. I will move for you, yes." He had an accent Grimble did not recognize, but his smile and nature seemed genuine.

Roche scrunched his eyebrows in confusion. He looked at the inn's sign and back to the young man, who was tending to his pack. Roche dismounted but held his hand up for the rest of the team to remain in their saddles. Flicker reached for his pouch. The other men continued scanning the area. Grimble pulled his reins in tighter. His horse tensed, its ears swiveling rapidly.

As Roche stretched the ride out of his muscles, the large barn door opened and a dark-skinned man built like Baz stepped into the late-afternoon sunlight. He and Roche looked at each other. The man beckoned Roche to him and quietly asked, "Did I hear you say your horses are tired?"

"Yes." Roche said. "We've had a hard ride this day."

"To me, your horses look fresh and ready for another day's ride," the man said. Roche smiled and the two clasped hands. The team relaxed. The new man eyed the young one by the well and ushered the team into the barn. Once inside he latched the door shut so it could not be opened from outside.

"Ahmed," the man said.

"Roche."

"I do not know that young man." Ahmed peered outside through cracks in the barn door. "He arrived with a merchant about half an hour ago. They were turned away. I've paid for the use of the entire inn for several days. But he remained. He's organized his travel sack and had his fill of water... Never mind. He's leaving now... Yes, back down the street toward north gate. To business."

"Kurt," Roche said. "Keep an eye at the door." Kurt switched positions with Ahmed. Roche removed his hood and the team followed suit.

"You're a day early," Ahmed said. "This is good." He paused a moment and mumbled some words with his eyes closed. He opened his eyes and pointed to the stalls. "Get your horses into the stalls. But not that one. Leave that one empty." He indicated a particular stall before continuing. "Your decoys will arrive in the next few minutes. They will untack your horses."

Ahmed motioned with both hands, shooing the men into action. Grimble and the others looked at him, then to Roche. Roche nodded, and the team sprang into action, posting their mounts quickly and gathering their items. Grimble took over Kurt's post, watching for movement outside, permitting Kurt to collect his kit while Flicker posted Kurt's horse.

"I know who you are," Ahmed said, looking sideways at

Flicker. "I've heard of you."

Flicker glanced over his shoulder at him, but said nothing.

"No. I am not allied to him," Ahmed said. "And not from your old guild, the Golden Quill. What was done was wrong. Others, too, have heard; you should know this. You have – admirers." He smiled. "You have support, too."

Flicker nodded to the man and wordlessly returned to sorting out his kit.

Grimble did another visual sweep of the courtyard and looked back in time to catch the other team arriving. He had only recently seen a mage teleport, or "portal," away; but never had he seen one portal in. Before his eyes, a group of five soldiers popped into the empty stall. The men seemingly zoomed into the space, growing from a tiny point around waist level to full-size in the blink of an eye. Dinger jumped. The horses danced and whinnied for a few seconds before calming.

Roche took his cloak off and motioned the team to do likewise. One of the men who had portalled into the barn, one matching Grimble's complexion and build, moved to take over the watch from him. He handed Grimble his new kit and Grimble gave him the garish cloak he had been wearing. The rest of the team handed their robes to Ahmed. Although the newcomers did not appear identical to Grimble and his teammates, they were of similar body types.

The new kits the men handed the team were different than the ones the team had been using. The bulging canvas satchels and thin canvas bedrolls used almost no leather in their construction. The new backpacks were made completely of waxed canvas and wood. The men also handed Roche and Baz two heavy rolls of canvas and one leather satchel before moving to Ahmed's side. Everyone moved with quick efficiency.

Grimble was forced to follow orders immediately and did not have the time to think about any of it.

Ahmed turned to Roche one more time. "I've hidden a small boat and some rope under the brush along the bank. It should not be hard to find if you walk straight from the old house toward the river. Other than the routine patrols along the river, there's been no activity around the house. River's Edge is quiet too." He looked at Grimble and the others. "Good luck, my friends. May Yahnn keep you close to her bosom and may Gavel light your way and guide you through this mission."

Under Roche's direction the team pulled tightly together, each holding their kits in one hand, and the wrist of the man to their right in the other. They made a tight circle to help the casting of the coming spell. Dinger looked at Grimble, concern in his eyes. He adjusted his grip on Grimble's forearm several times, each time with more strength. Grimble gave him a look of reassurance, but it seemed to have little effect.

Ahmed pulled a pouch from his belt and opened it. The aroma of sage escaped into the air. He drew a large pinch of powder from the pouch and with a flick of his wrist doused the team's hands and forearms with it. Ahmed moved his fingertips close together, turned them toward the team, and rapidly moved them apart.

The world blurred and swirled. Grimble thought he saw trees and fields, all in the space of half a breath. Then it was dark and he no longer felt hay beneath his feet.

*What the...*

"Shit!" said Dinger.

# CHAPTER FOURTEEN

Grimble could not make out any details. There was not enough light. However, he felt a flat floor beneath his boots, the air was colder than the barn, and the smell of hay and livestock was replaced with loam and —

"Kurt," Roche said.

"On it."

Grimble heard Kurt take a few steps away from the team. The shifting air brought the second aroma back to Grimble, a little stronger this time. It was light, but there was a hint of sage, garlic, and other aromatic herbs.

*A root cellar.*

It had been years since he had been in one, but he knew the smells. Away from the group, Kurt opened the trapdoor to the floor above and a soft light shone into the cellar. Grimble caught sight of Kurt's legs as he finished climbing the ladder to whatever awaited. He wasn't sure if his mind was playing tricks on him, but he thought he could hear Kurt walking on the wood floor overhead. The sounds were so faint Grimble could not be sure. For such a boisterous troublemaker, Kurt was surprisingly nimble and silent when necessary.

Grimble's eyes adjusted to the darkness, and little strips of light broke into the cellar between the floorboards over their head. It was not enough to get a look around the room. It merely cast thin, gray stripes upon his black-shadowed teammates.

The silence and the wait pressed on Grimble, but he knew not to speak. Roche would give the word. Minutes passed before the light shone through the trapdoor again and Kurt started down the ladder. He paused to close the trapdoor and the darkness enveloped him once more.

"We can afford a little light down here," Kurt said.

A yellow ball of light, small as a button, broke the darkness in front of Flicker. The light hovered over the mage's left hand. He closed his fingers around it, subduing it, and slowly moved his hand to the center of the group. Flicker opened his fingers again and released the light. The ball floated in midair, hovering around chest level. It provided as much light as a candle but was almost blinding in the darkness. Grimble admired the beauty of it. Dinger, across from Flicker, took half a step back.

"Report," Roche said to Kurt.

"Just like we were told: single floor, two rooms. Decent condition. No danger of falling through the floor. The shutters are all but closed. The gaps will betray any light inside. No light upstairs, and no fires anywhere. The smell of smoke will give us away too. Inventory of our new kits and any reading needs to be done down here. We should have at least one or two posted up top at all times, unless Flicker wants to Ward the area for us."

Flicker nodded indifferently.

"That won't be necessary, Flicker," said Roche. "But I want one of us above at all times."

"Outside is overgrown and unused," Kurt continued. "The

locals in River's Edge must think this place cursed or haunted."

"That was the plan when this shack was set up almost ten years ago," Roche said. "It was used for other purposes at that time. It's a safe house now. We're about two miles from the nearest farmstead."

"I used one of these places along the western border a couple of years ago," Baz said. "Very handy."

"They are," Roche said. "Still, I don't want to assume the locals or passing patrols will stay away. One on watch upstairs at all times. Keep lookout for unwanted visitors and listen out for our border patrols. I need to know if they come anywhere near this place. We avoid them as much as Renlar's patrols on the other side of the river.

"No fires. At night, the only use of light will be down here." Roche looked at everyone, meeting their eyes. "We stay here until well after dark tomorrow. That's when we cross the river into Renlar. Flicker…"

Flicker raised his chin but continued to stare into the darkness behind Dinger.

Roche continued, "While it's bright outside you can increase the flame's intensity, but keep it to a candle during the hours of darkness. When you choose your spells for the beginning two days of travel on this mission, all I ask is that you keep at least two Portals and one Message spell memorized. An Eye would be handy too, but that and the rest are up to you."

"Hmm," Flicker said.

"This will be our rally point until we're deep inside Renlar. Do what you can to make it here if we're separated. Kurt, we need to determine the patrol types and timing on the other side of the river." Roche gave Kurt a sympathetic look.

"I'll get across and be back by morning," Kurt said. "Relax.

It's what I do."

"Walk directly toward the river from the house. The path will look like a game trail. Be careful on your way back. The Warding spells are strong on this place. If you stay on the game trail you will hear noises. They're designed to make you feel uncomfortable. But if you stray off the path the Ward becomes aggressive when you get close to the cabin."

Kurt and Baz nodded.

"Prep your kit," continued Roche, "and head out after dark. Grimble, get upstairs now and take the first watch. The upstairs latrine is an old bucket or basin – it should be obvious if you need it. We'll have to dig one for down here."

"Yeah, there's a bucket near the door," Kurt said.

Grimble set his pack down and moved to the ladder. He heard Roche order the others to take an inventory of the kit and supplies they'd been handed in Brantsford. This felt familiar. Orders given and followed immediately. There was a sense of urgency now; the pressures of the mission were returning to the men. All Grimble had to do was concentrate on his part, follow orders, and be prepared to adjust as needed. He had this.

Grimble arrived at the base of the ladder and grabbed the risers before starting up. The rungs were wide, more like stair treads, but the angle was steep. At the top he pushed open the trapdoor and emerged, blinking, into the main room of the partially sunlit, two-room cabin.

It was much like his grandmother's house on the farm. Her main room had provided the living space, and the small second room had been merely a larder. Grimble took a quick look around the interior and checked the sightlines from the windows.

He settled into a routine of keeping watch using the gaps in the shutters. The person or team who had used the windows last had done an excellent job of leaving gaps that covered the game trails and open sections of the woods, the very avenues most humans would use to approach the cabin. The sun was low in the sky, and there was less than an hour of sunlight remaining. As Grimble tuned out the smells and noises inside the cabin and concentrated on everything outside, he began to pick up on the natural flow of the area.

The riverside, or west side, of the cabin was of most interest to him at first. He knew they would take that route the next night, so he worked to learn the area from his vantage point. However, it was the north side of the cabin that provided him with the most pleasant distractions. Two green-and-white hummingbirds vied for the nectar of azalea blossoms growing near the cabin. One chased the other away whenever it came into view: a dynamic display of dominance and territoriality from such diminutive creatures. Grimble couldn't afford to truly watch the constant show, but managed a glance here and there.

*Everything fights. Peace is a dream.*

On his fourth circuit around the windows, he found a rabbit had joined the north window troupe. Moments like these were impossible to come by when surrounded by scores of troopers. He remembered his days on the farm, days hunting when he became one with the woods. Like the time a squirrel had climbed the tree he was in and stared at him for minutes from an arm's length away. Or the many times birds had landed on his hunting bow. Or the time a yearling doe had walked up and laid down beside him. He recalled the walks in the woods with Ellie and wondered if he should give these animals names like the two of them had done.

*Don't get distracted. Move to a new window.*

The window looking east, the one beside the cabin's door,

afforded a view of tangled briars and not much else. The pines growing among the thicket were barren of branches near the ground. Several finches danced and darted about the forest floor under the thicket. Ellie loved birds. She had told Grimble several times that they were messengers from the heavens. The only thing these finches were telling Grimble was that they were hungry. He smiled. Looking deeper into the woods for any movement, his eyes returned to their work, but his mind went back to Ellie.

He'd joined the army hoping to run across her in his travels, or at least catch some word of her traveling merchant father. In all these years he was no closer to finding her than before. Had he grown complacent with his life in the regiment? Had he forgotten the primary reason he had joined? If he asked Kelban to leave the regiment with him at their ten-year mark, would he? Or did Kelban want to make it a career? They had always said they would stay in or leave together. Together, he and Kelban could take on anything.

A noise inside the house brought Grimble out of his thoughts. The trapdoor to the root cellar opened. In the fading light Grimble could make out Roche, Baz, and Flicker stepping into the room one by one. Roche and Baz moved to the riverside window, whispering about Kurt's nighttime excursion across the river into Renlar.

Flicker walked up to Grimble. "I'm your relief."

He gave Flicker the layout of the windows and what little information he'd picked up while on post, then stepped down the ladder and closed the door above him. The floating flame continued to provide light to the cellar. The room was about twenty feet long and no more than nine or ten feet wide. Kurt lay upon his outstretched bedroll at the far end, eyes shut and hands resting upon the belt at his waist. Six feet from Kurt, Dinger sat upon his bedroll, his back against his pack. He was studying a piece of parchment the size of a shoe sole. When he noticed Grimble stepping off the ladder, he motioned him over. Grimble sat on the boards next to him and Dinger showed him the parchment.

"Roche wants us to memorize the map," he whispered. "In case we get separated. He didn't mark it like a normal map, in case we are caught, so it takes a minute to figure out."

"It's the Divide, right?" Grimble said. "The one Renlar took from us in the Two Rivers War."

"Yeah. We're at 'Table' now. Headed toward 'Oven' and 'Market.' Each inch is roughly half a day's travel. The Vaster and Arnse Rivers are the long edges." He handed the map over to Grimble.

Grimble knew maps in the general sense, but the lack of landmarks and geographic features made him look harder at this one. A small, pointed line likely referenced north. Dinger pointed out the critical locations to him and identified their coded names. Once Grimble knew what to look for, the map made sense. He measured distances with his thumb. After that he set the map between Dinger and himself. The two eyed it together in the dim light.

Dinger was the first to lean away. He rubbed his face and looked toward Kurt. Turning back toward Grimble, he lowered his voice further. "You got a nasty injury at Steep Ridge, didn't you?"

"Yeah, twice. Spears in the right side and right knee. The one in the knee dropped me. I owe you – so many of us owe you and Roche our lives, brother. I hear you were the last two standing in our company."

Dinger waved his hand. "You'd have done it for us if the roles were reversed." He moved his face closer to Grimble. "You went to the Temple to see the priests after the battle, right?"

"Yeah." Grimble's brows furrowed, and he stared at Dinger. "What are you trying to get at?"

"I hear it's demons and phantoms that do the work when called by magic. Did you see them working on you?"

"Are you – where'd you hear that?"

"Everyone knows that. It's what I've been told my whole life."

"What did you see when you had to go to the Temple after a battle?" Grimble asked.

"I've never been to the Temple. Not after a battle or for any of the calls to prayer."

Grimble couldn't contain his shock. He stared at Dinger with wide eyes. "You've never been injured? You'd been in the regiment for years before I got here. Your platoon's been in the same shit as mine."

"I've had little nicks and scrapes," Dinger said, "nothing more than could be handled by sutures or a burn. Never hurt bad enough to end up in the Temple."

"Ihgel favors you, brother. Count yourself blessed."

"I did until this afternoon. That mage sent us out of the barn, through who knows what, into this cellar over a hundred miles away. Demons carrying us through their cursed realm... Who knows what disease or hex they might have placed on me?"

"That's not how it happens. I'm certain it wasn't demons or phantoms that brought us here," Grimble said with a slight smile.

"Don't mock me, Grimble. Even mages and priests don't know the powers they play with." Dinger's face was solemn. The corners of his dark eyes showed a hint of concern.

Grimble let his smile fade and looked Dinger in the eyes. "Brother, I'm not mocking you. I can assure you we were in good hands and never touched by evil." He adopted a wicked grin. "And if I'm wrong and the earth cracks and we're set upon by any creatures crawling from the Abyss, I'll be at your side, and we'll make those fuckers regret the day."

Dinger's face remained hard for several seconds as the two stared at each other. It finally softened, and the right corner of his mouth twitched. His eyes reclaimed their spark. "You're damn right. We'll give them something to remember us by and secure our spot at the table in Ihgel's Hall. Those shits won't know what hit 'em." He patted Grimble on the shoulder and turned back to his pack, fishing for something inside. He pulled out a sack with hard biscuits and a small block of pemmican, rendered suet with pulverized dried meat and berries. "Looks like we'll have to kill demons with frontier crap in our bellies."

Grimble smiled as he turned his attention to his own kit. He rolled out his bedding and began an inventory of pack items, laying them out on his blanket. The items were fairly standard but bore no resemblance to anything the Aenduran army issued its soldiers. The food was as Dinger described, typical frontier-style travel rations; not unsavory, but sure to become so after days of eating them at every – single – meal.

Two stacks of Vrelish coins, twenty each of silver and gold, lay wrapped in paper within a leather pouch. Grimble opened the packaging and poured the coins into the pouch. He'd never held so much money. He was uncertain how Aendura's money compared to Vreland's, but estimated it to be more than a year's pay. This made him wonder if they were supposed to use it to "buy" the Baker's loyalty.

His new kit included a new knife, one that was a touch

smaller than what he usually carried, and an arming sword. Both blades had been forged and finished in a manner different than his personal ones, and Grimble wondered if they had been made in Vreland, as their cover story was that they were part of a Vrelish free company answering Noreas' call for mercenaries. After the inventory, he repacked his kit, saving a couple of biscuits and some pemmican for his meal.

Perhaps two to three hours passed. The passage of time was near impossible to determine in the cellar. Grimble rested against his pack, stretched out on his bedding and staring, hypnotized by the floating flame. He worked to keep his mind occupied with anything but the dangers of the mission.

The cellar door opened and Roche and Baz made their way down the ladder, skirting along the cellar wall toward a supine Kurt. Right before they reached him, Kurt bolted halfway up, his legs cocked and his right hand resting on his knife handle. He blinked and relaxed. Baz nodded his chin upward. Kurt collected his cloak and a couple of items from his pack, and slipped in behind Roche and Baz as they returned to the ladder. Roche patted both men on the shoulder and watched them ascend the steps and close the door.

Roche approached Dinger. "Relieve Flicker. I'll relieve you when Baz gets back in a few hours." Dinger took a long drink from his canteen, grabbed his cloak, and made his way upstairs.

Before long, Flicker was down in the cellar, unrolling his bedroll between Grimble and Kurt's kits. The mage worked quietly and systematically, as if every movement required focus. Once his bedding lay across the boards, he removed his shirt, exposing an undergarment and a thin, small backpack securing his spellbook to his back. Grimble had run across only two other mages in his life and wondered if they had a similar harness system for their most treasured possession.

Once Flicker had settled himself and reclined against the wall, he opened the small pack and removed the leatherbound tome. It was a little wider than a loaf of bread, and about two fingers thick. Shadows moved in the room; Grimble looked up to see the light gliding toward the mage. It stopped a foot above his head. Flicker set the book upon his knees and opened it. A small, flattened white flower slid out. Flicker caught it with the adept nature of someone who had done so many times before. He replaced the flower against the inside of the front cover and thumbed through several thick pages before settling on one. Then he stared, unmoving, at the page.

Grimble shifted his position, attempting to get a better look. From where he was the page appeared to show a blue loop, or series of loops, nothing more. He craned his neck.

"Lost your spellbook, have you?" Flicker said, not looking up from the page. "Trying to borrow mine?"

Grimble's face warmed. He wanted to say something but couldn't find the words. Instead, he pulled out the map again and focused on that.

"Tell me," Flicker said. "What's your true story, Grimble Broadleaf of Minden?"

Grimble looked toward the mage again. Flicker's eyes remained on his book, but his left eyebrow was raised. Grimble swallowed. "I'm the son —"

"Don't tell me the 'son of a tobacco farmer' story you tell the other troopers. What is your life story? How did you come to be?" Flicker turned to look at Grimble. Dark clouds swirled in the whites of his eyes. His voice grew deeper, sounding more in Grimble's head than his ears. "What symbols are painted upon your soul?"

The hair stood up on the back of Grimble's neck and arms. The two men stared at each other. Time stopped, or so it seemed. Grimble felt the mage's eyes trying to peer into his mind, as through a window. They looked around as Flicker tilted his head this way and that. But his face showed frustration, as though a curtain blocked his view.

Finally, Grimble found his tongue. "I don't know," he said.

"You don't. Do you?" Flicker said. The harshness of his tone had faded, the hard lines of his face melted. "Curious."

"Do you pull that on everyone?" Grimble asked, embarrassment turning to frustration. "Did I pass?"

"Careful," said Flicker. "I'm not sure I can tolerate you yet."

"No disrespect meant, Flicker, but it was an honest question. We're knocking on Renlar's door. We need to concentrate on the mission, not play stupid games."

"I don't play stupid games. You should take great care before ever throwing that accusation at me again. I didn't have to test you. I got a sense of your worthiness before we left camp. Baz and Kurt should have taken my word."

"And the dark stare you just gave me?" Grimble asked.

"Dark stare? You saw the eyes? You are different." Flicker appeared intrigued. He sat up higher. "I will answer your questions if you agree to tell me what I want to know about you."

Grimble had a hundred and one questions running through his head. He knew the mage would not answer them all. What should he ask? Where should he start? "Fair enough. Explain magic to me. I was told you memorize those symbols, and they hold power, but it can't be that easy."

Flicker turned the book in his lap so Grimble could get a better look. "What do you see?" he asked.

"A blue loop with small circles near the bottom."

"Just one shade of blue, right?"

"No. There are different shades... and gray... and black. Black lines and – are those words in the colors?"

"Is that all?"

Grimble looked at Flicker, confused.

"Tell me," said Flicker. "Where do the lines of the symbol touch and not touch? Where do the words begin and in which direction do they run? What size are the letters? Do you see where the brushstrokes start? Where they end? When I move the book slightly, do you see the shimmer in some areas of the symbol? Does the ink remain within the lines of the symbol, and if not, where does it break free?"

"There's no way you can remember all of that."

"Not when you start, but you train with simpler symbols, simpler spells, and work your way to the more complex."

"How do they hold the energy to cast spells? Is the magic in the paper?"

"Ha. No. The pages and these symbols hold no power. The Great Bavan developed these symbols as they evoke the emotions a mage needs to cast the spell. Once we have the true feeling in our minds, we must rest. Our bodies then absorb the energy from all around us."

"What energy?" Grimble let the words out without thinking. Was he pushing for too many answers?

Flicker took a breath. "I should be more careful before offering to answer questions. That's another thing hard to explain to a non-mage. There is energy all around us. Like sunlight or air, it's there, and we can feel it. There is an entire school at the Institute dedicated to studying this energy. We call it 'vigre.' Some cultures, such as the Vrels, call it mana. It's in everything you see; although some things and some places have stronger or weaker vigre."

"And Bavan teaches this at the Institute?"

"No. Gods, no. Bavan lived over twenty-two hundred years ago. He was one of the Ancients, the first users of magic, and his son was born without the ability to cast spells using the ways of the Ancients. Bavan developed the symbols needed to give his son the feelings, the emotions, required to cast the spells. He called the magic Arcane, knowing few would be able to use it."

Flicker's hard face had softened. Grimble felt comfortable to ask more questions. "Roche said something about an ancient people who used magic. What happened to them?"

"They died off around the time of Bavan. No one truly knows how. Some say their time passed and they simply disappeared into the vigre. I've heard others say they were upset Bavan created Arcane magic and hunted him down. The ensuing battle consumed all of them, Bavan included." Flicker laughed. "Superstitious folks near the frontier, and people like your friend Dinger, call them elves or sprites and blame them for unexpected disasters or unexplained good fortune."

"Once you learn a spell, once you get the feeling, how do you cast it, and do you need to ever study that symbol again?"

"Each spell has words, or gestures, or some material which helps us summon the spell's power. The more experienced we become at casting that spell, the less we need to do to summon it; but when a spell is cast, the symbol is gone from our memory. What we could see in great detail in our minds moments before becomes lost to us. The casting and the energy take that feeling away. That's why the books are so important and why we protect them with our lives."

"If a mage loses his book?" asked Grimble.

"They are powerless. Rafel help them. Those who have lost their books spend the rest of their lives trying to get them back. The Spire and the Institute look very unfavorably on it. Very unfavorably. They'll never be trusted with another one. And when a mage dies, the Spire pays a healthy reward for their book. This keeps books from freely floating around."

"Who is in charge of the books used by the Temple priests?" Grimble asked.

"They don't use books. They use a different type of magic, one closer to that of the Ancients, I imagine. We're taught that the Ancients used chanting and songs to elicit the emotion needed to cast spells. No need for books and no resting or meditation. They gathered the energy from around them directly and cast their spells, but because they had to chant and gather the energy, their spells took time to cast."

"So, their magic was weaker?"

"No. Absolutely not. The Ancients were stronger, far stronger than the most powerful Arcane Grand Master. It's said a single Ancient singing or chanting over a long period could do more than our most powerful Arcane spell. And if a group of Ancients gathered and sang, they could do almost anything."

"Ah, and that is why the Temple priests pray and chant while casting their spells. They have no books. Are their spells based on emotion and feeling, too?"

"Yes, and no. The divinity scholars at the Institute say the praying puts them in tune with their god, who grants them their spells. Their praying does not always provide what they want. Sometimes the gods have different plans."

Grimble looked at the mage with new eyes. They sat for a moment in silence. Grimble, remembering Roche, glanced back toward their leader. He sat less than ten feet away, focused on touching up the edge of his knife with a stone and examining his work after every few passes. He showed no indication that he knew there was a conversation going on nearby.

"Now," said Flicker. "Your turn to tell me what I want to know."

Flicker and Grimble delved deeply into Grimble's life before joining the army. It was the same story he had told at the campfires, but Flicker guided the tale with his questions. Like everyone else, Flicker was intrigued by Ellie and most of his questions were about her, but as Grimble did not know much about her life he couldn't provide many answers. In the end Flicker gave no indication that he had found the thing he sought. Eventually, he excused himself from the conversation and dedicated his time to study.

Grimble felt more confused than before. He had many questions about magic but worried he had already pushed the mage for too much information. Then there was Flicker's repeated questioning about Ellie. Grimble's fellow troopers were always more interested in her appearance and her nature, but Flicker wanted to know what languages she spoke and from what country she and her father hailed. The mage also asked questions about the songs she sang.

*What was that about? I must have looked like a fool, not knowing the answers.*

Grimble peeked at Flicker. The man sat unmoving, staring at his book. Grimble thought of the energy mages used, vigre. He looked around the root cellar, wondering if any of it was around him, if he could feel it.

*Nope. Fuck it.*

He pulled his blanket over his body and allowed sleep to overcome him.

# CHAPTER FIFTEEN

The wind blew against Brother Bhen's back, mocking him as it raced up the hill. He lifted his eyes from the dirt path and swayed, thighs burning, mouth dry. Devout Mother Tara, several feet ahead, climbed higher, picking her steps, maintaining her pace. She did not slow.

She was praying, too. Her lips moved as steadily as her feet.

Bhen leaned against the coarse, ragged boulder beside him. "I understand we're in a hurry." He breathed deeply and spoke slowly, trying not to sound winded. "But can we not spare a few minutes – at just one of the stones – for me to kiss it and intone the prayers? I've not made the pilgrimage yet. I wish to honor the Father on High."

The Mother paused. Bhen could see her jaw continuing to move. When it stopped, she turned toward him. "That we take the Prophet's Path should be enough this time. We could have taken the main road to Aerndale, and you would have missed this opportunity. Recite the prayers as you climb. He knows your heart. Remember, the Spirit, the Path, is just as important. We climb instead of walk. That is important in itself." She stared harder at Bhen. Her eyes softened. "Do not struggle. Accept that you are on the Path."

*Accept that I'm on the path? I know I'm on the path.*

Bhen took a calming breath. "Yes, Mother." Silently, he admonished himself.

*Let not discomfort nor anger, struggle nor failure sway you from His word.*

She smiled at Bhen before turning away to look up the hill. She took her first step as her prayers started. Bhen looked at the massive rock beside him, the fourth since the bend in the trail. He kissed his fingers and touched the boulder before starting the Fourth Adjuration and continuing up the hill. That Devout Mother Tara placed the Spirit as important as the High Father made her part of a curious, but select minority in the Temple of Truth. The Mother believed it, but rarely brought it up. This intrigued Bhen.

The Grand Temple, the Temple of Raiyam, sat in the city of Aerndale, among the southern foothills of the Coastal Mountains. Travelers and merchants would take the main road with its wide construction and gentle incline to the city. Pilgrims typically took the Prophet's Path, a sometimes steep trail of dirt and rock winding through the grassy, craggy slopes. A thousand years before, it had been used by shepherds watching their flocks. It was the path of the Prophet Raiyam, the first Shepherd of the Temple. He had taken it to speak to his followers outside what was at that time the village of Aerndale.

When they reached the end of the Prophet's Path and emerged onto the main road outside the city gate, both Bhen and the Mother were winded and perspiring. Bhen hated being wet with sweat and looked forward to a bath later. The Mother didn't give them time to rest, pushing on. Bhen struggled to keep up with his teacher and mentor, surprised by her strength and endurance. He brushed off his robes while he picked up his pace.

The city watch allowed them access without paying a toll, as was customary for Temple clergy, and they walked through the large stone archway into Aerndale. All feelings of fatigue and discomfort fled as Bhen saw it for the first time: visible at the end of the street, which led straight from the gate and through the plaza, was the Grand Temple. It was large and beautiful, and Bhen smiled. He felt nearer to Abbyon. Even from this distance he could see the dark rock walls of the original Temple which made up part of the Grand Temple's eastern wall, obscuring the smooth granite there. It was all warm and inviting and larger than the city around it.

The stone-lined streets were well maintained but steep in this small, hillside city, and almost as fatiguing as the Prophet's Path. Still, the Mother did not slow her pace. They arrived at Temple Plaza, filled as expected with merchants and performers, each surrounded by residents and pilgrims. They wove through the crowds and passed Raiyam's Rock. The Mother touched the rock as she passed, placing her fingertips to her forehead, her lips, and her chest afterward. Bhen did the same, glancing at the tablet positioned in front of the rock. He didn't have to read it; he had memorized the inscription years ago at the seminary.

*Before the Time of Order*
*Before the Deum*
*Before the Arcane and Elder Ages*
*Before all*
*Was the One*
*Was the Father on High*

*His Prophet, The First Shepherd, Raiyam*
*Gave his sermons from this rock*
*Outside the village of Aerndale*
*1161 AA*
*520 PTO*

The Devout Mother and Brother Bhen entered the Grand Temple. "Before all," she said, again asking for Him to guide her mind, her words, and her heart.

"Before all," Bhen said, also gesturing.

A few brass floor candelabras provided what little light there was, lending to the sanctuary's mournful mood. The darkness of the granite Temple's interior did not surprise Bhen. Every Temple was maintained so, as was its modest exterior. That he did not feel a sense of awe, a connection to the High Father, confused Bhen. They moved to the front of the sanctuary, near the dais, and pulled out their olive wood beads to pray amid a handful of other faithful followers.

Bhen made his way twice around his prayer beads and was on his third transition when a Devout Mother entered the sanctuary from a side door. Her white robes, trimmed with red, indicated her position as a member of the Shepherd's Council.

"Devout Mother Tara," she said, "we are ready to receive you now."

Bhen's Devout Mother bowed, and they were led to the side door and through several dim passages to an inner chamber. A few high windows provided light in that room, their beams of sunlight illuminating a podium, beyond which were the two elevated wooden stands of the Shepherd's Council. On their benches were six small oil lamps, one for each of the three Devout Mothers and Devout Fathers.

Displayed on the back wall was the eight-foot-high symbol of the church's faith: a shepherd's staff set at an angle with an incomplete circle around its tip. It was made of tulipwood, and barely visible in the dark chamber.

Their escort motioned Bhen and his Mother to the pedestal, moved to the bench of Mothers, and took her seat at the right of the head Mother. The head Mother, at the center of her bench, looked to the bench of Fathers. She received a nod from the head Father and turned toward Bhen and Tara. "Devout Mother Tara, it is good to see you. How is your Spirit?"

"It is well," Tara replied. "May the Spirit be well with you too, Devout Mother Ameyna."

Ameyna strained a smile. "And how did you find the Prophet's Path?"

"I found it nurturing. Such is the Path."

Ameyna moved her left hand ever so slightly. The Mother to her left, and the corresponding Father at his bench, dipped their pens and began to write something down. Neither wrote long but Ameyna waited until they were finished. When their pens were down she continued, "You are here to petition to meet with the Shepherd, is that correct?" Her tone had Bhen wishing for more sunlight.

"That is correct, Mother Ameyna," Tara said.

The center Devout Father spoke. "You believe you had a vision?"

"I did have a vision, Devout Father Sean."

Murmurs rose from both stands as the councils whispered to each other. Mother Tara remained quiet and resolute at the podium. Bhen felt small. He wanted to support Tara, but was uncertain of his place. Never at any point had he expected to be in the Council's presence. And he had certainly never thought he would find himself in a position to be at odds with them.

Mother Ameyna lifted her hands from the bench and the councils quieted. Bhen held his tongue and returned his eyes to Tara.

"Mother Tara," Ameyna said, "the Shepherd is very busy. His mind and his time must not be disturbed for minor matters. You are not the first to arrive claiming to have had a vision."

"Mother Ameyna, Father Sean, Council members, I don't claim to have had a vision. I state emphatically that I've had a vision and that it came from Abbyon, the Father on High. It is of great importance that I meet with the Shepherd."

"Mother Tara," Sean said, "why would Abbyon Himself reach out to you? Why did He not speak directly to the Shepherd, as is customary? Can you see why we're cautious?"

Again, Bhen wanted to speak but remained quiet. *Who knows why he chose Mother Tara? It is not for us to question.*

"Father Sean," Tara replied, "I do not question the High Father's methods or His purpose. They are His alone and above our understanding." The plain-spoken reference to sacred texts struck the Council. Their postures became more rigid than before, and their solemn faces turned dour. Bhen stared in admiration of Tara's faith and strength.

"Mother Tara, you stood as a beacon in this church for years," Ameyna said. "So much so that you were given the opportunity to head the Temple in Delranon. You turned that down. Turned your back on those in that city, turned your back on those who are desperate and in need, to live among soldiers in King Saevar's army. To live in tents and walk in mud. To teach and proselytize to the base, the wicked, apostates and infidels. Those who neither need you nor want to hear His word. You abandoned your calling and lowered your state, yet expect us to believe He granted you vision?"

"Yes, Mother Ameyna," Tara said. "Prayer led me to that position. Prayer led to my vision."

"Do you know how many come to us claiming to have had visions?" Sean asked.

"No," Tara said. "I only know I —"

A door opened near the back of the Council room, and a Sister of the Temple entered. She remained in the shadows, her brown, red-trimmed robes barely visible to Bhen.

"Pardon, Council Mothers and Fathers," the sister said, "but the Shepherd's asked you all to come to his chamber."

"Pardon us, Mother Tara," Ameyna said. "We'll return shortly." Ameyna and Sean stood with the rest of the Council.

"Beg your pardon, Mother," the sister said. "He requested everyone in this room to attend."

Bhen noted the looks of confusion. *The Shepherd? We are to see the Shepherd?*

The Council hesitated at first, before motioning with an open palm for Tara and Bhen to join them. The members whispered with each other as they came together. Bhen overheard parts of their conversations.

"The Shepherd spoke? It's been more than a year."

"Almost two, by my count."

"These are interesting times."

"This Mother's having visions of Abbyon. We have a Mother in Grayfell leading her monastery in physical exercise..."

"I've never had a vision, have you?

"No. So how can this be?"

"...and the Shepherd speaks today. Today. First time in almost two years."

"What in His holy name is going on?"

They were led again through a dim and narrow hallway to a flight of stairs. At the top of the staircase stood a stained oak door. The sister led them through it without hesitation and light once contained by the room flooded into the stairwell.

On the other side of the door were living quarters with the same granite walls as the rest of the Temple; however, here they were whitewashed. Tapestries and artworks hung from hooks or sat upon small tables along the wall. Fragrant, burning incense hung in the air, and the room's light came from open windows and an abundance of lanterns and candles.

Motionless, in a high-backed lounge chair made of stained wood and red velvet, sat the Shepherd. Bhen did not expect the sight. The head of all the church appeared to be on the verge of starvation. His vellum skin and emaciated frame gave the impression of a broken man, not a wise and respected leader. The Shepherd was supposed to be around fifty years of age, but looked closer to ninety. His unadorned white robe weighed on his frail form and his eyes remained shut until the door closed behind the gathered group. When they opened, the lids struggled and hovered halfway.

Behind him stood two priests, the sister who summoned them, and a brother. "Shepherd, all are present," the sister said.

Silence fell and the weight of anticipation rose. The Shepherd's head lolled to one side. It appeared that he lacked the strength to lift it, but eventually he turned to face Bhen and the others.

"It is good," he said, his voice raspy and weak. "The vision – is true."

Everyone gathered touched their forehead, lips, and chest.

"Tara, Bhen," said the Shepherd, "please – to my side."

Tara did as he asked. Bhen looked about, trying to determine if he had heard the words correctly. The Council members turned to him, their faces marked by confusion. Tara, from beside the Shepherd, cleared her throat. Bhen looked at her and she motioned him over. He averted his eyes from the Council and slid from beside them, moving to Mother Tara's side.

They knelt beside the chair. The Shepherd's voice was quiet, but not for secrecy. Its very essence was weightless, and Bhen held his breath, worried the words would be lost to a breeze or even his own breathing. "Ever faithful." He paused to look into their eyes. Bhen felt the hard stare; it stunned him. But he was unafraid, for the eyes showed compassion. "You saw the white crane?"

"Yes, Your Excellency," Tara said.

"Tell me your vision, my lamb."

Tara retold the vision, describing what she had experienced and how she had felt afterward. The Shepherd smiled.

"What does it mean, Your Excellency?" she asked.

"We shall see. To be sure. But I fear. Conflict. Champions."

His eyelids drooped. It appeared sleep had taken him, but he spoke again, pausing for breath, his voice so quiet Bhen was certain the words were meant for their ears alone. "Desert the armor. Discard the shield. Yet save your spear. Struggles come." With that, he reached out and touched their arms. Bhen expected his fingers to be cold, but they were not, and he felt a flush come over him, starting from where the Shepherd's touch alighted.

The Shepherd took two slow breaths and looked at Bhen. "Faithful Bhen, please give me a moment, with your Mother."

Bhen bowed and stood, not knowing what to say. Silently he returned to the gathered group of clergy, avoiding their questioning stares. Tara's ear was close to the Shepherd's mouth and it appeared the two were speaking, as she occasionally turned her face toward him, her jaw moving. Perhaps a minute went by before Tara, on her knees, straightened. She placed her left hand on her heart and bowed to the Shepherd.

The Shepherd took a deep breath and in a raspy voice, said, "Before all…"

"…was the Father on High," all replied.

The Shepherd rolled his head to the other side and closed his eyes. The attending brother and sister ushered the clergy out, sending the group back down to the Council's chamber. No one spoke as they walked down the narrow hall. Bhen was lost in the memory of the meeting and he could not think of anything but the Shepherd's words, his eyes, and the touch of his hand.

An hour later Bhen and Devout Mother Tara had finished speaking with the Shepherd's Council. They stepped out of the Grand Temple and back into the day's fading light. Tara did not speak as they moved through the small city and out the archway's gate. The two started down the main road, passing the hillside path they had taken earlier in the day.

Bhen turned back to look at the archway and up the street to the Grand Temple. The Temple shone brightly to him. He smiled. But the archway seemed smaller now, the street narrower. He looked about. The city itself seemed less grand.

He glanced over his shoulder at the Prophet's Path beside him. Several pilgrims moved along it. He was happy for them. Bhen watched their steps. The dark, churned earth of the path stood out against the light green of the wild-growing grasses and the gray rocks.

Bhen started down the paved road again, following his Devout Mother, wrapped in his thoughts. He understood that what the Shepherd had shared with her alone was not meant for others' ears, but what about the words he had spoken to both of them?

Tara and Bhen were almost at their inn when one of his thoughts turned to a question and became too much for him. "Mother, you did not want to speak of the warning in the presence of others. Why? Do you understand the meaning of his words?"

"No, Bhen," the Devout Mother said. "I do not yet understand what the Shepherd meant."

"Desert the armor. Discard the shield. Yet save your spear? A struggle is coming? Are we to take up arms? Prepare for war?"

"That is not our way."

"I understand that, Mother. But what else could it mean? Why did you not share his words with the Council?"

"I'm not sure, but I had the feeling he wouldn't have spoken so softly if what he had to share was meant for everyone. After all, he had the energy to start the Declaration of Faith loudly enough for all to hear. Perhaps his message pertains to us alone. Perhaps we are not meant to understand it at this time. Its meaning will be revealed when its revealed. Work on your patience with this one, Bhen. Pray on it. The High Father guides not only our hearts and words, but also our..." She seemed to become distracted and did not finish her sentence.

"...minds," Bhen injected. "Yes, Mother. I understand."

Bhen focused on the paved road as they continued toward the inn. He admonished himself for being obstinate.

*Patience, Bhen. Don't let your curiosity get the better of you again. Patience. Patience.*

# CHAPTER SIXTEEN

Page, alone in her room of timber and white plaster, savored the silence and her supper of warm stew. Today's training sessions had been more rigorous than any prior. Hammer had specifically designed them so. He had worked the team physically, and afterward ran them through several sparring matches, first one on one, then four on three, and finally five on two. He had let Page use magic in two of the matches. Page liked the challenges and admired Hammer's adherence to the training regimen. She was particularly impressed at how he had fought on both the teams with the upper hand as well as the outnumbered ones.

The cold bath she had taken afterward had helped her worn muscles recover, but left her chilled. It did not help that her open window let in a soft breeze that blew on her wet hair and the back of her neck, chilling her further. But the window also displayed the fading light of day, and Page had always loved sunsets. They warmed her spirit. The stew warmed her body. Each spoonful reinvigorated. It healed. It comforted. She absentmindedly ran her fingers over the filigreed pommel of her dagger.

*I love my job.*

The arguments started in the room next to hers. Page rolled her eyes and sighed. The squabble interrupted one of the few moments of peace she had been afforded in weeks. For mercenaries such moments were rare, even more so for Page. However, she knew how it all started and couldn't help but enjoy the racket this time. She pushed back from the table and listened.

"Shut up, Axe," Dagger was saying. "I don't know and don't want to hear it."

"There's no proof it's true," Axe said. "Besides, just because he has a cousin who went to the Institute doesn't mean he knows about magic himself. And I bet they don't teach that shit in his *famous* University either."

"Ihgel help me," Dagger pleaded. "Go and argue with Badger. Don't bring that shit here. I'm trying to relax, asshole."

Page had learned that Axe had been second in seniority on the team and second in line behind Hammer. Badger had joined their ranks shortly before Page. He had been placed on the team after the loss of a recruit a few months before. Badger arrived with a long history of military and free company service in Vreland. He'd also been educated in Vreland's well-known Martial University. This made him a threat to the order Axe had once felt.

The other team members told Page that Axe had been throwing his weight around, trying to intimidate the slighter Badger. Badger, on the other hand, met Axe's bluster by casting shade and sowing seeds of doubt in Axe's mind, chipping at his overconfidence. When Page had joined the team things had heated up between the two, as she was a mage and instantly outranked Axe.

"If he's not careful, I'm going to kick his ass when this mission is over," Axe was saying now. "Everyone knows the best free companies come from Haldiland."

"Yeah," Dagger said, "and you know the best individual mercs are Vrelish. You're not going to challenge him, man. Even you have enough brains for that."

"Well, I'm just saying he's full of horse shit. I've never heard of a person being lost to the Abyss because a mage let go of them during a portal."

"I don't know. I don't care. Shut your fucking mouth."

Page stifled a laugh. Badger had checked with her before spreading the portal rumor. *I never thought Axe would buy it,* she thought. *And the dumbass is too proud to ask me about it.*

A stiff shoulder brought Page back to her room and her bowl of stew. She worked her arm in slow circles, massaging the muscle before getting another spoonful of warm potatoes and carrots.

The team had been content to plug along with training while earning their pay, but they all knew it could end any day since Chancellor Sala Nesar was growing visibly frustrated by his inability to locate the rogue general. Over the last five days they had received updates on the hunt, but the best information Nesar had received was a vague direction of "southeast," and that was from King Heselov's personal mage.

One thing that had pleased Nesar was the team's work in the apprehension and elimination of the conspirator Commander Rish Landar. Following that success, Nesar had continued to pay for their services, their room and board at the inn, and their exclusive use of the inn's barn for training. It was apparent that he wanted to keep them close at hand.

Page liked the money flowing in but did not like sitting idly by. Studying her spells and training with the rest of the team helped, but she wanted more to do. Today's hard training session was a good step in taking the team's mind off the wait. Now her muscles were fatigued, and her hand shook while holding the spoon, but she would be stronger and more dangerous tomorrow for it. She broke a roll in half and dipped it into the stew before taking a bite. The freshly baked bread was wonderful, and she took the time to enjoy it. With nothing else to occupy it, her mind quickly wandered again.

The thumping sound was light at first, but it brought Page's mind back to her room. It was louder the second time, and she realized it was someone knocking on a door. She heard a muffled male voice say something. There was a pause, and the process repeated, again getting closer. Page recognized Hammer's voice and pushed her chair away from the small table. She secured her spellbook to her back with its harness and opened the door in time to see Hammer step up to it.

"Quarter hour. My room. Light city kit only," Hammer said. He took a few more steps to his room on the other side of Page's and entered it without another word.

*A quarter of an hour* meant *immediately*, but gave you enough time to grab a few items. Page was practically ready to go. She threw her leather tunic over her head and wrapped her sword belt around her waist. Stepping into the hallway, she closed her door, but paused at Hammer's open door. She waited for Pike, the next teammate to step from his room, to join her, and they both stepped into Hammer's room.

Their team leader gathered several flat sheets of paper and stored them inside his logbook before looking up at the two arrivals. He motioned with a tilt of his head at the bed in the small room as he continued to secure the desk's items in his satchel. Page and Pike stepped to the bed and tilted it on its headboard, so it rested upright against the wall. They finished as the other members of the team streamed into the room. Axe, the last to arrive, locked the door and handed the key to Hammer.

It was a tight fit, even with the bed out of the way. Hammer slung the satchel over his shoulder and conducted a silent headcount as he looked each member in the eye. "The Chancellor's Hall."

"The Chancellor's Hall," Page stated. She stuck her left arm into the center of their group. Hammer grabbed her wrist, and one by one, the other members used one of their hands to grab hold of Hammer or Page. She counted as they did until she was confident the team was all connected. She felt a firm hand grab her left shoulder. Page looked over it into Badger's face.

"Just to be sure," he said.

Page smiled at the joke. She noted Axe's grip tightening onto her forearm, and her smile grew wider. She motioned with her right hand, collapsing her fingers and thumb together as if grabbing something out of the air.

The room spun and grew dark and was light again in the space of a heartbeat.

Chancellor Nesar stood with his back to a long table when the team arrived. Charts and maps lay on the near end, and a small buffet set upon silver trays sat at the far end. The shutters were open to the courtyard below, letting in the cool evening breeze. The fire on the opposite wall glowed warmly, and a dozen or so lanterns helped it provide a welcoming light. Page appreciated the contrast between the room's warmth and the meeting's cold purpose.

"My lord," Hammer said, and the team bowed.

"Hammer, my runner returned only moments ago. You and your team continue to impress. Join me." Chancellor Nesar motioned them over to the near end of the table.

The parchment holding the position of prominence was of Renlar's newly acquired territory, the Duchy of Beckland, the hard-won countryside between the Vaster and Arnse Rivers. Set upon the map near a town identified as Gandleton was a red token with a small pin and pendant atop it.

Hammer lifted his eyes from the map to the chancellor. "The Divide – pardon, Beckland, my lord?"

"Surprised us too. However, it makes perfect sense. He has some knowledge of the area, having fought the Aenduran forces there, and the king's influence there is weakest. We pressed Batal's wife and learned a cousin of hers attained land near Gandleton. A large farm, as I understand it."

"I was under the impression she was unaware of her husband's location," Hammer said.

"She wasn't aware. However, when pressed about connections in Beckland, she readily provided us with this new information."

"Readily?" Hammer raised an eyebrow.

Chancellor Sala Nesar's eyes grinned. Page gritted her teeth to keep from showing her displeasure. Punishing conspirators and traitors was well and good, but to torture and torment innocents, non-combatants, was cowardly.

"May I ask, sir," Hammer said, "how you knew to inquire about Gandleton?"

"That was a time-consuming affair. It appears General Batal did indeed procure a tattoo talisman to hide from our magic. It will protect him from detection for several more weeks. We were, however, able to track his horse. He did not take one from the barrack's stables, nor his own. Instead, he bought two from a breeder outside the city. That was the cause of the delay these past several days.

"Once we ascertained the source, we obtained hairs from the stalls and the last sets of shoes for our scrying spells. While he rides, we cannot detect the horses, but when he dismounts in the evening, we can determine their location. He is not yet to Gandleton but will arrive soon. We must leave in the morning."

"We, my lord?" Hammer said.

"Yes. I will accompany you."

"Sir, the travel conditions will be discomforting. The conditions austere."

"I will manage."

"We suspect he'll be meeting with other conspirators or enemy agents, dangerous persons. It will not be safe for you."

"I will be quite safe, I assure you."

"Sir, with respect, I cannot afford to assign even one of the team to your detail. We don't know yet what we will face." Hammer's voice was blunt, and without the diplomacy it had recently displayed. Page glanced at Badger and the others. Each looked concerned.

The chancellor took a breath and slowly exhaled. "Your concern is appreciated, albeit misplaced." Nesar turned, motioning toward the opposite end of the table and moving his hand back toward Hammer and the team. The platters of food slid along the table as if Nesar's hand had pulled them.

He moved away from the team while Page and the others stared at the trays of food sitting now among the parchments and maps. When Page looked up at Nesar, she found him suddenly accompanied by a monstrous wolf.

The entire team took a step back and reached for their weapons.

"Gods!" Dagger cursed.

The beast growled and bared its teeth. Its shoulders came to

Nesar's waist, and it lowered its massive head, ears and eyes fixed on the team. Drool flowed from its lips, collecting on the stone floor. Adrenalin spiked through Page. She was sure the creature was preparing to lunge at them. No one on the team moved.

Nesar calmly pulled a gold ring from his waistcoat and placed it on his finger. The ring bore the round setting of one trained at the Institute. The chancellor held his hand in front of himself, showing them the rare, blue stone in the setting. Nesar was a member of the Sapphire Order.

Page's attention was no longer on the beast but on the chancellor's ring. *A Grand Master. He hid that well, but why?*

"Now, away," Nesar said, and the beast turned into a mist, evaporating unceremoniously. "I have my own detail, Hammer. Does this convince you now?"

"Please forgive me, my lord," said Hammer.

"I'd have been disappointed if you did not show concern. But let's now get to the plans." He moved to the table and picked up the map of Beckland. "There is a newly built fort along the river less than two days' ride southeast of Gandleton. One of His Majesty's mages was there not long ago. We'll portal there in the morning, secure horses from them, and make for Gandleton."

"How do we coordinate our efforts once we find the general?" Hammer asked.

Nesar did not answer, but turned to the whole of the team. "Gentlemen, it is suppertime. Please partake of the food provided. Hammer, Page, please join me at the far end so we may develop a plan." Nesar grabbed a map and moved toward the far end of the table.

Page turned to Hammer. He raised an eyebrow and tilted his head, motioning to her that they should join their patron.

# CHAPTER SEVENTEEN

The extra day of rest had helped Grimble recover from the week's forced ride, but now he was stiff and eager to move again. The team packed their kits and bedrolls. They were meticulous, but swift from experience. The swish of fabric, jingle of buckles, and occasional squeak of leather were the only noises in the root cellar.

Since the noon meal, a morose mood had fallen among them. Even Kurt had adopted a sullen tone. They were about to cross into a country they had warred with less than a year earlier. During most of that war, Aendura's army had had the upper hand and dealt heavy casualties to the Renlaran forces. No doubt any soldier of Renlar who discovered them would exact some measure of recompense upon Grimble and the team. Capture meant death. A swift one, if they were lucky. The face of each man carried that reality.

Roche, as usual, was first to stand, and he placed his pack near the ladder. Grimble caught him wincing slightly as he set his pack down. As slight as the sign of discomfort was, it appeared the others may have missed it.

The rest of the team were not far behind Roche in preparation and each stood when their kit was ready.

"On me," said Roche.

The team fell in around him for the briefing. They had run through it several times before, making sure everyone knew the orders. This time, however, would be the last briefing before they left. The tension weighed on each man.

Roche spoke. "I can tell that I don't need to remind you of the dangers of this mission. But I know each of you, and I am confident we will be successful in completing it and returning home. This is a good team. We will succeed."

Roche paused and looked everyone in the eye before continuing.

"One more time, gentlemen. We're to interview a potential intelligence source, a high-ranking military officer named 'the Baker.' Our contact in Lagisborg places his authenticity at high. We won't know exactly who he is or what he has to offer until we meet him, but it's deemed important enough to risk our lives and possibly reignite the war. Baz, give me our organization."

"We move as one unit under the guise of a Vrellish group of freelances," Baz began. "We came together solely to answer Norea's call for mercenaries to expand their frontier. Like many other free companies, we've left our old identities behind. We only need to worry about this if we're caught, but our names are now the colors of the clasps on our cloaks." He pointed at his cloak's silver clasp. "Make up whatever given name you want, but we know each other by our colors. *If* we are caught.

"Roche has our papers of travel through what Renlar now calls 'Beckland.' If we need to separate, we'll break into two three-man teams. One will be made of Roche, Kurt, and Grimble. Two is me, Flicker, and Dinger. If we are forced to scatter individually, the mission is aborted, and the rally point is this cabin. To return here from the Divide, travel due east, cross the river, then move north along the river back to the cabin."

"Flicker. Travel," Roche said.

Flicker spoke in his passionless voice. "Travel is west by southwest. This has us passing south of the village of Arhus, which is about halfway to Gandleton. Then we skirt north of the swamp to the east of Gandleton. We will hit the road south of Gandleton where there are two prominent hills in the area. A fallback, 'Oven,' will be set up on the eastern hill, and our basecamp, 'Market,' will be on the western. The target house is the second farmhouse moving west from Market. The houses are separated by a few hundred yards. We stay in the area until the mission is complete. Even after I've seen Market or the Baker's house, we don't portal back to the regiment or any other safe area. We hold our ground. We don't want to create too many ripples, accidentally portal back into an ambush, or surprise locals who will raise an alarm. Once the mission is complete, that's when we can portal out."

"Dinger. Communication."

"Communication is plain talk when necessary, and no Aenduran military shit that could give us away, especially in the presence of others. Hand signals if distance requires more than normal talking voice. If we are discovered by anyone, patrol or otherwise, and cannot slip away, we cooperate and provide our cover story. Kurt will act as our leader in that instance, as he can mimic a Vrellish accent. The rest of us will feign the inability to speak Aenduran and will focus our attention on him. Flicker and Kurt will converse in Vrellish to bolster the story if the need arises. If detained and the command to attack or flee is about to be given, the preparatory command will be 'Wish we had some horses.'

"Once at the Baker's, we will identify him by asking, 'May we use your well?' He will reply with, 'I just watered the animals. Come back in the morning.' We will then touch our hands to our foreheads, and he will rub his hands together. Flicker will make regular reports to regiment nightly using his – magic."

"Kurt. Support."

"Essentially, we are it. However, if it is approved by the watch commander, there is a small team of mages and soldiers available if we get into a situation that requires serious combat support, but the commander's been instructed to consider the political consequences. Flicker must portal to their location at Fort Anjermott, then portal back with them. If he does not have two portals available, that plan is useless, as the mages at Anjermott won't be able to portal to us themselves. Response time for support could be seconds to never. We cannot expect support from the locals, as any Aenduran who remained after the pull-out likely switched allegiance."

"Grimble. Risks and concerns."

"There's the overall danger of being in enemy territory. Then there are the risks associated with the Baker. First, the Baker may have been discovered by Renlar, and there could be an ambush at the farmhouse. The Baker may also be a false spy and may provide misleading information, trying to use us to identify any spies operating in Renlar. Next, our travel papers are signed using a seal over two months old, and Renlar may have different papers now.

"There's information Renlar's found a way to use dogs as roaming patrols and lookouts, much like magically trained birds are used for sending messages. Lastly, the swamp to the east of Gandleton is to be avoided. Locals, ours and Renlar's, say it's cursed. They call it Eblees' Fane. During the war both armies avoided it."

"Excellent," Roche said. "I don't know how much weight I put into the rumors of a cursed swamp, but I agree we avoid it. We'll reassess the plans once set up at the Market. Check each other for noisy buckles and gear issues. I'll check up top and give the word when we're clear." With that, Roche shouldered his kit and started up the ladder.

Each member of the team checked the straps of two or three others and readied themselves at the base of the ladder. Grimble took a deep breath and let it out slowly. One or two others did the same. Now was the time to focus on his job and not the "what if"s. Focusing on the negatives usually led to their realization. He moved the shoulder straps of his backpack to a more comfortable spot and prayed to Abbyon, asking for the team's safety.

The team started toward the ladder and Grimble fell in behind Baz. Flicker, the last man, took one last look around to verify nothing had been left behind and that the latrine had been refilled with dirt. Grimble was halfway up the ladder when Flicker grabbed the side rails. At that moment the hovering light disappeared and lonely darkness reclaimed the root cellar.

On the main level, Roche held open the cabin's front door, and Kurt led the team outside and toward the river. After the extended stay in the small cellar, the cool night air felt good to Grimble. The smell of spring in the forest lifted his spirits and briefly took the stress of the mission from him, leaving only the backpack's weight on his shoulders.

The first quarter moon hovered halfway toward the horizon already, not long from setting in the cloudless sky. What moonlight made its way to the forest floor did so in streaks and splotches. But it was more than enough for Grimble to see Baz in front of him. The broken moonlight danced over the large man's head and down his back, disappearing and reappearing.

The team was experienced. They were quiet. The silence comforted Grimble and he listened for the other sounds of the woods, but the forest itself was quiet too. That discomforted him. His tension returned.

Deeper in the woods an owl called in lament.

Grimble smelled the river before he could see or hear it. Like every other creature on the land, the Vaster River and its banks had its own smell. He had ridden over it during the war, using one of the stone bridges. The smell was the same now as then, and when Grimble was close enough he could tell the river sang the same hushed song, too. It reminded him of the day the regiment had crossed into the Divide during the war.

The team spread out when they arrived at the riverbank. Visible in the silver light was the other side of the river, almost a hundred yards away. They found the boat as described, upside down under bushes along the bank. Grimble helped flip it upright and the team placed it sidelong into the river. The boat was wide-beamed, so they could fit two abreast, but shaped like a canoe. It would take effort to keep it moving in a straight line across the river, but with four of them rowing it could be done.

The team embarked upon the boat one by one and Kurt, the last man, picked up a large, angular stone before he stepped aboard. He tied one end of a cord to the rock and, shortly after they pushed away from the bank, dropped the stone into the deepening water. Roche steered while Kurt gave course corrections and let the cord out as the team made their way across the cold, swift-moving water.

Grimble and the other rowers pulled as hard and as fast as they could, fighting the current without making any undue noise.

Their paddles knifed into the water with precision, lifting clear before bringing them forward again. Dinger made a little noise at the start, but quickly learned the technique.

Before long Renlar was fast approaching, shadows under moonlit branches. The team pulled into a slow-moving pool protected by a downed tree. There wasn't much dry land next to the eddy, and the bank was a steep nine or ten feet high. Grimble and the team disembarked and stood by while Kurt tied the other end of his cord to the stern of the boat. He and Roche tipped the canoe and filled it over halfway with water, turned it upright, and pushed it back into the moving water of the river.

Without a word, Kurt dropped his pack. Grimble watched as he pulled himself up onto the trunk of the downed tree, crawled across it to the level ground above, and disappeared. A few moments later he lowered a rope. One by one, they climbed up the bank. Baz, the last man, brought Kurt's kit with him.

The team paused to check their kits and get their bearings. Grimble thanked Gavel for their good fortune getting across the river and hoped it would continue. They shouldered their packs and made their way to the road that ran parallel with the river. Kurt had reported that the patrols had come through twice the night before and that their horses could be heard long before he had seen them.

The men took the time to drink a little water and eat some of their frontier rations while waiting for the first patrol to pass. The former was refreshing, but the latter was purely out of necessity. They were already past the novelty of the taste and texture.

As Kurt had said, the noise of the patrol announced their presence long before they came into sight. Twenty mounted soldiers moved north along the road. They were disciplined, but their speed indicated that they searched for large groups or precursors of an invasion, not small teams. Two dogs loped along at the front of the patrol. They were not thick-bodied war-dogs, but a trimmer version, and Grimble was glad they were upwind of the team.

The team's maps were accurate, as the land had been part of Aendura less than a year before. This helped them stay on schedule, and a few hours later, they were about seven miles into the Divide.

They were preparing to move around a farmstead community when Kurt stayed Roche. "There are no lights here. None."

Grimble noticed the untended fields; what crops remained were brown from the winter. The team was moving west, generally into the wind, and he should have picked up some scent, but the typical farm smells were subdued or absent. "We can save time cutting through this one," he said.

"My thoughts too," Kurt said.

"Alright," Roche said. "Kurt, take point. We'll follow at a distance but keep you in sight."

With that, Kurt snuck to the front and moved toward the nearest building. The team slunk behind, leaving a gap.

This farming community was comprised of a half-dozen homes spread over roughly a half mile. Grimble took note of the fencing and equipment left behind and surmised that the former inhabitants had been ranchers, raising mostly sheep, from what he could see. The land was eerily quiet. No chicken or geese to raise the alarm, nor any cry of surprise from any other livestock. Something skittered into one of the barns. The hair stood on Grimble's arm, and the others peered about cautiously, looks of concern upon their faces. The land felt dead.

When the trailing team rounded the third house they found Kurt standing in front of it, staring at the ground. He looked to Roche and motioned the group to him.

A human skull lay on its side at Kurt's feet, a section of it cut away. Its jaw was missing. Grimble soon noticed the other human bones and skulls lying about.

"Heh," Kurt said. "Well, these dumbasses missed the harvest festival."

"Watch your fucking mouth," said Baz.

"Not my fault. Everyone was told to leave."

"Easy, you two," Roche said. Baz nodded, but the scowl on his face remained. Kurt raised his eyebrows and showed his palms, pleading innocence.

Many Aenduran families with relatives in the Divide had lost contact with them after the war. Any news, good or bad, was usually welcomed. Grimble continued to look around at the bones. He counted six skulls. Two were smaller than the others. He nodded toward the farmhouse. "Should we see if we can identify the family?"

"No," Roche said. "We don't have the time. I'll make a note of the community on the map and hope the evacuees from this area will be able to identify the family or families. No doubt the place was looted by the soldiers who did this." He looked up at the team, waiting until everyone's eye was upon him. "We knew some families stayed behind. Whether it was because they didn't care who their sovereign was or simply because they weren't going to be 'forced off their land', they made their choice. I don't care if you had family in the Divide or not – save your personal opinions on it all until we're back home. You hear me?"

"Yes, sir," the team replied.

Roche had them move out again, continuing along their prior

bearing. Grimble noted three more skulls before they left the farmsteads behind.

A star streaked northward across the sky.

For the rest of the night, the team moved as quickly as they could. At one point they nearly walked into a guard post set near a crossroads, but thanks to Baz, leading on point, they successfully moved around it. A little while later, walking around a working farm, Kurt offered to grab some eggs from a chicken coop – something to give them a break from the pemmican. Roche nixed the idea quickly, stressing that the team didn't need to raise any suspicions.

Soon the moon had set. Whether in the open or in the woodlands, the lack of moonlight made their passage harder to detect, but it also required them to take trails and roads when traveling through forested areas. To risk off-road travel when they could not see would make them as noisy as a herd of cows.

Roche halted the team on the side of the road for another check, bringing them into a circle around him. Grimble knelt and faced outward like the others. He glanced skyward briefly and noted the stars and constellations above, before turning his attention back to his watch area. By his estimation, they had an hour, maybe two, before the eastern sky began to brighten for the dawn.

"Flicker," Roche said, "did you memorize an Eye?"

"Yes."

"Good. Find us a place to camp." Roche moved to Flicker's spot and Flicker moved into the center of the team. As he knelt, the mage covered his eyes with his left hand and held his right hand cupped in front of him, as if it were holding something. He opened his hand and moved it forward, as if turning loose a bug or bird. Then he dropped his arms to his side and kept his eyes closed. He didn't move for several minutes. Grimble continued to scan the area in front of him, occasionally checking on Flicker and his other teammates. It was dark and he could not see much.

"On me," Flicker said. He stood and moved further down the road. One by one the team followed, Roche bringing up the rear. Flicker moved to the south side of the trail and studied the woods for a few seconds before stepping off the road. The team followed single file for more than fifty yards before the underbrush cleared, and the hardwood gave way to tall pines. They moved up a gentle slope, which leveled off, and the pines began to give way again to hardwood. Flicker led them to an area near some undergrowth.

"Camp here," he said. "I'll set up a Ward, but we should also keep an eye on our path at the top of the hill back there."

"Kurt," Roche said, "take the first watch on the hill. The rest of you, cloaks only, no bedrolls."

Kurt moved to take his watch shift while everyone else found a spot of ground and removed their packs. Roche and Baz met off to the side while the other three choked down the pemmican and hard biscuits, water helping the latter go down a little easier. Grimble watched Roche working with Baz while he ate.

The sun was up when Grimble went to relieve Kurt at the watch post on top of the short hill. He could see the sign of the team's passage earlier, and he followed it toward where the slope started down. With the sun up, he expected to spot Kurt immediately, but could not find the man. He knelt and scanned the base of the trees, the branches above, and the scattered litter along the ground. Something was out of place to Grimble's right, but he could not identify what it was. Not wanting to get locked into a bad search, he dismissed it and turned his head to search the left side again.

A few seconds later a small twig whizzed over Grimble's head and landed where he was looking. Grimble turned back to the right. It took him a few seconds to catch Kurt's hand poking out from the ground beside some downed branches. It was closed, its thumb poking out between the middle and ring fingers. Grimble smiled, and Kurt emerged from a depression in the ground. Leaves and pine needles fell to the ground as he lifted himself up. He motioned Grimble over, and the two sat and whispered.

"Something seemed out of place," Kurt said, "didn't it?"

"Yeah, but I couldn't see you. Good job."

"Next time, trust your instinct."

Grimble wondered what had caught his attention, but it eluded his conscious mind. He dropped it from his thoughts. "I'm your relief."

"I hope you don't mind if I hang here for a little while longer. This is a nice spot. Peaceful. Besides, I'm not tired yet and not really looking forward to my dinner of greasy goo and tooth-killers. I've got new respect – or maybe it's sympathy – for frontier folk. They're a hard lot. You'd think they'd pray to Gavel to come up with some better food. He's a bastard making them eat that crap."

"It is nasty," Grimble agreed. "It's taught me to never complain about the food in the regiment again. Still, this frontier stuff is giving us what we need – better than starving. I can't believe you thought about stealing some eggs from one of the farms here."

"Relax. I'd have made it look like a fox or other predator got into the hen house. They wouldn't have been looking for human thieves. I promise you that."

"We'll be fine eating the pemmican."

"You, maybe. Not me." Kurt smiled.

"I guess your job in the Ravens never called for embracing the misery. You're far more into taking risks than most soldiers."

"I embraced enough misery before the army. Don't plan to embrace any more. Not going back to —" His face relaxed, and his eyes got a faraway look. He blinked. "Enjoy every moment, take what I can, and beat the unbeatable. No more embracing shit."

"Is that why you fuck with Flicker?"

"That's more curiosity. But, yeah, it's fun too." He smiled again.

"And the horse race?"

"You're a bastard. Hoped to add beating you to my list."

Grimble looked at Kurt in confusion. "What?"

Kurt chuckled low. "You're the best rider I've heard of."

"You're full of shit." Grimble picked up a leaf and started tearing it into pieces.

"No, seriously. You've quite a reputation in the regiment, enough so others in the army have heard of you. They may not know your name, but they've heard of 'that rider in the 209th.' I planned to beat you and add that to my list of accomplishments – the 'Immortal Labors of Kurt Melovet.' Not one of the grander ones, but something to brag about all the same."

"Immortal Labors?"

"That's what I call them now. It may change when I pay the bards to write my song."

"Okay, I'll bite. What amazing tasks have you performed?"

Kurt smiled and counted on his fingers. "Let's see. I beat the prize bull at Delranon's Harvest Festival in a tug-of-war. I've walked on water. Caught lightning in my hand. Spent the night in a coffin filled with venomous snakes —"

Grimble's face shifted slowly from amusement to incredulity.

"I'm serious, you little shit. I beat Roche in a wrestling match. Climbed the Spire's Glass Wall with bare hands and feet. Kissed a Devout Mother full on the lips…"

Grimble threw the leaf away. "Now you're pushing it. There's no way."

"I did. Flicker was there for that one, ask him. Best, and worst, kiss of my life."

"Walked on water?"

"Did that one at the end of the war, when the king abandoned this land to our enemy."

"Abandoned? King Saevar would never have abandoned his people. Watch your tongue, Kurt."

"Don't tell me you're still devoted to king and country? Gods, one Baz is enough."

"Don't tell me you believe any of the rumors," replied Grimble. "That the Spire threatened to leave Aendura for Renlar if we didn't give them the Divide, their way of balancing power in the region; or that the king's family was threatened by an assassin who ordered King Saevar to pull out of the Divide. Those stories are nonsense."

Kurt smiled, but it quickly faded. "You need to wise up, trooper, or you'll suffer horribly when reality hits you."

"My eyes are open. I see what's before me. I'm not as naïve as you think."

"You need to see the unseen, hear the unspoken. The deeper you are in His Majesty's work, the more vulnerable you are."

"We lost. Plain and simple. We only thought we were winning the war. Renlar's new offensive, supported by Noreas and free companies, was more than we could handle. Why else would we sue for peace and abandon this land? Why lose and ruin so many lives?"

Kurt rubbed his chest, looked back toward the rest of the team, and turned toward Grimble, a dark expression upon his face. "You're deep in this now. You should know better the lay of the land."

This was the first time Grimble had seen such a look of resolution on Kurt's face.

"Every coin you earn," said Kurt, "every loaf you eat, takes a toll greater than money alone. Not everyone shares our admiration for the king. Yeah, you heard me. Now, I admire him, but not the same way you do. Takes guts to make the sacrifice he did. The war cost the king dearly. We outnumbered Renlar's military and our soldiers were more skilled, so it was expected to be a short war. As Renlar continued to fight for access to the ocean and the war dragged on, levies were called. The people were burdened with more taxes to pay for it all.

"You're right that Renlar received aid from countries to the south and added manpower from Noreas and mercenary groups, but we didn't learn of that until later. Certain noble families began to use the length of the war against the king. Whisper campaigns started as a means to undermine His Majesty's authority."

Grimble could not believe what he was being told. He had never heard of such things being cast about. "Like what?"

"One rumor said King Saevar was going mad and carelessly throwing lives into the war, hurting the western and northern duchies the most, rendering them susceptible to attack from the wildlands and even Haldiland. Another claimed he levied the western earldoms most in order to deplete them of healthy men,

239

making it easier for him to swoop in and remove the duke and earls, replacing those nobles with members of his own house. There were others, but those two were the strongest." Kurt paused and tilted his head, as if listening for something. He dismissed it almost as quickly and continued.

"We suspect they all started in Vasterland. That duchy has been a thorn in the royal family's side for two generations. You've been spared the trouble of knowing this because you're in the army and not forced like the others to pay more taxes, to see your son conscripted against his wishes, to hear the rumors. If it wasn't bad enough, our spies to the south reported Noreas was building up its military in earnest. Working to make it larger than mere support for Renlar."

"No," Grimble said. "They're calling for mercenaries to help them push farther into the frontier, to increase their land. It's not for war. We may not be allies, but we trade with each other. They have no need to attack us."

"You only hear what they want you to hear, damn it," Kurt said. "Listen for what's not spoken openly. Our spies report shiploads of flax and linen arriving, an increase of ore mining, and citizens along the Arnse River forced to store barrel upon barrel of provisions. These, among others, are not signs of a desire to push into the frontier. These are signs of a plan to cross the Arnse and invade Aendura. Probably by the Gathering Season or perhaps Wanting, trying to take advantage of our weakened state."

Grimble looked doubtfully at Kurt again. "Probably false rumors or grandiose pub talk."

"I hope you're right. But I'm not betting my life on it. His Majesty sacrificed this land, and yes, many lives, in the hopes we could rebuild and recover before Noreas launches an attack. He's also counting on Renlar not permitting an army to march through its newly acquired land. My bet is the king hopes Renlar will weaken or possibly turn back the Norean forces before they try to cross the Vaster River into Aendura."

Grimble thought about it all for a minute. "But our people would never tolerate an invasion. If we'd stuck out the Two Rivers War and were then attacked by Noreas, there would have been support for the defense of the homeland. No family would have denied the call to arms."

"You're right, but if our forces had been depleted or greatly weakened winning the Two Rivers War, the horns calling our people to arms would have rung across empty fields and shaken empty beds." Kurt paused a moment. "Then there's the politics of the court. Let's say we continue to fight against Renlar, and we win; and then we win the war with Noreas. Somehow we survive the attack with a stalemate or even manage to defeat their forces. Aendura would be weak and practically helpless. The king's enemies in court would seize any opportunity they could to usurp his crown."

"If what you say is true," Grimble said, "I can't trust anyone. We could be left behind out here, or return after a successful mission and find ourselves a pawn in some game of the court."

"You can trust the men fighting beside you. You can trust us. I care more for you five than I do this mission or the Baker. I'll abandon it before I see any of you sacrificed. You, me, and the others, we're all going home. I wouldn't trust the nobles. Fuck them. They don't care about us. And fuck this mission. I won't leave you behind. You can hope the king is doing what's right for Aendura, but if I were you, I'd be ready to drop the mission and save your skin and mine if the weather changes."

"Still, doing something wrong for the right reason is

dishonorable. He shouldn't have abandoned his own people. We should have fought 'til the end."

"Open your eyes," Kurt said. "You shed that cloak of innocence a week ago. You're deep in the shit now."

"What?"

"You've invaded a foreign land. You're on your way to meet a spy in the hopes of gathering information to help our country and hurt his. You're doing wrong for right here. You, my friend, are being dishonorable. *You* are the 'bad guy' now." With that, Kurt took a look around and slowly got up. "Tastes worse than the pemmican, right? Don't worry. Unlike pemmican, it gets easier the more bites you take." He walked toward the camp.

Grimble sat stunned for a few moments. Then he returned his stare to the woods around him and back down the path to the day camp. He would wait until he was back at the camp before thinking about Kurt's revelation again. He did not want to be distracted.

The time passed more quickly than Grimble expected, and it was before noon when Baz relieved him. He found everyone asleep when he returned. Roche stirred and lifted his hood high enough to see it was Grimble approaching, dropping it right after to hide his eyes from the daylight. By his actions it seemed Roche was preparing him to become a sergeant. But Grimble could not get over how efficient and observant Roche was.

*How could I ever be as good a leader as him?*

Grimble set his pack for a pillow and wrapped himself in his cloak, covering his eyes like everyone else. He wanted to think some more about the king intentionally sacrificing lives and allowing land to fall into the hands of the enemy. But he felt himself melt into the ground as his body relaxed. Sleep overtook him, sending his mind from thought to dream.

# CHAPTER EIGHTEEN

Shortly before dusk, the team readied themselves for the next night's travel. They weren't far from the town of Arhus and would need to take care while skirting it before continuing their westward journey. Although they were glad to see the warm day end, Grimble noticed the overcast sky through the canopy above, as well as the birds moving into the brush and lower branches of the trees. He smelled the air. It didn't smell like rain, but he had a feeling it was coming.

*Probably not going to see the stars tonight.*

He reached deep into his pack and removed the small brass box holding his compass needle, placing the box in a pouch on his belt. Once the straps were tied down again, Grimble slung his pack.

The team made one last attempt to return their camp to its prior condition before heading back to the road. Roche pulled out a lacquered wood box, a little bigger than the heel of a man's boot, hinged on one side. He flipped it open, revealing his own dry compass.

Roche took the team farther south, dipping even farther away from Arhus than they had expected, as a new farming community sat along the route they had planned to take. Once the team had moved around that community and a few outlying homesteads on the outskirts of town, they were free of the influence of Arhus. Occasionally a dog barked or bayed in the distance, but it was always too far to concern them. The men traveled in the open now, paralleling the road as it made its way westward. They stayed about thirty yards off the road, but kept it in sight.

The thunder of hooves sounded long before an approaching group of horses could be seen. Kurt gave the sign and each man found a ditch, tree, or another means to hide or disguise himself.

It was a mounted patrol of six soldiers. Thin clouds collected most of the moonlight, which made it difficult to get a good look at them as they rode by, but two of the riders wore uniforms or armor different than the others. The six riders all focused on the road. In contrast to the patrol the team had seen along the border, no dogs accompanied these soldiers. They passed the team and continued east toward Arhus. The sound of their horses' hooves was a memory when Roche gave the signal to move again.

Grimble remembered a wooded area on the map that gave way to the large swamp west of Arhus. They planned to move beside the road, using a bridge to cross the swamp's river, and afterward hike the edge of the swamp as they moved southwest. They were inside the woods and making good time when Roche paused and raised his nose to the air. Grimble sniffed and caught it too – rain. He knew the sound of rain would hide what little noise they made, but would do the same for others along the road. The team would be in danger of running into a patrol or guard post before they could detect it.

Roche sent Kurt to lead the team again and ordered the pace doubled. They hastened along the road for a mile or more before flashes in the sky heralded what would soon follow. Another two miles later, the wind picked up and the temperature dropped. The team slowed. The tops of the trees, some with leaves, others budding, whipped one way before snapping back as the wind set the music for the dance. Percussive thunder, deep and snapping, accompanied it. The flashes brightened.

Kurt turned to check on the team, and Roche waved his arm in a circle before leading them off the road. Grimble removed his kettle helmet from his back, setting it upon his head. Dinger and Roche did the same. The deluge started, and the men found a place to sit, huddled close to each other, before the ground was soaked.

"We'll wait out this wave," Roche said, "and hope it lightens up so we can move again. We need to be on the other side of the swamp by midnight."

The rain drenched them, soaking through their wool cloaks and their gambesons within minutes. It was uncomfortable, but no one wanted to hear a complaint.

Grimble made the discomfort a game in his head and thought of other things to keep his mind off the rain. He reached into his pack and drew out a few hard biscuits. He set them in his cup and let the rain run off the front of his helmet into it. Placing the cup under his bent knees, Grimble wrapped his cloak around his legs again and set to refilling his canteen.

The downpour continued for an hour, maybe more, coming in waves with the wind. Grimble ate his partially reconstituted biscuits in the lulls. A few others followed suit.

Kurt was the first to speak, his voice ever so light. "My father wanted me to fall into his line of work, but that life wasn't for me. I hated it."

There was a pause.

Dean Radt

"What's your father do?" Dinger said.

"He's a fisherman," Kurt said, "but I can't stand getting wet. I showed him."

The rain continued.

Time slowed. It tick-ticked with each drop upon their cloaks and helmets. It trickled down the tree trunks and through the leaves of the forest floor. They sat and bore what the clouds loosed upon them, left with the reflections and haunting memories that minds replay when given the opportunity.

Roche's voice brought Grimble from his thoughts. "It's slowing down. We need to push the pace when we get going."

"That wasn't so bad," Dinger said. "Stood on guard post all night through worse showers."

"That's all you got?" Baz scoffed. "Let me know when you've spent two days submerged in a swamp with nothing but your head and hands out of water. Then you can talk about bad conditions."

"Please," Kurt said. "Gentlemen, neither of you have anything on me. It rained for fourteen days and nights on one of my missions. I had nothing but a nightshirt on. I was so wet by the sixth day that the nightshirt dissolved, and I was covered in moss from head to toe." He spread his hands about. "I became part of the very ground around me."

"Right," Dinger said, his eyebrows peaked.

"I do not jest, my thick friend. The only reason I stand here before you is that I was harvested to repair a patch on a farmer's roof. Once I was cut free, I jumped up, completed my mission, and made it back to barracks by the end of the next day. I hear there's a farmer in Haldiland who's mocked by his neighbors for going on about the moss monster that nearly attacked him."

"You're full of shit," Dinger said.

"Are you calling me out? I have a permanent green spot on my scalp from the ordeal." Kurt moved his hair about, searching with his fingers.

"There's no way." Dinger looked at the others, but received no support.

"I can suffer more than any man. It's what I thrive on. It drives me. My very nature is such that hardship seeks me out. In fact, the rain doused me twice as much as you just now."

"Sure."

"I'll bet a dula I have twice as much water in my boot as you do. Your choice, left or right."

"Dula? Let's make it another crown. A crown calls you out. Left boot."

"Alright, you first," Kurt said as he stood up.

Dinger remained seated and smirked. He carefully removed his left boot. "No. Together."

Kurt leaned back against the tree behind him and gently removed his left boot. Together the men grabbed their heels and slowly turned the boots over at the same time. A trickle ran out of Dinger's boot, perhaps enough to fill the bottom of a small cup. Water poured free from Kurt's, gushing onto the ground in front of him. The boot held what appeared to be over a pint of rainwater.

For a few seconds everyone simply stared. Grimble wouldn't have been surprised if a fish had fallen out at some point.

"I'll collect when we get back to Anjermott," Kurt said, putting his boot back on his foot.

"Enough fun, people," Roche said. "Let's get moving."

Dinger, putting his own boot back on, stared at Kurt. "You pissed down your leg."

"I'd like to see you prove that," Kurt replied. "But don't play if you're not ready to play dirty."

A drizzle continued as they left the wooded area and moved around the swamp. Their waterlogged gambesons and cloaks weighed on them, but the team moved on at a slow jog. They were fortunate that the rain seemed to keep other travelers off the road. This made it easier to cross the hundred-foot-long bridge running over the swamp's river, and they didn't have to dive out of sight once while running parallel with the road.

They had recently left the road and were making their way around the west side of the swamp when the rain stopped and clouds broke, revealing patches of the night sky. Grimble looked to the stars when he could and realized they were a few hours from sunrise. Roche kept them moving. Breaks, what few they got, were short, and they arrived on the eastern hill – their fallback location, 'Oven' – about an hour before sunrise. The hill showed signs that a fire had moved up its east side, the one facing the swamp, sometime near the end of the war a year earlier. They were able to find an area where the underbrush was not burned away and stored a couple of knives and some rations in a hole the team quickly dug. They marked the location by cutting two notches into a low branch on a nearby tree.

Not wasting any time, they moved as quickly as they could across Gandleton's southern road and up the more densely wooded western hill, the one they called 'Market.' The town was two miles north of their position and well out of sight, but the team took no chances and kept low and quiet.

The sky began to brighten as they found a flat spot near the hill's crest. It was out of sight from the road to the east and the farms to the west. Flicker complained that the area had low vigre, but he set up his Warding spell all the same. Roche and Kurt left the team to get a look over the farmsteads on the western side.

Everyone else worked to move branches, laurel bushes, and other materials to help hide the camp from anyone straying too close. After that they dug their sleeping trenches, their "spider holes," and set up a watch schedule. Then those not on watch settled in for some wet but much-needed sleep.

Everyone was up a few hours later. Wet clothes and armor did not lead to deep sleep. They kept their conversations to whispers, knowing voices traveled far. Grimble was spreading out his kit, drying it, as he saw Kurt preparing to leave. He remembered Roche had ordered him to confirm the house's location, get a lay of the land, and check for any indication they were headed into a trap. Kurt was to return mid-morning the next day.

The scout stripped out of his wet clothes and lay them to dry on the low branches of a laurel bush. This was the first time Grimble had seen him without his shirt. Like so many other soldiers and troopers, Kurt's body was lean and hard. He did not have the large build and muscles of Baz, but Grimble could tell the mouthy rascal was fit and powerful. The tattoos and scars along his arms were nothing new, but the whipping scars on his back and the dark red tattoo encircling his midsection were a surprise. The tattoo, an unbroken, braided rope, wrapped its way around his body below his pectoral muscles. The ink looked new and wet and seemed to shimmer when the sun hit it.

Kurt pulled a dry shirt over his head and started pulling up his pants. Grimble looked at Dinger, who shrugged. A glance at Roche caught a subtle shake of the head and slight wave of the hand.

Grimble raised an eyebrow at Roche. All he got in return was a mouthed *Don't ask*.

Kurt pulled on his boots, grabbed a small pouch from his

pack, and with a nod to Roche, left Market. Roche spoke to Grimble and Dinger before they could say anything. "One day he may tell you about it, but until that time it's not my place to explain. And don't ask him, either."

"Yes, sir." They went back to work, shaking their heads.

The weather was favorable, and the team used it to dry out as much of their equipment as they could. They dried and oiled, polished and sharpened in preparation for what may come. Flicker's nose was in his book. Baz strung the team's second bow and opened the bamboo tube holding the arrows, checking each one.

Grimble was turning his gambeson over to let the sun dry the other side when he was reminded of the soldiers on horseback the night before. He went back to oiling his blades and turned to the group. "Did you notice the two soldiers riding with the Renlar patrol last night?"

"Yeah," Dinger said, "the helmet silhouette was different, but it was too dark to get a good look at their armor."

"Norean," Baz said. He placed the arrows back in the tube and recapped it.

"You sure?" Grimble asked.

"Yeah, we scouted and ambushed a group of them during the war. I recognized their helmet. It's like ours, but the brim flares out farther in the back and the front has no brim. They have a visor there that slides down to cover most of the face when they fight."

"Lose some vision, but get better protection," Dinger said. "I think I'd prefer being able to see."

"Me too," Baz said. "But they use it to its full advantage. We were clearing the field of battle after our attack and several of their wounded popped up when we got close to them – looked like they rose from the dead. They could watch us through the visor slit and we couldn't see if they were alive or dead. Then *snap*, they sit up or jump up and run a sword or spear through the nearest guy. Trying to kill at least one more of us before succumbing to their own injury. They took out quite a few infantry that way and made the others think they were zombies or demons from the Abyss."

"Shit," Dinger said, his eyes wide. "You mean the rumors were true? Noreans refuse to be taken prisoner?"

"I don't know if it's the gods they worship or their culture, but what you heard weren't rumors. Those bastards fight to the end."

"How did you search for teammates and survivors?" Grimble asked.

"The 108th Infantry had the most encounters with them. I watched the battalion send teams onto the field after an engagement with Norean soldiers. Those teams ran spears through every single dead and wounded Norean before litter teams could collect our wounded. The 108th continued to lose men. Some bled out. Some were killed while dispatching the Noreans."

Dinger's face reddened and he glared at the ground before looking up at Baz. "What sick gods do those fuckers worship?"

"The Lightbringer, or something like that. The Church of Light. I don't know all the gods' names."

Grimble spoke up. "Eblees – he's the one they call the Light or the Lightbringer. They also worship Zebul, Ashmedai, Aszag, Sheroth, and, uh, Gresle."

Flicker continued reading, but the rest of the team stopped what they were doing and looked at Grimble.

"What?" he said.

"T'Abyss! How do you know all that?" Dinger asked.

"School. And I asked our town's priest, Brother Loben, about them after Temple one day."

"You're not a Norean spy, are you?" asked Baz. The large man stared at Grimble with intent. Grimble wondered if he should have kept his mouth closed.

But Baz broke into a wide grin.

"You're a dick," Grimble said.

Baz slapped him on the shoulder and laughed as loud as he dared. "Just giving you Kurt's ration of grief, brother. The poor guy's not here to dispense it himself."

"Blessed shit! Who knew you had a sense of humor? You're an asshole, man." Grimble's smile grew as the stress fled. Dinger and Roche grinned. Flicker continued to read.

"Well," said Baz. "What can you tell us about their gods, Grimble?"

"Not a lot. I don't remember what each god patrons, but their virtues are things like confidence, ambition, power, fortune, uh… strength. Brother Loben said the southern gods admire displays of individual greatness. Rise to the top. Be the best. No loyalty is expected in their chain. If the community, or a member of the community, sees a leader as weak, they are expected to challenge them, to kill them. Supposedly they believe that's the best way to grow a strong nation."

"The biggest asshole becomes the leader. Got it," Dinger said with a smile.

The team let out little laughs. Even Flicker smiled from behind his book.

Grimble sheathed his knife and sword and turned to Roche. "Hey, is Kurt going to need relief?"

"No," Roche said. "None of us are capable of doing that job.

Even you with your hunting background can't do what Kurt's doing."

"He can be a pain in the ass," Dinger said, "but he gets shit done, doesn't he?"

"You have no idea," Baz said. "The man can do some unbelievable things. And some amazingly stupid things, too. He had me nail him into a coffin full of diamond-skins, rattle-tails, and other venomous snakes. Whole crowd of folks as witnesses. I opened it up the next morning, and out he pops like he'd come back from a holiday. He won a small fortune on that bet."

"That really happened?" Grimble said. "I only half believed him when he told me that. He told me all about his 'Immortal Labors.'"

"What did he tell you?" Baz said.

"Well, he said he beat Roche in a wrestling match."

"We don't talk about that," Roche said. "Ever."

Grimble and Dinger looked at each other. Grimble continued, "He said he beat a bull in a tug-of-war."

"Heard about that one," Baz said. "But I wasn't there."

"Kissed a Devout Mother on the lips."

Flicker chuckled and looked up from his book. "Yeah, I was there for that one. I thought he was going to die or be committed to the Abyss, but she slapped him, then smiled and walked away."

"*What?*" said the others.

"It's a true story," Flicker said.

The rest of the team looked at each other, trying to figure out how such a thing could be done without some form of holy retribution or cursing of the soul. Grimble and Dinger shrugged at each other with crooked smiles and resumed caring for their gear. Silence fell again as everyone went back to their tasks.

When they were done with their own kits, they worked together to take care of Kurt's.

Even though they were all awake that night, they once again set a series of watches, allowing folks to get some rest. When it was Grimble's turn, he paid attention to the sound of the wildlife in the area while he ate his pemmican and hard biscuits. The animals were cautious about their presence, but not alarmed. He hoped it meant they occasionally ran across humans, but that the hill was not a frequently hunted area. It would be unfortunate if a local hunter stumbled upon them.

The next morning most were out of their spider holes, enjoying the daylight. The trees' shadows were short by the time the Ward alerted them to someone's approach. Kurt walked up to Market using trees and undergrowth to hide his approach as much as possible. None of the team heard him until he was practically inside the camp. His eyes were red and he held a bundled cloth in his hands.

"Morning, all," he said. The group nodded at him and smiled at his safe return.

"Alright, give me the report," Roche said.

"We were given good information on the farmhouse. It is the second house and is as described, wattle and daub, small, with only one floor, doors in the front and back." Kurt scraped a bare area on the forest floor and used his finger to sketch the house. "Windows on each side. The Baker's there, or at least someone matching his description is there. Didn't see or hear anyone else at the house. He stayed inside most of the time, shutters open during the day and closed at night. He comes out to chop wood, gather water, and care for his two horses, which are in a small, three-sided barn near the house, on the west side." Kurt added the barn to his diagram.

"The house faces north, with a short rock wall around it. The farm fields are to the west and north, and wooded areas on the south and east side come within ten yards of the rock wall. We should be able to approach out of sight."

"So, we're good for tonight?" Roche asked.

"Yes."

Roche looked at the bundle in Kurt's hands. "What else do you need to report?"

"Oh. Right. I know we're tired of that frontier crap – thought the team would enjoy something different." With that, he gently lowered the bundle to the ground and opened it, revealing eight brown eggs.

"I ordered you not to do that. It's going to raise suspicions."

"Relax, I made it look like a raccoon took 'em."

Roche's anger did not diminish. His eyes were locked on Kurt in a manner too familiar to Dinger and Grimble. They became nervous themselves.

"This will raise morale," Kurt said. "It'll give us all a boost before the negotiations. The farmer will never know."

"You'd better be right," Roche said.

Kurt set about digging a fire hole and a connected air tunnel. Before long, he had a hot, practically smokeless fire burning. When he had enough coals in the bottom, he stopped feeding the fire and placed a layer of dirt over the coals. He put the eggs in the hole, covering them with leaves and more dirt.

Half an hour later, the eggs were dug up, and the men enjoyed their first hot meal in almost a week. It even made the hard biscuits and pemmican tolerable. After eating, they all got some sleep while continuing the watch, in preparation for the coming night.

A few hours before sunset, Roche brought them together again. "Grimble and Dinger, you're both coming as far as the base of the hill. Kurt will show you the holding area for the man on close support. Grimble, you're it tonight. Dinger, you get back up here right after and keep watch on Market."

Dinger and Grimble nodded.

"Remember, Flicker and I are the Baker's contacts for this. Baz, you're the watch from inside the house, Kurt the watch outside. Kurt, if things go bad, get inside with us if you have time, or tap the house with a rock or arrow and get back to the close support man right away. If we hear something impact the door or shutters, Flicker will portal us to the close support location. We'll then move to Market and reassess the situation. If things are bad enough that we need to abort, we will portal to Anjermott from Market. Close support is there if we need extra manpower at the farmhouse or Market, but you are not to close in on the house unless you get word from one of the four of us in person or by a spell.

"If Market is compromised, Market watch links up with close support and the two of you get to the western stone wall at the rear of the farmhouse. Kurt will link up with you once he sees you by the wall. We'll assess if extraction or relocation is necessary."

Roche paused, but no one had any questions. He continued. "Flicker will communicate with regiment at the end of each session, but we will also keep written notes, for more detailed items and as a backup. The papers will be placed in this satchel, which will stay at Market until we leave." Roche held up the brown leather haversack and handed it to Dinger.

"If we need serious help," he went on, "Flicker will portal to regiment and return with a small backup team, but they will only come if the highers deem it necessary and prudent. If all goes well, in a few days we extract from this site with Flicker and portal directly back to regiment. Understood?"

Roche received a circle of nods and "Understood"s.

With that, the team made their way to a spot near the bottom of the hill, less than a quarter of a mile from Market. It was an hour before dark, so they were able to negotiate the way without difficulty. Two downed trees provided a perfect blind at Kurt's designated spot for the close support. Grimble made himself as comfortable as he could among the trunks and Dinger moved back to Market.

Kurt got Grimble's attention again. "Listen for our signal when we return." He and the other three moved west into the woods and disappeared.

Hours went by. The sun was long below the horizon and the moon was past its zenith. Other than several deer and a few small animals in the silver light of the gibbous moon, Grimble's post saw no activity. He continued to find ways to keep his mind focused on the surroundings, while listening out for Dinger at the top of the hill and the rest of the team several hundred yards to the west.

A dog barked somewhere between Grimble and the team. It was the alert bark dogs give to their pack when they notice something and want to draw the others' attention. The sound was in the distance and did not stop for several minutes, but it didn't seem to move. Wherever the dog was, it was not chasing anything.

Many more minutes passed, and Grimble tensed as he heard something approach from the south. He silently drew his sword and waited. Before long, Kurt's cricket chirps sounded from the west. Grimble gave the response. Roche came out of the darkness, followed by Flicker and Baz. Kurt brought up the rear. It was hard to see, but the first three appeared angry. Kurt's visage was less tense.

"Everything okay?" Grimble whispered.

"It's not my fault," Kurt said. "It's not."

They made their way back to Market and settled in. The five who had returned to camp took time to eat some of their rations. Dinger, too, seemed to notice the tension among the four who had been to the farmhouse.

"You know what would taste good right now?" Baz said.

"Don't," Kurt said.

"Some eggs."

"It's not my fault. Besides, the dog's not out there looking for people, he's on the watch for a raccoon or some other animal."

"We were sent off the game path and into briar patches and worse."

"How was I to know?"

"Shut it, you two," Roche said. "Stay focused on the mission. We'll deal with this when we get back home." He looked directly at Kurt. "Disobey my orders again, and I'll have Flicker send you back to a waiting tribunal. You hear me?"

"Yes, sir."

"Other than that," Roche said, "we made progress tonight. The Baker appears to be legitimate. He was as nervous about us as we were about him. Took an hour before we were comfortable with each other."

"He doesn't trust us," Baz said. "He didn't want Flicker beside you at the table."

"I don't think we'll need magic to determine if he's telling the truth. He's a soldier and a plain speaker, one of Renlar's highest-ranking generals. I'm getting a pretty good read on him."

"Did he reveal what this is all about yet?" Baz asked.

"Not much. He's playing his cards close to the chest right now. I get the feeling it's about Noreas, possibly confirming what our spies have already told us: that Noreas plans to invade. He doesn't want to betray his country, but he needs to tell us something important.

"What I found intriguing is that he's not interested in money or an Aenduran title. In fact, his first option is to return to Renlar, and if that can't happen, he wants us to facilitate his family's relocation to Vreland. We did set up contact and drop locations, signals and communication codes, and he gave us some items as proof of his word. So, progress was made."

"What was the talk about the goblin raids?" Baz said. "I overheard that mentioned."

"That was while we were testing each other. He brought up the raids, saying what he needed to warn us about was related to that too. I wasn't impressed that he knew about the raids. After all, they were near Renlar's border as well. But he told me about a new metal Noreas has discovered – they call it Elder Steel. He said the goblins were capturing healthy men and selling them to Noreas to work the metal."

Roche pulled a small cloth bundle, the length of a large knife, from his shirt. "He gave me three bodkin arrowheads and a spearhead made from this metal." He unwrapped the bundle and displayed the four items. The bodkins arrowheads were longer and sleeker than usual, but the spearhead was shaped as expected. All were dark gray and had no luster. They seemed to soak up the light of the moon.

"Goblins kidnapping folks to work metal doesn't make

sense," Flicker said. "They took men and boys from all crafts and trades. Most of them had never worked metal in their lives."

"Apparently they don't need them to work the metal. They only need them to work the furnaces. The workers heating the metal are dying, and Noreas needs more. The Baker said King Saevar would gladly grant an earl's land and title to anyone with the knowledge he's prepared to give us. Yet, he's not asking for land or title."

"Odd," Flicker said.

"Very," Roche agreed.

"I'm not impressed with these things," Baz said. "They're too light and they don't look special."

Roche grabbed the spearhead by the shank and effortlessly backhanded it into a pine tree. The tip sunk several inches into the trunk. Grimble was surprised by how deeply it penetrated.

Roche stepped away. "Try to bend it."

Baz walked over and pushed on it with one hand, trying to bend the blade sideways. When it didn't budge he grabbed the shank with both hands and pulled on it, grunting. The spearhead flexed ever so slightly. His face glistening in the moonlight, Baz gave up on his efforts and stepped back. The spearhead remained straight. "I'm impressed."

Roche pulled the spearhead free, knelt, and drove it into the ground several times. He wiped the dirt from it and used it to shave the hairs on the back of his arm.

"Ihgel's arm," Grimble said.

"Yeah. It caught my attention too." Roche bundled the items back in their cloth.

"What else did he say about this metal?" Dinger asked.

Roche motioned for Dinger to hand him the satchel. "Nothing yet. It's one of his bargaining chips." Roche placed the bundle and a leather-wrapped cedar tube containing a roll of papers into the satchel. He handed it all to Grimble. "Grimble, this is yours for the next day. Dinger, you're close support tomorrow. I'm trusting the dog won't be protecting the chicken coop until after dark. So, our approach to the house shouldn't be affected, but we need to sweep wide of that farm whenever we return to Market from now on. Because of the dog, close support will be very close from here on out."

Roche looked at Kurt and received a sullen nod.

# CHAPTER NINETEEN

Over the previous two nights, Kurt had painstakingly cut and bent the inside of a wild-growing holly tree into a near perfect observation blind. Even he would have a hard time seeing himself in the spot from outside it, and his comings and goings were aided by numerous pine saplings and an abundance of undergrowth. He was proud of the location and lamented that it would serve its purpose for only two or three more nights.

He scanned continuously from inside the branches of the holly, his left hand ready with the bow, an arrow already nocked. The wattle-and-daub house was not more than twenty yards away and his view of the south and east sides was practically unimpeded. Kurt also had the path to the front door partially in view, even if the door itself was not. It was a good spot, with only a short stone wall between him and the house.

An hour passed. No signs.

The horses in the barn whinnied, followed by the dull chime of metal on metal and the pounding of feet on the tall grass. Running around the corner of the house, moving from the west side to the south's back door, were two men in light armor, swords on their hips and crossbows in their hands. Kurt drew and loosed the arrow at the wooden shutters. His shot was accurate, but struck the shutters the same time a commotion started from within the house.

The soldiers took up a position near the rear door, facing opposite directions, left shoulder to left shoulder. They moved their crossbows wherever their eyes scanned. They ignored the noises in the house and visually swept the yard and woods.

Movement in front of the house caught Kurt's attention. Another soldier with a crossbow stood ready by the front door. Beside him was a bear – no, a massive dog, a...

*Bollocks!* he thought. *Time to get to the close support and rally.* He snuck away, his movements unnoticed by the dancing crossbowmen at the rear of the house. A second round of noise emanated from inside and died again within seconds. Kurt kept moving.

A minute later he was within earshot of Dinger and gave the signal. Dinger replied. When Kurt stepped out of the shadows, Dinger whispered, "What the fuck's going on?"

"Where are the others?" Kurt said. "Did they already move out?"

"No, it's just you and me. Thought I heard some yelling and banging. What's going on?"

"Shit. The team's compromised."

"Let's go help them," Dinger said, and he tried to stand before Kurt brought him back to a knee.

"The ambush is over. Rushing in won't help. They're captured or dead already, or they'd be here."

"Then let's get Grimble down here and plan a rescue." Dinger looked at Kurt, waiting for a reply. Kurt lowered his eyes and his view of the world faded. He rubbed his chest with his left hand and thought he heard himself mumbling.

*Best option. Get Dinger and Grimble to safety. Then make these new fuckers pay.* Kurt's upper lip twitched into the beginnings of a snarl. *Oh, yeah – and make it hurt.* He lifted his face to look into Dinger's eyes.

Dinger's head snapped back and his eyes widened. "Are you okay, buddy?"

He had received that look from others who had never seen him truly work. He ignored it. "Get to Grimble, and be ready to leave."

"Uh. But..."

"Listen to me. We don't have time to argue. The attackers had a mage. They portalled in. Had to. I didn't hear them until the last second, and they may have portalled away already. Are you with me now?"

"Rah, sir."

"Get your ass to Market. If that's been attacked too, get to Oven. I'm going to check on the others. If they are still there, I will do what I can to get us to Market. If they're already gone, I'll be right behind you, and we'll need to move out right away."

"Got it."

"One more thing. The soldiers looked well trained and their mage is probably a Grand Master. Only a Grand Master can summon a beast, and this one summoned a varga wolf. Keep alert and watchful going back. Now go."

With that Dinger was off, weaving his way around the trees on the way back to Market.

Kurt reapproached the house from the east, moving toward his holly. If the attackers were there, he anticipated they'd be on alert. He checked the front. Clear. At the back of the house he found four men standing near the door. Two held crossbows; the others stood off to the side, arms crossed, talking.

The rear door opened and lamplight streamed into the night. Kurt got a better look at the four men. They all wore armor, but each man's suit was different.

*Fucking mercs.*

A fifth man, one who had been inside, threw a small table into the grass, stepped back into the lit room, and came back with two chairs, which he unceremoniously tossed in the direction of the table. "Pike," he said. "Give me a hand with this one."

One of the men with crossed arms entered the house. A minute later he stepped out, carrying the legs of a limp man. The fifth man carried the body by its arms. The lolling of the head and bloody neck declared the man's status.

*Well, don't have to worry about the Baker anymore.*

An arm reached out and closed the door. The two mercenaries carrying the Baker moved to the west side of the house. They returned empty-handed moments later. One of them knocked on the door once, then twice. The door opened, and he stepped inside. The man called Pike rejoined his companion in conversation.

In the east, hundreds of yards away, a dog barked his alerts, which continued for some time. One of the crossbowmen knocked on the door, using the same rhythm as before. The door cracked.

"Are you catching this?" the crossbowman said. "Could be in response to a deer or something, but just the same, are you sure there wasn't a fourth man?" The door closed again, but only briefly. When it reopened, it did so fully, and the varga wolf ran out of the house into the yard.

It paused, standing on three legs, one paw raised. Even though the head and lines were more wolfish in nature, the broad beast with its thick hair reminded Kurt of a bear. It cast its head about, facing east, toward the noise. Its ears peaked, and it growled low, lips curling to expose its white teeth. The creature took off toward the east – toward Dinger and Market.

A lightly armored woman popped out of the house too. She pointed toward two men. "Badger, Axe," she said, "with me." One of the crossbowmen and the other talking man fell in behind the woman as she ran after the creature.

The door closed again and the men left behind went back to keeping watch. One near the door, the other closer to the middle of the yard. Their awareness level had peaked. This made it more difficult for Kurt to move, but he could also use it. With three mercenaries and that beast no longer around, the odds were much better than before.

Kurt slinked toward the front of the house. When he was out of sight of the guards by the back door, he vaulted over the rock wall. He paused a moment and grabbed one of the loose stones – not a big one, but one that would do the job.

With the stone in his right hand and the bow and arrow in his left, he moved toward the rear of the house, pausing by the east window to listen and look through a gap in the shutters. Someone's muffled voice screamed in pain. A kneeling, well-dressed man blocked Kurt's view, but the cloak clasp told him who was being tortured.

*You're going to pay for hurting Roche, asshole.*

Roche was having a hard time getting air through his gag, but he was alive. Baz lay on the floor, bound and gagged, scowling at the torturer. Flicker, beside Baz, was similarly bound, but he also had a hood over his head. One mercenary stood near the window.

From the east side of the house, Kurt tossed the stone in a high arc over the roof toward the south-west side of the property and estimated its flight. *Three*... He drew his knife. *Two*... He moved along the wall to the corner of the house. *One*... The stone landed with a gentle thud. The mercenaries turned in that direction, weapons ready.

*Go*...

Kurt stepped around the corner behind Pike and drove his knife into the base of the man's skull. Pike twitched and dropped, his body and sword crashing to the grass. The crossbowman turned at the noise of his partner hitting the ground, prepared to shoot, but Kurt's arrow pierced through his neck. His legs wobbled, and he fell to his knees, then the ground.

Kurt drew his arming sword and retrieved his long knife from Pike's skull. He stepped to the door, knocked once, then twice, and took a deep breath.

The door opened. The light assaulted Kurt's eyes. The man standing there wasn't surprised until after Kurt's knife and hand had passed by his neck. Kurt pushed the door in and picked up speed. The door flew open to the right, cracking against the wall. The man by the door grabbed his throat with one hand. Blood ran down his neck and between his fingers as he gasped. His attempt to take a breath made a wet, honking noise. With his free hand, the dying mercenary grabbed the handle of his sword, but drew it only partially out of its sheath before falling to the floor. Kurt, already in the room, picked his targets. Two remained.

The rectangular room ran off to Kurt's left side, where his teammates lay supine upon the dirt floor near the wall. At their feet, three steps from Kurt, was the fancy-dressed man. "Fancy" flinched at the sound of the door, but had not yet started to turn.

*He's slow.*

The other man, another armored mercenary, was two steps in front of Kurt, his back against the far wall. That man drew his longsword.

*He's quick.*

Kurt split the two and dropped to his knees on the dirt floor. Fancy stood and began to turn. The mercenary finished drawing his sword. Kurt thrust his blade at the mercenary and, with a forward slice of his knife, cut the tendon of Fancy's right ankle. Fancy dropped to his knee, screaming.

*Slow and unused to pain. A dandy.*

The skilled mercenary parried Kurt's attack and countered.

*Quick and skilled.*

On the backswing of his knife, Kurt stabbed into Fancy's side. He raised his sword and, blocking the mercenary's swing, kicked at his left knee. The merc jumped back and drew his own knife in the process. Kurt stood and stepped away from both men, facing off against the only opponent who remained standing. The man who was quick, skilled, armored, and whose sword had a reach advantage.

"Pike! Dagger!" the man yelled.

*He's still shocked.*

Fancy gasped. Kurt knew the punctured lung made it difficult for him to breathe, and the sliced tendon would make it impossible to stand. Fancy doubled over, trying to catch his breath.

*Better hope you die before I start working on you, foppish fuck.*

While Kurt's opponents were distracted, Baz, with his feet bound and hands tied behind him, slid himself into the best position he could manage. He drew his legs toward his body, rocked back onto his shoulders, then rocked forward, kicking his legs out as they fell down. His boot heels fell down onto the back of Fancy's head and neck, collapsing the man entirely to the ground. Fancy screamed, and blood ran from his mouth. Baz continued to stomp and kick his downed opponent.

Baz's attack on Fancy distracted the merc for a fraction of a second. The tip of his sword dipped off its line, and that was all Kurt needed. He moved in with a series of strikes from both blades. The merc defended well, but Kurt managed to slice the inside of his left wrist, which disarmed the man of his knife. Once that was out of the equation, Kurt bound the man's sword with his own and drove his long knife home, coming in at an angle through his opponent's armpit and into his chest. He knew he had struck true when he felt the beat of the heart in his handle.

The merc yelled and struck out at Kurt with his left hand. But he could not make a fist with his cut tendons and the hand slapped against the side of Kurt's head. He ignored the pain as his opponent's heart twitched for the last time.

Baz, breathing hard through his gag, stopped kicking. Fancy didn't move. Occasionally he gasped an agonal breath. He was as good as dead.

To Baz's left was Roche. He was breathing but did not move. A knife stuck perpendicular out of his right knee, the joint no longer functioning. His lower leg was bent at an odd angle. A growing pool of blood gathered beneath it. To Baz's right was Flicker.

"Hel' 'rimmle ahn 'inger," Baz said through his gag.

Kurt removed his knife from the dead merc. "We'll get to 'em as soon as I cut Flicker loose." He knelt next to Flicker and pulled the hood off of his friend and was cutting Flicker's hands free when there was movement at the door.

The crossbowman Kurt had shot staggered into the doorway, the arrow still protruding through his neck. His breathing was labored and noisy. He brought his crossbow up and pointed it at Kurt and Flicker. The bow wobbled as he took aim.

Baz threw all his weight into a lunge and slung himself in front of his two friends as the crossbow fired.

The bolt struck Baz in the center of the chest. He slumped on the ground by Flicker's feet.

Kurt raised his knife to throw it at the mercenary, but the man teetered and fell back against the open door, sliding to the ground. His head slumped to his chest. Kurt brought the knife back down and finished cutting Flicker free of his bonds."Hold on, Baz," he said. "We're almost out of here."

Flicker removed his gag as Kurt freed his legs. "My book and the intel notes," he said, pointing to a storage shelf on the opposite wall. "They're on that shelf. We need them."

Kurt moved to stand, but paused at the growing sound of something fast approaching. The varga wolf burst through the open doorway and slid to a stop a few steps from the team. It took a cursory look around the room and its gaze settled on Fancy's body.

A growl started deep within the beast. It turned its head and locked eyes with Kurt. The growl grew into a snarl as it opened its mouth, its lips curling back, drool pouring from its lower jaw.

"Grab them," Flicker said.

Flicker gripped Kurt's shoulder as Kurt grabbed Roche and Baz's legs.

The beast lunged.

Page ran as fast as she could across the uneven ground and through the woods, trying to keep the chancellor's beast in sight. She had no illusions of keeping pace with it; that would be a lost cause. Badger was right behind her – she knew his breathing. Axe would be behind him.

Fortunately, the creature occasionally paused to listen or sniff, giving the three chasers time to close the gap before it ran off again. Page practically crashed into the beast on one of those occasions. It held its position on the other side of a large bush and cast its head from side to side. When it started forward this time, it moved at a slow jog, nose low, eyes forward. To their left, a dog barked. The varga wolf and the team ignored it.

They all moved forward cautiously now, Axe ready with his crossbow, the others with swords drawn. The beast took off at a run again, and Page lost sight of it. She listened as best she could while chasing it down.

The beast suddenly yelped in pain. The mercenaries ran to the sound. In the gray light, they found a man in gambeson armor holding the varga wolf at bay. He half-sworded in a low guard, his left hand grasping the middle of the blade. The beast circled him, its steps measured. A dark mark on its right flank dripped blood onto its paw and the forest floor. Page was impressed by the man's courage and that he had been able to wound the wolf, but that wouldn't stop her. He must be caught or killed.

"We'll call it off if you surrender now," she said, though she had no idea if the monstrous wolf would listen to her.

"Fuck off," the man said. He stood ten yards away. The wolf worked on circling him, but the man kept moving backward, keeping the beast and the three mercenaries to his front. With her left hand, Page drew three darts from her pouch.

"You can't win," she said. "Work with us."

"You're outnumbered, asshole," Axe said. "Listen to her."

Page watched in admiration. Every step the man took was textbook, every position and grip perfect.

"Fuck off," he said again.

"Is that all you got?" Axe said.

At that moment, the varga wolf stopped pacing and cocked its head, ears pointing back. Without warning, it turned and bolted away, headed back toward the farmhouse.

"At least one of you understood what I was saying," the man said.

"That's it," Page said, and she lifted her left hand.

With that the man yelled and charged her, releasing the hold at mid-blade and turning side-on, putting his left arm behind him. He ducked quickly with his first step, and Axe's bolt missed him. However, Page's three darts found their mark and stitched up his side and chest. He managed to attack Page with a thrust, but Badger knocked it away.

Page swung at his right leg, cutting him behind the knee. The man dropped. He grunted from the pain and blood spat from his mouth.

Axe drew his sword, and the three Iron Leafs stepped toward the downed man, swords pointed at him. The man swung his own sword, trying to knock the others away, trying to make an opening; but he weakened, and his efforts failed. He grunted and coughed in defiance. The light, frothy blood glistened in the dim light.

"What did the general tell you?" Page asked.

"Okay, okay," the man coughed. "He said, 'Fuck off.'"

At that moment, a loud, unnatural howling rose from the west, from the direction of the farmhouse. The dog that had barked at them earlier started howling.

"Oops," the man said. "Bad news – for you – I think." He started to chuckle and cough. More blood sprayed from his mouth.

Page knocked his sword aside with her own and stepped on his arm, pinning it to the ground. Badger and Axe thrust theirs into his chest, the gambeson slowing the blades until they put their weight behind them. The man went limp and spoke no more.

"This isn't some internal feud," Axe said. He paced back and forth, staring at the body.

Badger looked back in the direction of the farmhouse. "This shit's getting weird. We need to get back to Hammer and talk to him."

"I'll portal us back," Page said. "Same place, north side, by the stable." With that, they grabbed Page's arm, Axe using a death grip. She cast the spell, and together they left as if pulled through a hole in the air.

———————————————➤

A tranquility lay across the hilltop that night, a noticeable blanket of peace. It spread wide, and Grimble noted the absence of the many sounds to which he'd become accustomed. Even the crickets and frogs were muted. Most might have appreciated the calm. Grimble was unsettled. It was as if a storm approached, but the sky was clear and the treetops silent. Grimble kept watch over Market and listened for any signs of life.

To the west a dog barked, the same dog as before. The rhythm was much the same, and Grimble wondered what had caught its attention, as he knew the team would never chance straying too close to that farm again. Its excited cacophony lulled, telling Grimble whatever had caught its attention was moving away from it. But before the dog stopped barking altogether, it renewed its warnings. Its calls grew frenetic this time. Something was different.

Grimble moved from Market to the edge of the hill, affording him a better view of the route the team had taken to meet the Baker. He hid near a laurel bush and nocked an arrow onto his bowstring. He sniffed the air, checked his surroundings, and waited.

The dog's barking slowed. Another dog yelped in pain, but this one was near the base of the hill. Grimble imagined another farmer's dog had chased a buck and the two had squared off. It was probably nothing more than that.

Voices, dim and unclear, climbed the hill to Grimble's ears. He strained to hear them. The team would not be so careless as to be heard. Grimble made certain his cloak covered him and got more familiar with the laurel in the event that a group of locals were making their way up the hill.

The farmer's dog howled.

Dinger's battle cry rang from the base of the hill and struck Grimble's soul.

He knew that call as well as he knew any sound in his life. In training and in dozens of battles, Dinger's cry had risen above all others. It made Grimble want to fight, and he found himself looking for a target to shoot. With none in sight, Grimble slid out from the bush and started down the hill. Dinger would not have given away his position unless the situation was dire. He had sent a message.

Grimble moved beside the path and weaved around the trees and bushes. The urge to run was strong, but the disciplined soldier in him knew that was folly. So he maintained as fast a pace as he could, silent, his bow at the ready.

The ground leveled off. He moved among the trees toward the position he had manned the night before. The two downed trees and the opening in the woods came into view. The toe of a boot was visible in the clearing. He paused and scanned and listened. He started toward the boot. More came into view: the legs, the body.

It was Dinger.

Grimble moved to his friend. Even in the dim light, Dinger's body showed the many wounds he'd suffered in the fight. Black blood covered his chest and right leg. It fouled his face. But Dinger's unstained white eyes stared unblinkingly at the moon through the canopy above.

"Shit," Grimble mumbled. "No, no, no." He scanned the area. Even in the limited light, he noticed the fresh toe and heel scuffs of multiple people in the leaf litter. He knelt and checked for signs of life, signs he knew would not be there.

*We knew you'd never be taken one on one, brother. Hope you gave them something to remember you by.*

Grimble closed his friend's eyes and focused on his next step to stop anger and grief from overcoming him. He looked about. He listened again, straining his ears for any signs of the team or this unknown enemy. Only the farmer's dog made itself known.

He thought of checking the farmhouse, but dismissed that idea. The orders were to meet at Oven if Market was compromised. The others may already be there waiting for him now.

"Not going to leave you here, brother," Grimble whispered. He stuck Dinger's sword in the ground so it stood up, and propped his bow and arrow against the hilt. Then he positioned Dinger's body and pulled him up into a shoulder carry.

Grabbing the weapons, he looked around one last time, and the two men started their final journey together.

# CHAPTER TWENTY

Bleeding and broken, the Raven team emerged through Flicker's portal into the 209th Light Cavalry's training hall. The whitewashed walls with their racks of weapons and the cold, stone floor were in stark contrast to the dirt floor and wattle-and-daub walls of the farmhouse's small pantry. A guild mage and six troopers met them.

"No, no, no," Kurt muttered. "Dinger. Grimble —"

"We've got wounded," yelled a trooper.

"Market!" Kurt said. "Get us to Market."

"I can't," Flicker said. "That was my last portal."

"Last one?" the guild mage said. "We're not returning now?"

"No," Flicker said. "May Ihgel and Yahnn help them."

"Shit!" Kurt burst out. He rubbed his chest with his left hand.

"Get the Duty Officer," a trooper yelled.

"No, no, no —" Kurt repeated.

"This one's done," said a trooper kneeling beside Baz.

"Get him to the Temple anyway," Flicker said.

"No! No!" Kurt stood and yelled. It was a scream of desperation and frustration, and the emotion in it caused everyone to pause.

"I got him," Flicker said. "Get the others to the Temple." The troopers placed Roche and Baz on stretchers and redoubled their efforts, carrying the casualties from the room.

Kurt turned with a purpose, a wild look in his eyes. He focused on a wall rack holding weapons. He moved to it and grabbed a war hammer. His shoulders and chest heaved as he yelled again, beating the stone wall and weapon racks with the hammer.

The guild mage raised his hands for a spell.

"No," Flicker said. "He needs this. If you delay him, it will be worse."

"Worse?" the mage asked.

"Yes," Flicker said. "Much worse."

The mage lowered his hand and took two more steps away from Kurt, keeping his wide eyes on the man determined to destroy the stone wall.

"Two are left behind," Flicker said to the mage. "Do we have anyone in the regiment who can get us close to Gandleton?"

"Glastrup's as close as we can get you," the mage said, eyes on Kurt as he continued to attack everything in front of him, chips of rock and shards of wood flying about. "Almost eighty miles away from Gandleton. There are only three of us here. We've already discussed options, and that's the closest we can get you."

Kurt had broken the hammer's head free from the haft, but he continued to beat the wall with the wooden stick.

"Give me a second," Flicker said. "I'll contact Dinger and let him know what's going on. Tell him to get to the fallback location with Grimble."

He closed his eyes and mumbled words only the other mage understood.

"It's not working," Flicker said after a moment. "Can you reach him?"

Kurt's swings slowed, and he swayed. He grabbed one of the broken racks for support.

When the men had been selected for the mission, each had supplied a personal item. This was so a mage may have a strong connection to them in an event such as this. The guild mage picked up the personal item belonging to Dinger: the silver spearhead he had received as an award for valor in combat. Few troopers earned it, ever. The mage cast the spell, but could not contact Dinger either.

"I don't think he's alive," the mage said.

Flicker nodded solemnly. "I agree."

"No. No! NO!" Kurt screamed a hoarse, demoralized wail. He punched the stone wall with one fist, followed closely by the other. Cracks echoed through the room but the wall did not yield. Kurt managed a dozen punches, smearing red upon the stones, before his legs buckled and he slumped to the floor.

The mage turned to Flicker. "Try Grimble."

"Can't."

"I'll try," said the mage, picking up Grimble's personal item – a steel buckle with a portion of leather strap connected to it.

"It won't work."

A look of confusion washed over the mage's face. "All I get... All I see..."

"I know," said Flicker. "Running or rearing. It's all I get too."

The duty officer ran into the room. The trooper sent to fetch him followed right behind. The officer looked at the blood smeared upon the stone floor, a look of concern growing on his face. He turned to his right and saw Kurt sitting amid the splintered wood and broken stone, and the look turned to anger.

"Please ignore that for now, Lieutenant," Flicker said.

"What happened?"

Flicker provided the duty officer with a brief report of the situation.

The officer nodded toward Kurt. "What happened to him?"

"He doesn't like to lose," Flicker said.

"What do you need?" the officer asked.

"I'm embarrassed to say, I need a spellbook."

The looks Flicker received in return were not promising.

---

"Fuck me."

"Shut up, Axe," Page said. They had found Pike dead in the grass behind the house and knew things had gone wrong at the farmhouse. Axe only became more agitated when they found Dagger slumped against the house's open door.

A whimpering noise came from within the pantry, accompanied by someone's agonal gasp for breath. They turned the corner to find Snake face down on the dirt floor. Against the far wall, lying on his side, was Hammer. Blood pooled around both men and soaked into the ground. The varga wolf nuzzled Chancellor Nesar. It whimpered and bleated. A long, raspy breath left the chancellor, and a second later the wolf turned into a wisp of smoke and disappeared.

The men they had captured earlier were nowhere to be seen.

"Who could do this?" said Axe.

"The one in the woods, his accent was Aenduran," said Badger. "These were probably the King's Ravens."

"Ravens?" repeated Axe, a look of concern on his face.

"Shit."

"Axe was right," said Badger. "This wasn't an internal problem. This is bigger."

Page recalled the dying words of General Batal, accusing Chancellor Nesar of betraying Renlar. Nesar had killed him before he had said too much. This was indeed a thick mess. She looked around the room and saw the shelf with the papers and spellbook they had seized from their prisoners.

"This shit's fucked." Axe jittered and jerked his head about as he scanned the room.

"They left the mage's spellbook and the documents," Page said.

"So?" Axe said.

"A mage wouldn't leave that behind. They're probably coming back," Page said. That got Badger and Axe's attention. "And if they were Ravens, we don't want to be here when they do. A quick sweep of the house – grab what we can and get the bodies together."

"On it." Badger started moving into the main part of the house.

"Fuck that. Let's go now," Axe said.

"No. We sweep then go," Page commanded.

"Who are you to give orders?" Axe said. "I'm senior on this team."

"Are we really going to do this now?" Page lifted her left hand. Little arcs of lightning danced and crackled between her fingers.

Axe's eyes popped wide and his face paled. "Uh…"

"I didn't think so. Put your fucking ego aside and get your shit together. A sweep, people. Now."

The three of them performed the sweep of the house and

collected the loose items taken from General Batal and the spies, including their books, papers, and personal items. They dragged the general and Pike's bodies into the farmhouse and secured all the bodies together in preparation for Page's portal to the stable they had rented outside of town. Page performed the spell, and they left the house.

Their horses whinnied and danced in their stalls when they arrived. Page summoned a magical flame, as bright as a lamp, and it hovered in the center of the barn. Badger moved to calm the horses.

"Axe," Page called. "Help me move the bodies." They had time to move three to the back of the barn, laying them side by side, before they were interrupted.

"Who's there?" came a call from outside the barn. "Announce yourselves."

"Badger," Page said. Badger moved to the barn's door to greet the proprietor and prevent him from entering. There was a mumbled conversation outside while the last two bodies were moved. Badger reentered the barn and gave the "all clear" sign. Page waved him over.

"I've been thinking about the situation," she began. "Whoever attacked the house while we were gone was part of the original group of spies, but not one we captured and not part of a rescue group."

Axe's mouth twisted. "How do you know one of the captured spies didn't get loose and do all that? The mage we caught might have done it."

"Highly unlikely with Pike being backstabbed," Page said. "They may have gotten loose and participated, but there was some kind of outside help."

"I agree," said Badger. "Pike and Dagger went down in a

surprise attack. Snake might have stepped away for a second and came back to help. That's when he got it. There was someone, I'm thinking at least two, on the outside."

"Looked like the chancellor was caught by surprise too," Page added.

"Don't give him too much credit," Axe said. "He wasn't that tough. Remember the ride from the fort? We could have made it much faster without him slowing us down."

"Axe has a point there," Badger said.

"He was not used to roughing it," Page said, "that's certain. But he was effective in the two fights when we captured the general and the spies tonight. He was no pushover." She looked at both men, but neither countered. "It was not a large rescue group, either. If they were well prepared, they would have taken their paperwork, and the spellbook at the very least. Yet those items remained. My thought is the varga wolf interrupted the rescue, and they had to leave in a hurry – another indicator it was a small group."

"They must have fallen back to their camp," Badger said. "The same place that mouthy fuck was trying to reach before we stopped him." Everyone nodded in agreement.

"What now?" Axe said. "Our patron's dead."

"Our patron's another matter," Page said. "You were right. He didn't tell us everything."

"Noble assholes and their games," Badger spat.

"He didn't just withhold shit from us," Page said. "He's withholding things from his people, too. Nesar didn't want us to hear what the general had to say. As soon as the general was ungagged, he accused Nesar of betraying King Heselov and Renlar. He said Nesar was setting Renlar up to be occupied by Noreas."

"What?" Axe said.

"The general said he would never let his king be hurt, or his country fall. That's when Nesar killed him. I think he wanted to silence him before he said too much in front of us. Remember back in Lagisborg? He spoke with that commander at the far end of the hall, away from our ears, and had us kill him. He didn't want us to learn what was going on or what his plans were."

"What did he do after killing the general?" Axe said. "Did he try to explain away what the general said?"

"Nesar said nothing. Didn't try to argue with him, didn't explain anything. Nothing. He simply moved over to the one we caught talking with the general and went to work on him."

"Went to work?" Badger asked.

Page nodded. "You know what I mean. While I was there, that man didn't speak, and Nesar was working him like a butcher, from his foot to his knee. But we were interrupted by the dog's alert. Don't know if he finally said anything."

"Still," Badger said, "our patron is dead. We worked for Chancellor Nesar. We don't need to get in the middle of his, or Renlar's, politics."

"We need to report to someone," Axe said. "We need to tell them about the chancellor's death and what the general was up to."

"Give me a minute," Page said. She stepped away from her teammates, deep in thought. Straw crinkled and swished under her feet. Badger and Axe remained silent until she returned. "We send the chancellor back to Lagisborg, along with the general and our brothers. I'll write a quick report to King Heselov's Chief of the Court detailing what we learned and how this all played out, then seal it with Nesar's ring. The letter will accompany his body, and it must remain sealed until it reaches the chief. Axe, you'll have to go with them in the event that they have questions, and to take care of our brothers there."

Axe did not look happy, but nodded. "Understood."

"Badger, you and I will try to locate the conspirator camp, see if we can learn any other information about them before we portal back to Lagisborg."

"You sure you want to go after Ravens, just the two of you?" Axe said. "Send the note explaining things, and say that we'll follow after. I should join you and Badger. You don't want to be shorthanded if you run into Ravens."

"I agree with Axe," Badger said. "We all go to Lagisborg and end this thing, or we all investigate further. Whoever hit the house, they killed four of us and a Grand Master mage."

"Alright," Page agreed. "In the morning we send them back to the Chancellor's Hall. I'll memorize a Message spell and let the chancellor's attendant know to expect the bodies before I send them. You both need to keep watch while I prepare the spells and rest."

Before they bedded down, the three of them secured the personal effects of their deceased teammates. Around the neck of each Iron Leaf mercenary was a braided necklace holding a silver elm tree leaf about two inches in length. Etched into the leaf were a date and a number. The date signified their time with the company, and the number was their identity. Sometimes the bodies of fallen members of the company could not be returned to their headquarters. In those cases, the leaf was taken from the dead warrior and placed on a wall of honor as a record of their death in the service of the company. Badger and Axe cut the men's leaves free, unsure if they would be returned to the Anvil in Haldiland, or buried in Renlar.

Page secured the chancellor's items, placing his signet ring in her pocket. It would be needed after she wrote the report. She also secured his mage's medallion and spellbook; both would be turned over to the Spire. She considered keeping the Raven mage's spellbook, weighing its benefit against the financial reward she would receive from turning it in to the Spire. That determination would have to wait until she had more time to study the spells in it.

Page continued to check the chancellor's body, finding his brown-and-yellow worry beads in a vest pocket. When she touched them they vibrated. She pulled her hand back, thought for a moment, and glanced at Badger and Axe. The two men continued their work securing the belongings of their teammates. They were oblivious to her.

Page reached into the chancellor's pocket again and grabbed the beads.

*"Sala... No... Who is this?"*

A voice, measured and deep, rang in her head. It seemed as if a Message spell was communicating with her. She knew the others would not hear it.

*"I see your thoughts, young mage. Where is Sala Nesar? Ah, he is dead. That is very unfortunate."*

Page dropped the beads. Strength was in the voice, and power, and that concerned her. However, she was intrigued and wanted to communicate with it again. The voice did not sound or feel menacing, but she resisted the urge to touch the beads – for now. She scooped them up with a stick and let them slip into one of her pouches.

Once the deceased's items were secured and tied to their bodies, the team prepared to get some sleep, with Badger and Axe trading watch shifts. Before studying her spells, Page opened the pouch containing the worry beads. She peered into it. The beads stared back unremarkably. She set the pouch down.

Page opened her spellbook, knowing she needed to concentrate on committing several difficult spells to memory. Fleeting thoughts and transient curiosity interrupted her, breaking the concentration she needed for study. She took another breath and let it out while returning to the page containing the symbol for the Portal spell. Her finger traced over the pommel of her dagger.

*Who is on the other side of those beads?*

She closed her book and looked at the pouch again. She needed to confront the beads or understand her trepidation before she could do anything else. It took great power to create items with enchantments on them. This one put her in touch with another mage, a strong one. One from whom she was unable to shield her mind.

Was the mage another member of King Heselov's advisory council? Would they learn what Page knew already, and would that put her and the team in good standings, or jeopardize their lives? If Chancellor Nesar had been part of some nefarious plot, had the mage on the other end been controlling him – and if so, how likely was it that Page would fall victim to that power?

Her mind had been linked with the other mage for a short time, but she had not felt a sense of foreboding. On the contrary, the other mage's mind had been calm. No, Nesar had not been under their control. He had been able to willingly hold and release the beads, rather than wearing them like a bracelet.

Once again, Page reached for the pouch and this time pulled the beads from within. The familiar sensation met her fingers. She calmed her mind and waited.

*"I'd hoped you would reconnect with me,"* the voice said. *"What happened to Sala?"*

Dean Radt

*"Ambushed,"* Page answered in her mind. *"The best we can tell is one or two people, possibly Aenduran Ravens. They rescued the spies we caught talking with the general. May I ask who you are?"*

*"Sala and I worked together. He reported to me and asked for my counsel. That is all."*

*"You're not King Heselov."*

*"No, my dear."*

Page got the feeling the chancellor had respected this mage. *"You were like a teacher to him,"* she said.

*"You could say that. That's a good title. You may call me Teacher too, if you'd like. How should I address you?"*

*"My company calls me Page."*

*"That's a good name for you. I see your real name as well, Emma. But I like Page. Anonymity cannot be overrated. Please, I need to know about the general and what he told the spies."*

*"That is for King Heselov and his council now, I'm afraid."*

*"You do not fully trust me. I respect that."* The voice was not upset. It remained pleasant.

*"Why should I trust you?"*

*"Sala trusted me. We were committed to the same goal. He sought me out for advice on complex matters. I helped him. I can help you. You can trust me."*

There was a pause. Page wondered if the connection had been lost. But a calm came over her, like the sensation she felt right before falling asleep, and she realized everything was alright. She could trust Teacher to help her and the team. She could trust Teacher.

*"You remain a member of the Ruby Order and wish to finish your Arcane education. You wish to become a member of the Sapphire Order."*

288

*"I do."* Page's heart ached briefly. She wanted desperately to attain the final level of Arcane training.

*"My dear,"* the voice purred. *"That can be arranged."*

Page felt the truth in the statements and somehow knew Nesar had trusted this mage, his teacher, completely. She could trust Teacher. Nesar had held the beads almost every time they had met with him and again before he had interrogated the general. She could trust Teacher. She decided to relay to the mage what she had heard during the interrogation. She could trust Teacher.

She told Teacher everything.

*"This is disturbing news, but it can be managed. You plan to return tomorrow and find the spy camp?"*

*"Yes, Teacher."*

*"Keep in touch. I can help. If there are any conspirators still in Renlar, they must be found."*

*"Yes, Teacher."*

*"I sense you work hard and study long to be good at your work."*

*"I do."*

*"I work best as a silent advisor. Do not betray my presence to anyone, not even your companions. They do not understand the Arcane arts. They may misunderstand how I am able to help. You can trust me."*

*"Understood,"* said Page.

Sensing she was no longer connected to the mage, she set the beads back in the pouch, opened her spellbook again, and studied.

The next morning the team sent Chancellor Nesar and their fallen comrades to Lagisborg. Once the bodies were gone, they prepped and saddled their horses. Page did not like the animals. She hadn't liked them when she'd lived on the farm, and it was all she could do to put up with them when it was necessary now. They were feculent, foul creatures, and it seemed they could always tell how to frustrate and annoy her. However, they were needed for fast travel, so she got through the tacking of her horse as quickly as possible.

Together they rode to the farms southwest of Gandleton. In the light of day, the cheerful land was at odds with the events of the night before. The farmer from the house next door was nowhere to be seen, but a woman stood outside with several small children. Chickens and goats mingled about. Before the target farmhouse came into sight, the three mercenaries dismounted and tied their horses to a fence post. They approached on foot. Cautious. The woman they had passed had moved to the road with her children to watch them.

Together, Page and her companions entered through the front gate and made their way around to the back of the house. Flies zipped about and gathered where the area had been fouled. The door remained open, and a slow, careful check of the house showed all was as they had left it.

They exited and weaved their way through the woods, much more slowly than they had the night before. They worked their way to the clearing where they had fought and killed the mouthy man. In the sunlight, they had no trouble locating where the fight took place. The three mercenaries were not surprised to find the body gone, but it displeased them. The patch of blood-covered leaves attracted flies and other bugs. Their weaving flights and incessant buzz repulsed Page. They were another reminder of growing up around animals.

"Over here," said Badger, pointing at a piece of ground. "I'm no tracker, but even I can tell one person carried the dead one away." Page and Axe looked at the series of deep impressions in the forest floor, footprints heading away from the area and up the hill.

Slowly and on the alert, the team followed the tracks to the top. The tracks continued across a flat portion of the hill until they abruptly ended. There was no camp in sight. Page and the others looked about, but could not see anything.

"Hold on," said Badger. "Don't move." He didn't look alarmed, but instead appeared to be listening. "Buzzing. More buzzing."

Page could hear it too. The three of them searched until Page noticed flies gathering around a patch of the forest floor. They approached it together. The ground looked a little different than the rest of the area, but it wasn't until a fly landed and crawled under a leaf, not to return, that Page understood why. She drew her sword. Instinctively her companions did too. Using her blade, she poked into the ground, and her blade met no resistance. She lifted the tip of her sword up, and a thin trapdoor made of tree branches lifted off the ground.

All three jumped back as they spotted a man beneath the branches. When he did not move, they picked up the cover again. Revealed was the man they had slain the night before. He lay in repose in the shallow pit, his hands across his chest, holding his sword. A backpack was at his feet.

"Check the area," Page said. They kicked the ground around until they unearthed another five spider holes. Four contained backpacks; one was entirely empty.

"We caught three," Axe said. "Killed one. Are we looking for two more?"

"No," Page said. "No more than two were left behind. This dead one and another. Most likely a male, and he's not a mage.

The one who rescued the other spies may have been a mage, but they had to leave the dead one and the missing one behind. They didn't come back for either of them. Otherwise, the dead one wouldn't be here."

"We've got one on foot?" Badger said.

"Yes," Page said. "Hold on." She moved to the empty spider hole and grabbed some of the soil. She concentrated and started the incantation for her spell, but something wasn't right.

"What's wrong?" Axe asked. "Who're we looking for?"

"Give me a moment," Page said, and concentrated again. She sensed a male, but she could not see him. She received flashes of images – images of a horse. A horse running. A horse rearing. "A horse?" she said out loud.

"We're looking for a horse?" Axe said.

"No, a man," Page replied tersely, trying to maintain her concentration, but the image was gone. "A horseman. We're looking for a horseman."

# CHAPTER TWENTY-ONE

*The earth was damp and raw deep beneath the leaves, and with his nose so buried he could not help but inhale the essence of the forest floor. Grimble knew his mother searched for him. She did not call. She did not need to.*

*It was not because his chores were unfinished, nor because supper was soon to hit the table. He was thirteen now and knew better than to run about before finishing his chores. And he never needed anyone to call him twice when the opportunity to eat presented itself. No, those were not the reasons she searched for him.*

*Somehow a squirrel had found its way into the house. By now it must be frantic, desperate to escape. Grimble knew his mother would suspect him first, especially if she caught him close at hand. Years before he had learned not to use livestock, little pigs or chickens, for these tricks on his mother. The suspicions always landed on him, and he could not figure out how they knew until he realized that farm animals needed help to get inside. He never liked the punishment, but he thought the game was good fun. Wildlife, on the other hand, were crafty in their own way. A lost bird or a curious squirrel caught in the house was not out of the realm of possibilities.*

*He simply had to remain hidden while his mother dealt with the squirrel, yelling at the innocent creature and searching for Grimble near the house. This time she found the squirrel mere moments after he had set it loose. He managed to duck into the woods and kiss the ground beneath the low holly branches before she could catch him. The prickly leaves poked him through his handed-down shirt and pants, but he endured the discomfort and hoped his mother would never suspect that he hid nearby.*

*"Get out, you!" she called. "Out, you!"*

*He remained hidden, nose in the soil, breathing deep, earthy breaths.*

*"Out you! Out-roo! Ah-roof! Ah-roof!"*

Grimble opened his eyes and shifted his head. He gazed upon a wooded hillside, not his home. The leaves covering his head fell to the ground. On the other side of the wide draw, a hound sniffed the ground and gave an occasional call, notifying all within earshot that it was on the trail.

Last night Grimble had zigzagged while making his way to Oven, the team's fallback location. It had delayed his arrival but allowed him to see if an enemy soldier or magically enhanced dog had followed him. He had done his best to stay awake, to look for his teammates for the rest of the night and almost half the day, but between the monotony of watching nothing, his fixed position, and his sleep deprivation, he had slipped in and out of wakefulness.

Now he studied the hound from his side of the draw. It was bad news that a dog tracked him, but good news too. He could not imagine Renlar training hound dogs to hunt and attack humans. All the same, Grimble prayed to Ihgel. He waited to see if the hound took the path up the hill, the path Grimble had taken himself the night before. If it did, he had mere minutes before it would double back and track its way to his current hiding spot.

*Shit!*

The dog moved up the side of the hill, its nose pulling its body. Grimble waited until it disappeared over the ridge and slid out from under the bushes. He grabbed a hard biscuit from his pack and tossed it into the laurels, hoping the food and his scent would be enough to delay the dog. He checked that the satchel remained about his body, shouldered his backpack, and grabbed his bow, looking once more at the ridgeline.

*No dog.*

He circled the bush several times, put the wind to his back, and moved about twenty paces away from his hide. At that point he turned and hastened down the hill.

At the bottom, the woods thinned into a rolling grassland. As he recalled, the field stretched more than a mile between the bottom of the hill and the swamp to the east. His plan was to skirt the woods, moving north long enough to get away from the hound. Once clear, he would bed down and wait for nightfall before moving out again, paralleling the road east, toward home.

The swamp would help him put the dog off his trail, but he

hoped to avoid it if possible. He did not know the area and being wet on a cold night with no fire or other trooper's body heat to warm him could prove fatal.

Grimble convinced himself that avoiding it had nothing to do with the superstition that the swamp was cursed.

To keep himself from feeling tiny and abandoned in this unknown land, he used memories of being alone in the woods, hunting and hiking. Every time fear inserted itself into his thoughts, he stopped and took a calming breath. He knew fear would feed panic, that unwanted beast. And panic would hurt him. Grimble told himself he was merely on a hunting trip, but questions popped into his head.

*Where's the team? Why didn't they meet me at Oven?*

If he was the only one alive, how long would it take for one of the regiment's mages to reach out to him? A cold, lonely feeling like none he had ever felt before slithered around his heart. It squeezed. Grimble froze. He questioned and doubted. He took a deep breath, again.

*I'm hunting. Let's see if we can shoot a rabbit or a squirrel for lunch.*

He drew an arrow and held it in his bow hand. His lips smiled; his eyes did not. He pressed on.

He had not moved far when two men on horseback came into view several hundred yards ahead. He knelt beside a tree, using it for cover. The riders moved southward, toward him along the tree line. They stopped and looked about discussing something. They were too far away for a good look and he could not tell if they were soldiers. The horses' gait and posture led him to think they were not.

*Move back north, assholes. Nothing down this way.*

Grimble contemplated moving back into the woods and up

the hill, but he was not yet sure if his attempt to sidetrack the hound had worked. As though prompted, it barked a few times. It was far to the south behind Grimble, but now on this side of the hill. The men on horseback turned their heads in his direction and started closing the distance.

*Drought and blight!*

Should he risk the dog or the riders? He could not be certain that the dog wasn't magically enhanced, but he felt confident that the horses were not military-trained. That, combined with the casual nature of both riders, made up his mind.

*The swamp it is.*

Grimble took a moment to pray to Ihgel and Gavel for success and for guidance. His pulse pounded in his ears. He took a steadying breath and stepped into the open, hoping a casual pace would convince the riders he was a local out for a stroll or on a hunt. He sauntered onto the grassland, his stride perhaps a bit too jaunty.

The dog barked and bayed. The calls came from where Grimble had overnighted.

He wanted to keep the men in his peripheral vision, but his cloak's hood made it difficult. They called to him. He was too far away to make out the words. Grimble looked their way, raised his left hand, the one holding the bow and arrow, and waved it warmly, as if he knew them. He continued toward the swamp.

The men kicked their horses to a faster pace. Grimble picked up his own, but he would not make it to the swamp. He was barely a quarter mile across the field when the riders closed on him.

*Shit. Is this going to happen?*

"Halloo," the leading rider called. He wore farm clothes and rode in a saddle. The other was dressed similarly, but younger and riding bareback. Grimble realized he would appear more suspicious if he ignored the men. Besides, the rider's call was friendly, not challenging, and they looked like farmhands. Grimble stopped and moved his left hand to his belt, pivoting his sword's handle backward to hide its profile with his leg. Woodsmen did not hunt small game with swords.

"Hallo, friend," the older rider said as they stopped a dozen yards from Grimble. "You're not from Gandleton, are ya? Ya come from up north?" The man's Renlaran accent was heavy. Grimble could not mimic it like Kurt could, but he turned to the riders and gave his best effort.

"Nah, passin' through ya area. Headed west. Like to shoot a rabbit or squirrel for my meal tonight. Might try to catch somethin' in the swamp."

*I don't want to shoot you.*

Both men's heads rocked back. "Gavel help ya friend," said the young man riding bareback. "You're a strange one. Everyone knows to avoid the swamp. It's cursed. Some say alive. Weird noises there. Eblees' Fane, that's what it's called. Best to avoid it. They say anyone who's gone in's never been seen again."

"Thanks, friend," Grimble said, a genuine touch of concern in his tone.

"Hmm," the older man murmured. He smiled and appeared relaxed, but his horse's head rose up and its legs shifted its weight side to side. The man stared at Grimble's neck, smiling, saying nothing.

Grimble angled the arrow with his fingers, edging the nock toward the string.

"We're looking for our dog, friend," the younger man said. "Ya must've heard him just now." His horse behaved like the other, but the young man was oblivious to the signals.

"He ain't seen 'em," said the older rider.

Grimble scratched his belly with his right hand. It remained there, closer to the bow.

"But, Dah," said the younger, "he can't be far. We heard 'em. He went crazy last night, friend, then bolted as soon as we opened the gate this morning."

"He ain't seen 'em," the older stated firmly. The younger man scrunched his eyebrows and looked at his father. The look he got in return told him to stop talking.

Grimble gave a look around. "I ain't seen 'em."

"We thank ya," said the older. "Good day." He backed his horse away half a dozen steps before turning it to lope south toward the hill and the hound.

The younger man nodded at Grimble and followed, calling after his father. "Dah...Dah..." He received no answer.

Flushed and starting to sweat, Grimble took a calming breath. He moved to unclasp the top of his cloak to get some air to his chest and realized the top was already open, exposing the gambeson armor beneath. If his poor attempt at an accent had not caught the riders' attention, the armor most certainly had. He looked back toward them. Their pace had quickened.

Grimble started again toward the swamp, taking glances at the two men over his shoulder. When they were no longer in sight, he returned the arrow to a comfortable grip and quickened his pace until he reached the boggy edge.

Along the verge of the swamp brittle grass, tall and straw-colored, swayed in the breeze like chest-high trees. Green grass peeked out from their bases. The familiar scent of plant decay and stagnant water wafted from the swamp. Gray tree trunks, knotted undergrowth, and a maze of waterways met his stare. He walked north looking for a game trail or a path of some kind. He saw none. Leaves rustled in the light wind.

Grimble thought about turning away. He thought about heading north toward the road and taking his chances there. A chill stiffened his spine, as if someone had trickled cold water down the back of his neck. He whipped around. No one was there. The field was empty.

*Can't turn back. Those two will waste no time notifying the local reeve or any passing patrol.*

The breeze stilled. The grass and the trees quieted. Grimble turned back toward the swamp. His apprehensions eased. A trail he had missed earlier stretched out before him.

*Thank the gods.*

He started forward, feeling light. The trees ahead swayed in a renewed breeze, their heads nodding over their shoulders, beckoning Grimble to come along. He managed dozens of steps without faltering, without looking down, without getting wet.

It was too easy.

Grimble paused. His feet felt chilled. He looked down at his boots. Dark water ran over the top of them. It slinked into the seams and wet his toes. It did not bring comfort to his hot feet; instead it made his toes curl reflexively.

Grimble turned around to examine his path into the swamp. He could not find it. He could see where he had taken his last two steps, but the rest were lost. Skirts of tangled vines around the trees and the moss hanging from their outstretched arms blocked his view of the field. Everything around him was strange, strikingly unfamiliar. He did not feel like the hunter anymore.

*Guys, I could use you now. Find me and get me out of here.*

Committed to this route, Grimble inched forward, doing his best to stay on the dry patches. A wail emanated from someplace farther into the swamp. It started low and guttural and ended in a high-pitched scream, the waves of it penetrating his skull.

Grimble's blood lost its warmth. His mouth dried. He could not swallow. He nocked the arrow and scanned in front of him.

The swamp screamed again. Grimble froze. His breathing quickened. Inside him fear shoveled nourishment into panic's waiting maw. His breaths staccatoed in his throat as he worked to get air to his lungs. The tip of the arrow shook.

"You're not five anymore, dumbass," he said to himself. "Probably an owl or a fox. Remember, you're the deadliest thing in this swamp right now. Act like it, damn you."

It was one thing to say it, another to feel it when everything around him felt rotten. He moved forward again, using tufts of ground, downed trees, and claw-footed roots to stay as dry as possible. But try as he might to stay out of the water, he too often found himself venturing into the veins of muck and channels of opaque waters. He slogged through ankle deep mud that seemed determined to hold him. The satchel he bore snagged on every branch and twig like a condemned man dragged to the gallows, reaching out for whatever he could to stave off his doom.

The weather cooled. The water chilled. Grimble, wet to the waist, told himself to appreciate it; snakes and other creatures preferred warm weather. But his mood was tainted. Something told him snakes were the least of his problems. The sun started its downward track. A nagging seed sprouted doubt. Worry prepared to bloom.

Someone was following him.

Grimble whipped around. Eyes were upon him. He could feel them, yet he could not catch them. They were close, and he was exposed. The unseen gaze made him shudder and raise his shoulders in a futile attempt to protect the back of his neck. Every few steps he snapped his head around. When that did not work, he stayed in one place for minutes, scanning the path behind him.

He might have seen a dark shape, but he could not be certain. He listened, but heard only his own heartbeat and heavy breathing.

*How could they have gotten on my trail so quickly?*

He had been moving northeast for a while, and decided to cut back southeast to see if he could spot his pursuers. He moved slower now, making even less noise than before, conserving his breath and slowing his heartrate. He took more time to listen. And watch. Although he felt someone, he saw no one.

*Who's that sneaky? Kurt?*

Perhaps Kurt was back there, trying to catch up. But why would he try to avoid Grimble? "Kurt," he called in a loud whisper. "Kurt."

No reply.

*Not Kurt.*

Grimble's legs ached. Slogging through the water and scrambling over the broken terrain had worn him down. His muscles burned. Despite the cool weather, sweat poured down his face and back. He pushed on, challenging himself to reach the next tree or the next patch of ground.

It was hours past noon when he found a lap of dry ground with barely enough room to stretch out and rest his head. But it was enough for him to take a break. He looked back once more and did a sweep of the entire area before he removed his backpack and sat down.

His gambeson was as wet as his pants, one from sweat and the other from swamp. Each spoke of what had soiled them through the aromas they gave off. Grimble did not like their conversation. He drank from his canteen and looked at the dark, unmoving water around him. He recapped the canteen before drinking too much. He did not want to refill it here.

Several nights ago it had taken the team hours to make their way around the swamp. Grimble knew going through it would take much longer. He thought of that rainy night and Dinger's bet with Kurt. Then a different image of Dinger slipped into his mind. The last image he would have of his brother in arms: a wan and chalky body in a spider hole. Grimble pushed it back. He could not think about it now.

He focused on the swamp. He estimated it at ten miles across if he moved in a straight line, but he would zigzag while crossing it. That would add miles to the distance he had to travel.

There was a lake at the swamp's southern end. He could try to make his way south and skirt it, but that would mean traveling through more of the swamp; eventually it would mean a lot of swimming, too, and it would put him in the open. Going through the swamp or risking the road to the north were his best options. He preferred the idea of traveling beside the road. It was closer than the lake and moving along it would allow him to move faster. Besides, he could dodge into the swamp if someone approached.

*Hit the river in the middle of this thing and follow it north to the road.*

Grimble's stomach growled. He thought about eating, but he had limited water. He elected to go hungry. Two days of food remained in his pack and it had to last. When he had arrived at Oven last night, he had not taken any of the supplies from the cache. He had his pack. If others from the team were on foot, they might not be so lucky.

The longer Grimble remained still, the more the swamp came to life around him. Some sounds were familiar, some strange, but he was thankful for both, as they were signs that no one else was near. That did not comfort him enough, however, as the all-encompassing feeling of dread that permeated the air and the water and the land lingered.

He removed the helmet from his pack and thought about the gambeson he wore. The armor made him stand out. He could remove it and put it with his helmet in the pack, but if he were caught and needed it for protection, he would not have time to put it on before the fighting started. At this point it was no more to him than weight, weight that stank and made him sweat. And the more he sweated, the more water he would need.

Grimble slid the gambeson over his head. As soon as his chest and back were exposed, a chill hit him, but it was gone before he could set the armor down. He wrapped his helmet in the gambeson and wedged them into a root system under the water. No matter how hard he tried, a small portion peeked above the waterline.

*I am your dutiful soldier, Ihgel. May it be good in your eyes that no one finds this.*

Wrapping the helmet in the cloth armor had given Grimble an idea. He unrolled his bedroll, placed his sword across it and rolled it up again, securing the blade inside by strapping the outside tightly. He left the pommel accessible, hidden by a flap of his bedding. He would be able to draw the sword if the need arose. He felt relieved to be free of the armor, but vulnerable.

Grimble opened the satchel, reaching past the cloth bundle of Elder Steel items to withdraw the leather-wrapped cedar tube containing the information from the team's first meeting with the Baker. He uncorked the tube, unrolled the parchment sheets, and examined them. The four sheets were covered with codes and locations comprehensible only to those familiar with Lagisborg. He rolled them up, slid them back into their wood tube, and recorked it. He placed the tube in the satchel and secured it again.

*This shit had better be worth Dinger's life.*

Grimble ground his teeth and curled his upper lip at the thought that he and his team had been sacrificed like the thousands who had called the Divide home before the war. He didn't mind dying while fighting "the enemy," but the idea of being cut loose, to wither on the stalk because it was convenient, angered him. Baz had warned him. He heard the Raven's voice again: *"You need to be ready to cut us loose or be cut loose. The mission is bigger than us all."*

*Did that fucker cut me and Dinger loose?*

Grimble looked to the heavens.

*If he did, he'll pay for this, Dinger.*

His eyes shifted to the branches above him. The trees peered down, their gaze disapproving. He was small and guilty and unwanted, like a boot. It reminded him of years ago, of his first weeks in the regiment. The scowls. The insults. He felt the cadre's disapproval. He heard their voices on the wind, soft at first, but growing. *"You're worth less than horse piss. You'll never make it. You don't have what it takes to become a trooper. You're not strong enough. You'll never leave this swamp. You will die here, in my arms."*

The trees stooped over him. Grimble held up his fist with his thumb poking between his middle fingers and showed it to the trees. "T'Abyss with ya!"

The swamp wailed again. Grimble felt a hundred ants crawl upon his neck and shoulders. He shivered and flinched. The sensation faded.

He was alone.

A chill remained. An emptiness took hold. Not the feeling one gets in an empty room but the deep, internal emptiness that exists in the dark places of the heart and the abyss of the soul. It was the pit that drew you to the edge, a thousand comforting voices calling from within, telling you it was good to peer inside. And when you listened to them and looked, against all better judgment, you teetered and fell head first, trapped forever.

The sky darkened. Grimble's shoulders slumped. He would never get out of the swamp. He would die here, alone. Why had he left his saddle buckle behind? The regiment's mages were not going to use it. Maybe they'd had no intent ever to use it. The buckle had made him feel like they cared, like the regiment would try to save him. But they would not.

*"It is better that you die here. It is good for you here. The army is not good for you."*

Maybe that was true. Maybe it was good that he had come here. The army was not for him. He thought of his best friend, Kelban. He heard Kelban's voice. It floated on the water. *"Worthless. You're worthless, Horsepiss. I'm better off without you hanging around."*

But it was not Kelban's voice. Something was wrong. He pictured Kelban laughing. Laughing at the minstrel's songs in the pub at Cairn Cross. Laughing when they had sewn Thom inside his tent. Laughing when three soldiers from the 108th Infantry had said they were going to kick his ass. Some of Grimble's gloom faded. Kelban had a great laugh.

What had happened to the team? They were formidable. And Flicker? Flicker was a mage. They could not have been taken easily. He remembered Kurt crawling from the pile of leaves the first time they had stopped to sleep in the Divide. Kurt was different, not like Baz. His promise, his words, were different. *"I'll abandon this mission before I see any of you sacrificed. You, me, and the others, we're all going home."*

306

*It must have all gone to shit.*

Home, the farm. It was warm. Family was always within the sound of his voice, friends too. He remembered Ellie. He would find her. He would make it back to his buddy, Kelban.

*Just stay alive. Just keep moving forward.*

Gazing about, Grimble noticed a bush with blue flowers a few steps away. He had never seen anything like it. It reminded him of a cabbage plant, but larger, over three feet in diameter. Its leaves were broad and light green, emanating from a central core about two feet high. Instead of a head of cabbage, three stalks rose from the center to a height of about four feet. A half-dozen blue flowers grew along each stalk, all facing different directions.

As he investigated it further he saw that its root system was exposed. The thin pink and purple roots lay on top of the ground and stemmed out several feet from the plant. Grimble followed the glossy roots to the base of the plant and was surprised to find that it grew atop an animal's skeleton.

The bones and teeth resembled those of a medium-sized dog, but the skull, or what he could see of it through the roots, was different. The muzzle was shorter and the entire skull was broader than that of a dog or a wolf.

"Are you locked into the ground some way, like a vine? Or can I move you to look at the skeleton?" Grimble asked. He reached out and picked up the nearest root. It stung his finger and thumb. He dropped the root, but it was too late; his index finger and thumb cramped, contracting into his palm. "Son of a bitch!"

His hand shook and the rest of his fingers cramped. A burning sensation grew inside his hand. A few moments later his forearm twitched, and he could not move his hand or forearm, no matter how much he tried. Grimble gritted his teeth as the burning pain and cramps crept up his arm to his shoulder. There they stopped. He was certain his arm would snap under the intense cramping. Sweat built up on his forehead. His clenched jaw ached.

For several minutes he rubbed his forearm and pulled on his fingers, trying to release the grip. Progress was slow, but after a quarter hour he regained use of his limb. The pain subsided shortly after that.

"You're a fucking bastard, aren't you?" he said, looking at the plant again. The stalks appeared different now. He scrutinized them.

Every one of its flowers now faced him.

*Ahh, shit! You gotta be kidding me.*

Keeping an eye on the plant, Grimble shouldered his backpack, made sure he had the satchel, and grabbed his bow. He took a quick reading from the mid-afternoon sun and, taking one last look around him, he moved northeast, away from that damn plant.

Two hours later, he was wet to the waist again. His bow was strapped to his pack and he used a long stick to judge the depth of the water before taking each step. Occasionally something bumped his leg under the water or splashed atop it nearby. He remained prepared to react.

By his estimation, night would fall in the next few hours, and Grimble knew he needed to overnight on dry land. The cool temperature and his wet clothes worried him. He hoped his wool cloak would keep him warm during the night.

A patch of land peaked above the water's surface ahead of him. Several thick trees and less undergrowth grew upon it. Grimble's stick helped him negotiate the shallowest approach toward the bank, but he was almost chest-deep in the water, and another twenty yards or so stood between him and dry land. He paused. Something moved to his right, about fifty yards away. He got no more than a glimpse of it before it dipped below the water's surface.

Grimble scanned the area around him and started again, maintaining his pace toward the land. A softer splash sounded. He did not see movement, nor did he see a ripple. Dry land neared. A call came from somewhere behind him: a high-pitched bark. It sounded like a hoarse dog. The creature called, paused, and called again. Grimble hoped it was a mating call.

He made his way up the sloping bank onto the dry land and paused behind a tree. He checked to see if he was followed. After several minutes he emptied his boots and moved away from the water, continuing further onto the raised, dry ground. The barking creature continued its call. The sound faded farther and farther behind him as he made his way across the patch of land.

It was the largest island he had encountered so far, about a hundred yards on each side. Ash, maple, and oak trees grew in the ground here, stoic and strong. They were spread out, permitting lower branches to grow.

Grimble walked across the land and arrived at the next stretch of water. This one was wide, about fifty to sixty yards across. The bank, about a foot above the water, dropped off sharply. He looked up and down the waterway. To the north, his left, the river emerged from the trees like a small creek among the legs of a herd of horses. To the south, the slow-flowing river disappeared into a similar tangle of trees.

Leaves and other debris drifted slowly from Grimble's left to his right. They would eventually make their way to the lake at the south end, far out of sight and miles away.

*This has to be the river in the middle.*

That meant he was halfway through the swamp. Using his stick, he tested the water's depth. The bank was steep and the stick did not touch the bottom.

He would have to swim across.

The water suddenly rose several inches up the bank and receded as quickly. Yet there was no movement in it save for a few eddies near the middle.

*What the...?* Grimble backed away from the riverbank. Nothing more happened.

Hoping he was indeed halfway through, he decided to take advantage of this place for the night's stay. He walked back toward the trees a few yards from the water's edge, but kept a watch on the river. The way the water had moved unnerved him. Grimble set his pack in the crook of a moss-covered ash tree. He did not know what kind of creatures called this swamp home and wanted some space between himself and them. He figured the best way to make that happen was to be off the ground during the night.

He climbed partway up the tree and checked the branches for suitability before climbing back down. Hungry and tired, he needed some nourishment as well as sleep, but that meant he needed water. He had downed the last of his canteen about an hour earlier and had sweated more than that in the meantime.

Grimble found a stick and whittled it to about two feet in length with a chisel edge on one end. Grabbing his bow and two of his four arrows, he made his way back to the spot where he had walked out of the water. There, he started a rover's well with his digging stick. He worked a little more than a foot from the water's edge, watching and listening for signs of anyone following him.

During one of his checks, Grimble caught movement in the

middle of the water, about thirty yards away. It was a beaver, or an otter, and definitely the largest one of either he had ever seen. Only the top of its head was above the water, but it was as large as a dog's. A second head popped up, followed by a third. Grimble looked about. Nothing else was nearby. A few birds cried from their branches and flew away. A fourth head popped up not far from the first three.

Grimble stopped digging and stood up. He raised his hands above his head and hissed. He would have yelled, but didn't want his voice carrying through the swamp. The creatures continued to stare at him, their ears twitching. Farther off to his right, a fifth and sixth head popped up. Grimble sensed that they were working to circle him. He backed toward the tree line, and the creatures drifted toward him. He stopped, but they continued.

This was not curiosity. He was prey.

Grimble dropped the digging stick and began his retreat toward his kit and the tree. It was a methodical effort. He nocked an arrow in preparation. The creatures emerged, one, then two at a time. These were not beavers. They were dogs, about the size of a coyote, with elongated bodies and short brown-and-black fur coats. But their heads were different. Their ears were small and round, and their muzzles and lower jaws were compact. Long whiskers jutted from above their eyes, under their chins, and along their muzzles, giving them the appearance of otters. Grimble was reminded of the skeleton he had seen under the plant.

The large one in the center called out with the same hoarse bark Grimble had hoped was a mating call. Those around it replied. More calls came from the woods to Grimble's left and right.

*Shit. Definitely not a mating call.*

He reached the tree with his backpack. The water dogs, now nine of them, moved closer, creating a semicircle around him. The river was behind Grimble. The dogs had closed to within a dozen strides. They paced back and forth, growling, their heads low. One moved toward him, testing him. Grimble stomped his foot. The water dog tucked its tail and retreated.

He hated to use an arrow at this point, but needed to send a message to the pack that he was dangerous. Grimble waited for the next one to move closer and when it did, he fired, striking it between the neck and shoulder. The creature yelped and limped away, the fletching protruding from its chest. The rest of them backed off a few paces.

The one Grimble had shot flopped to its side and stopped moving. The others kept their eyes on Grimble. They continued to pace. Using the opportunity he had paid for, Grimble nocked the second arrow. Keeping an eye on the dogs, he grabbed his backpack and lifted it into a higher crook. He did the same with his walking stick. A few dogs barked, and the pack closed in again.

*Shit! Didn't scare 'em.*

He could not climb while holding the bow, so he removed the arrow and quickly slung the bow over his head and shoulder. The dogs paused and canted their heads. As Grimble jumped and lifted himself onto the lower tree limb, they charged. He managed to get his feet up onto a limb six feet above the ground, but the movement dislodged his backpack, and it slid. He reached for it but missed. It fell to the ground below. The dogs scattered briefly. His walking stick too started to slide, but he managed to save it.

Growling and snarling, the dogs jumped at Grimble. Their thick heads reached the stout branch he stood on. It was too close for Grimble's comfort, and he moved to a higher branch.

One dog sniffed at his backpack and tried to claw and root its way into it. This drew the attention of a few others, and before long, several were fighting over it, tearing into it with their teeth. The frenzy drew the attention of the rest of the dogs and they all set upon the backpack, until the big one barked and snarled, causing the rest to cower away. The big one sniffed the torn pack, dug its nose inside, and emerged with one of the pemmican tubes. It jogged away from the group and ate, growling at any who dared come too close.

The others attacked the pack and emerged with biscuits and the other pemmican tube. Those that had failed to secure food fought with those that had.

*I hope you choke on that greasy shit.*

The dogs fought over the rations. One, looking back at its pursuers with a hard biscuit in its mouth, ran into the deep water. The chasers immediately began a desperate bark as they backed away from the edge. The sound was similar to the alerts of farm dogs. The rest of the pack stopped what they were doing and barked along. A few moved toward the water, but none drew closer to the bank than five or six feet.

The dog in the water thrashed for a second, before swimming to the bank. The mud and the steep wall made climbing difficult. The dog struggled. The rest barked. It disappeared under the surface and reemerged, springing up and leaping onto the level ground with its front legs. Its back legs kicked and dug at the mud, trying to find purchase.

Finally obtaining the grip it needed, the wet dog arose from the river and shook the wetness from its fur. An upheaval of water caught Grimble's eye, and as the wet dog stepped away from the bank, a massive creature emerged.

It was mottled brown and moss green, about seven or eight

feet wide and no more than four feet high. Black, bulbous eyes stared from behind a huge, flat mouth – a mouth as wide as the creature itself. It looked like a monstrous catfish. Tentacles several yards long writhed from above and below its mouth. Its head rested on land while its tail thrashed in the water. Grimble believed it to be thirty feet long or more.

The wet dog yelped and ran, but two tentacles wrapped around its body and legs. The creature opened its jaws and pulled the screeching dog toward its waiting mouth, then slid backward, disappearing beneath the water. The other dogs fell silent. The creature was gone.

The water had calmed again before the dogs returned their attention to Grimble's rations. A few set upon the body of the dog Grimble had shot, tugging and ripping at its flesh. Eventually the whole pack fought over the body, dragging what parts remained back toward the shallow water from which they had emerged. The yips and barks faded away to the south. It seemed that Grimble had been forgotten.

The light waned. From his perch Grimble took an inventory of the things strewn about beneath the tree. Not hearing or seeing any more activity, he lowered himself to the ground and salvaged his bedroll and a few other items before returning to the safety of the branches. Using the remnants of his backpack and his bedroll, he did his best to create something somewhere between a hammock and a sling. He made certain it was secure among the branches before entrusting his weight to it.

Grimble looked at the darkening sky and took a few moments to assess his situation; but a few moments were all sleep would allow, and he nodded off.

# CHAPTER TWENTY-TWO

Grimble jolted awake at the sensation of something alighting on the branch supporting his back. He whipped his head toward the end of the bough. The thin branches at the end jiggled, but nothing was there. The sun was almost down; the light was low and his eyes were bleary. He blinked and rubbed his eyes, looking again. Nothing.

Had he imagined it? Had he caused the branches to shake? Or had something been there? Darkness waited at the edges of his vision and he knew it would envelop him soon. A cold breeze blew on his neck. He shivered and scrunched his shoulders against its bite.

Behind him a voice whispered, *"Grimble."*

His hair stood on end. He sprung sideways to look, nearly falling from the tree. No one was there. He peered toward the river and scanned beyond it: the woods, the swamp, the sky, the ground. The voice had been strange, neither male nor female. Grimble's hands shook. He felt that he was being watched.

The wail he had heard when he first entered the swamp howled out again, low and guttural. It was not far away. It ended, as before, with a high-pitched scream. Grimble shuddered. He was too scared to move his head to look about. His eyes flicked this way and that and he slowly bunched his cloak around his neck. He listened, but heard little more than his breathing. Even the frogs were silent. Grimble watched the last light of day slip away between branches and leaves. It left him alone. In a tree. In the middle of this malignant swamp.

Grimble stayed awake. He knew in his mind and in his heart that if he fell asleep, he would not wake up. The darkness blanketed everything. He felt like a child walking through the woods beside a stranger with a cold heart.

*Where's the moon?*

The darkness was total, though he saw shapes emerge and disappear. He resisted the need to sleep, but the shapes were hypnotic. Grimble closed his eyes. His mind fogged. His head nodded —

He bit his tongue to wake himself up. He had to stay awake.

Time crawled.

Grimble found himself breathing slow and rhythmic. He shook his head and took a quick, deep breath. How long had it been now?

Hours?

Minutes?

Heartbeats?

High above, and unfelt, a breath pushed a cloud and exposed the moon. The darkness melted into long shadows, and silver beams struck around Grimble, muting what colors they touched. A steady, gentle current shushed through the trees. Sweet blossoms perfumed the air. All was serene. Hushed. Calming. His eyes locked onto a stream of moonlight shining down on the water below. The image blurred. It was beautiful, relaxing.

*He was outside. His mother called. Her voice, clear at first, changed to a bird's chirp.*

*He sat on the woodchopping stump behind his home, watching a chick peck at insects in the dirt. Ants crawled about beneath its feet, first a few, then more. They crawled along the dirt toward the chick. He watched the ants. Lots of ants. It pecked. They swarmed. They crawled up the chick's legs, surging onto it until its yellow down disappeared. The mass pulsed. The chick kicked its leg. It fell, letting out one last cry.*

*His mother called for him. He should go to her. That was the right thing to do. She opened the back door and looked out at him. She stood in the half-open doorway, flour and wet dough covering her hands. She wore her Templeday dress.*

*"Suppertime, Grimble," she said, a smile on her face. "Come along." But he did not want to eat. He did not want to go with her. Why was she cooking in her best dress? Why were her hands doughy if supper was ready? He looked at her again. Her mouth smiled, large and toothy, lips pulled taut. Her eyes were wide and blank.*

*"Suppertime, Grimble. Come along." Her grin widened. Her skin stretched.*

*Someone behind the door pushed it closed and shouted, "NO!"*

*His mother opened the door again. Her mirthless smile grew large and corrupted. The door started to close. She fought it. Her expression persisted as she struggled.*

*As if possessed by the strings of a puppeteer, her hands slapped at the door. Her head slumped forward onto her chest. The door almost closed. Her arms wiggled through the opening. It sprung open.*

*"No," the unseen person said again. His mother backed away from the door. Her walk was wrong. Her knees bent the wrong way. She quivered and convulsed.*

*The door closed.*

Grimble woke to the grating of claws scratching and moving up the trunk of his tree. He blinked his eyes clear and looked about. The noise stopped. Shades of gray lay all about him, from the ash of the tree branches to an impenetrable charcoal deeper in the swamp. He saw no threat, but reached for his knife anyway. The scratching started again, below him. It grew louder. He glanced around his legs and prepared to strike.

A raccoon edged its way by his boots, its claws scraping at the bark as it crept by. It eyed Grimble and slunk onto a branch inches from his feet, squatting in the crook and holding onto the trunk. The two stared at each other as if coming to an agreement.

"You bunk here too, little brother?"

The raccoon stared at him. It comforted Grimble to see something familiar, something normal. But this was not a normal swamp, and he wondered if this was not a normal raccoon. The gray-and-black creature near his feet could be venomous or menacing in some other way. A thought of killing it crossed his mind. Even if it were not dangerous, he could kill it for food. But he quickly dismissed that idea – a fire would give him away.

Grimble was getting ready to attack the racoon when he noticed that its gaze was moving repeatedly between him and the ground. It made no noise. Grimble started to move and the creature growled. There was enough light to see it was not taking an aggressive posture. The growling stopped.

*What the —?*

Grimble started to move again and once more it growled. It was a low growl, quiet, but intentional. The creature stayed where it was, gripping the trunk with its front paws. It stared at him, looked to the ground, and back to him. Grimble peered over his shoulder to the ground below. He jolted.

A glowing blue mass moved across the ground ten feet beneath him. The glow was brighter than the coals of a campfire and pulsed every few seconds. The light kept him from recognizing the source at first, but when he focused beyond the blue haze, he saw it. Gliding across the ground below was a plant with blue flowers like the one he had encountered earlier.

The stalks glowed brightest, and the rest of the plant's radiance diminished from the edges of the leaves to the base. The roots were all but invisible in the darkness, but there was enough light to catch them slithering like snakes. The plant circled Grimble's tree. Its stalks undulated and rippled independently, unnaturally.

*T'Abyss! That thing can move?*

He looked back at the raccoon and nodded. It blinked and returned its gaze to the plant below. Grimble looked about, trying to judge the time. It was hours from daybreak. He turned his attention to the swamp and thought he saw two or three other glowing patches farther away; at least one was on the other side of the river.

The plant below moved away from the tree, heading south.

319

Grimble watched it until the glow faded entirely and it disappeared from view.

He turned back to the racoon. "Thanks, little brother. Looking out for me like a tiny Kelban." The raccoon stared at him, its ears twitching and scanning. It turned and looked around before climbing a few feet higher into the tree and wedging itself in the crook of two branches.

Grimble settled back down in his bedding. He was too awake at this point to return to sleep, so instead worked the stiffness out of his muscles bit by bit. He was thirsty and had a headache, and knew water had to be a priority in the morning.

The sun was distinctly above the horizon before the raccoon climbed down the trunk. It sniffed around and took a few bounds away from the tree, then paused and looked back up at Grimble. The two stared at each other for several seconds before its ear twitched and it turned away, bounding off to the west.

Understanding what he'd been told, Grimble lowered himself to the ground. With the full light of the morning sun he was able to examine his backpack in detail. It was as he had feared. Rips along the seams and gouges as big as his fist had been torn in the fabric. It would no longer serve him. Grimble secured the straps and cords from the backpack, determined to make use of them in some way. He consolidated his kit by rolling items into his bedroll or placing them in the satchel.

The swamp wailed.

Grimble ducked. The origin of the sound was not far. The wildlife grew quiet and all movement stopped. His skin crawled.

*T'Abyss! What is that thing?*

It felt wrong to move immediately afterward. Grimble waited until the sounds of the swamp returned before he budged.

A comforting, fleeting thought of heading south whisked through his mind. He had no idea why, but looked in that direction. It was darker, and he knew more swamp and a lake lay that way. He picked up his bow and walking stick and set out north, toward the road and the bridge across the river.

It was warmer than the day before. Grimble slogged through the murky water and muddy islands with their thickets of twisted roots, keeping his distance from the river and the creature it hid like a snake under a log. The river held a relatively straight course, but did not run perfectly north to south, and on a few occasions he found himself walking toward it, only catching the mistake a few yards from the bank. There was a multitude of animal sign in the shallows and along the dark mud of the swamp side of each pocket of land. But it seemed everything in the swamp knew of the creature in the river; there was an absence of any life along the riverbank.

Well, an absence of anything that crawled on land. There was a handful of birds and an abundance of buzzing and biting insects. As troublesome as the latter were, they did not bother Grimble as much as the tedious exertion of trying to move through the thick mud. Once again he was sweating, even with his cloak removed. His heart pounded in his ears. It was difficult to keep his mind focused. He needed water and decided to make that his priority, rather than the speed of his travel.

Spotting an area with vines growing up the trees, he made his way to them and spent the next few hours digging rover's wells, collecting water from them and any suitable vines. His headache subsided, and his canteen was a quarter full, but his stomach growled. This worried him, as he was unsure if what he had drunk from the wells might hurt him later.

*Please, Gavel, show me the way. Let me be home before I*

*find out whether this water was good or not.*

While Grimble had been collecting the water he had removed his boots and socks, trying to air and dry his feet. They had been wet for more than a day and their appearance was as bad as he had expected, macerated and pale. He knew the swamp would take him by way of his feet, if he did not get out of it soon.

As he donned his socks and boots again, he looked back toward the river and wondered if the monster ran up and down the entire length – or worse: could there be more than one of them? He had to know. Grimble finished with his boots and slinked his way to the bank, remaining crouched and prepared to move.

The dark water hid its secrets well and nothing could be seen below the surface. Using his walking stick, Grimble first moved the end around slowly in the water, and when that elicited no reaction, he thrashed it about. There was a ripple several yards away and the water level rose along the bank. Grimble darted back. When nothing else happened, he knelt and reached out with his stick, rubbing it back and forth in the soil a few feet from the water's edge.

Four thick, gray tendrils slipped over the bank toward the stick.

If he hadn't seen them the day before, Grimble would have thought them to be large snakes. He pulled his stick back and stood. The tentacles slithered to where the stick had scraped the ground and paused, eventually retracting and sliding back from where they came. The water rippled and a minute later was calm again.

*Shit!*

Grimble looked up and down the river. The view had changed little. He checked behind him and when he saw nothing, heard nothing, he pressed on, wondering if the father and son he'd met had told anyone about him.

He pressed north, paralleling the river, grabbing cattail roots and harvesting water when he could. After the morning's encounter with the river monster, Grimble enjoyed the mundane wildlife he spotted the rest of the day. Several of the trees he encountered were new to him, but one was more intriguing than the others. It looked like a willow tree, but it bore leaves and blooms at the same time. He examined its yellow-and-white catkin flowers and dark-green leaves. That each thin leaf was edged with barbs, longer than those of a holly tree, made it all the more curious. Their points were aggressive and Grimble ended up with scratches on his hands trying to handle them in the breeze.

He turned northbound again and was hundreds of yards from the spiked willow when his hands began to burn where the scratches were. Grimble found his legs heavy. The further he moved, the more fatigued he became. There was another scream, this one high-pitched. His head spun. Dizziness and nausea overtook him. He fell to his knees. His mind clouded and blackness threatened to steal his vision.

Instead, his sight cleared and he took several breaths. The world around him was familiar, yet unknown. Grimble could not remember why he was kneeling in dark mud amid tangled roots and broken trunks.

*Where am I?*

The sun was on its downward path. Grimble remembered he was headed home and realized he was going the wrong way. He had been walking north, but he needed to cross the river if he was going to make it home. His mind struggled. Thinking was like trying to breathe through several layers of wool cloth.

A hushed voice spoke to him. *"The river. Cross the river."*
*I should be headed east. Home is in the east.*
*"Cross the river."*
*Why haven't I crossed that damn river yet? I need to cross the river.*

Grimble looked north and wondered why he had been traveling that way. His head hurt. He rubbed it, pulling at his hair. His scalp was hot. His head burned. Even on his knees he swayed. Sweat snaked down his head and face, stinging his eyes. His heart pounded in his chest, in his ears. He should cool his head. Yes. He should soak it in the cool water of the river. Then he could swim across. He was a good swimmer. Why had he not crossed it already?

He crawled to the bank, ready to reach down and splash water on his head. He thought of the time he and Ellie had crawled out of the creek, soaked and laughing. He had enjoyed that walk, even when they had fallen into the water. He smiled. That water had been clear, however, not this dark, murky, ominous —

*What?*

He remembered where he was.

*Shit!*

Grimble scrambled backward, crawling away from the river on all fours. He slipped and fell on his back. He kicked his legs out. The satchel bound them. He rolled away from the bank until he was sure he was no longer near it.

He sat up, breathing heavily, gulping for air. He remembered the crawling plant and whipped his head around. Nothing was nearby. Grimble unwound the satchel's shoulder strap from his legs and got up. His head hurt, but the fog had lifted from his mind.

*What in the Abyss was that? You aren't a boot. Stay focused.*

Remembering he was being hunted, he checked for signs of pursuers. He found none. Grimble shouldered his pack and started north again. North to the road. North to the bridge.

The absence of any sign of humans was a blessing; however, as the day warmed, more of the swamp's biting and blood-sucking bugs awakened. They loved Grimble. When their numbers rose to a swarm, he covered his skin in mud and endured the bites the coating did not stop.

Not to be outdone by the insects, the satchel tried its best to help the swamp wear Grimble down. As if almost trapping him by the riverbank had not been enough, it continued its practice of snagging on branches, sticks, and vines. Grimble did *his* best to show the swamp it would not beat him as he trudged through muddy grasses and waist-high water, reclaiming his dominance over the satchel every time it tried to assert its will.

Grinding through the swamp and constantly checking for pursuers distracted Grimble from the time and before he was ready for it, the sun threatened to dive below the horizon. He did not have much water remaining in his canteen and used the last hour of light to dig a rover's well and find a suitable sleeping tree. He had no idea how far he had come, but he did not want to push into the night. He was not going to be caught on the ground after sunset.

Strapped into the branches of the tree, Grimble removed his boots to dry them and his feet. Two days of walking through water was taking its toll. He knew blisters and sores would soon follow. He rubbed cattail gel on his feet and chewed on the last of the roots. When he had no more food, he sipped water while thinking on the next day's tasks.

325

A white cloaked figure appeared at the corner of his eye.

He turned. No one was there.

*Now I'm seeing things. Gods, I need sleep.*

He had been there before – awake so long he'd started to see things. But he did not feel safe falling asleep in the swamp. He'd survived the previous night, but the dream he'd had unnerved him. He also feared some creature would find him and crawl up the tree. He was determined to stay awake.

It wasn't long before sleep threatened his awareness, but Grimble was ready for it this time. He focused on keeping his mind aware and refused to give in to indiscriminate slumber. He made up little games to keep his mind occupied, telling himself was not going to fall asleep again.

He was wrong.

*Ellie sat on a large rock, reading a book near the tobacco-drying barn. Her light-blue dress covered her knees but allowed her calves and feet to enjoy the warm, sunny day along with her arms. She held her book in one hand and with the other played with the honey-colored hair draped over her shoulder, twisting it between her fingers. She loved her books. She had a few, but the book of poetry was her favorite. At least that was the way it appeared to Grimble, because she read it more than the others.*

*During a few of their walks she had read to him from that book. It was written in a language he had never heard of. He didn't know the words, but by the way she read each poem, he could feel the joy or misery or love or loss that it recounted.*

*Ellie saw him looking at her and smiled. She
put the book on her lap and gave him one of her
funny faces before waving for him to join her.*

A leg cramp woke Grimble from the dream. He clenched his teeth to stifle his scream; forgetting he was in a tree, he tried to stand. The absence of a floor quickly reminded him of his mistake. He began to fall. He reached for the trunk, grabbling it and wrapping his arms around it, pulling himself to it like a frightened child to his mother. His face grated on the coarse bark as it ground along the trunk, a foot or more, before he was able to stop his momentum.

He clutched the tree, trying not to grunt, trying not to make a noise, while his right calf contracted in waves. When he thought it was over he started to move, and the muscle cramped again. Grimble pushed his face into the bark and hoped it would catch any curses he uttered or sounds he made.

The cramps diminished again, but he was not going to take a chance. Hugging the trunk, he used his good leg to search for a branch to gain a foothold. Once his foot located one, he put his weight on it and relaxed a little. It was several more minutes before he climbed back into his makeshift bed. He rubbed his calf and hoped it was done.

The rest of the night passed in monotonous misery as Grimble rubbed his legs for the next several hours. There was an occasional interruption from the local wildlife and two visits by the glowing blue plants, but for this swamp, the night was rather unexceptional. Shortly after sunrise, as the sky brightened and brought colors back to the world, Grimble climbed down from the tree. He wondered where the raccoon had spent the night. Did it always use the same tree?

"Missed you, Kelban."

He walked around the tree and stretched the stiffness out of his limbs. His calf and back remained sore. His feet were cracking and stung with every step. Upon his left cheek and jaw he discovered caked blood from scraping his face on the bark. Grimble shook his head.

*Even the trees are kicking my ass.*

He readied his kit and checked his boots and socks. Although both were damp and the wool socks were wearing holes in spots, they looked like they would hold up for a few more days. Looking at the sores and cracks on his feet, he realized he needed to harvest more of the jelly from the next cattails he came across.

Grimble's stomach growled as he finished readying himself for the day, and he felt the weakness brought on by two days with almost no food. Water was essential, even though it was only going to make the hunger pains worse. The foot-deep rover's well he had dug the previous night was full, but the mud had not fully settled and the water was murky. Without any better choices, Grimble used his cup to scoop some out, smelled it, and gave a taste. Beyond the grit and taste of mud, there were no other adverse indicators. He prayed to Rafel for the water to heal and not hurt him as he drank from his cup and used it to fill his canteen.

Once again Grimble headed north, paralleling the river. Before midday the terrain changed. Instead of meandering in stagnant streams, the water and mud hid beneath grass and other ground cover, and the patches of dry land were becoming larger. The river remained, narrowing slightly, but every time Grimble tested the water, he saw signs of something substantial moving beneath the surface.

He ran across another plant with blue flowers. This one's

roots sprawled over bare ground, no prey within its grasp. Grimble gave it a wide berth.

He thought he heard something and stopped. His breathing and heartbeat were the only things he caught. He moved again.

Someone whispered.

Grimble dropped to the ground. He listened and heard it again: breathy whispers, coming from the west, too far away for him to make out the words. Had he been distracted and let his pursuers get too close? His blood chilled, and he crawled to an area of tall grass and exposed roots to hide. The sound stopped. Grimble looked about and listened. He saw no one. He heard no one.

The whispers started again. This time they came from the east, across the river. He stayed low, straining to hear. A hushed conversation was taking place, but Grimble could not make out the words. Had they seen him? He crawled north, staying behind the grass. The satchel snagged on every clump of grass and exposed root. His clothes tore and ripped. He continued until his arms and neck gave in from the exertion.

He listened, his breaths heavy, but the voices were no longer there. Grimble raised to a crouch. Nothing. He drank some water and prayed that he had eluded them, whoever they were. He continued north, moving slower now, constantly looking and listening.

He had to get home.

# CHAPTER TWENTY-THREE

Once again Grimble found himself surrounded by standing water. Over the next hour he waded through it, sticking to the shallow sections of the swamp as much as possible. Sparse beds of green ground cover mottled the dark gaps between the trees. Eventually, voices – not the whispering he had heard before, but discernible voices – wove their way to his ears. He slowed his pace and paid closer attention to the sounds. He could not make out anything intelligible, but before long he smelled a campfire, and the voices became clearer. Grimble crouched lower and crept forward. One of the strange willow trees with its spiked leaves and catkin blooms loomed in front of him. He swept wide of its branches.

The bridge over the river came into view. Grimble slid into a prone position behind a beech tree with a clump of bristly sedge growing near its base. He spied through gaps in the sedge and between the trunks of the oaks and beeches to the elevated roadway ahead of him. The wooden bridge that connected to that road was gray from the weather and the sun. It was a striking difference to what he remembered of it from that rainy night when he and the team had crossed it. Although that had been only a few days ago, it seemed like a lifetime. Grimble thought of the team, but quickly shut those memories down before they took over.

A single soldier stood on the western end of the bridge, spear in hand. Another paced along the wooden beams, a crossbow in his arms, looking south into the swamp and down at the river, which flowed four or five feet beneath the bottom of the bridge.

"There it is again!" screamed the soldier with the crossbow. Grimble prepared to run, but the soldier was looking down over the railing, at something under the bridge.

"Where? Where?" said the one with the spear. He rushed onto the bridge.

The crossbowman aimed his bow at something below him, moving it slowly as if tracking a target. "Riiiiiiiiight – *there*!" He fired and whooped. "Eat that, you slimy fuck! Hope you rot and die." The spearman hurried to his partner's side.

A voice from the other side of the road cried out, "Ya pig-shit eatin' son of a whore. Stop wastin' ya bolts. I told ya to let that thing be. T'Abyss with it all! If ya shoot at it any more, I'll dock ya a day's pay."

"But Sarge," the spearman said, "that thing's unnatural. It'd eat us if it could grab us."

"Alright," said the sergeant, his voice overly sweet, "both of ya are docked one day's pay. Shoot another bolt or flap ya lips again and it'll be two. And ya know what? Just 'cause I'm feelin' generous, both of ya are on cleanup tomorrow. Got it?"

"Yes, sir!" the soldiers shouted. They pushed each other and whispered harshly, both clearly accusing the other of being the cause of the sergeant's wrath. The spearman shook his head and moved back to the road. The crossbowman wound and reloaded his bow.

Grimble waited for an hour, watching their routine. He waited for something to change, but the soldiers kept diligent watch and were true to their tasks. They scanned the road and swamp equally.

The ground vibrated under Grimble. Subtle at first, it increased in intensity. A low groaning started from the base of the spiked willow yards away from him. It grew to a guttural wail. The trunk shuddered. The wail rose to a high-pitched scream as the leaves shook, sending a cloud of pollen drifting along with the breeze. Grimble twisted, drawing his arms to his chest, his head toward his right shoulder. His bones vibrated and ached. His breathing was hard and labored. Every part of him trembled uncontrollably, as if he were covered in ice.

"GODS ABOVE!" the spearman yelled.

The wail ended and the leaves stopped shaking. Grimble lay on the dirt and grass, still shaking. He moaned softly, hating himself for it. He was not five years old anymore. Why was he so scared?

"Ihgel's arm!" shouted a soldier.

"What the fuck is that?" yelled another.

"T'Abyss with this post, Sarge."

"Gods above!"

"I'm serious! What the fuck is that?"

"It's gotta be a hole to the Abyss. It's gotta."

"Calm down," called the sergeant.

Grimble blinked, trying to clear the tears from his eyes and focus on what he could see of the soldiers posted on the bridge.

"Demons. Fey creatures —"

"I said calm down. Easy."

"— fell beasts. All sorts of evil shit coming to suck our

souls."

The sergeant screamed, "EASY! Get ya shit together!" The others stopped shouting. The sergeant continued. "I don't like it either, but we don't do each other good when we act like snot-sleeved, whiny brats. Ya're soldiers. Act like it. Ya got that?"

There was a spiritless, but collective, "Yes, sir."

"Now, switch out. Next team. Ya're up."

Two new soldiers relieved the ones guarding the bridge. They moved slowly to their positions until a man who looked like their sergeant stepped onto the road. The ones being relieved wasted no time leaving the bridge, hustling down the far side of the embankment and out of Grimble's sight. The sergeant looked about, hands on his hips, and shook his head before following the others down to their encampment. Grimble watched the new ones as he collected his composure and stopped himself from shaking. He spent the rest of his surveillance dividing his time between the soldiers and the spiked willow near him.

Shortly after the jitters had stopped and Grimble was feeling close to normal, he heard the rhythmic beating of hooves approaching. The new spearman at the end of the bridge craned his head, looking west, and grabbed his spear with both hands. "Riders approach!" he shouted over his shoulder.

His partner moved to his side. Four riders appeared, leading two other horses carrying packs. They pulled to a stop a few yards from the bridge. A half-dozen soldiers appeared from the other side of the road and made their way to the packhorses. The soldiers unstrapped some of the parcels and sacks and carried their provisions back down the other side of the road.

"Hey! One parcel of meat per outpost," the lead rider said.

"We got two last time," said a soldier holding a parcel in his arms.

"Well, ya only get one this time. Where's ya sergeant?"

"Here," the sergeant said, walking up to the road.

"Report."

"No sightings, nothing to report." The sergeant took the second parcel of meat from his soldier and tossed it to one of the other riders. "Thanks for the resupply."

"Have ya patrolled the swamp as ordered?" the lead rider asked.

The sergeant's posture tensed and he drew himself up to his full height. "Don't take that tone with me." He closed the distance with the rider and speared a finger at him. "We've been the ones out here. The ones hearing things. Things that make even my skin crawl. The ones getting eaten up by these damn bugs. The ones putting up with this cursed swamp and the damn creature-fish-thing in the water. Bigger than an ox. It almost grabbed Niall."

"Sure as the Abyss," came a yell from the other side of the road.

The sergeant continued. "We've done what we've been ordered to do. I want to catch that assassin bastard as much as *you*. Shit, the month's pay for spotting 'im is motivation enough. But the locals say that swamp's cursed. And I believe it. If ya have the balls, ya walk into it. Ya haven't heard or seen what we have the last few nights. Abyss and curses, I'll give ya a month of my own pay if ya walk a mile in yaself."

"Alright, alright, a simple 'yes' would have done," the rider said. "Just carrying out orders."

"I'll continue to send in patrols, but they will remain within sight of this bridge. Shit. He's probably long gone. Likely picked up by a mage and portalled out two days ago. Any of the other patrols reporting anything?"

"No. Like you, most think he's back in Aendura. The rest

hope to cash in on the bounty. A year's pay for catching or killing 'im has motivated a few to enter the swamp, but they never go far. What good is a reward if ya can't spend it, right?"

The sergeant chuckled. "My point exactly."

"Anyway, we have four more drops to make. See ya on our way back." The rider gave the order and the mounted soldiers headed east toward Arhus. The horses' hooves made a racket crossing the wooden bridge. The other soldiers went back to their routine.

*Shit. Doesn't that beat it all? I've got a price on my head. Fuck.*

Grimble thought about waiting for dark, about stealing some food and trying to sneak past the guards. He thought about crossing the bridge. He tried to think of ways to do it, but his mind would not stay focused on the problem. He was so tired. He had to use the bridge. It would save so much time.

But the soldiers were motivated to get a glimpse of him. They would love nothing more than to be the ones to catch him or shoot him. T'Abyss, he would be lucky if they shot him instead of capturing him. He did not want to imagine the things they would do to him if he were taken prisoner. Simply being spotted would be his end, too. These soldiers were rested and fed. He would never be able to outrun them in his condition.

Still, Grimble was desperate to take the bridge. It could take days to find another way across the river, and he was losing strength. He thought of attacking the outpost, trying to sneak up in the darkness and take them out in their sleep, or shooting the ones on the bridge with his own bow. But he knew the reality was that one of them would not die quietly. He would be discovered, and even if he fought only one of them he was at a disadvantage, unarmored and fatigued. They were armored and had spears, which outreached his arming sword.

His mind continued to wander. He ordered it to focus on the problem, but it was recalcitrant. Grimble promised himself he would punish it with lots of beer when he got home. He smiled. It was a little smile, but it briefly helped his mood.

Could he climb or crawl under the bridge?

*You're not thinking. Your back would be inches from the water at that point. That damn river monster would get you.*

His shoulders and head slumped. He knew he would have to spend many more days in the swamp. More days sludging through the muck, while he weakened with each passing hour. He would have to head south. He had to try to make it to the lake or come up with a plan to cross the river along the way. Grimble headed back into the swamp, thinking about the route he would take.

*It's more than a day's travel back to the tree I slept in that first night. Then several more days to get to the lake, more still if I have to avoid any patrols. I can't make it that far without food. I'm getting weaker by the minute.*

His stomach growled. The idea of the soldiers at the bridge enjoying a hot meal frustrated Grimble. Even though he was over two hundred yards away, he could smell their fire. It gave him an idea.

If he started a small fire and kept it smokeless, the soldiers' fire would mask his. He'd seen fish in the shallow waters – nothing too large, but big enough to eat.

Using his knife, Grimble split the end of his walking stick into quarters and fashioned a fishing spear using two smaller sticks and some lashings from his backpack. Making sure he was deep inside the swamp, he found a good spot in the shallow water and waded in. He waited.

It took several attempts before he was successful, but by mid-afternoon he had a handful of cattail roots, three small fish and a frog to show for his efforts. Grimble returned to land and gathered some dry wood. In a shallow pit he started a small fire and worked to prepare the fish and frog. He monitored what little smoke the fire made and was satisfied it wasn't enough to give away his position. Before too long he had cooked and eaten the fish, burying the evidence afterward in the shallow pit containing the fire's embers.

The swamp wailed.

Now that he knew how the cry was made, the fear of the unknown was not there, but the sound still made Grimble's skin crawl. Seeing no signs of pursuers, he moved south again to get away from the location. Hunger continued to nag him, but the protein had renewed his spirit.

Soon he heard the whispering again and ducked behind an oak tree. The whispers were not accompanied by any other sound, no noise of passage, no odors, and he could never see anything. Grimble began to wonder if it was the wind.

He pressed on, careful not to run into a group tracking him, and reached the tree he had slept in the night before. The rover's well he'd dug was still there, the water clearer than it had been this morning. Refreshing his canteen and drinking his fill, he climbed into the tree and removed his boots and socks. He checked his feet, rubbing some of the cattail gel on them. Once his feet were covered in the slime, he stretched out his legs and prepared to act like a bird for another night. The smell of sweet blossoms did not visit him, nor was he lulled by the trees.

Darkness fell. Before Grimble could fall asleep, his legs cramped, first one then the other. He was working them out when he caught sight of a blue plant at the tree's base. The manner in which it moved gave him chills. Not knowing if it could hear, he stopped moving, suffering the cramps in silence. He was sure if he were on the ground the thing would move quickly, but it lingered before crawling away. Grimble was glad when it was out of sight.

Not long after the plant left he heard scratching on the tree's trunk. He reached for his knife and looked down. "Kelban?"

The raccoon climbed the tree and tentatively crawled by him before taking position on a higher limb. They looked at each other. Grimble was confident this raccoon looked like the one before, and he smiled at its company. His furry companion straddled its legs over the limb, laid its chin upon the branch, and closed its eyes. It did Grimble more good than he could have expected to have the raccoon nearby. He smiled to himself and relaxed.

*"Grimble, pass the bread to Jenn," Dad said. Grimble picked up the basket in front of him. It was lighter than he expected and he lamented that only a few pieces of the loaf remained. He passed it to Rose, who sat to his left, and it began its journey to Jenn, who sat near Mom. Grimble stole a look at Ellie on the other side of the table before returning his attention to his plate. She sat between her father, Dahl, and Grimble's grandmother. Ellie caught his glance, and a hint of a smile met her lips before she took another bite of her greens.*

*She and her father had arrived almost three hours prior. It was their fifth visit with the family and Grimble's mother and grandmother had set a fantastic table in their honor. Grimble did his best to eat slowly, but the aromas of the roast chickens, sausages, bread, and fresh vegetables, combined with his never-ending hunger, made it all too much for a fifteen-year-old boy to suffer. He wanted to show Ellie he could be as polished –* well, almost *as polished as she was with table etiquette.*

*"It may be the Rising month of Tending," Dahl said, "but Tending is clearly here. It was a hot one today. We needed to stop and water the mules more times than I'd like to count."*

*"It surely was," said Dad. "Likely to be hot the entire Tending this year."*

*"Oh?" Dahl said. "Do tell." A look of genuine interest was in his eyes. Curiosity flowed through his voice. Dahl and Ellie loved to learn about local traditions and proverbs.*

*"Ha. I wish I could say the birds are nesting high or the squirrel tails are less bushy, but no – the old-timer in the village has seen a lot of years and can predict the coming season three times out of four."*

*Dahl continued to smile but appeared disappointed.*

*"Well," Mom said, "I don't know about the rest of Tending, but it's just started, and I already had two robins get into the house today. I wish I knew what was drawing them inside."*

*Grimble hid a smile and did his best to look surprised. He looked across the table to Ellie. Her eyes locked onto his, her face emotionless. She rolled her eyes and turned her attention to Grimble's mother, all but showing Grimble the back of her head.*

*His heart sank. Ellie saw right through him. She traveled and knew things he didn't. Her etiquette and grace were all Mom talked about. Why did he try?*

*The food didn't smell or look appealing anymore. He pushed his plate away from the table's edge, taking care not to knock over the water pitcher. With its red-and-white artwork, the pitcher was the only item remaining from Quincy Geldirn. It was the family's most prized heirloom, only brought out when they had special guests.*

*Soon everyone had finished, and Grimble helped clear the plates with his sisters. Ellie stood to assist, but a simple "I wouldn't hear of you helping. Please relax." from Mom encouraged her to sit back down.*

*When Grimble returned to his seat, he found a small paper-wrapped item, no bigger than a robin's egg, at his place. He looked around and saw everyone had one. Dad looked intrigued. Mom appeared giddy with anticipation.*

*"This," Dahl began, "is a special Nyrlish treat, from Aabenraa. It's only available for a few weeks in early Planting, and we were fortunate enough to be there at that time this year. You pop the whole thing in your mouth and allow it to slowly dissolve. Please, enjoy." With open palms,*

*Dahl spread his arms out, motioning to everyone at the table.*

*Grimble opened his wrapper, and the aroma of the delicacy hit his nose and woke his senses. It was egg-shaped, almost-white in color, like sheep's wool, and the texture reminded Grimble of pressed sugar. The candy appeared mundane; however, the potent fragrance suggested that a singular adventure awaited.*

*He popped the whole thing in his mouth, as instructed, and sucked on it. It was sweet, but the flavors were muted. Without warning, the candy collapsed in his mouth and Grimble was struck by the experience. It was spicy, like cinnamon and nutmeg, and warming, like a sip of sherry. Yet it did not taste like any of those things. He peered about the table, and one by one his family members' expressions changed. Looks of interest were replaced by surprise and delight. Ellie and Dahl enjoyed their candies with smiles as they watched everyone savor the treats.*

*When Grimble's had finished dissolving, a pasty, oily film covered his entire mouth. It had no flavor, but he rubbed his tongue around the inside of his mouth, hoping to dislodge the unexpected sensation. Every family member did the same. All around the table, mouths popped open and closed as tongues worked to remove the film. Dahl's smile turned into a light laugh.*

*"Forgive me, my friends," he said. "It is an amazing treat, but the after-effects can be more*

*than some care to experience a second time. Unfortunately, they are a necessary evil."*

*"Oh," Dad said, sucking on his tongue. "How tho?"*

*"The blubber and glands of a whale are used in the making of the candy. They wouldn't tell me how, but it's responsible for some of the wonderful flavor as well as the coating in your mouth."*

*Grimble's sisters sat unmoving, eyes wide. They were in their late teens; Jenn was curious about the world, but Rose showed little interest in exploring anything outside the village of Minden. "You mean," she said now, "what we feel in our mouths is..."*

*"Yes," Dahl said. "Whale blubber."*

*"Ah!" Rose screamed. "May I..."*

*"You may be excused," Mom said. Rose bolted from the house toward the water bucket outside. Jenn remained seated, moving her tongue about inside her closed mouth, a quizzical look upon her face.*

*"I did not mean to upset anyone," Dahl said.*

*"It's quite alright," Dad assured him. "It's good to experience things."*

*"The Nyrls tend to drink heavily after they eat these," Dahl said. "Maybe one of the reasons is to get rid of the sensation."*

*"The Nyrls tend to drink heavily most nights, Father," Ellie said with a smile.*

*"This is true. This is true."*

*"Delightful, yes?" said the strange man to Grimble's left. He was smiling, too. "I find it delightful. Thank you for it. Yes. This was good."*

*The man must have been sitting between Rose and Jenn, as Grimble hadn't noticed him before. He was perhaps twenty, with hair cut close to the skin, close enough to see his scalp. He wore a white shirt with dark-blue embroidery. His accent was foreign, like the style of his shirt, but his smile was genuine, and Grimble felt a familiarity with him. Looking around the table, he saw Mom and Dad speaking with the man as though his presence was natural. Ellie, too, was comfortable with him.*

*"You're most welcome," Dahl said.*

*Mom smiled. "We're so glad you could join us tonight."*

*"Absolutely," Dad agreed. "You're always welcome at our table." Smiling, he scratched his cheek, a happy look in his eyes. A rumble started deep in his throat. He continued to smile, but a growl emanated from him, growing little by little.*

Grimble blinked awake to find "Kelban" sitting on its branch, looking down at him. The familiar throaty growl was coming from the raccoon. Grimble peered over his shoulder toward the base of the tree and saw another blue plant slithering by, its stalks undulating. Both he and the raccoon watched it move by before they relaxed.

It was not long before sunrise and the first hint of a glow could be seen through the trees. Grimble used the remaining darkness to ready himself. The raccoon scratched the side of its head with its hind foot and watched him.

Grimble's legs and feet were sore, but at first light he managed to pull his damp socks and boots over them. He descended the tree when the sun burned through the branches. His condition made the effort arduous and painful, but he welcomed the pain, knowing it meant he was alive. The raccoon followed him, then bounded away to the north.

Grimble knew he would not last long in his condition. He needed more food. He thought about killing the racoon if he saw it again. The meat would do him wonders, but he was unsure if he could safely make another fire.

He had to cross the river. He imagined he might have to do so by swimming as slowly as he could to avoid creating vibrations or ripples. Grimble didn't like that idea. He was weakened, and there was no telling if the creature could sense the slightest movement even if no noise was made. The idea of being dragged underwater and swallowed alive by that thing made him shiver.

Grimble finished the remaining roots he had gathered the day before, refilled his water, and set out for the day. While he walked he thought about the team and mages. He wondered again why none had located him by now. For all their amazing power, was it true they could not locate and save him? Or had he been left out here alone by the king, abandoned like the residents of the Divide? How many days had it been? If hunger or thirst did not do him in, no doubt the water dogs or the river monster or one of the blue plants would. And there were soldiers hunting him.

Grimble cursed under his breath. He wanted to shout, wanted to release the tension, but he could not risk the chance he would be heard. Every time he thought about the matter, it ate at his spirit and resolve. He reminded himself to focus on the path ahead.

*Do not look at the whole. Remember your training and focus on the next step. Get out of here and you'll have stories to tell.*

Since he did not have to harvest water from vines as he moved today, Grimble made better time, despite his bad feet and aching muscles. He found no sign of pursuers, but along the way he encountered a blue plant. This one was on a mound. A few roots spread out over the ground, but the majority of them disappeared down a burrow. A person unaware of the plant's nature might find the scene peaceful, even beautiful; but Grimble knew the burrow's occupants were in terror – that was, if they had not already died that way.

Although the plants didn't appear to move in the daylight, Grimble skirted wide around this one as well, and continued south. He passed the tree he had used to escape the water dogs that first night; however, it was hours from nightfall. He had the urge to keep going and heeded it, moving in and out of the water as he traveled. He was not sure the dogs moved north of that location, but he knew he was in their hunting area now. Grimble moved slowly. Listening. Looking. The bow and an arrow ready in his hand.

Several hundred yards past the tree, in knee-deep water, Grimble felt the urge to move west, onto a strip of land to his right. It made no sense. Not ten yards in front of him was dry land in the direction he wanted to travel. He looked right, dismissed it, and turned south again.

A hawk screeched high above, several times. Grimble paused. The hawk called again. Something flittered through the treetops. It caught Grimble's attention, and he watched its irregular flight as it tumbled to the ground west of him. Drawn to it, he moved onto the strip of dry land to see where it had landed.

Grimble waded out of the water onto dirt and grass. A hawk's primary wing feather, an abnormally large one, sat atop a bush in front of him. He moved to grab it and stepped on something, glancing down to discover the shaft of an arrow buried headfirst into the ground. Less than a foot of it showed above the dirt. The shaft, weathered and bent, was almost imperceptible among the undergrowth.

He returned his attention to the feather among the branches of the small bush. He picked it up, and that was when he noticed a large object, elongated and dome-shaped, on the ground on the other side of the bush. Sticking the feather in the satchel – it was too long to fit, and poked out from under the flap – Grimble moved around the bush and found an overturned canoe. Moss and other vegetation grew on its bottom and along its sides. He looked about the plot of land. A few yards from the canoe was a tree with a crudely made wooden hunting blind in its branches. It stood about fifteen feet off the ground.

As Grimble took more time to explore the area, he noticed white stones among the grass and undergrowth around him. He moved about and found what appeared to be the base of two stone walls, which came together near the tree with the hunting blind. Along the way, he discovered two more arrows shot into the dirt. Their angle indicated they had come from the blind. Grimble began to climb the tree.

He was almost level with the blind when a boot came into view. Preparing himself, Grimble finished the climb.

"Gods," he muttered. "May Gavel and the High Father bless you."

A human skeleton lay upon the floorboards of the blind.

Weather, bugs, and other creatures of the swamp had deprived the man of his flesh and most of his clothing. Near him was a bow; its string had snapped and now hung loose from the ends. Grimble wondered how desperate a hunter had to be to hunt within this swamp.

*You don't need this anymore, brother. But I do.*

Grimble returned to the ground with the man's bow. He used it to scrape the canoe free of plant growth and examined the wood. It was not ideal, but might be viable. He turned it over to find a paddle wedged among its framing. Maybe he wasn't as cursed as he thought. He thanked the gods, all six of them, for his good fortune. He put the canoe down, dug a well, and returned to the blind for the night.

While settling in and trying to find a comfortable place between a tree trunk and a skeleton, Grimble thought of the hunter and what might have caused him to spend his last minutes in the blind. He thought of how the falling feather had brought him to the spot and the hunter's canoe. Grimble pulled the hawk's feather out of the satchel and examined it. It was black and gray and longer than any others he had encountered in the past. Normally such feathers were shorter than the distance from his elbow to his fingertips. This one was as long as his arm, from shoulder to fingertips. Its shaft was firm like a tree branch, the vanes stiff like a brush or comb.

*That's one big bird.*

The sounds of the swamp grew around him, and Grimble was sure he heard the barks of the water dogs and the swamp's guttural scream among it all. Since he had no company, he set to conversing with the skeleton. He found the dead man easy to talk to, although the conversation was one-sided. The skeleton had made one thing clear to him: he should not wait too long to cross the swamp.

The cramps started early that night, but Grimble did not suffer as much, as he had the advantage of standing in the blind to stretch out his legs. The cramps did not ruin his mood, either.

He had a plan, and the morning could not come soon enough.

# CHAPTER TWENTY-FOUR

It was past noon, but the overcast sky made it seem much later. A savor of roasting meats offset the gloom as it whirled through the narrow streets of Khvoron. It edged the aroma of baked bread into the shadowless town's recesses. Not to be upstaged by the cooks, several groups of musicians performed along the main street and inside the buildings, and if someone were positioned in the right spot, the tumult of all the songs would blend into one. But in most cases the noise of the crowds that choked the street dampened the music. The wind carried hints of it all, song and smell, to nearby Fort Anjermott.

The throng in front of Commander Loren Dek was a mix of soldiers wearing their crimson-and-tan garrison uniforms and townsfolk in their finest attire. They mingled as one body, the mass moving in and around the booths and buildings in a strange dance. Banners of crimson and blue and gold waved above them all. It was a first for the town, as they had never entertained the entire garrison. All had gone well. So far.

When someone looked his way Dek smiled, but when no eyes were upon him, his face gave away the conflict within him as he thought on the unit's history. Beside him was Mayor Yadier Ebi, the man who had organized the impromptu send-off for the men and women of the 209th Light Cavalry Regiment. Both men's eyes were bloodshot, but the mayor was less accustomed to the lack of sleep, and his shoulders sagged.

"What will they do with the fort?" he asked Dek. "What'll come of our town?"

"I'm afraid I don't know. I've never heard of a permanent unit being dissolved. This is new to me."

"Loren, please do what you can. Without trade from the fort…" Ebi left the rest unsaid.

"I know, my friend," Dek said. "I know."

A loud bang, like the crack of two pieces of lumber slapping together, shook the men from their thoughts. Somewhere in the middle of town a war cry rang out and the crowd cheered. Ebi gritted his teeth and looked at Dek from the corner of his eye. He had already expressed concern over so many carousing troopers in his town. The old soldier waved his hand, attempting to dissuade the growing worry that the festival would get out of control.

"Yahnn's grace," Ebi mumbled in prayer.

Dek kept his eyes on the crowd and tilted his head toward Ebi. "The captains and lieutenants are out there. If anyone complains to them, or if they see anything requiring intervention, they will act. They too could face discipline."

"Even the officers?"

Dek nodded. "The men and women need this. They've earned this. In two days they leave the fort. Many will never see their friends again." Another cheer rose from the crowd, followed shortly after by a loud hoot. "The officers have been told to let them have their fun, but to come down hard on any who get out of line. The troopers and staff have been warned: violators will be dealt with harshly. They'll keep each other in line."

"How can you be so confident about that?"

"I know my men, and I know the ones who will keep the others in line. I let it slip to those few that anyone causing damage or injury will have their pay taken and may find themselves placed into indentured service."

"How can you be sure the word will be spread?"

"This is an army camp. Trust me. The word got around."

Dek's eyes faced the revelers, but his attention was on the attractive tailor in his peripheral vision. She shook an orange cloth from the front stoop of her timber-and-stone shop. She examined it and shook it one more time before returning to her shop and shutting the door behind her. Dek noticed Ebi looking at him, waiting for an answer.

"I thank you for this celebration," Dek said. "All will be well. You have my assurance, Yadier. You can hold me responsible."

Ebi smiled. "Thank you, my friend. I worry about my people."

"That's why you have my respect." Dek shook his friend's hand. "Now, if you don't mind, I must attend to a few more things before returning to the fort."

Dek spoke with a few captains before taking leave. Under the guise of checking for errant troopers, he moved through the alleys and behind the buildings along the main street, until he was sure no one paid him any attention. At that point he stepped to the back entrance of the tailor's shop, lifted the wooden door's latch, and stepped inside.

A dimness fell over the room as he shut the door. What little light there was came through a thin sheet of muslin covering the single window, and from a fire in the small stone hearth. The light was not really necessary. He knew his way around the small backroom. He had shared meals and tea at the table many times. Dek looked around, knowing this would be the last time he would see it. He took in the swatches of fabric, the old spools repurposed as pegs, the leather punches and brands, the bottles of dyes and jars of waxed oils.

Light footsteps approached. They weaved their way from the store in the front. He knew they would have to negotiate their way around the tables and bolts of fabric in the workshop before reaching the backroom. Dek listened to her, hoping to remember the sound. The loose floorboards creaked. Her steps were light, soft. The fire cracked and popped. Breathing deeply, she stepped into the doorway, leaning her slim figure against the frame.

Her face was alluring – it always was – with its cute nose, long eyelashes, and soft, brown eyes. Svana was not yet thirty, at least twelve years younger than him, but she stared into Dek with a maturity that always surprised him.

"I wasn't sure you got my message," Svana said.

"I saw it the first time. You didn't have to shake it twice."

"Well, sometimes you men are oblivious. A woman can never be sure."

"Not oblivious. We're merely accustomed to ignoring the prattle you women so often dish out."

Dek knew immediately he had made a tactical error.

She cocked her head, giving him a dangerous look. "I prattle?"

"Not you, dear, but sometimes your words are as bold as an orange banner."

Svana said nothing. She looked at him with that face she used for negotiating her business dealings, the face he had never learned to read.

"Bold and welcoming – and the most beautiful banner in all the land," Dek went on.

"You're in full retreat, aren't you?"

"I can clearly see I need to regroup."

Svana moved to him in that feminine, caring way of hers that Dek loved to watch. Not like a lover, but like a partner. Her smile was muted. His was likely the same. Their smiles told of times together in each other's arms, of long conversations alone, of secrets and fears known only between them. They hugged, pulling each other in tightly. Her hand rubbed the back of his neck. He smelled her hair and rubbed his cheek and nose against the top of her head. Svana made him feel young, but he knew his younger self would not have appreciated her.

They pulled apart and Dek cleared his throat. "I see you have a kettle heating."

She turned from him and walked to the hearth, rubbing her eye. "Uh, yeah. Thought you might like some tea. Or would you prefer something stronger?"

"No. Tea's good."

She checked the kettle and pulled it away from the hot coals. Dek reached into the cupboard and pushed aside the wooden cups and dishware until he found what he was looking for. He smiled as he pulled out the two clay cups reserved for these moments. They were a light brown with small blue diamonds painted around the middle. He ran his finger over the chip on the rim of one and looked up at Svana.

She finished spooning the tea and set the crock back on the shelf before she saw him looking at her. "What?" she asked. Then she saw the cup and smiled. "That was two years ago. I wish you would let me throw it out." She lit a candle from the fire and set it in the holder on the table.

"I like being reminded of your temper."

"You were about to see it again with that 'prattle' comment of yours."

"I know," Dek said with a wry smile. He loved her feisty nature and her confidence.

"Yeah, that's why I didn't give you the pleasure." Svana waved the metal spoon at him as if preparing to throw it. "You should be thankful. My aim has improved." She brought the kettle to the table and the two sat down. Dek placed the undamaged cup in front of her. They sat in silence for a few moments.

He spoke first. "Mayor Ebi and the town did an excellent job putting this festival together."

Svana cut to business. "What will happen to the town?"

Dek looked her in the eyes. "I don't know."

She sighed. "Well, I'm not waiting around to find out. One of my suppliers from Agderon has been telling me of opportunities in the capital."

"Oh? I hear Agderon's trade guilds are vicious. Especially to newcomers."

"That's just business. I've got that worked out."

"I have no doubt," Dek laughed. "Wish I could be there to see the shock on their faces and the chaos in their houses when you hit them."

"I've already reached out to some brokers and have a few folks there gathering details for me. Arje's term nears its end, and I was thinking we'd move to the capital anyway. I'll have to speed things up is all."

"How is your brother?"

"Infuriated. He enjoyed being a Raven. All that sneaking and killing, it suited him."

"We're all giving up things we love." Dek looked toward the fire. "Arje will find something new."

Svana kept her eyes on Dek. "But will he love it?"

"It will never be the same. Nothing ever is." He returned his attention to the table and lifted the kettle. Steam rose from Svana's cup as the bronze liquid filled it. Dek poured a cup for himself before setting the kettle out of the way. Svana reached out and took his hand.

"What about you?" she asked. "Will you – where will the army send you?"

"They haven't told me yet."

"They're cutting it close, aren't they?"

"That's the army."

They looked into each other's eyes and drank tea in silence for several minutes, their fingers studying each other's hands.

A coy smile lifted Svana's cheeks. "Your men know how I make extra money. They think you're paying to bed me."

He shook his head, pulling his hand away. "I was worried they might think that if they caught us together. How do they know? I've been careful."

"It's an army camp, Loren."

He chuckled. "Well, better they think that than the truth."

"There's nothing wrong with our arrangement. I like it when we talk and when you hold me. I've never had that. It's tender."

Dek's face warmed and he sat up straight. "These are not tender men, Svana. They need to see me as strong and unbreakable. Better to be virile and crass than weak and tender."

She let out a little laugh and Dek shook his head. He worked to calm himself while he drank his tea. Svana knew what strings to pluck when it came to playing him.

"I would never have tried to replace her."

"I know. And I'm sure she knows that too." He glanced upward momentarily. "You've made me a better man, and I bet she's thankful for that."

Svana's brown eyes twinkled in the candlelight. "You've been good to me, too."

He nodded his thanks and reached out to hold her hands. "Thank you for bringing a woman's light into my life."

She pulled her hands away, pushed her chair back, and got up. He watched as she slid around the table, her leg pressing against the edge, her dress pulled tight to her form. She leaned down and pulled on his knee, moving his leg from under the table. The copper skin of her neck and chest gleamed. He breathed in her perfume. She sat on his leg and leaned in to him. They hugged again, his face on soft cotton and the smooth skin of her chest, her head on top of his. He pulled her in tightly.

"A woman's light?" she said.

"Your light," he whispered.

They embraced. Candle wax dripped and pooled in the base of the holder. Dek felt her nuzzle his head. He ran his hands along her back and leg. She played with his hair, breathing warm breaths in his ear.

"I have to go," he said.

"Shhh." Svana didn't move. "One more minute."

He took it all in. Wanting to remember it all for the rest of his days, but knowing the memories would fade. He hoped to take in so much of her – her smell, the feel of her body against his, the sound of her voice, her breathing; anything and everything, so that something would remain years from now.

Svana pulled away from him, enough to look into his eyes. For the first time, she leaned in toward his face. For the first time, they kissed. It was soft at first, their lips touching and lingering. Then they pulled each other in tightly. Their lips explored. Their feelings erupted and they kissed passionately. Their pulses surged, their breathing became deep and quick. Their hands rubbed and grabbed and played.

She seemed to know the same time he did that it could go no further. The kissing slowed and ended as tenderly as it had begun. Svana got up, grabbed the kettle from the table, and stepped to the hearth, her back to Dek.

He stood and cleared his throat and smoothed his hair. The room seemed foggy to his eyes. "I'll miss you, Svana."

She turned and looked at him. Even in the low light he could see her eyes were red. "I'll miss you too, Loren."

Dek turned toward the door, but stopped. He stepped back to the table and grabbed the chipped clay cup.

"Take that old thing. I've been trying to throw it away for two years now." Svana sniffed and rubbed a finger under her eyes.

A smile tugged at his cheeks as he looked upon her. He paused at the door and pulled a stack of gold coins from his pouch. They chimed as he placed them on a shelf near the door.

She stood tall. "I've been telling you, you don't owe me anything."

"I have no one else to spend my money on."

"I'll probably give it to charity."

"Good. Then someone will appreciate it." He took one last look around, then unlatched the door. "After all you have been through, I never would have asked for – well, I never would have asked." Dek opened the door, peeked outside, and left. The door shut quietly behind him.

Svana's shoulders sagged. "I would have given it to you."

A quarter of an hour later, Dek rode up to the gates of Fort Anjermott on his horse, Oak Warden, where the two sentries waved for him to enter. He slowed to a jog, rode through the gates, and made his way to the stables and Warden's designated stall. Halfway through the untacking prayers and rituals he was interrupted by his adjutant, Trey.

The younger man was breathing heavily. He looked about the stable, his eyes lingering on a groom at the far end of the building. Trey turned toward Dek. "Welcome back, sir. How were things in Khvoron?"

"The festival goes well. It'll be a loud night and a quiet morning, I think. Any word from down south?" Dek eyed the groom too. He had never seen the man before, but new staff had arrived to help the 209$^{th}$ disband. Dek dismissed him as one of the new workers.

"No bird has arrived yet. No update on Corporal Broadleaf."

"What about the extra resources I requested from Agderon?"

"Turned down again, sir. And Marshal Chedwick says he'll forward no more requests."

"No more? Understood." Dek was upset by the decision, but had expected it to happen eventually. He was thankful for the two requests Marshal Chedwick had forwarded up the chain. Dek would have to keep praying and hoping Grimble would be found by one of the other army units or a militia in the south. The good news he'd had so far was that the increase in Renlaran activity along the border probably meant they had not found Grimble either.

Dek wondered what more Trey needed to pass along. The young man had obviously run to the stable, and there had to be something more pressing to impart.

"I'll finish with the Warden here," Trey said. "Constable Dressel asks for your presence."

"Thank you." Dek brushed his clothes off with Trey's help and tucked in everything that needed it. "How do I look?"

"Presentable, sir."

Dek left his adjutant to finish caring for his horse and stepped through the door, emerging under the gray sky. He moved with purpose toward the command building in the center of the fort. Along the way he prepared his mind to respond to queries on the search for Grimble Broadleaf and for news on his status in the army.

He passed a group of men outside the warehouses, unloading crates from the tail of one wagon and placing them into the bed of another. Dek took a few steps more before instinct told him something was off. He cast a second glance at the five men and could not determine what had drawn his attention, other than that he knew none of them.

The command building lay ahead. Dek felt light as he thought on the many times he had climbed its granite steps. He smiled, remembering the first time: striding into the building as a newly transferred lieutenant from the 202$^{nd}$ Cavalry. It had been the best move of his career and he thanked Ihgel for such a blessing.

Near the building's left corner was a laborer splicing two ropes together. The man held his head low, concentrating on the ropes, shielding his face with the wide brim of his hat. His sleeves were pulled above his elbows; his forearms were large and defined. To the right of the door, another laborer swept the stone porch. That man too appeared to be fit, and he stood tall and proud as he brushed back and forth.

Before climbing the steps Dek gave himself the time to

sweep his gaze over each of those men again. Their clothes were those of a laborer's, but not as torn or dirty as one would expect. But the men seemed to pay him no mind as he bounded up the steps and breezed through the front door.

Many of the plaques and banners that had lined the whitewashed walls of the lobby had been lowered to the floor, where they now rested, leaning against the walls. Another laborer, again unknown to Dek, used a flannel to wipe dust from the wooden and stone plaques – dust that Dek knew was not there, because the regiment dusted and cleaned them daily. Yet this man acted as though he had found a stain. His movements were precise, like a soldier's, as he rubbed and buffed and polished.

On the far side of the lobby stood the constable and his aide. The former dismissed his junior officer. With only a slight nod, the younger man left through the same door Dek had entered. Dek cast his head left and right, peering over his shoulders, looking for the source of his discomfort.

Constable Dressel's baritone voice shook him from his thoughts. "Loren, any word on our missing trooper?"

The constable summoned Dek with a small wave of his hand. The senior officer of the entire regiment was younger and heavier than Dek, but the extra weight did not come from muscle. He was of nobility and his position in the regiment had been appointed, not commissioned. The gold braiding on his shoulders reminded everyone of that, even if his physical conditioning did not. Dek, who had served his way to his rank, was always thankful King Saevar had appointed a good man, if not an able man, to lead the regiment.

"Nothing new to report, my lord. No bird today."

"And the festival? Well managed, I hope?"

"Yes, sir. The captains and lieutenants remain in place to address any issues, which I expect to be few and minor."

They walked toward the constable's offices and talked about other matters related to the logistics of the 209th's disbanding. At the end of the hall a man rested against a mop handle, the head of which sat inside a bucket at his feet. What little daylight there was outside oozed through a window behind him. It cast him in silhouette in the dim hallway and exposed the uniform dullness of the marble floor. Dressel seemed to pay him no mind, and that brought a small measure of comfort to Dek.

When they arrived at the door to the office, Dressel paused. He rubbed his hands together and the look on his face changed. All manner of warmth disappeared, and a grave but not unfriendly face turned toward Dek.

Dressel's voice lowered to a whisper. "Loren, you are a good man." Concern over what awaited grew within Dek. The constable continued. "No matter what you hear and how things play out in the near future, please know you have my respect and admiration."

"Yes, sir," Dek said.

"I must know that you believe me."

Dressel's demeanor was honest, and Dek had known him for years. If that were not so, he might have worried some horror lay before him. He could feel something ominous at hand. Perhaps he was going to be set as an example for the failed mission in Renlar. However, his history with the constable and the memories of their honest exchanges helped him believe the nobleman now. "I do, my lord."

Constable Dressel stepped away from the door and motioned for Dek to open it and enter. "I cannot enter with you. And regrettably, our relationship from this point forward must be different than it has been."

A chill took Dek. He wondered why Dressel would speak to him in such a way. It was unlike the constable. He flexed his fingers, lifted the latch, and pushed the door open.

Normally the inside of the constable's office was well lit, but the windows were shrouded and the lamps were turned low. Dek looked back to Dressel, and found him walking away. He gritted his teeth and entered the room.

In the center, on the other side of the planning table, was a cloaked figure. Dek took a preparatory breath and stood tall, awaiting his fate.

"Close the door, please, Commander Dek," the man said. The voice was calm and Dek could not find any hint of aggression. He closed the door and the figure lowered his hood. "Thank you."

A gold ring with a round medallion and blue stone rested on a finger of his right hand. His dark face was angular and his gray hair was cut short. Dek estimated him to be between fifty and sixty years old.

From behind him stepped another cloaked figure. As that figure removed his hood, Dek found himself face to face with his liege, King Saevar the Wise.

Dek dropped to a knee. "Your Majesty."

"Rise, Commander Dek," the king said. "I need the leader of warriors, not the subject."

"Yes, sir." Dek stood and waited.

The king moved further into the light. He had aged noticeably since the last time Dek had seen him – two years ago, when the king had arrived at Fort Anjermott to inspect the massed regiment. He was tall, over six feet in height, and his muscular build and medium complexion were as Dek remembered. His dark eyes retained their hard stare, but his black hair and beard showed flecks of silver, unusual for a man in his early thirties.

Both the king and the other man were dressed in brown-and-white travel clothes and nondescript gray cloaks, but the cut and quality of the clothing revealed their wearers' stations. A passing glance on the street may miss it, but anyone truly looking at them would see the coin in the cloth. The king moved his cloak to his favored location, freeing his right arm and keeping his left covered. Every painting, statue, and public appearance showed him that way. The only time Dek had seen King Saevar otherwise was when he was dressed in plate armor.

The king smoothed his hair with his right hand. "I'm afraid the deception was necessary. No one can know Hrafnal and I were here. You do understand?"

"Yes, sir. This conversation never happened."

"Good. Everything I hear about you says you're a man of action, but have you thought about retiring?"

"Sir. I will retire if you wish it."

"Commander Dek, I need you to be honest with me. Honest like you are with Constable Dressel. Honest like you are when you say things others don't want to hear." Dek felt a chill and worried he had spoken too plainly at some of their meetings. The king continued. "You must be that honest with me. Trust is the key."

"I have no intent to retire, sir. I have a few more years of service in me."

"And how would you feel about an administrative assignment? Something that pulls you out of the field."

"I would not like that, sir."

"And what is your opinion of the Lord High Constable Zahn Avengard, and how he's handled matters recently? Specifically, how he's handled your regiment?"

"He's related to Your Majesty, is he not?"

"Yes. He's married to my sister-in-law." There was a pause. "Out with it, Commander. What is your opinion on the dismantling of the 209th Light Cavalry Regiment?"

Dek drew himself upright. "It's a terrible decision and makes me wonder if His Lordship is fit for the post, sir."

King Saevar nodded and looked at Hrafnal. "And how so?"

"Sir, we are… *were* the last light cavalry unit in the army. No other regiment has our capability to scout enemy positions, disrupt enemy supply lines, or delay enemy movement and protect our main body. Without light cavalry Your Majesty's army is at a severe disadvantage. And if an enemy attacks, we will be hard-pressed to train enough troopers to field a new light regiment in time."

He waited for King Saevar to reprimand him. Instead, the king smiled.

"I heard you would speak the truth to me. Constable Dressel knows you well. He admires you and respects you, Commander Dek. You should know this."

"Thank you, sir."

"Were you aware the constable is of royal bloodline? That his family is one of the crown's greatest supporters?" The king walked toward the wall to Dek's left. Weapons of various types and makes were displayed there.

"I'm aware of his nobility, sir, but not of the matters of court."

"Now you are." Saevar plucked a long sword from a display. He waved it, feeling its weight and balance. He looked down the length and pulled the hilt close to his face, turning it to examine the edge. Dek could tell by the way the king held the sword that he was well trained with the weapon. He was proud to fight for such a king. "Commander Dek, your performance has pleased me too. What you were able to do in Talas was the very thing the kingdom needed. You did precisely what I asked of you."

The tone was genuine, but Dek sensed it held a hidden meaning. That concerned him. He felt something unpleasant awaited. But the king was not threatening. He did not approach Dek or move the sword about in his direction. "Thank you, sir."

"I wish I could be like you, Commander – lead soldiers into battle."

"But you do, sir. I've seen you on the field."

"That's what everyone is meant to see." The king placed the sword back in its rack with reverence and care. "What you don't see —"

Hrafnal interrupted. "Sir —"

"Your concern is noted," the king said, looking at Hrafnal over his shoulder. He turned back to Dek. "What you don't see is a portion of my guard surrounding me and secreting me from the field. It is the most difficult thing for me to tolerate, but it's for more than my own protection. It is ultimately for the protection of those around me."

"I don't understand, sir. You are clearly well trained. You have the best armor. And I've seen you ride."

Hrafnal cleared his throat. King Saevar raised a hand to silence him. "I'll show you, and you will become part of a very small circle, Commander."

The king used his right hand to move his cloak and reveal his left arm and gloved hand. Dek watched as he rolled his left shirt sleeve, displaying a thin and bony forearm. Lastly, he removed the glove from his left hand and revealed his withered and gnarled fingers. Dek knew there could be no way the king would be able to lift a shield or hold a weapon with that arm.

"Your Majesty, I had no idea," he said.

"It's been hidden since my birth. On occasion, magic helps maintain the secret. But as you can see, I would put others in harm's way if I entered a battle. I would rather be known as Saevar the Bold or Saevar the Strong, but I have learned to accept my strengths and weaknesses." He put the glove on his hand and rolled his sleeve down. Hrafnal helped him return the cloak so it covered his left arm and side.

The king looked Dek in the eye. "We both want to lead on the field, but we serve better in other positions."

"I'm at your service, sir," Dek said. "What do you need of me?"

"You will be assigned to Lord Zahn's office, in Agderon, and become his aide. In that position, you will be able to monitor him and provide me with information should Lord Zahn take actions that hurt Aendura. To get this done, we had to convince Zahn you would be no threat to him or his goals, and that you were no friend to the crown. Constable Dressel spoke against you at our last meeting, claiming you had a battle lust and that was the sole reason you held your position. He claimed you were of low intelligence and low character, and showed no loyalty to the crown."

Dek now understood why the constable had spoken with him in such a way before he had entered the room. He did not like the idea of his character or competence being challenged. That part stung – no, it *infuriated* him. He took slow breaths and focused on his king, who was still speaking.

"...necessary – unfortunate, but necessary. Zahn had to believe you were not loyal to the crown or to the family of His Grace, the Duke of Grayfell. Your sacrifice will be recognized and all will be remedied when this is over. You do understand?"

"Yes, sir." *What am I getting into?*

"Your thoughts? Remember, I'm asking for them."

"If you distrust Zahn, why not simply remove him or give him a different post?"

"You have studied Inpilis' Treatises on War and Bruwn's Conflict Theory?"

"Yes, but this is more complicated. You're talking about politics and people." Dek waited for an explanation. But the king remained silent. He was clearly giving the commander time to think.

Dek thought through the texts. He understood that the king was trying to trap Zahn; but that would not solve the issue of the unit being disbanded, or help them learn Zahn's purpose if the king removed him too early. Dek considered the various problems Zahn had created for King Saevar and his army. He thought of it as a battlefield, with each person and element being different resources. He imagined the pieces on a map and how he would have to employ units to counter their efforts until the time was right to attack.

The king smiled. "It's no different than preparing for a battle, is it?"

"No. It isn't," Dek said. "It is just like preparing for battle. The elements are different. That's all." The king nodded and turned to Hrafnal. The man bobbed his head. Dek spoke again. "But I'm not trained for this. I meet my enemy face to face. I've never had to hide my intentions from them. I might be able to do it for a short period of time, sir, but not weeks and months."

"Let someone you know inspire you. Model their actions. Surely you must know someone who can hide their intentions and their true nature from others."

Dek was surrounded by warriors. He could not think of anyone he knew who could play that game. But his recent interaction with Sir Albert reminded him that he had learned to do things he'd been unaccustomed to just years before. And he knew that turning down a position in the army, especially one assigned by the king himself, would mean the end of his career.

He nodded and looked at King Saevar. "I can do this, sir."

"Good. You help Aendura by taking this post. You help me." King Saevar stepped to the side and motioned Hrafnal forward. "Commander Dek, this is my personal advisor, Hrafnal Ové. He served my father and I trust him more than my personal secretary, more than my chief of the court." Saevar gave a knowing smile to his advisor. "Her Majesty the Queen is the only one who holds more trust than this man." He turned back to Dek. "From this point forward you will meet with him. What he says is my word. What you tell him, you tell me."

"Understood, sir."

Ové moved to Dek and reached out with his right hand, the hand that bore the ring with his mage medallion. They shook hands and Dek was impressed with the older man's grip. The mage looked up into his eyes while their hands clasped. He grunted. "I look forward to working with you, Commander Loren Dek."

"And I you, my lord."

"Your reputation is strong, and I truly enjoyed your handling of Sir Albert of Lanrik."

"How did you hear of that, sir?"

A glint of amusement lit his eyes. "This is an army camp, is it not?"

# CHAPTER TWENTY-FIVE

"Ain't no way he's still alive," the reeve said. "I've lived here my whole life. Nobody who's been in after nightfall ever came out."

"Oh dear," said the mayor.

"And you say the man you hunt, this 'Horseman,' went in three days ago? Ain't no way." The reeve was a stout, bearded man, his clothing one bad day away from being rags. He drew a small knife from his belt and peeled a wrinkled potato, allowing the brown skin to fall freely to the wooden floor. The mayor looked down and moved his shoe to keep the peels from landing on it.

Page hoped neither official saw her display of frustration. She looked back to the maps on the table and the Renlaran officer, Lieutenant Commander Verus, standing across from her. Verus looked at her and rolled his eyes. At least they were in accord.

"Be that as it may," Verus said, "we're not going to count on his death until we have a body. So, the swamp will be searched."

"Well, the three who work for me ain't goin'," the reeve said. "Can't spare 'em. As far as town volunteers, you ain't got any

Dean Radt

yet. Word's spreadin'. Those who know of the Fane been tellin' those who don't." He took a bite of his potato.

At the sound of horses coming to a stop outside the public house, Page and the others turned their heads. Page looked through the haze of tobacco smoke to the doorway, and a few moments later it darkened as Badger and Axe entered the log building. Soldiers sitting at the tables and gaggled in pockets eyed the two men suspiciously. A chill hovered in the large room that none of the day's warmth could touch.

The two mercenaries ignored the glares and scanned the crowd until they saw Page. They made their way to her, passing a table with baskets of food along their path. Both men grabbed a meat pie and broke the top crust. Axe fingered the chunks and dark paste into his mouth. Badger used a small knife to spear cold hunks from the crust bowl. Outside, a tumult of voices and the rattle of equipment picked up.

"Lieutenant Commander Verus," Page said, "these are my Iron Leaf brothers, Badger and Axe." The men shook hands. "What's the racket outside?" she asked.

"A platoon of regulars arrived. They've brought a handful of militia, too," Axe said.

The mayor's eyes shot wide. He hurried to the door and peeked out. "Oh dear." He pulled an unlit pipe from his belt and began to suck on the stem.

"Who's the pussy?" Axe asked.

Page smirked. "That's the mayor."

"What's wrong with him?"

They all looked at the mayor, who sucked and nibbled and shifted his weight from one foot to the other. His eyes darted back and forth between the men outside and the ones inside.

"Got a notice from Lagisborg last month," the reeve said.

"Everyone in Beckland runnin' an office paid by the crown got one. His Majesty, King Heselov, doesn't want these towns to dry up. Wants to see production. Told us he won't tolerate new settlers changing their minds and returning to upper Renlar. Told us we'd be held responsible if Arhus fails."

The reeve took another bite of the potato and continued, his lips wet and chunky. "Since your soldiers have been arriving, the mayor's tighter than his wife's —" He looked at Page and cleared his throat. "He's worried folks will be scared off, thinking the place ain't safe, or won't come if they hear about this."

"Boys," Page said, "this is the town reeve."

"You're not worried?" Badger asked.

"Nah, it'll all work out." The reeve wiped his mouth with his sleeve.

"It'll work out better," Verus said, "if ya can talk some of the townsfolk into helping us out. Two days, that's all. I won't even put them in the swamp. They can act as extra eyes, maybe help distribute food."

"I'll try again." The reeve's tone betrayed his words.

Verus stood to full height. He was a tall man, lean with a firm jaw. As he stood, so did every soldier who had been sitting. "See that ya do." Verus' eyes were determined and cold. "General Batal and Chancellor Nesar were assassinated. Your cooperation, or the lack of it, will be in my report to Lagisborg. I'm losing my patience here and my report will be detailed."

The reeve's jaw set harder and his look of complacency washed away with a red flush. He swallowed, nodded curtly, and left, bumping the mayor with his shoulder as he walked out the door. The mayor stood in shock for a few seconds before putting the pipe back in his mouth and skulking back to Page and the others. The Renlaran soldiers took their seats and returned to their conversations.

Page turned to Badger and Axe. "What did you find?"

"Coverage on the east side of the swamp looks good," Axe said. "It's a tight perimeter. We're gonna switch out the horses and check the bridge and the west side."

"I put one of my first patrols on the bridge," Verus said. "That's covered. Haven't been able to send many to cover the west side yet. There'll be gaps there. Ya let me know where they are and I'll send men there as they arrive."

"I thought you sent that last platoon, the mounted ones, to the west side," Badger said.

"That's what I wanted," Page said, "but the commander thought it better they patrol the roads."

Axe huffed and glared at Verus. "Did you not hear who we're working for?"

"Fact is I did," Verus quipped. He looked hard at Axe. "I saw the orders. I saw the seals. That's why you're getting access to my men and making *some* of the calls. So far. But even if the chancellor trusted ya, I don't. I don't even know ya. I'm responsible for these men and I'm gonna look out for them. If you have a problem with how I lead my men, better have it out now." Verus kept his eyes locked on Axe. Wood squeaked as soldiers stood again, this time taking a step closer to their commander and Axe.

Page glared at her fellow mercenary. Axe eyed the soldiers to his left and right, his head tilting. He smiled. "No, sir. We're good."

"Another thing I know better than ya is this area. If this assassin broke out of the perimeter before we had it closed, if he made it out of the swamp, the patrols on the roads will act as an outer perimeter and hopefully pick him up or keep him contained."

"We appreciate all you're doing, Commander," Page said. "East, the way home, is cut off right now. It makes sense."

"In two days we'll have all the men we'll need," Verus said. "We'll have the swamp secured and we'll start sending in patrols to find him."

"The men you sent for will be here in two days?" Page asked.

"Yes. Got their dispatch this morning."

"I have an idea." Page pointed to an area on the map. "Searching the entire swamp would take too long. When the soldiers arrive, let's open a gap here, move those watch posts to the west side. I'll place some Warding spells along the gap to warn us if anyone moves through it. Place a small patrol here and another here." Page pointed to gaps between three farms east of the swamp. "As for the rest of the force arriving, they take positions on the western side. When everyone is set, the whole line pushes into the swamp, making as much noise as possible doing it. If the Horseman moves through one of those gaps, he'll be ambushed by one of these teams. If he stays in the swamp, we'll catch his ass there."

"They'll never sneak up on him that way," Axe said.

Verus and Badger nodded in understanding. Badger chuckled. "Like scaring fish into a net."

"I was going to say flushing a deer with dogs," Verus said with a smile. "You don't expect him to stay in the swamp, do you? You're counting on him being flushed out."

"If the swamp's as bad as they say, he won't want to stay there," Page said. "He won't take the road. It's too much in the open. We've been warning the locals about him, so he won't find any friends at any of the farms or houses. He'll have to take one of those gaps."

A look of concern crossed the commander's face. "Ya sure ya'll be able to tell if he pops out of the swamp?"

"Absolutely," Page said, "and he better hope one of your men catches him before I do."

"Right now, we work to contain," Badger said, "but hope to capture him. Either way, in two days his time is up. You sure you have enough men coming?"

"Oh, we'll have enough. And they all fought under General Batal. They're looking for some payback. Five companies of pissed-off veteran infantry."

"Five companies?" the mayor said. "I need a drink." He made his way to the counter.

The commander of the newly arrived mix of soldiers and militia entered the pub and was directed to Verus. The two saluted and shook hands before Verus briefed the new arrival on the mission. Page and her teammates excused themselves and made for the door. Every soldier eyed them as they passed. A few curled their upper lips.

"Dumbass mercs," one said, just loud enough.

Axe slowed and tensed, but Badger's hand on his back kept him moving. The mayor mashed his back against the bar counter to step out of the way of the three mercenaries. The pub's owner locked his gaze upon the departing trio. He stood next to the mayor, placing a full mug on the counter while blindly tapping the mayor's arm.

Outside, the three mercenaries found a private area along the side of the public house. Axe finished his meat pie, tossed the shell aside, and licked his fingers. Badger speared one of his few remaining pieces of meat. "I still don't like this," he said as he bit the chunk from the end of his knife.

"Me either," Axe said. "We've done our part. Our contact is

dead. The army can handle it from here."

"Iron Leaf completes the mission, lads," Page said.

"The mission is complete," Badger said. "Like Axe told you, we did our part."

"And another thing," Axe said, "why haven't you corrected them?"

"About the general being assassinated by the enemy?" Page asked. "That's the story King Heselov's Chief of the Court wants told." Teacher had told her so.

Both men shifted their feet. Axe kept his gaze on Page. Badger looked over his shoulder and back to her. "That lie – that lie gets us involved in their politics. That's not our job. I don't like it."

"Me either," Axe said.

Badger continued. "We completed the mission. We got Chancellor Nesar to the meeting spot. We captured the traitor general and those he spoke with. We interrogated them. We have nothing ordering us further. Besides, something doesn't feel right here. Why was this Horseman left behind? Someone or some group ambushed us and rescued the others – why are we assuming they haven't left him here for a reason? He could be leading us the wrong way. We could be heading into a trap."

Page couldn't believe there was any concern. "We have an army helping us hunt him down now. We'll be alright."

Axe threw up his arms. "She doesn't get it. I told you it was no use talking to her." He walked toward his horse, in front of the pub.

"Do we have a problem carrying out orders?" Page asked Badger, crossing her arms.

"That's not the issue."

Page was losing her patience with the two men. "Go ahead,

then. What's the issue?"

Badger made sure Axe was out of earshot. "The night of the attack, you agreed with us that the chancellor was acting suspicious and this whole thing stank. We were going to portal back to Lagisborg the next day. It's three days later and we're still here. Something's changed in you. What is it?"

"I don't know what you mean," she said.

Badger's face darkened. It was as angry as Page had ever seen him. He took a breath. "Nesar was never open with us, you said that yourself a while back. Iron Leaf protects. Iron Leaf fights. We don't get into the drama of court or the bullshit of politics." He checked again to assure they were alone. "You have two reputations in the company, Page. The first one is known by everyone. We know you're tough and get the job done. We respect you for that. We're all proud to call you a teammate."

"Okay." Page worked to quell her frustration. She could feel her face flush and worried she may start shaking out of anger. "What's the other side?"

"The other one is known only to folks who've worked closely with you. Those folks know you're motivated to finish your training at the Institute."

"What's wrong with that?"

"It's wrong when you take it too far. You're motivated to the point that you put yourself at risk, and that puts the rest of us at risk."

Page was furious now. They did not understand. She felt her lips purse, trying to keep herself from sneering at Badger. "I can trust Teacher."

Badger stepped back, his face the picture of confusion. "What?"

"What?"

"You said, 'I can trust Teacher.' What does that mean?"

"No, I didn't."

"Yes, you did. Who's Teacher?"

"I don't know what you're talking about." She stepped away from Badger, her mind in a fog. Teacher was helping her, but she didn't remember bringing him up. Absentmindedly, she put a hand in her pouch and played with the worry beads there. They helped calm her. She understood now why Chancellor Nesar had liked them.

In her core Page knew following through on this was the right course of action. She was in charge of the team now and it would be her call. She stepped back to Badger. "Your apprehensions are noted. Five more days is all I ask. I get the feeling he's still in the swamp. Several companies of infantry arrive in two days. We will continue the hunt for three more days after that. Give me five days, Badger. Five more days at rate and a half. If he's not caught by then, we return to the Anvil."

Badger looked like he would not have made the same call. But he nodded. "Agreed."

"I'll work out the plan from here and Ward the areas I discussed with Verus. Are you good telling Axe about this and checking the western edge of the swamp like Verus asked?"

"We'll take care of that. But what if the Horseman triggers one of your wards while we're separated from you? What's your plan for that?" Badger was shaking his head, as if he could not believe they were going to continue the search themselves.

"I'll use a spell to communicate with one of you. If you're near a place I know, I'll portal there and pick you up and we can go after the Horseman together. If you're not someplace familiar, I'll advise you where I'm headed. I'll portal to capture or head him off. You get to me as quickly as you can."

"Alright," he said. "I'm keeping you to that. We're done in five days. That's it."

Page was certain they would be done before that time. She could trust Teacher, and he was going to help them find the Horseman.

# CHAPTER TWENTY-SIX

*The afternoon kept the morning's promise of another hot day at the farm. Grimble's and Ellie's fathers had headed into Minden for supplies. Having completed the day's chores, Grimble and Ellie took advantage of some free time and were deep in the woods on another of their walks. Ellie was behind Grimble as he led them along the path.*

*"Why are you so mean to your mother?" she asked.*

*"What are you talking about? I love my mother."*

*"You don't show it. All those tricks you play on her."*

*"I'm just having fun."*

*"They upset her, Grimble. She's not having any fun."*

*"What?" Grimble stopped and turned toward her.*

*"You're lucky to have a mother. You should be nicer to her." The sincerity in Ellie's voice and the look in her eyes reminded him she had lost hers.*

*"Alright, but don't ask me to stop teasing my sisters."*

*"Fine. You keep on being a jerk. Stubborn little..." Ellie's words faded as she mumbled under her breath.*

*Grimble smiled. The cold shoulder she had given him at last night's supper was gone, replaced with something that didn't sting as much. He felt better.*

*They would have to cross a stream along this path, and Grimble didn't mind getting wet to mid-thigh; but he elected to lead them to an area where one could hop across the stream on a series of rocks. Ellie wore a modest dress, as she did almost every day. It was light in color and fabric, perfect for the warm weather, and stopped below her knees. He was certain she would not appreciate getting it wet.*

*They arrived at the rocky crossing and found the water level higher than Grimble had expected. He was embarrassed for not having taken into account the heavy rain over the previous few days. The large rocks, usually several inches above the water level, now hid beneath the surface. They weren't the best footing when dry, and one of them teetered when stepped on, but now they posed a real risk of toppling anyone trying to cross. To their left the water pooled deeply, and to their right the rocks and fast current made crossing even more dangerous.*

*"I was going to suggest we hop across the rocks," Grimble said. "But now I think we should go back downstream to a shallower section where I could carry you across."*

*"Who do you think you're talking to?" Ellie looked at the rocks, nodded, and removed her sandals.*

*"Ellie, I know you're no coward, but why—"*

*Without a look back, she jumped to the first stone and nimbly leaped from one to the other until she reached the far side. Her feet made little splashes along the way. Grimble was mesmerized by her catlike grace.*

*"You go down to where it's safer," Ellie called. "I'll wait for you here."*

*He smiled and started across himself. "Please. I've been hopping these rocks since —"*

*Grimble forgot to count the rocks, and the one that teetered caught him by surprise. He lost his balance as it tottered. Worried he might fall toward the sharp rocks to his right, he leaned left, waved his arms in vain, and plunged sidelong into the stream.*

*He was distracted from his embarrassment by the cold water. However, when he surfaced to find Ellie giggling at him, the flush of shame trumped the water's temperature. How could she laugh at him? He'd thought better of her. The back of his neck warmed as the frustration and anger built. He found his footing, and with the water at waist level, he started to climb out.*

*Grimble scowled at Ellie. "Why are you laughing?"*

*"It was funny."*

*"Now you're being mean. I wouldn't laugh at you."*

*"I wouldn't fall in." She giggled.*

*As he looked at her, his anger softened. She was as pretty as ever and her laugh was not mocking. It was innocent. It was as enchanting as her voice. He couldn't stay angry. But she had to pay for the affront. He ran his hands over his head and wrung the water from his hair. Then he locked his eyes onto her and stalked forward.*

*Ellie's giggles subsided. "What are you thinking?"*

*"Just need your help with one thing."*

*"Don't you dare." She threw a sandal at him. It bounced off his shoulder.*

*"What?" He continued toward her. She backed away.*

*"Don't you dare throw me in." Ellie threw the other sandal at him.*

*Grimble ducked. "I'm not going to throw you in." He reached out and grabbed her arm, pulling her in.*

*"You're not? Argh! You're all wet and cold."*

*Grimble picked her up and carried her toward the stream. Ellie fought against him. Her strength surprised him.*

*"Don't throw me in, Grimble." Her voice was stern but touched with worry.*

*"I'd never think of throwing you in. I promise."*

*They neared the edge.*

*"You better not."*

*"Never." Grimble approached the deep section. "I promise. I won't throw you in." And he lunged off the side of the stream, carrying a very shocked Ellie. She screamed, and for the first time sounded like a girl his age.*

*Underwater, she pushed away from him. A couple of her swimming kicks struck his head and chin, but he didn't mind. He surfaced to find her treading water. She splashed him.*

*"You... you... you —"*

*"Jerk?"*

*"Yes. You jerk! How could you?"*

*"I only wanted to show you I would never laugh at your misfortune." Grimble put on a faux sympathetic look with his eyebrows. "See?"*

*"You little shit!" Ellie screamed. Her eyes, full of rage at first, took on a look of shock as she realized what she had said. She covered her mouth.*

*Grimble, just as surprised at hearing Ellie curse for the first time, stared at her, his eyes and mouth wide open. "I think the water rinsed all the goodness off you. Most people get clean in water – you get dirty." He smiled.*

*She started laughing. "Oh, shut your mouth."*

*They swam to the shallows by the rocks and climbed out. As Ellie emerged, her dress clung to her, revealing her form and all the curves that had been concealed moments before. Grimble caught himself staring and turned away as she grabbed the front of her dress.*

*"I'll lead us back, if that's okay," he said.*

*"Good idea."*

*Grimble collected Ellie's sandals and emptied his boots while Ellie wrung water from her dress. They walked back barefoot, still laughing over the whole incident.*

*The two emerged onto the farm to find their fathers had returned in their absence. Ellie's caravan sat in its usual place, the front facing the house and the rear backed up to the hay barn. Their mules were already unhitched and in a paddock. Grimble escorted Ellie to the open door at the back of the caravan. She walked up the steps and peered inside.*

*"Father's not here. I'll change and be right over."*

*"Alright," Grimble said.*

*She stepped into the caravan and Grimble headed toward his house. On the way he remembered Ellie had hung some laundry out to dry before they had left for their walk. Wondering if she had anything to dry off with, he rushed back to ask before she had a chance to undress. He turned the corner at the back of the caravan, prepared to call her name, and was rendered speechless.*

*Inside the caravan Ellie stood nude, her left side to him, her arms raised as her fingers ran through her hair. The light of the day shone through the door, caressing her, accentuating her lines, her body. Grimble had never seen anything so beautiful. He had always admired the grace and physique of thoroughbred horses, but he would never again think they were the epitome of beauty.*

*Every creature in the world should be envious of her.*

*He darted back to the side of the caravan and stood at the corner, trying to decide what to do. His heart was pounding so hard he thought his chest would burst. The caravan creaked as Ellie stepped off the last step onto the ground in a dress of yellow. She looked at him curiously.*

*"Tow— I..." Grimble said. "Um. You. You were, uh, wet, you were wet. Um – towel. We have towels."*

*Ellie's brows dropped in confusion. She cocked her head and looked back at the caravan's door. Her eyes sparkled. She smiled. "We have towels too," she said. "There are lots of things in the caravan. Did anything grab your interest?"*

*She walked toward the house, not waiting for an answer.*

*Grimble watched her walk away. He stood planted to the spot, his mouth open, hoping the words would land on his tongue. She was weightless. Her steps were like a dance. He would never again miss the shape of her in whatever she wore, and he would never again underestimate the speed and efficiency with which a woman could get undressed and dressed again. Ellie looked over her shoulder once more and smiled.*

*The evening air cooled, but Grimble did not notice. He continued to watch her walk away. They would sit for dinner, like they always did. They would eat and talk with the family, like they always did. But this time they would exchange secret glances and knowing smiles. And, being the inexperienced youths they were, their wordless, inconspicuous conversation would be most conspicuous.*

Don't go inside yet.

*She was already walking across the water of the swamp.*

Don't argue with your father tonight.

*Her steps were light. The mist closed around her.*

Please don't let this be the last time I see you.

Grimble was half awake and dreaming of Ellie. He dried his eyes and looked into the swamp again. She was no longer there. A mist lay all about, and he realized the temperature had dropped overnight.

He pulled his cloak closer about his body and bumped into the skeleton again. "Pardon," he said, then shook his head in disbelief.

*Speaking with the dead? Have I lost my mind?*

Grimble let out a determined breath and climbed down. He stretched and set about preparing to cross the river, all the while keeping an eye out for the water dogs or any other threat. Testing the canoe for leaks in the shallows, he found a few small ones, which he addressed with pine resin and leather trimmings. It was as good a fix as he could imagine.

*Gavel, please let it hold.*

It was almost midday by the time he had finished with the canoe. The fish he'd eaten two days ago were a memory. Their energy no longer helped him, and the few roots he had gathered provided little energy themselves. Grimble had it in his mind that by midday he would be on the other side of the river, or he would be fish food. He hoped his plan meant the former, but he would have to wait to find out.

The second part of the plan wasn't falling into place. Grimble had counted on one of the water dogs to show itself by this time. He'd heard them the day before and expected his scent or the noise he made would draw one or more in. The last time he had encountered them, he'd been given up by a single dog signaling the others, and this time he'd wanted to catch one or two away from the pack. Now, with the canoe ready and no water dog at hand, he was forced to speed things up. This was a process he had hoped to avoid, as there was no telling how many might show.

Grimble climbed up into the hunting blind. Using a blade of grass between his thumbs, he mimicked the distress call of a small animal. He blew a few times and waited for signs of an approaching predator. He repeated the process until movement caught his attention.

A single dog crept toward the tree. It peered around it, looked left and right, and sniffed the air. Grimble was ready. He loosed his arrow. It pierced the dog behind its shoulder blades and buried partway into the dirt. The dog yipped and kicked its rear legs to start running, but merely pivoted on the shaft of the arrow. Wood snapped. The dog somersaulted onto its back. It lay upside down and kicked the air a few times, then stopped moving. Grimble waited several minutes to see if other dogs were close before climbing down.

Once on the ground, he approached the creature and examined it. There were no signs of life.

"Forgive me, little sister."

Grimble readied the canoe and moved everything to a dry area near the river. He unstrung his bow, not wanting it to snag on anything, and placed it and the two remaining arrows in his bedroll next to his sword. He placed the bowstring in his tinderbox to protect it from water if he fell in the river. Finally, he checked on the satchel and its contents and secured it to his body as best he could. Once his kit was in order, he placed the canoe near a shallow area of swamp that fed directly into the river.

Grimble carried the dog's body about twenty yards downriver from the canoe, set it on the ground, and cut away its two hindquarters. His stomach growled as he cut the skin away from the muscle and examined the red meat. The creature seemed healthy. The meat looked free of disease. He had never butchered a dog, but it looked like every other creature he had. The part that would be the rump in a deer or cow appeared soft and juicy. Grimble's mouth watered, and he cut the section away. He washed it in the shallows and wrapped it in part of his bedding. If he could not find food soon, he would at the very least have this hand-sized piece of meat.

Ensuring everything was in place – his kit, the canoe and paddle, his destination on the other side of the river – Grimble walked back to the butchered dog. Picking it up by its front legs, he spun around once, and heaved the body as far into the river as he could. He immediately bent to pick up the two hindquarters. The water heaved and rippled. He threw the first hindquarter downriver, beyond where the dog had landed, and threw the second farther still.

Grimble didn't wait. He ran to the canoe and slid it into the water. Stepping in, he paddled hard with a few strokes, built up strong momentum toward the opposite bank, and gently set the paddle in the canoe. He drew his knife and bent low, watching all about.

The turmoil where the dog parts landed had settled, and the water began to calm. The canoe's speed dropped off. Grimble looked ahead. The bank neared, but he was only two thirds of the way across. The patches he had made in the canoe slowed the water coming in, but they did not stop it. Already the bottom was covered.

The canoe all but stopped. It turned as the gentle current of the river pushed it along. Water seeped through the leaks. Grimble was about fifty feet from the other side.

He picked up the paddle and slipped it into the water. Pulling, he straightened the canoe's heading, getting some forward motion. He pulled the paddle free, and it bumped against the side. The *thunk* of the impact sounded as loud as thunder to Grimble.

Off to his right, the water rippled.

Abandoning all attempts at stealth, Grimble paddled hard, pulling with what energy he had left. A handful of strokes put the canoe on a collision course with the roots of a tree growing along the riverbank. Grimble dropped the paddle, stood, and took two steps before jumping for the tree.

The canoe collided into the roots. The water behind him churned and over his shoulder, Grimble saw the beast's tentacles turn the boat sideways. It filled with water and was dragged below.

A week ago, the leap and subsequent climb over the tree roots would not have been an issue, but in his current state Grimble was slow, and several times he nearly fell backward into the river. The bank was no more than three feet high, but it might as well have been ten. He looked again at the water and saw the massive tail of the creature as it thrashed about.

Grimble tried climbing further but was held back. The satchel's strap had caught on a root, keeping him from reaching the safety of dry ground. The water rippled again.

He knew he couldn't think about what might happen.

*Smooth. Smooth motions.*

Grimble took the tension off the strap and freed it from its captor. He pushed hard with his legs and clawed for purchase in the soil, crawling free of the tree and away from the edge of the river. He collapsed, his strength depleted.

*The satchel tried to kill me. The little fucker tried to kill me.*

Grimble felt around to make sure he still had it. He held his bane in front of his face and whispered, "I'm burning you to ashes when I get back."

Remembering the swamp was a dangerous place, Grimble forced himself to his knees, caught his breath, and worked to stand. The effort it took surprised him. His knees nearly buckled, but he didn't quit until he was on his feet.

Slowly he started east, avoiding the spiked willow trees, and walked until he found a good tree to rest in. He used the remainder of the day to recover. His sleep was interrupted by cramps and worry. He never had the chance to dream.

The next day Grimble made a beeline for the eastern edge of the swamp. He collected what roots and plants he could along the way and harvested water from vines and a rover's well. His clothing, weary, torn, and worn thin, exemplified his condition. The starvation and lack of sleep tugged on him. He did not move quickly.

"*Grimble,*" a voice called.

He ducked low and snapped his head around, looking for the caller. No one was there.

"*Stay, Grimble.*" The voice was beginning to sound like Ellie. "*Stay with me.*"

He longed for her voice and thought about staying, if only to hear it. It was comforting. Loving. Warm. But how could she be here?

"*Stay with me, Grimble.*"

Hunger no longer chewed at his insides. A calm overtook him. "Where are you?" he asked.

"*I'm right here with you. I'll always be with you. Stay.*"

He strained his neck, looking. Nothing but trees and bushes and bugs and dank water met his eyes. She was not there. But he wanted her. To see her. To hear her.

"Sing. Sing for me."

"*Songs are for children. I don't sing anymore, but I will make you feel good, Grimble.*"

"Ellie would sing. You're not Ellie."

Harshness stole the warmth from the voice as it snapped at him. "*Your Ellie is a dream. She's not real. Your Ellie has moved on without you.*" The words stung his heart. The voice laughed.

It was cold and gripped his bones. *"You broke Ellie's heart when you didn't find her. She lost faith in you. She lost her love for you."*

The voice was convincing. It made him feel its words were true. It had been a long time. Could that be true? He had failed to find her. He'd grown neglectful in the army and should have tried harder. The voice was probably right.

*"Your Ellie doesn't even think of you anymore. She sells herself. She's spread her legs for countless men. She is an empty shell used by the wretched and vulgar for their pleasure."*

"No. No."

*"Men take their turn with her in soiled beds and bent over tables and on all fours in the mud of filthy streets. She laughs at your memory."* The voice laughed. *"You did that to her. It is your fault."*

Tears welled in his eyes. In his mind he could see Ellie being mistreated as the voice described. In his heart he knew it was a lie, but the images felt real and tangible. He could see her dead eyes as she let misshapen sadists and soulless boors have their way. Grotesque, unnatural, demonic creatures crawled over her body, her skin. The images crushed his heart. Dispirited, Grimble wept. He fought against the burgeoning ache, but the hole within him grew. It consumed everything good and warm. The hunger he had known for days, every pain he had suffered before, was a shadow of the agony he now felt inside.

*"Stay and I will make the pain go away."*

"You lie," Grimble spat through gritted teeth. "Ellie is stronger than that."

But what if the voice was right? No. That was not the Ellie he knew.

*"Stay with me. She doesn't want you."*

"No." Grimble was determined. "You lie. I will never stay here."

Deeper in the swamp, a tree wailed. A wind blew against Grimble, shaking his cloak. It was cold and smelled of acrid death and bitter decay.

He looked about. The swamp was quiet. The horrors he had felt moments before were gone, and his heart knew the voice had lied. Grimble took a deep breath and released it. He could no longer feel the swamp's presence.

He was alone.

Grimble picked himself up; he felt lighter than he had expected. Moving eastward, he soon arrived within sight of the swamp's edge. He smelled a campfire, but could see no camp. He watched and waited. Counting. Memorizing.

Once or twice an hour, a two-man patrol walked by. Grimble could not hear every word between the soldiers, but he knew the tone and could tell they would rather be in town or even at the barracks than camping next to a wailing, bug-infested swamp. This was good news to Grimble.

He moved out of sight of the swamp's edge and sat on the ground, huddled against the base of a tree. He was more comfortable than he'd been in days, and as he waited for the dark, he nodded into a numb slumber.

Grimble awoke with a jolt. A look at the moon and stars told him it was hours past nightfall. He was on the ground – at night. Grimble lumbered to a crouched position and drew his knife. He breathed easier when he noticed nothing around – no blue plants. Nothing.

Over the next few hours clouds moved in, shielding the moon and stars. Grimble crawled through the swamp to the edge where the grass was cut low by farmers and grazing animals. He slipped through the grass and by the patrols, staying low until he had left the swamp far behind. Thinking on the map Roche had made them memorize, Grimble pulled his compass out and, using touch alone, formulated a heading to the town of Arhus. He hoped he was headed in the right direction. A fox's cry skimmed across the field behind him.

Grimble kept low as he traversed the field. He found a remote farm and watched it for movement before he approached. The farmer's garden, protected by a short wattle fence, might have kept out rabbits, but not hungry troopers. Grimble stepped over it and collected a few lettuces and carrots. The chicken coop was near at hand, and he removed a half-dozen eggs, replacing them with a silver coin. He snuck to the blind side of an outbuilding and downed as much of the vegetables as he could before cracking and drinking the eggs. The rush of energy hit him within minutes. Grimble chuckled to himself.

*Best damn meal I've ever had.*

He put his sword on his hip and used some of his rope to make a hackamore. The next part was tricky, but he managed to "borrow" one of the horses without waking the farmer or his family. Grimble left the rest of his coins in the stall and walked the horse away from the farm. Using a fence to lift himself onto the horse, he rode bareback with the hackamore toward the river. A dog barked in the darkness.

The Vaster River was over ten miles away, and he pushed the horse as hard as he dared. The eastern sky in front of him was losing its darkness. Time was running out.

It was gray overhead as Grimble approached the final crossroad. If he could make it past there, he would have perhaps a mile of farmland between him and the river.

He heard shouts of alarm. Movement on the north side of the road drew his attention. A watch post there came to life and soldiers scrambled to ready themselves.

"The Horseman!" a soldier yelled. "The Horseman!"

Another soldier rang a bell. Grimble kicked the horse to a gallop and rode by them. He swept wide and caught the soldiers off their guard and unprepared. None were ready in time to engage him.

He galloped across the intersecting road and into the field that lay before the river. The tilled land churned beneath the horse's hooves and its mouth foamed, but it gave everything Grimble asked, keeping the speed. The sky continued to brighten.

The river came into sight. Grimble slowed his mount and brought it to a stop along the bank. His dismount was anything but graceful as he fell from the horse. He crawled, then stood and scrambled down the river embankment. The sound of the hooves behind him grew louder. His pursuers were not far.

Grimble entered the water. It stole his breath. He treaded and swam as best he could. The swift current pulled him south, away from the soldiers on his trail. Grimble saw the trees of home. The sight motivated him, and he focused on them as he swam. He heard nothing but the water. He breathed wet air, half coughing, half choking. His strokes were sloppy, but sloppy worked as he slipped toward his country.

Grimble reached the shallows of Aendura's side of the river and dragged himself onto the muddy bank. He wanted nothing more than to collapse and catch his breath, but shouts behind him pushed him onward. He feared they were almost upon him. His arms and legs behaving like a newborn calf's, Grimble pulled himself up the riverbank onto the grassy field.

He was home.

Grimble collapsed onto his back, heart pounding. He breathed great gulping breaths.

The faraway cries stopped. Grimble turned his head toward his pursuers. They stood in defeat on the far bank about seventy yards away: five soldiers and a dog. Grimble rose and stood in wobbly triumph, regaining his strength. He showed them what he thought of them, raising his fist and thumb.

One of the soldiers was more slender than the others. As the stouter ones turned and left, the slender one, a woman, stayed. She motioned with her right hand, tossing something away. The hair on Grimble's neck stood on end.

A moment later, several objects whizzed past him. He crouched defensively and looked harder at her hands to see if she had a bow. He pulled his own bow stave from his bedroll and tried to remember where he had stored the string. Maintaining his focus on the woman, he ran his hands over his pouches and pockets, searching for his tinderbox. As he stared, a streak of white-blue lightning leaped from the woman's hand. It crossed the river with a resounding crack, striking the tree next to him. Splinters and shards of barks sprayed onto Grimble.

*Shit! A mage!*

He backed away, keeping the mage in sight.

She disappeared.

Grimble put the stave in his left hand and drew his sword. He looked about.

The mage appeared next to him, forcing his back to the river. She swung at him with her sword, and he managed to parry it away, but just barely.

"Who are you?" the mage said. She followed through and made a thrust attack, followed by another swing.

Off balance and on his heels, Grimble struggled to defend against them at first. But he soon gained his footing and managed to counter an attack. The mage backed away, giving him a moment to recover. She made a buzzing noise with her voice. Grimble heard a series of pops and cracks. It smelled like it was going to rain.

The mage stepped in to attack again, making her thrust obvious. Grimble moved to parry it, prepared to counter or step back if it was a feint. A spark of light emerged from where the two blades touched, and a sharp crack rang in his ears. Grimble felt a strange vibration and pain in his right arm. He called out as his arm went limp. The sword fell from his hand.

The mage attacked in a fury. Grimble did everything he could to defend himself with the bow stave in his left hand, but she was too well trained, and she did not let up. With his right arm useless and no real weapon at the ready, Grimble knew he would not last against her. He managed a strike at her weapon hand, before hurling the bow at her face. She moved out of the way of the strike to her hand, but was caught off guard by the thrown bow.

When she dipped below its path and backed away, Grimble slid down the riverbank and jumped into the river, praying to Ihgel her armor was too heavy for her to follow.

# CHAPTER TWENTY-SEVEN

Page chased down the riverbank after the Horseman until he ran headlong into the water. Even though it was crafted to be lighter than most, the metal plates in her brigandine armor made it too heavy for her to swim. She watched him for a few moments. When it was apparent he wasn't going to drown, she spied down the riverbank. The footing was not good, and she would have trouble following him, so she made her way back to the grass field. Looking to the river again, she spotted the Horseman riding the current.

Page ran along the bank and managed to keep him in sight for a few hundred yards. A gully made by a stream feeding the river cut off her path, delaying her. It was twelve or fifteen yards across, but downed trees and undergrowth would make crossing it slower than going around. Page cursed how long it took; by the time she reached the riverbank on the other side of the gully, the Horseman was nowhere to be seen. A second check of the river and both banks was as fruitless as the first. There was no sign of him.

The sound of approaching riders drew her attention. A half-dozen men riding parallel to the river neared. Page uttered a profanity under her breath and portalled back to her horse before the riders could see her.

Thinking about her next steps, Page cursed the Renlaran soldiers for leaving so quickly. If they had stayed, they could have helped her search, covering more ground. Since the Horseman had defied her ability to locate him through Arcane means, she would have to search for him on horseback. That he eluded her frustrated her, even more so now that she needed to spend more time on a sweaty, smelly horse to conduct that search.

When Page had first seen the man crawling from the river this morning, she'd known he was as good as dead. Her darts never missed. Her lightning strike was similarly effective. They may be blocked, but never had they missed. Until today. Could it be that she was not powerful enough to strike him, or that he was himself a mage?

Teacher was another option. He was more powerful than her. He had even told her he was an advisor. At first Page resisted the temptation to reach out. She wanted desperately to report with good news, to report success. She was embarrassed at losing the chance and letting the Horseman slip away. But she realized her good news would have to wait. Better to get some help than miss this chance altogether.

Page reached into the pouch on her belt, pulling the beads from it. The familiar tingle returned to her fingers, and she waited.

*"What news?"* Teacher's deep voice penetrated her mind.

*"A setback, Teacher,"* Page said. *"I funneled the Horseman into a trap and tried to take him down, but he escaped. Somehow, he's protected from my spells. He's nearby. I know it. But I can't*

*find him. I know his secret now and next time he won't get away. The trouble lies in finding him. Your guidance may help."*

*"Allow me into your mind to see what troubles you."*

Page relaxed to let Teacher in. She felt the pressure as Teacher reached into her mind. The muscles on her skull twitched. She saw flashes of lights. She smelled wet clothes and a man's sweat. The search was not aggressive, but it was unpleasant.

*"I see him in your mind. I know this man... We faced each other,"* Teacher said.

*"Who is he?"*

*"He is a cavalry soldier, my dear. Nothing more. His charms cannot be strong. Give me a moment. I will find him, and when I do, you must not fail in dispatching him. It's peculiar that he has encountered us both, and I don't like it."*

Page felt that Teacher was no longer connected to her. It lasted several minutes, perhaps more.

*"Page,"* said Teacher upon return, *"he must die. You'll find him on the western bank of the river. He has the smell of death and does not move. Find him. Finish it."*

*"On the western bank, smell of death? What does that mean? Did you have trouble as well?"* Page asked.

*"I have given enough. Prove yourself."*

Page sensed frustration. It was the first time she had felt emotion through the beads' connection. Teacher wasn't telling her everything. He withheld something, and Page wondered if she should trust him. Something in the way he spoke reminded her of a reprimand she had once received from her mother.

Page hated her mother.

But none of that mattered. Page had been hired to complete a job, and she would see it through. She was a professional. She would earn the tuition and sponsorship for her final year of training. She was going to be a Grand Master, and this Horseman was not going to stop that from happening. She would also make him pay for killing Hammer. Yes, she would hurt the man.

Already on the western side, she mounted her horse and kicked the dull beast forward. South she rode, examining the bank for any movement.

*Smells of death... Is he dying?*

His right arm useless to him, Grimble kicked and struggled with his left arm to stay afloat. His only thought was on breathing, on keeping his head above water. The first time he went under, all concern about the mage fled his mind. His opponent now was the Vaster River.

The current was swift, but manageable for a few hundred yards. After that the river's pace quickened, and Grimble found himself shifting toward the right bank, the western bank. Renlar's bank. He didn't care. He yearned for dry land. The river tossed him about as he tried to swim. It taunted him with what he could not have, spinning him, showing him both banks, but preventing him from reaching either.

Along the banks were dead trees and branches deposited by storms and flooding. As Grimble approached one, he reached his left arm out to grab it. The branch snapped in his hands as the river hurried him by. He went under again.

The water was peaceful. The sound beneath the surface was muted and inviting. He was so tired. The days and days of little sleep, of little food, of constant fighting... Everything had gone wrong. His body was exhausted. He wanted it to be over. All he had to do was breathe in the water. It would be easy. He could rest. He had given his all and put up a good fight. Rest. Grimble simply wanted to rest.

*Ellie.*

He kicked with all his might and pulled with his left arm. He emerged and gasped for air. His lungs ached. His leaden legs slowed. He could not get enough air. He coughed. White water lay ahead. Grimble focused on staying above water and not letting the river win.

His shins struck something hard under the water. It spun him to face upstream. Grimble paddled with his arm and turned back downstream in time to collide face-first with the trunk of a downed tree. The rushing water pushed him under the trunk, popping him up on the other side. Grimble grabbed a branch as he surfaced. The water on the downriver side moved slower. He took a moment to catch his breath.

He tasted blood and spat. The water turned red and rushed away behind him. He looked to the dirt bank not more than a dozen feet away from him. Rocks and boulders spread along its edges and up the steep embankment. Instinctively he reached out with his right arm to help stabilize his grip on the branch. But before he remembered it was useless, Grimble noticed he had managed to make the arm move a little. It moved and it hurt.

Taking his time, he made his way to the bank on Renlar's side of the river. By the time he reached it, his arm moved where he wanted it to, albeit slowly. The pain was excruciating.

Grimble chuckled. *At least I know I'm alive. I'm not done.*

He crawled from the water, looking first at the opposite side of the river, then the top of the ten-foot-high embankment where he had emerged. He saw no signs of anyone, mage, soldier, or witness. His eyes found nothing, but his nose told him something was wrong. The air around him was putrid.

Grimble looked at the dark rocks at the base of the steep bank and noticed they were shades of black, brown, and white. He blinked a few more times, trying to focus. The rocks were, in fact, cows – three decaying cows. He finally separated the noise of the flies from the rush of the water behind him and saw the maggots crawling around holes in the sagging skin on the shaded side of the corpses.

The stench hit him full force, and he retched.

Grimble had become accustomed to horrible smells in the regiment and knew how to take his mind off the matter, but his abrupt deposit in the middle of such fetor caught him off guard. He focused on putting the scent out of his mind. The bank was too steep to climb in his condition, and he was not ready to move along the edge of the river in search of a better location. Grimble crawled under the trunk of the downed tree, using it for cover. He wrapped himself with what remained of his cloak and took a few minutes to catch his breath, mere feet from one of the decaying cows.

Once he felt strong enough to move, Grimble extracted himself from underneath the tree trunk. He was nauseous from breathing the rancid air, but he recovered enough strength to move further down the river, looking for a way across or a way up the bank.

*The satchel!* Grimble stressed. He reached down and found it secured around his body. His bedroll and canteen, however, were missing. His water, his food, his supplies. Gone. Grimble needed to get across the river, and he needed to do it soon. Without the mage seeing him. Time was running out. Keeping watch for anyone on the riverbanks, he moved on.

A few hundred yards from the dead cows, Grimble found a

long, thin, dried-out tree, just over an inch thick. It was tangled among the branches and items washed up on the bank. Its trunk was straight. Grimble remembered the mage using a spell that hurt metal, but not wood, as he had fought her. He secured the sapling, hacked out a seven-foot section, and smoothed out the bark with his knife. Opening the satchel, he pulled out the cloth bundle with the Elder Steel items.

He thought about the trouble he could get in for doing this.

*Fuck it.*

Grimble needed to get home before they could bring him up on charges. He would take the chance.

He pulled the spearhead out of the bundle and replaced the rest in the satchel. Using his knife, he shaved the end of his pole so it would fit inside the shank and cut strips of cloth from his cloak to secure it. It was far from ideal, but it felt good to hold a spear again.

*This… this I know how to use.*

The river ran wild here, and as far as he was able to see. Grimble pressed on, but the going was slow due to the rocks and debris. He had moved perhaps half a mile downriver before he found a game or cattle trail, affording him the chance to reach the level ground above.

His legs, obstinate at first, eventually accepted their orders and he started up the dirt trail. The first few steps were an effort and his feet slipped in the clay and dirt, but he reached the top and took a look around. Seeing no one in sight, Grimble continued downriver. He hoped to find slow-moving water, and to reach it before being caught in the open.

He reached a small grove of trees and used it to get a lay of the land, moving his right arm as he did so. He could move it freely now, though pain shot through it every time. But the more he did it, the better it moved – pain be damned. Grimble set his spear against a tree, sat down, and massaged and worked his arm.

Above him, a chickadee called. It sounded upset, almost as loud as a squirrel barking. It kept going, on and on. They usually made a quick call, but this one sang, "Chicka-dee-dee-dee-dee-dee…" It must have completed two dozen "dee"s before repeating its high-pitched "chicka" call. Grimble kept working his arm.

The chickadee alighted on his spear. The little bird was close enough to touch. It started its call again, repeating the final note dozens of times.

He got up, and the little bird flew further into the grove – right by an armored woman, slinking toward Grimble with a drawn sword.

Grimble's blood ran cold.

"Once I found those dead cows," the mage said, "I knew you had to be close."

She was Aenduran. Her accent shouted it this time, but it was clear her allegiance was elsewhere. Grimble was about to kill or be killed by a countryman.

His spear's reach was its benefit; it would be hampered by the trees. Grimble grabbed it and backed into the open field, glancing at the dull gray spearhead and its improvised binding. With the weapon held low, he uttered a prayer to Ihgel that it would remain secure.

The mage emerged from the shadows of the grove, stepping into the sunlight. Her sword gleamed in her left hand. A bright green gambeson jacket covered her arms. Her black brigandine armor covered her body and the top of her legs. The mage paused, reached out with her right hand, and grasped the air, as if she were showing Grimble how she would crush him. A strange sensation ran like a chill through his body. His hair stood on end. He cocked his head to one side as he looked at her. She scowled, switching the sword to her right hand.

Too many elements were in her favor. She was armored, rested, nourished, and a wielder of magic. Grimble was none of those. His one benefit was his weapon's reach. He picked his targets and hoped to make his first strike count.

Outside Grimble's range, the mage uttered her buzzing words again. She lowered the tip of her blade toward the ground beside her as she stalked toward him. Tiny bolts of lightning arced from the sword to the ground, snapping and popping. The grass smoked. Her impassive focus on Grimble never changed. She reminded him of a wild cat. If he weren't a seasoned trooper, she might have intimidated him.

Using his right hand at the back of the spear, Grimble kept the tip moving, circling, making little adjustments. When the mage arrived within a few steps of his reach, her sword came up and she turned side-on, making herself a smaller target.

Grimble advanced a step. The spear tip feinted low and circled to strike at her head. The mage backstepped, dodging her head to one side. Both went back to their guard. Grimble watched her back foot step forward in preparation for her front foot to move. Before it could, he stepped in, stabbing at her head. The mage was quick; she knocked the spear to the side and leaned in to close the distance, taking away his advantage.

Grimble stepped off the line and used the parry to carry his spear around to attack her front leg. Catching her mid-step, her right thigh exposed, the spear pierced her thin leather cuisse and cut her above the knee. She grunted and staggered, backing away. Grimble pressed, thrusting at her head again. The mage ducked the tip, and took another step back to gain space.

*She's not trained to fight against a spear. Let's give her something else to think about.*

Grimble brought the spear back and switched his grip, his breathing heavy, his head pounding. He raised the butt of the weapon over his head, using it as a staff, and brought it crashing down at an angle across the mage's body. She brought her sword up in a high parry, but the momentum of Grimble's blow knocked it out of the way and the spear shaft connected with her left shoulder. A steel plate there protected the collarbone from breaking, but she groaned at the impact.

Grimble backed away to bring his hands back to their original position. He held the spear point out, moving it around, never stopping. The mage, a slight limp in her right step, moved back too. She reached into her pouch and pulled out several darts, like the ones Flicker used. She mouthed a few words and tossed them in the air. They bolted at Grimble. He ducked, and they narrowly missed him. Her look of frustration told Grimble she was on the defensive now.

"Who the fuck are you?" she said, breath heavy.

"A man who wants to get home."

"You can't go home."

"That may be so."

He watched her breathing. They circled each other. She breathed in. He moved the spear point about, prepared to strike. Sword outstretched, she searched for an opening. She breathed out, and Grimble charged in.

He feinted high, then low, drawing her defenses into two rapid responses. She stepped back as he thrust high with his actual attack and brought his right hand forward, pushing the point of his spear into the joint of her right shoulder, striking where the brigandine didn't protect her. The spear penetrated her gambeson. She cried out and dropped her sword.

The mage tried to back away, but stumbled on her wounded leg and fell. Grimble thought the fight was over, but the mage motioned with her left hand, as though asking for her weapon's return. Her sword flew to her hand as if tossed to her. He took a quick look to his left, fearing a new opponent had joined their fight.

That was all the time she needed to levitate to her feet and press Grimble while he was distracted. She thrust, piercing him below his ribcage on the right side.

The mage's left hand wasn't as adept as her right, but it was lethal enough. She moved to withdraw before Grimble could counter. She staggered on her injured knee. He raised the spear over his left shoulder and struck her chest with the butt end.

The mage stumbled back and fell again. Grimble stepped forward. She crawled backward, trying to gain some space, but her right knee, covered in blood, didn't appear to have the strength she needed. Her right arm disappointed her, too. A red blossom grew where it connected to the shoulder. Grimble closed in and switched his grip.

Ignoring the pain in his side, he thrust at his downed opponent's hip. She tried to block the attack while on her back, but the spear made it under the defense. The Elder Steel spearhead pierced through the metal plates and gambeson protecting her. It struck deeply into the joint of her left hip. The mage screamed in agony. "No, no, no!" she cried, dropping her sword and drawing her dagger.

Grimble pulled the spear back, raised it high. The mage shouted something and flicked her dagger in the air, her eyes on the tip of the spear. The blade shot skyward, slicing the straps securing the spearhead. The impact vibrated the pole and the head shook free, falling to the grass behind Grimble. He switched his grip again, infuriated at losing the spearhead. The mage used the moment to grab her sword from the grass with her left hand.

Grimble raised the pole higher and brought it crashing down like a club. The mage lifted her sword to redirect the impending attack on her head. He had anticipated that she would try to block his strike, so he aimed for and struck her wrist. She winced as a sickening snap rang out. She dropped the sword, her face red.

"No! I've trained too hard. No. No!"

Grimble used the pole to knock her sword farther away from her. She tried to crawl backward again, but managed only to claw and rip the grass with her right hand and dig troughs in the dirt with her left heel. Blood ran from her hip, her thigh darkening. The green grass was covered in a sheen of red. The mage looked to her right and reached with her hand, trying to locate her sword.

Grimble raised the pole for another strike. He held it with both hands near the very bottom, and brought it crashing down. The mage raised her right hand, palm open, and shouted a word. The pole snapped as it struck some unseen barrier between the two warriors. The top half tumbled through the air. The vibration of the pole stung Grimble's hands. The mage kept her right hand in the air, palm facing him.

She tried to inch her way backward, wincing and grunting between deep breaths. Blood drenched her gambeson's right sleeve and armpit. Her left wrist was swollen and red and unnaturally angled. Grimble looked at the portion of the pole in his hands. The broken end was splintered and raw. His side burned and he grimaced. Rubbing his fingers across it, he pulled back a warm, wet hand covered in thick, dark blood. Grimble put his hand back over the wound, bunching his shirt over it and trying to stem the flow.

"You're as good as dead with that wound," the mage said.

Grimble looked at her. Beads of sweat ran down her forehead. Bright red blood flowed freely from the wound on her hip.

"So are you."

He poked at her and met hard resistance a foot or more from her hand. He flung the broken stub at her and watched it bounce off the unseen barrier. She kept her hand up.

"You're from Aendura," Grimble said, putting pressure on his wound again. "Why are you trying to kill me? We're countrymen." He drew his knife and moved left and right, but she spun on her back and kept facing him.

"It's my job. I couldn't care less for Aendura. Besides, you're going to pay for killing Hammer."

"Who? Did he fight for Renlar in the war?"

Frustration seemed to take her and the hand almost fell, but she lifted it again. The shoulder injury appeared to be sapping her strength. "No, jackass. Back at the farmhouse."

"I haven't killed anyone since the war, you ignorant shit."

The mage's face reddened. She clenched her teeth. "Your friends did, then. May the Abyss take all of you bastards. You're spies and have no honor."

"I'm a spy? You're working against your own country." Grimble's legs were growing weak. He stopped moving, looking at his shirt and the blood running down his right pant leg. The mage's hand began to falter, but she snapped it back up with a grunt when he looked back at her.

Grimble fell to his knees. He peeked over his shoulder to the river and his country on the other side. "I was home."

"You can't go home."

"Did you kill the others?"

"I killed the one you carried. That asshole had an attitude."

Grimble knew Dinger was dead, but the words stung. He nodded, accepting the news. "You and a few others, from what I saw."

"Yeah. Three of us. Three and a varga wolf."

"A varga wolf?"

"It's a wolf as big as a bear, you illiterate dunce."

Grimble laughed, but winced at the pain and stopped. "We always said Dinger's death would be worthy of song."

"You'll be joining him soon, you know."

"Not before you. And I think you know that."

The mage's arm wobbled, but she kept it in the air and laughed. Her face revealed pain and concern. "Ha. I'm just waiting for you to die. When you do I'll take you back to my camp and heal before claiming my pay."

Grimble was impressed with her determination and inner strength. He shook his head. It made him dizzy. He decided not to do that again. "You're bluffing. You're well trained. I'm sure you know your injury will probably take you before me. A blood wound of the leg will take someone in minutes. The liver takes longer." Her eyes showed fear for the first time. "If you had a portal spell you would have already used it, I think. What spells you have left must be useless to you now, and this – thing, this barrier, is your last-ditch effort to survive."

"Did you train at the Institute?"

"No."

"Then how do you know these things? How do you have such strong protection from magic?"

Grimble recalled his talk with Flicker back in the root cellar. "A friend." He thought about Roche and the other Ravens. "Do you know if my other friends are alive or dead?"

"No." Her mood had changed. She was straining to keep her hand up, but something seemed to be on her mind. "The chancellor killed the general and tortured one of your people, but he was alive when I last saw them." She shook her head. "The chancellor was a piece of shit. What he did was wrong. I never really trusted him anyway."

"Well, at least we can agree on something."

The mage winced in pain. Her face paled and her hand shook and dropped. She started breathing in short, rapid breaths. Grimble crawled toward her. Her eyes grew wide with fear. She threw out her right hand, but it fell immediately. "No. No. No."

"It's okay, it's okay," he said, sheathing his knife. "I'm done fighting. We're both dead. Nothing will stop that now." He continued to crawl toward her. No barrier stood in his way.

The mage relaxed and lowered her head to the grass. She was shaking; her teeth chattered through her frantic breathing. Grimble removed his cloak and laid it over her. She looked at him, teeth still chattering, and uttered a "thanks" that hovered somewhere between statement and question.

"Well, at least we won't die alone."

She rolled her eyes and coughed. "Not much comfort. This is not what I wanted."

"What did you want?"

She looked at him in anger. "What, are we friends now? You did this to me, asshole."

"We did it to each other, horseshit. What's done is done. I was trying to distract us from what's coming."

She paused. The anger softened and she looked off somewhere else. A smile of lament lifted her cheeks. "I wanted to become a Grand Master. I was so close."

"That's a good one. One of my friends wanted to become

one too." He grunted through a spasm of pain. "I wanted to see Ellie again. That's all that kept me going through that damn swamp."

The mage looked up at him. "They said that place is cursed."

"Cursed? Yeah, that place is cursed. It may be the Abyss itself."

The look in her eyes changed. He did not understand it. "And thinking of this woman got you through it?" She winced again and gasped for breath. "If you survive —"

"I won't."

"Shut up," she said. Her breathing seemed to be making it difficult for her to talk. "If you survive, please take my Iron Leaf medallion back to Camp Redemption." She pulled on a chain necklace under her armor, making a section of it visible. She did not seem to have the strength to pull it free. "Tell Niko – tell Niko he was good to me. Better than family."

"I..." Grimble paused as she tried to take a breath and convulsed. She stopped. Her gaze locked on his and a long, shallow breath left her. Her eyes did not look away. Grimble closed them.

The pain in his side brought him out of the moment. Remembering Flicker's flask of healing liquor, he searched the mage, hoping she had some, or maybe a field aid kit. He unstrapped her backpack, the one like Flicker's. To his surprise it was stretched taut and contained several books. A quick search found it did not even have room for anything else. He put it aside and searched the rest of her. In the end, he found a few items he didn't recognize, but no flask.

Grimble pulled on the silver chain at her neck. He bent to pull it over her head and the pain was excruciating. His head grew light and he caught himself before falling over. He took a few breaths and lifted the necklace free. It dangled from his hand, the mage medallion's ruby glinting in the morning light. Beside it, from a small chain, hung a silver elm leaf.

Grimble remembered that when he had seen the mage across the river she had been standing next to a horse. She had no water on her person, and no food; her horse must be nearby. He was dizzy, the world hazed. He looked toward the grove, hoping to see her horse.

He saw Ellie in a sky-blue dress running toward him, but no horse.

*Ellie? That's weird.*

A chickadee alighted on the mage's backpack. It danced, drawing Grimble's attention. "Tseet," it called.

*... tseet... tseet... tseet... tseet...*

Darkness began to take his sight. "Hey." His head was heavy. "I meant to thank you." Grimble fell sideways to the ground. He thought of Ellie, how much he loved her and never told her so. He had thought he would have time, that he would live to an old age. He hoped she was well and happy. He could hear her singing. It was the most beautiful sound in the world.

Grimble opened his eyes. His head rested in Ellie's lap. The soft folds of cotton caressed his neck. She sang and looked off into the distance. He wished he knew the words. She knew so many languages. How many times had she sung to him by the creek or under the beech trees?

*If I am to reach Ihgel's Hall today, I couldn't ask for a better send-off.*

Grimble fell asleep.

When he opened his eyes again his head was still in Ellie's lap. He was weightless. She stroked his hair. He wished he had told her he loved her years ago. He wanted her to know.

"I missed you, Ellie," he said. His voice was dry and thin and light. She stroked his hair and sang. He gazed up from her lap, trying to look into her eyes, but her focus remained on the horizon.

Grimble took a painful breath. "I wanted to find you." He took another. "I love you."

She sang. A tear rolled down her cheek and fell onto her blue dress. The intoxicating song was better than any he remembered.

"It's okay," he said. "I got to spend the last few days with you. You brought me some joy in that cursed place." He took another breath. The pain was not as bad as before. He had to be dying. "I hope you find happiness. I hope you find someone who'll love you as much as I do."

Her voice cracked mid-song. Tears ran freely down her cheeks. They fell upon her dress and onto Grimble's forehead. He lost consciousness once more.

Grimble woke in a field. He blinked in the sunlight and felt the grass around his head.

He sat up. The mage was nowhere to be seen. Neither was the grove. Earlier the river had been to his right, as had been the sunrise. The sun remained on his right, but the river was now on his left. There was no blood on the grass, no sign of a struggle; but the satchel and the mage's items were right beside him.

*Gavel's eye. How'd I get so turned around?*

His side didn't hurt anymore. He reached down to feel his wound, finding a blood-crusted shirt with a hole in it and no injury beneath.

The thud of heavy boots brought him out of his thoughts. A dozen soldiers approached. The whole image looked familiar to

Grimble. They wore cheap armor and carried spears and a banner, much like one of the militias his regiment sometimes worked with.

Militia or soldiers, he was not going to give up. Not after all he had been through. He was going to find Ellie.

Grimble sprung into a crouched position and picked up the mage's sword, drawing it from its sheath.

The soldiers recoiled and stopped well out of reach. Their formation was sloppy and loose. Grimble glared.

"What's your name?" one of the men called.

Grimble growled. He moved the sword back and forth in front of the line of soldiers.

"That can't be him," said another. "We're looking for a cavalry trooper. Look at him, he's a homeless beggar."

"A beggar with a sword," said the first. "Don't be daft. What's your name, friend?"

Grimble realized his tattered clothes, unkempt beard, and filthy appearance belied his true self. He looked at the soldiers, wondering why they did not overwhelm him or try to kill him. And why did they sound Aenduran?

"Hey, Sarge," a woman said. "What was that question we're supposed to ask?"

"Oh, yeah," said the first man. "Hey, friend. Who owns the battle?"

Without thought, Grimble growled, "Wicked Spears."

"Thank the gods!" said the sergeant. "We've been looking for you for days, Corporal. We're the Halton County militia. You're safe now. We'll get you to Fort Northbridge." He turned to the others. "Get him some food and water."

# CHAPTER TWENTY-EIGHT

For over a century, Fort Anjermott's War Room had served as the strategic planning center for the 209th Light Cavalry Regiment. The large room was linked to Constable Nicholas Dressel's office and contained two square tables, each side measuring six feet. They immediately grabbed the attention of anyone who entered the space. Colored blocks with tiny pennants lay atop the tables, each one representing a unit on a battlefield or their position inside the country.

Maps hung on the whitewashed walls beside trophies and banners earned by the regiment. Lanterns circled the room and dangled from the soot-covered ceiling. They burned whenever the room was in use, as it had no windows to grant access to sunlight or the gaze of a spy. The room's thick door was the only entrance and egress. Constable Dressel, the highest-ranking officer of the 209th Cavalry Regiment, held the door's sole key. There were few other rooms like it in the King's Army.

On this day, one table was littered with inventories, finance sheets, and orders from King Saevar's Lord High Constable. The other table, the one covered with a painting of the Kingdom of

Aendura, proudly displayed the blocks and pennants that always sat atop it. However, instead of noting military units, the pennants waved strips of paper indicating tons of food, horses, farrier equipment, spears, swords, tents, and other inventory items of the 209th.

Bhen, Priest of the Temple of Truth, stood inside the War Room beside Devout Mother Tara and a handful of other military officials. Constable Dressel had requested their presence. The Temple delegation had arrived ahead of the mages and waited patiently for them. Bhen had begun to sweat. The room had limited ventilation and was hot and muggy from the bodies and open flames.

"The noble took the remainder of our horses," a captain said. "First Division will accept the entirety of our food stores, but they don't have room for the wagons. They'll have to unload and return."

"That doesn't help us," a commander said.

"Can we send the wagons to Fourth Division?" Commander Dek asked. "They unload and head to Fourth. Fourth always needs to move heavy loads."

"Alright," Dressel said, "check with Fourth. What about the shields and armor?"

"We added to the storage in Chatham," Dek said, "and still have wagonloads of shields, helmets, armor, barding, and assorted tack. Here are the numbers, if you want to see them." He held a sheet out for Dressel to examine.

The captain spoke again. "The shields are the wrong type for infantry. Let's reach out to the 202nd, see if they'll take the shields and barding, and then check with the 108th about the armor and helmets."

"No," Dressel said. "I don't want to send wagons all over the kingdom. That'll slow this whole thing down. Send word to the 202$^{nd}$ and 203$^{rd}$, tell them what we have. They take it all or get nothing. First to reply gets the goods."

"Rah, sir." The captain wrote on some parchment, looking up as the Arcane delegation walked through the door.

"Excellent," Dressel said. "Thank you for coming. Please excuse the conditions." He handed the Head Guild Mage and the Devout Mother a sheet of parchment each. "I've had our clerical supplies inventoried and divided. There is a good deal of parchment, ink, and writing instruments. If you are interested in them, and the few other items on the list, please let me know by tomorrow evening. It would honor me if you were to benefit some from this too. Your support has always been indispensable, especially in fighting to preserve the kingdom and the regiment."

"Thank you, Constable," Devout Mother Tara said. "We're as shocked as you that they would dissolve such a storied and successful unit. We will miss doing Abbyon's work beside you."

"We too offer our thanks," the Head Mage stated, "and will miss working alongside you."

Dressel nodded. "How goes the process?"

"Smoothly," a mage said. "Almost everything is removed or claimed. We are ahead of schedule."

"There was not much for us, either," Bhen said. "The artifacts and relics will leave with us, and the Temple will be empty tomorrow."

A knock sounded. A trooper stood at attention outside the door, catching his breath. Dressel motioned for him to enter.

"A bird just arrived," the trooper said. "Dispatch for Marshal Chedwick."

The marshal stepped forward and accepted the small, rolled-up piece of paper. "Dismissed."

"Rah, sir." The two saluted, and the trooper turned on his heels and left the room.

Marshal Chedwick broke the seal and unrolled the tiny scroll. As he read, a smile pulled his usually dour face from its perpetually gloomy appearance. He turned toward Constable Dressel.

"It seems," said Chedwick, "the last of our spears is coming home. They found Broadleaf yesterday. He's at Northbridge Fort now."

Bhen noticed the Devout Mother lift her head and change her focus from Chedwick to the door. He wondered what she was thinking. She turned to him and lifted a hand as if to say, *Not now*.

---

Both banners flying over the wooden walls and towers of Northbridge Fort – the red and light-blue quadrants of the royal house, and the blue of Dalemark – showed Grimble he was almost home. They also showed him the fort was under the watch of His Grace, the Duke of Dalemark. The soldiers in gambesons and blue garrison tunics, and the officers in their blue surcoats, further showed Grimble who his benefactor was.

Grimble's quarters faced the main gate. Beyond that was one of two remaining bridges that crossed the Vaster River. So far today, a handful of merchants and travelers had made their way across that bridge into Renlar, or had come from that country and been granted entry into Aendura. Of course, this was after they had been taxed by Duke Rooker's men.

Construction of a stone wall had yet to start, and Grimble found that peculiar. Renlar, on the other hand, appeared to be in a race to erect a proper stone wall for their fort on the other side of the bridge. Construction there was well underway. The foundation appeared to have been completed and gray stones were being lined and set.

*Why have we not started on this side?*

The wet smell of fresh lumber brought him back to his room. Its construction was so new that sap seemingly seeped from the walls. The aroma, natural and inviting, did more to ease Grimble's mind than the chair, bed, and other conveniences in the room. The furnishings were all a sharp diversion from his last two weeks. Even more so were the walls, which were barely four steps from each other and felt more like a prison than a comfort.

Two soldiers stood guard outside his door, and guards followed him wherever he went. It all furthered the sense that Grimble was living in Northbridge Fort as a criminal rather than a repatriated countryman. He watched one of his current minders shifting his weight back and forth on the stoop. Beyond it, a small patrol marched in formation across the courtyard and a horse rode past in the other direction. The rhythmic clop of the hooves comforted Grimble and he listened until they faded away.

He brought his attention back to the room and moved his chair so he could sit beside the wood-plank bed. The individual items of his kit sat atop a folded brown blanket. The only things missing from his ordeal were his tattered clothes and leather satchel. Last night he had been given a new set of clothes and a pair of leather sandals, and he had wasted no time burning his ragged clothes in the room's fireplace. His ceremonial burning of the empty satchel took more time. He had made sure there were plenty of embers, and had watched the damned thing burn down to the buckles, making sure no leather remained. Justice served. After all, it had tried to kill him.

Grimble picked up the mage's sword – the very thing that should have killed him. While he had bathed, he had examined the place where his injury should have been, but no evidence of it existed. He touched his side again, poking gently first before pushing firmly. Even though his disbelief remained, the wound did not.

The mage's sword and its scabbard were beautifully constructed, no doubt custom-forged for her. Brass rope inlays in the leather-wrapped handle wound between the engraved pommel and crossguard. Its blade was slightly narrower than most arming swords, which made it a little lighter. Well balanced, the sword moved and swung well. Dried blood on the blade and the blood on the shirt he had burned last night told Grimble the day before had not been a dream. He cleaned the blade off and secured the sword and scabbard to his new belt.

He picked up the mage's necklace. Her gold mage's medallion needed no explanation. Grimble had learned about them recently. The ruby stone in the center told him she was trained to the same level as Flicker, but the writing etched into the gold surrounding the stone was foreign to him.

He might have thought the silver elm leaf hanging alongside the medallion was simple jewelry, if the mage had not told him what it was. The back revealed two rows of writing. One looked like a date, but the other he could not decipher.

Grimble had worked beside and fought against mercenary groups before, but never Iron Leaf. They were well known and well respected. He knew each free company had their own traditions and protocols. To return this pendant to their headquarters was likely one of Iron Leaf's. Grimble wondered how they would react to him. He wondered how he had defeated a mage in the first place.

*She said I was protected in some way. Is that how I defeated her?*

Another gold mage's medallion sat on the blanket. This one was in the form of a ring, not part of a necklace. It bore a dark-blue stone, possibly a sapphire. The writing around the outside of the stone was the same as the one on the necklace. Grimble wished he had asked Flicker for the meanings of the different stones. He put both medallions in a pouch.

The mage's pack, the one he had unstrapped from her armor, was next. Grimble put it on the floor and opened it to find three books within.

*Flicker never mentioned mages needed more than one.*

One by one, he pulled the books from the pack. Their design was all the same, but their adornments and coloring made each stand out from the other. Although he understood the purpose of the symbols, the words written within were of a language unknown to Grimble. All three held roughly the same number of pages, but two contained blank sheets. Those two had some spells and symbols that matched, but several pages bore different symbols. Only one of the books bore images of elm leaves on the cover. He was certain this one had belonged to the Iron Leaf mage.

One of the others looked familiar to Grimble, though. He'd seen it before. He opened the front cover and found a pressed small, white flower.

*This is Flicker's? Gods, no! No. Can't be.*

The mage Grimble had fought had told him one of his friends had been tortured. Could it be that Flicker had eventually died of his wounds, and his book was left behind? But if that was the case, why did she not know of Flicker's death? She could have been lying all along, but Grimble felt her admissions were the truth. She did not seem the type to hide her intentions. Besides, if Flicker were dead, where was his medallion? She had his book, but not that. Realizing he would not be able to come up with an answer, Grimble set Flicker's book aside, hoping and praying the man was alive.

The third book contained the same number of pages, but where the others held blank sheets, this one was filled with symbols and writings. The front and back were gilded and bedecked with colored stones. It reeked of wealth and nobility. Grimble placed all three books back in the pack and secured it.

*What in the Abyss was she doing with two extra books and an extra mage's medallion?*

Grimble ran through a number of scenarios in his head, trying to explain how the mage he had killed came to possess these things. It was too much to try to piece together. There were too many questions and too many ways to answer them. None of the scenarios ended favorably for Roche and the Ravens, but he held out hope that some had survived.

He turned back to the items on his bunk. What remained were a set of prayer beads, made of brown stones with yellow stripes running through them, the long feather, and a few small tins of powder and dried herbs. Grimble picked up the tins and placed them into the pouch with the medallions. Next he studied the gray and white feather. It appeared undamaged for all that it had been through, making him even more curious. He slid it into his new backpack, its stiff barbs scratching against the leather wall.

He reached for the beads and they vibrated against the tips of his fingers. "What the —?" he said aloud, dropping them.

"Pardon, sir?" one of the soldiers asked.

"Nothing." Grimble grabbed a stick from the bundle by the

hearth and used it to transfer the beads to his pouch. He placed the pouch and spellbooks inside the backpack alongside the feather, papers, and Elder Steel items from the meetings with the general. He had been carrying the backpack with him everywhere, never letting it out of his control. The soldiers had been giving him odd looks, but Grimble was beyond caring. He was not going to risk anything getting lost or stolen.

Late afternoon arrived. The soldiers outside Grimble's door were new, having changed out with the morning watch hours before. Grimble, not wanting to suffer any questions, was delighted to learn these two men were equally distant and silent.

Excitement at the side gate drew the attention of the guards and Grimble popped his head out the door. From here, neither Grimble nor the soldiers could see the gate. They watched the body language of the other soldiers and staff, but those folks simply turned their heads to see what the commotion was and returned to their business.

"Shit," a soldier said, "ain't nothing."

"Nothing's been happening since we built this place," the other said. He turned to Grimble. "Except you, Corporal."

"Ain't supposed to talk to him."

"We're not supposed to ask him questions, jackass. Nothing says I can't speak to him. We address him by rank only and ask no questions about him or why he's here."

Grimble slipped back into his room and laid back on the bed, his hands behind his head. The soldiers assigned to him obtained whatever Grimble needed, but they didn't speak with him much. Now he understood why. Grimble didn't mind, though. He wanted to be left with his thoughts.

"Ten-*shun*," one of the soldiers ordered. The boots of both men slid and snapped into place on the stoop. Grimble turned his head toward the door to see a group approaching. Their uniforms and dress indicated that someone thought highly of them. Walking ahead of the group was the captain Grimble had met when he had arrived the previous evening. The captain was the highest-ranking officer in the fort. His body language, the antithesis of yesterday's bravado, said everything Grimble needed to know about his status among this new group.

Grimble got up and met the delegation at the threshold. The captain and the four who followed stopped a few steps away.

"Lord Cabral," the captain said, "may I present the corporal. Corporal, this is His Grace Duke Rooker's advisor, Lord Cabral." Grimble dipped his head in a short bow. The captain motioned to the others: two men, a captain and a priest, and a female mage. "I believe you know the delegation from Fort Anjermott."

"Corporal," Lord Cabral said. "I trust you were treated well. The duke is honored to have been a small part of your rescue and recovery and wishes you well. May the gods be with you."

"Thank you, Lord Cabral," Grimble said. "I am indebted to Duke Rooker for the care I received. Please express to His Grace my sincere gratitude." He had heard the officers talk like that to the nobility from time to time, and hoped he had said everything the right way.

"I most certainly will. Now I must leave you in the hands of the delegation from your regiment." Cabral turned to them. "Please reach out should you require anything further." With that, he turned and walked away. The captain motioned to the two soldiers beside the doorway and led them away behind the advisor.

Grimble recognized two of the delegates. One was Captain Marin, from the logistics battalion, and the other was Brother

Bhen, from the regiment's Temple. Grimble did not know the third person, a woman with an unreadable face, wearing the attire of a guild mage. Her aspect was different than Flicker's, but reminded Grimble of the man he had come to know.

Grimble stepped back into his room and invited them in. He turned to the mage. "Please tell me Flicker and the others made it back."

"A discussion for another time and place," she said.

Captain Marin kept his voice low. "Corporal Broadleaf, we were overjoyed to learn you made it back. Constable Dressel can't wait to shake your hand and welcome you home to Anjermott."

"Thank you, Captain," said Grimble.

"Are you prepared to leave?"

"Let me grab my pack." Grimble picked it up and turned back toward the officials.

Captain Marin held out his hand. "Let me take that for you."

"No, sir."

Marin's posture stiffened and his face hardened. He was clearly caught off guard by the determination in Grimble's voice. "Pardon, Corporal?" he said. "Is there going to be an issue?"

"No disrespect meant, Captain. But Commander Dek assigned this mission, and I won't turn over the documents to anyone but him or his superior."

The mage was unfazed by the dialogue, and Brother Bhen watched in earnest. The captain paused and nodded.

"Juta," he said, "when you're ready, please."

The mage reached a hand out to Grimble. He clasped it with one hand and held onto his pack with the other. The captain and the priest grabbed Juta's arm. A moment later, they stood in the courtyard of Fort Anjermott.

# CHAPTER TWENTY-NINE

Grimble could not hide his disappointment. He had arrived expecting to see a fort stocked with horses and men, and hear the rattle of arms and armor. Instead, there were no troopers within sight and the few horses he saw were beasts of burden. Wagons loaded with goods left the fort instead of stocking it, and servants, not troopers, crisscrossed the courtyard.

"Thanks for your help, Juta," the captain said, looking at her and Bhen. "I've got it from here. Neither of you need to bother any further."

Juta paused, staring into Grimble's eyes, her hand holding his. She cocked her head and nodded, her unreadable face softening. Then she thanked the captain and left.

"Thanks, Captain Marin," said Bhen. "However, I believe I will join you."

The captain breathed in, preparing to speak, but let his breath out and shrugged. He led them to Constable Dressel's office, where Commander Dek dismissed him.

The two highest-ranking officers in the regiment, Marshal Chedwick and Constable Dressel, stood beside Dek. They greeted Grimble with firm handshakes and warm smiles, welcoming him back as a returned hero. They asked a few general questions about his escape. No one mentioned Grimble's other team members.

"Constable," Grimble said, "we lost Dinger. He was slain during the mission. I'd really like to know if the others returned."

Dressel's happy face turned dour. "I'm afraid we can't share that information with you at this time. You'll have to trust that we have good reason."

Grimble saw Dinger's dead body again. Dinger, laid out in the spider hole. He remembered the pain he had endured after touching the blue plant. The dogs. The water monster. *"You should not be here."* He felt the presence behind him. His hair stood on end. Cold fingers ran up his spine. *"Grimble,"* the swamp called to him again. It screamed. It mourned and moaned, lost and lonely. He saw her eyes again. The eyes of the countryman he had killed. Grimble's blood ran cold.

*Trust them?*

A dump of adrenalin filled Grimble. His anger rose. His head throbbed. His voice raised in anger. "Trust? A lot of good my trust did me over this past week when I trusted you to find me, sir. Tell you what, how about you trust *me* now, and tell me about my teammates."

Dressel and Chedwick's demeanors changed. Dek put his hand on Grimble's arm and spoke up. "Constable, please give me a moment with him."

"Granted," the constable said. "You're dismissed, Corporal."

Dek escorted a fuming Grimble outside. Bhen followed, receiving a look from Dek. "May I have a moment with my trooper, Brother Bhen?"

"I must insist on staying by his side," said Bhen.

Dek raised an eyebrow and looked between the two men. Bhen's solemn face remained. Grimble's anger turned to confusion, his eyebrows twitching. Dek turned to him. "I understand you've been through a lot and you grieve, but you know better than to take that tone with superior officers, especially some of the highest-ranking officers and nobles in the King's Army. You need to suck it up and watch your step. You did good out there. Don't ruin your hard work by getting sent before a tribunal. Rah?"

Grimble breathed out and nodded. "Rah, sir." His anger was fading, and the reality of what he had said to his commanding officer – and its accompanying trouble – hit him.

"Since your lieutenant and captain are no longer on post, if you need to get something off your chest, let me know. I'll meet with you, one on one. No rank. Better you talk with me than snap like that again. As for your questions, you'll be given a briefing after you've had a night's rest. I'll express your deepest apologies to the constable, but I need you to get your head together." Dek waited for Grimble to look at him and nod before continuing. "Scribes wait for you at your barrack. They'll write your report on the mission. Give them everything."

"Understood," said Grimble. He was still angry, but Dek's words rang true.

"Now, I believe you have something to turn over."

Grimble took his pack off and reached inside to grab the tube with the sheets of parchment he had been protecting, and the Elder Steel spear and arrowheads wrapped in cloth. He handed them to Dek.

"Excellent. You did your king proud, Grimble. Now, report to the scribes. Dismissed."

Grimble saluted the commander, and turned to the priest. "Thank you for your help, Brother Bhen."

Bhen shook Grimble's offered hand. "Stop by the Temple, Grimble. The Devout Mother would like to see you one more time."

"Yes, sir," Grimble said. His look of curiosity matched Dek's.

For the remainder of that day and half of the next, Grimble relayed his story of the mission three times. He told them everything, save for his dreams of Ellie, the voices he had heard in the swamp, and the items he had taken from the mage. The scribes were forced to write furiously, as Grimble didn't slow for them. He was tired of revisiting the last two weeks.

Once the inquisitions were complete, Grimble reported to the logistics office. It shocked him to find Commander Dek waiting and not Captain Marin or another member of that battalion. Grimble moved to within a few steps of the wooden table and came to attention.

"As you were," said Dek. He motioned for Grimble to sit. "Relax. We've got too much to get through and the formalities will slow us down."

"Understood." Grimble set his pack on the floor and sat in the wooden chair.

"I knew you were not the same man I sent off three weeks ago, but I had no idea what you'd been through until this morning. I read yesterday's reports." Dek pointed to a small stack of papers sitting among other documents on the table. "Gods, you've been through a gauntlet! We tried to find you, Grimble, but there were complications."

"Complications, sir?"

"Flicker, the mage who knows you best and therefore would have the best chance to locate you, couldn't detect you with his spells. He was even further hampered by the loss of his spellbook. Don't tell anyone that, especially any mages."

"Sir, Flicker could find a clearing in the middle of a forest at night. And he can do it without taking a step off the road. He can portal half a dozen men hundreds of miles. How could he not find me? And what about the items we left for other mages to locate us? Why did they not work?"

"Grimble, there is something – a magic, most likely – that stopped their attempts. I don't understand it. T'Abyss, I don't think the mages understand it either."

Grimble thought about Flicker shaking his hand for the first time and the questioning he had received in the root cellar. The Iron Leaf mage had failed to strike Grimble down, too. It had frustrated her. Why? "We were blessed by the Devout Mother before departing on the mission. That must be it, sir."

"We talked to her," said Dek. "That's not it. You may have had some favor in your chances, some extra determination, but it would not have protected you from magical attacks or attempts to locate you. I'm told that whatever is on you is powerful magic, beyond the Temple's abilities. Something's at work here, Grimble. But it seems to favor you. I think you'll be alright."

Grimble remembered the spellbooks in the backpack. "Flicker made it back. Where is he now?"

"I'm afraid I don't know. He out-processed and disappeared. Both he and Kurt. Gone. No word as to where they went. Kurt has time left on his term, and he's going to pay the price if he doesn't report back soon."

"Kurt violated his term of service? Why would he do that?"

"He was upset that they left you and Dinger behind. Upset

enough to destroy the weapons racks in the training hall and break both hands punching the walls. But I don't understand why he'd risk violating his term."

"What about the others, sir? Can you tell me if they're okay?"

Dek's posture straightened and he looked hard into Grimble's eyes. "You cannot repeat anything we talk about. There are strange things afoot and it's important none of this gets out. I'm violating orders here. They could hang both of us if they learn I told you." He turned and looked at the closed door.

"Understood."

Dek lowered his voice. "We've learned the Baker was one of Renlar's most respected generals, Endo Batal. Roche, Flicker, and Baz were meeting with him when they were ambushed at the farmhouse and captured by the mercenaries. The mercs had a magic-using nobleman or high-ranking official with them when they attacked. We believe he was Renlar's chancellor, Sala Nesar. Whoever he was, he killed the Baker and tortured Roche, attempting to learn what the Baker had told him. The mercs had a second mage with them, too – a woman. We're pretty certain she's the one you fought and killed by the Vaster.

"She and two others left the farmhouse to hunt down you and Dinger. They took a varga wolf with them. While they were gone Kurt was able to effect a rescue, but it was interrupted. Baz took a bolt to the chest protecting Flicker and the team. They were forced to portal back here, hoping to get aid for Baz and Roche.

"The Temple priests could not help them. Not even the Devout Mother could sway the gods. We lost Baz, and Roche lost most of his right leg. The Temple prayers did help close Roche's wound. He's convalescing at a farm in Grayfell. He didn't want to leave until we found you, but I had to send him away.

"Flicker was out of portal spells and the two mages we had here could not get a rescue team anywhere near Gandleton. We tried, Grimble. In the end, the only thing we could do was increase military presence and patrols on our side of the river."

Grimble's mind ran between the faces of the men he would never, or may never, see again. Two of the toughest troopers Grimble had ever met were dead, and the man he admired most was irreparably injured. His mind flashed to that night. He heard the echo of Dinger's war cry in his ears. Relived finding him dead. Grimble had not had much time to think about Dinger's death in the last week, but the thoughts and feelings rushed in as he listened to Dek.

He should have run down the hill; he should have gotten to Dinger faster. He could have made a difference in that fight. It was his fault Dinger was dead. He should have been there for Roche and Baz. They would have been there for him. Dek continued talking, but Grimble didn't hear him. He looked at the regimental colors hanging behind the commander. He looked at his legs, both legs.

*I shouldn't be here. I let them down. I should be dead too.* Grimble's head sunk to his chest. An unbearable weight pressed on his spirit.

"Grimble," Dek said. "Grimble. Grimble!"

Grimble raised his head. He faced Dek, but his eyes did not focus on the man. He felt the slackness in his jaw, the numbness of his eyes and cheeks. A foul haze covered his mind.

"Snap out of it, Grimble! I've seen that look before. This is not your fault. Mourn them, but do not think their deaths were caused by anything you did or did not do." Grimble nodded listlessly. "When you leave here this afternoon, I want the Temple to be your first stop. The Devout Mother asked to see you, anyway. Go talk to her and Brother Bhen after this. That's an order."

"Yes, sir," Grimble whispered.

"Who owns the battle?"

"Wicked Spears," he muttered.

"Swifter than wind."

"Harder than steel."

"What?"

"Harder than steel," Grimble said, louder.

"Do I need to jump over this desk and kick your ass?"

Grimble cracked a wry smile. "You'd better bring some help, sir."

"That's more like it." Dek smiled too. "I was about to promote you to sergeant, but your attitude could change my mind."

"I'm good, sir. We lost some good men is all — Wait a minute. What?"

Dek stood. "Roche said he was preparing you to take his place. On your feet, Corporal. You've got some big boots to fill."

The commander called Grimble to attention. In a ceremony lacking its usual luster, Dek presented Grimble with his extra stripes and ceremonial sash. He made everything sound as official and august as he usually did, as though Grimble were standing in front of the entire regiment, but it did not feel real until Dek shook Grimble's hand. The solemnity of the grasp and the look in Dek's eyes told Grimble the promotion meant something to him, and that was more than enough for him. He was honored by it.

"Go ahead and sit back down now," Dek said as he returned to his chair. "I have to inform you of some news that surprised us all. No doubt you noticed the lack of personnel and the unusual activity here."

"Yes, sir. I asked the scribes about it, but they told me someone above them would have to answer that."

"Indeed. King Saevar's Lord High Constable, Zahn Avengard, has ordered the 209th disbanded. This is due to the coin burden on the kingdom and the overall downsizing of His Majesty's military."

Grimble couldn't believe what he had heard. It was lunacy. "Sir, we are the last light cavalry unit. That doesn't make sense."

"I told you strange things were afoot. As far as you are concerned, it doesn't have to make sense. Those are simply the orders."

"Yes, sir."

"However, like all of us, there are some in power who are apprehensive about the decision. For that reason, I'm placing you in what we're calling a reserve status. Only a handful of the regiment knows about this."

Grimble tilted his head. "What does that mean?"

"It means that because I trust you to keep your mouth shut, you get to go home for the next year and collect one-quarter pay. Maintain your fitness and training as best you can, as you may be called back to service at any time. I stress that no one may know about this arrangement. Everyone must believe the 209th is fully disbanded and you're out of the army. I'm trusting you to never reveal this conversation."

"Understood. Sir, I have to warn you – there are some troopers who may not be able to keep that promise."

"I'm aware of that," Dek said. "I've made arrangements for men who fall into that category. As for you, you can return home to work on the farm or earn some extra coin in any way you see fit, but you must remain in Minden for the next year. I will have

436

a courier bring you your pay monthly. You must be there, Grimble."

"Understood."

"There is another reason you must remain in your small town. We fear King Heselov will send agents in an attempt to locate you and the other members of the team."

"Sir?"

"We know the Baker was killed by the chancellor and we know Kurt was the one who killed the chancellor, but they don't. Renlar's army is looking for you. Or rather, they're looking for an assassin they call 'the Horseman.'"

Grimble's eyes shot open. He remembered the soldiers at the watch post he had passed while escaping to the river. They had yelled "the Horseman" when they gave their alarm. At the time he had thought it was simply because he was riding a horse, but now it made more sense. They were looking for "*the* Horseman." They were truly looking for him.

Dek continued. "No one alive saw Kurt. You are the only person they could put at the farmhouse or in the area. You're their scapegoat. Their story states that our mission was a plot to assassinate General Batal, and that the chancellor, who happened to be visiting the general, got caught up in the incident and was killed as well.

"We don't know how determined they are. Keep your head low and don't talk to anyone. Roche is aware they may be looking for him too. We haven't been able to warn Flicker or Kurt."

"If they're looking for me, won't going home put my family in danger?" Grimble asked. "If the other troopers went back to their homes, maybe I could join Kelban in Agderon. I could find work there."

"No. You are not to meet up with any other members of the

209<sup>th</sup>. That is one of the orders given to every trooper. Look, Grimble, Renlar doesn't know your name. Going home will make you less visible than trying to hide in the city. If someone strange shows up in Minden, won't your neighbors notice?"

"Yes, sir. Everyone seems to know everyone else's business there."

"All villages and small towns are like that. But a stranger can walk around a large city without drawing attention. If Renlar sends agents looking for you, home is the most out of sight you can be. However – they have a rough idea of your appearance. I don't know how they got it. Merchants crossing the border from Renlar into Aendura report seeing 'Wanted' decrees posted in communities and along roads. Some of the postings include a drawing of a hooded and bearded man. That's the best they have. I wouldn't worry about them using magic to find you. It didn't work for us, and the mages tell me it won't work for them.

"Go home. Enjoy some time with your family. Maybe that girl of yours will show up. But keep your mouth closed and your eyes open. If you leave Minden, you'll be arrested and charged. Don't let me down, Grimble."

"I won't, sir."

Dek had Grimble put his name to some papers and handed him a few to keep for his own records. He also presented Grimble with several awards for his service. First, the Regiment's Service Award: a lacquered wooden spearhead. For his part in the mission, Grimble received the Grand Lance, a bronze spearhead, noting extraordinary heroism; and finally, the silver Service to the Crown Medallion. He had never before received any recognition beyond extra pay or extra leave. The awards were almost too much for him. He took care in placing them in his pack.

"There's one more thing," Dek said. "Those Elder Steel items were very interesting, and they have drawn a great deal of attention. Thank you for bringing the spearhead and the two bodkin arrowheads back with you." Grimble was about to remind Dek that there were three arrowheads when the commander handed him a cloth bundle. "Keep this as a trophy. We don't need three."

Grimble opened the bundle to find the dull gray arrowhead within it. He thanked Dek, secured the bundle, and stepped out of the logistics office. His heart was heavy and his mind swimming as he walked to the Temple.

The regiment's Temple of Truth, like every other building in the fort, was stone-built. The interior, never ostentatious before, was strikingly barren when he walked through the doors now. Nothing remained, not the shepherd's staff nor the altar.

Grimble had not been inside more than a few moments when Bhen and the Devout Mother entered. Both walked at a relaxed pace, Bhen following the Mother. But where Bhen's stride was clear, the Devout Mother, her feet hidden by her robe, appeared to float toward Grimble.

Grimble smiled and bowed his head. "Thank you for being there yesterday," he said to Bhen.

"Ever in his service," Bhen said.

Grimble turned to the Devout Mother and tried to find words. Her presence affected him. She rarely spoke directly to anyone, and a friendly glance was enough to lift a person's spirits for weeks. He closed his mouth and gave her a short bow.

"Your thoughts are heavy." The Devout Mother looked at him, her sky-blue eyes soft, her voice ethereal.

"Yes, Devout Mother."

"Their weight is unwarranted. What happened in Renlar

happened as it needed to. You are not responsible for anything but your own effort in completing the task. In that, you did well."

The burden of Grimble's sorrow became too much, and his head fell to his chest. "I can't help but think I may have saved them, or that I should have died with them. That if I had acted in some way, did something better, things would be right. Or at least, things would be the way they're supposed to be. Not like they are now. I should not be here. It's not right that I'm alive."

"You're placing too much on your shoulders, Grimble. And you have not given yourself the time to grieve."

"I've mourned for them, Mother. But I don't understand how that helps."

She reached out a hand and placed it below Grimble's ear. Her touch was cool and reviving against his warm head and neck. The Mother started praying, and the light in the room faded to darkness.

*He sat beside Baz at the creek after their fight. Grimble felt close to him. They had shared something that day. Baz's voice, deep and strong, sang through Grimble's soul, and he could now see that the large man accepted him.*

*Next he watched as Baz and Roche removed the loud drunk from the tavern in Whitby. As Baz and Kurt argued about the dead family in the Divide. Baz had lost family when the Renlarans took it over. He was a commanding man, and his rare smile was genuine. Grimble would never see it again.*

*A hundred memories of Dinger played through Grimble's mind. Battles won. A battle lost. Dinger standing over him, protecting him when he had fallen at Steep Ridge. Grimble had never thanked him properly. What he owed Dinger was beyond measure. The memories ended with Grimble finding his friend, carrying his dead body, placing him in the spider hole.*

Every time Grimble had felt like grieving over the past week, had felt the need to mourn his teammates, he had suppressed the emotion, telling himself, "Later."

It was later.

He fell to his knees and wept.

Gradually, Grimble became aware of Bhen and Devout Mother Tara. The Mother held a hand out to him. He took it, and she helped him to his feet. She returned her hand to the sleeve of her white robe.

"You are not responsible. They are glad you live, and they hold a spot for you in Ihgel's Hall."

Grimble composed himself and stood. He wiped his face on his shoulder and sniffed hard to clear his nose.

The Mother paused and looked skyward. When her eyes locked again on Grimble's, they were several shades darker than before, blue like a deep lake. "You have drawn the attention of many, and most wish you ill. Your life will never be the same, Grimble Broadleaf. But Abbyon and those with him know you, too, and look upon you with favor. Remain true to yourself, even in the darkest times, and you will retain their blessings. Go now with Abbyon's grace."

With that she smiled one last time and left the sanctuary. Bhen followed behind.

Grimble waited several minutes. His mind was nowhere, and he felt a relief he had not known in a long time. He turned and walked out the door, stepping into the light of the courtyard. It took a moment for his eyes to adjust to the sun.

His mind wanted to think on the Devout Mother's words, but he could not focus on them now. He was in this moment and then the next, never lingering in any one place or any one period of time. His burdens had been lessened. He breathed in the fresh air deeply and let it rush out.

That afternoon Grimble settled his account with the regiment. He didn't spend much, nor had he gambled in almost eight years. He received his coin and a Royal Monetary Note for what he couldn't carry. Grimble lightened his purse by buying a horse, tack, and a pair of riding boots. He had hoped to buy Havoc, but all of the cavalry horses had been herded away four days earlier.

He was tacking his new horse as Commander Dek approached. Dek nodded to Grimble, but turned his attention to the horse, taking a few moments to look it over. Grimble watched.

"Nice dun," Dek said. "Been trying to see why you chose this one."

"What do you think it is?" Grimble asked.

"Can't find anything that stands out – physically. She's a good horse, cold-blooded, it appears, but really a typical example of the breed. Yet she has a look in her eye that caught me off guard at first, like she's watching you. She's a smart one."

"I believe that, too. I'm impressed, sir."

"Don't be. I've spent over twenty-five years in this regiment. If I hadn't picked up some ability to read a horse, I'd have disappointed myself."

"Commander, thanks for everything."

"I should be thanking you. You helped a lot of lads become better riders. Made my job easier." He paused and rubbed the horse's neck. "Shit, I loved the job. I'll miss the men and women."

Grimble nodded. "Me too, sir. I'll miss a lot of this." He thought about those who never got the chance to out-process. "But some things I won't."

Both men smiled and nodded in understanding.

"I'm intrigued by your relationship with the Temple," Dek remarked.

"I seem to be in the middle of a mystery, sir. I wish I understood that too."

"You don't have to 'sir' me any longer. Please call me Loren. You're supposed to be out of the army, remember."

"Will do. You always did right by us, Loren. We'd have followed you to the Abyss."

"Thank you. If I was headed to the Abyss I'd want no other unit with me. I'd be proud to ride with you again, Grimble. Once you're truly out of the army and all this shit is finished, if you need to reach me, I've accepted a post at Draeger Hall in Agderon." Loren Dek offered his hand. "Take care of yourself, rah?"

"Rah."  The men shook hands and parted.

Grimble checked his mount and equipment. He took another look around the courtyard, hoping he'd see one of his friends, maybe one of the Ravens, but no one stood out. He had mounted his horse and was readying himself to go when a wagon driver near him called out.

"Hello there. Which way you headed?"

"North," Grimble said.

"We're headed to north to Chatham when they finish loading the last wagon. If you wait a couple hours you can join our caravan."

"What're you hauling?"

The driver looked at the other wagons and his own. He shrugged. "Crates."

Grimble shook his head. "Thanks, but I think I'll head out now."

"You'll be alone."

"I've been alone before."

Sergeant Grimble Broadleaf kicked his horse and left Fort Anjermott for the last time. He thought of Ellie, and how the memory of her had helped him get back home.

*One way or another, I'll find you.*

THE END

# *EPILOGUE*

"He's still there. They're still there."

Sister Hegdora scurried away from the open door and rushed to the observatory's side window, her brown robes flowing behind her. She stopped before reaching it, one hand on the stone wall. She craned her neck and peeped carefully through the window to avoid discovery.

"What does it matter if they see you? You needn't skulk."

"Yes, Mother." Hegdora blushed and made room for her abbess.

Devout Mother Jeenne stepped up to the window with confidence. She peered out to the monastery's main entrance three floors below. A man stood in front of the doors, both palms pressed against them. He was lean and hard, with salt-and-nutmeg hair and lines on his face that told of life and death. His knees wobbled. Every few minutes he lifted a hand, only to bring it back down, slapping the door. He opened his mouth to call out, but his voice had been taken from him in the middle of the first night. All his throat managed to produce was a hoarse whistle.

Behind him was a small cart and two imposing men. They

had arrived with the one at the door, appearing like soldiers, wearing mail and brigandine armor. They had since removed their armor in favor of their traveling clothes. Their swords and knives remained on their hips, but the men showed no indication that they meant any harm. One stood at the head of the cart, close to the monastery's entrance. The other sat in the shade beside the cart, his back against the wheel. He ate something from a sack.

On the small cart was the body of a woman, covered with a thin sheet of muslin and adorned with a collection of flowers and aromatic herbs. If a hard wind disturbed the sheet or the display of flowers, the man at the door would step away to put everything back in order. Other than that, he had hardly left the door.

Hegdora tiptoed, trying to get another look at their visitors over the Mother's shoulder. She wondered what her abbess would do.

Jeenne kept her eyes on the men. "Two days and two nights now."

"Yes, Mother."

"Has he left at all?"

"Only when necessary."

"And food? Water?"

"His companions offer it to him. He's taken only water, and not enough of that, I'm sure."

"Did he say why he doesn't seek Rafel's healing?"

"He said he's a follower of Yahnn and seeks her compassion for his child, and her wisdom on how to manage the loss."

Jeenne turned from the window to Hegdora. "Child? I thought they were wedded, or perhaps lovers?"

"No. He claims she was like a daughter to him. Please, Mother Jeenne, I – we – we all believe he is being truthful, and that he is here for the right reasons."

"Hmm." Jeenne looked back out the window. "And the others? What of them? Why do they remain?"

"They worked for him. Employees of some kind. He wasn't their lord. They display a respect for the deceased that makes me believe they too cared for her in some way." Hegdora watched her abbess intently, trying to read her thoughts through her actions. Jeenne tapped a finger on her lips and said nothing. She continued to watch.

The sister looked hopefully toward her superior. "He's brought a small chest of silver and gold coins as an offering and to offset the costs."

"You know —"

"I know we have little use for money ourselves," Hegdora inserted quickly, "but imagine those we can help with it. The healings that could be purchased, and the preparations that could be secured." When that solicited no response, she continued. "He's also offered to remain with the monastery and to serve in whatever capacity we may need."

"A small chest of gold and silver, but not a nobleman."

"No, Mother. We overheard him talking with one of the soldiers the day they arrived. He called that one Bear – no, Badger. Anyway, the soldier told the man they'd look out for him, since he sold everything for this chance to bring the woman back."

"Generous himself, and has the love and generosity of those under him." Jeenne spoke softly, as if to herself.

"He's willing to serve. The potter could use help in the workshop."

Hegdora waited. The silence was long and bordered on unbearable.

"His name is Niko, correct?"

Hope returned to Hegdora. "Yes, Mother."

"Tell Mr. Niko we will do what we can. But he must understand that whether it is successful or not is out of our control, and even if it is, there will be unseen costs."

Hegdora hurried away, leaving Jeenne alone in the room.

The abbess frowned, gazing down at the body beneath the sheet. "There always are."

# About the Author

Photo by William Lüc

Dean grew up in a military family, traveling the U.S. and Europe in his youth. He's now retired from a twenty-five year law enforcement career and currently lives in central Virginia with his wife and the couple's problem child, their Australian Cattle Dog.

Dean's working towards his MFA in Creative Writing and was awarded the Dennis Lehane Fellowship for Fiction in 2020.

*TRIALS of the HORSEMAN* is his debut novel.

Visit his website for information on future releases.
DeanRadt.com

www.ingramcontent.com/pod-product-compliance
Lightning Source LLC
Chambersburg PA
CBHW031958120726
47898CB00004BA/1209